THE MEANING OF LOVE

"You're a clever man, but you're not always smart. Don't you know how important love is?" Alexis said.

She was all seriousness again, and Jon found himself getting lost in her eyes. He also found himself unable to answer her. The truth was, maybe he didn't know what love was—had never known, until this moment at least.

She was very much a woman, sitting there with her ivory satin negligee clinging to her arms, her shoulders.

Alexis leaned toward him. Or had he leaned toward her?

Their lips met.

Also by Paula Paul

Sweet Ivy's Gold

Available from
HarperPaperbacks

For Brenda

ACKNOWLEDGMENTS

I wish to thank Betty Orbeck, archivist for The Permian Basin Petroleum Museum in Midland, Texas, for her enthusiastic assistance in my research of this book and for the loan of tapes and transcripts from the museum's oral history archives, particularly *The Ford Chapman Interview Project* (Permian Basin Petroleum Museum, 1985). I also gratefully acknowledge the use of Walter Rundell, Jr.'s, *Oil in West Texas and New Mexico* (Texas A&M University Press, 1982) and *Early Texas Oil* (Texas A&M University Press, 1977).

1

Alexis Runnels had told herself that a woman should have no qualms about using whatever means she had to get what she wanted. But she had learned that looks and sex could only get her so far. What she needed was money. So, in the spring of 1920, two years after she had returned from France and the war, Alexis decided to ask for her inheritance.

She'd had her fill of war and death, and lately she'd tired of life among the fast set. She was especially tired of the tight rein her papa kept on her allowance. She'd whittled her bank account down alarmingly since the war, on cars and clothes and ocean voyages and smuggled champagne and bootleg gin.

She knew she'd been foolish, just as Papa had accused her, but the war had been reason enough to want to run away from reality, at least for awhile. Be that as it may, she still couldn't allow herself to slip into abject poverty, so she'd decided to become a businesswoman.

She was not entirely surprised, however, that when she left New York and returned home to Houston to ask for the money, she met with resistance.

"But Ali, I don't understand why." Ivy set the blue china bowl of fresh-cut daisies on the cherry table and turned toward Alexis. "You have everything you could possibly need, and if you got the money now, it would only—"

"Please, Ivy, let's not argue." Alexis was arranging a similar bowl with roses. She stood in front of the French windows that overlooked the lush front garden of the family home, Green Leaves, in Houston's fashionable River Oaks section. "I thought you would understand."

"Darling, must you call me Ivy? You know I prefer Mama, and your papa doesn't like being called Langdon, either." Her voice was softly southern, warm and languid. "I'd blame it on the relaxed standards so many of you young people took up after the war, except that you started doing it after that letter—"

"It has nothing to do with the letter, Mama. That was a long time ago. I'm sorry. It was just a slip."

Ivy's eyes held hers for a moment, and Alexis saw a flicker of some dark sadness she tried to ignore. "Of course," Ivy said quietly.

"Besides," Alexis insisted, turning away, "you're getting off the subject. I have a wonderful opportunity to invest my money, and I don't want to lose it." Through the tall windows, Alexis could see Langdon getting out of the Cadillac. Another man was with him, one of his business associates, no doubt. "I'll speak to Papa about it, of course, but I came to you first because I thought you might speak to him on my behalf. You know . . ." She broke off, distracted when she noticed that Langdon and the gentleman seemed to be arguing. "After all, you made it on your own in your business before you and Papa married. If you speak to him before I do, things might go easier."

"But Ali, dear, I'm not sure I do understand. My circumstances were so different. I was desperate. I had to get into the business world. But you have everything you need, except—"

"Mama, please don't say 'except a husband.'"

"I wasn't going to say that. God knows I would never want you to marry just because it's expected of you. The truth is, I don't know what I was going to say. I don't know what's missing from your life. You've changed so since the war."

"Nothing's missing, of course," Alexis said quickly. She didn't want to talk about the war, about the year she'd spent in France as a canteen worker. Many of the young women in her set had volunteered for such duties, partly out of patriotism and partly out of hunger for adventure. It had been mundane work, but it had brought the war close enough. And Ivy was right, the war had changed her. She'd learned to be a survivor, both physically and emotionally. "You wouldn't suggest that something was missing from Miller's life if he asked for his inheritance early so he could set up a business," she added.

"There is a difference, Ali. Your brother is—"

"Is what? A male? Should that really make a difference?"

"But a nightclub? It's hardly fitting."

"Hardly fitting? May I remind you again that you ran a saloon?"

Ivy sighed and looked down at her hands, folded in front of her. Slender and well cared for, they belied her fifty-eight years. They were, perhaps, her only vanity, but they were tense now. "It was all I could do under the circumstances," she said finally. "You have plenty of choices."

"Do I?"

"Of course. And I would hope you would make a wiser choice than a nightclub, even if just for practical reasons. Prohibition is bound to make it harder to make any money, unless you break the law and run one of those . . . what do they call them? Speakeasies? That's the wrong kind of crowd, Ali."

"How do you know what kind of crowd a nightclub attracts? Have you ever been to one?"

"Of course not, but I—"

"A better class than your saloon, I should think. At least no worse. Why don't you just come out and say it's because you're afraid I can't handle it as well as you. Can't keep my morals intact. After all, there's a bad seed to consider. Look at what my real mother did. Gave birth to a bastard. Or is it bastardess?"

Ivy's face grew very pale and Alexis was immediately sorry she'd brought up her true parentage. Yet, it seemed she hadn't been able to stop herself.

"Mama, we're only going in circles," she said. "I'm almost twenty-five years old. I should think I've proven to you by now that I'm perfectly capable of being my own woman."

"Of course you have," Ivy said. She looked suddenly weary, saddened. Alexis felt a twinge of guilt, knowing she had been the cause of that sudden change in her. "And I suppose you're right. We wouldn't hesitate if it were your brother asking." She sighed heavily. "But I won't do it, Ali. I won't go to your papa and approach him as if I approved of your scheme."

"Then I'll do it without you," Alexis said sharply. "I only thought you'd want to be included. I'll speak to him at dinner." She was still doing it—hurting her mother—this time by implying that she didn't need her. Why couldn't she ever make it come out right?

"Oh, Ali, can't it wait? All the family will be here for dinner, and that was Jon Calahan you saw coming in with Langdon. Your papa's always in a foul mood after a meeting with that man. He'll be looking forward to a pleasant dinner."

"I'm afraid it can't wait, Mama. This is important to me. I'll talk to Papa before we eat if you don't want your dinner party disturbed."

There was a moment of hesitation and that hint of darkness in Ivy's eyes again, but only for a second. "Darling, do whatever you must," she said, "but don't be surprised if Langdon's not any more receptive to the idea than I've been."

Alexis felt a growing tightness in her chest as she watched Ivy walk away. It had not gone well. She had not meant for the letter or any of the past to come up, and she hadn't wanted to cause any hurt. She had simply wanted to let Ivy know she planned to ask for the money, and, of course, she had hoped for her support.

She could hear Langdon and his guest entering the front hall as Walter opened the door. Walter and his wife, Marie, were the only servants in the Runnels household, although they could well have afforded a full staff. The two of them were treated more like family than staff. It was an arrangement that had amused Alexis' school friends from the east, whose relationships with servants were usually long established in a more formal custom.

"Come in, Mr. Langdon," Walter said, sounding as if he were inviting Papa into his own house rather than performing the duties of a butler.

"Thanks, Walter," she heard Papa say. Alexis walked to the double doors leading to the entry hall and saw through the glass panes a man, perhaps in his middle forties. He was not quite as tall as Langdon, and he possessed a squarer, stockier build, so that the fabric of his coat looked strained across the breadth of his back. His dark hair was graying at the temples, and his face had a weathered, aristocratic look.

"I'll be upstairs in my study with Mr. Calahan for awhile, Walter," Langdon said brusquely. Obviously Ivy had been right. Mr. Calahan put him in a bad mood. Alexis stared at the man, wondering what it was about him that did that. "Make sure you don't let us stay up there past dinnertime," Langdon added. "Ivy'll be all over me."

"I'll be gone before dinnertime," Mr. Calahan said.

Langdon didn't respond, but started up the stairs with Calahan following behind.

Alexis knew that meant she would have to wait until after dinner to talk to Langdon about the money. She would respect her mother's wishes and not bring it up during dinner and ruin the family reunion. In fact, she intended to do her best to make the gathering as pleasant as possible. In spite of what her mother might think, she did not enjoy being the rotten apple that spoiled everything.

She decided to slip upstairs to freshen up before dinner. Diana was sure to be back from her walk with the children soon. She would join her sister and her mother in the drawing room in a little while and do her best to make amends for the barbs she'd thrown her mother's way earlier.

In her room, she splashed her face with water, then applied fresh makeup and ran a brush through her bobbed blond hair. She started to go downstairs in the dark blue serge dress she'd worn all day, but changed her mind. Pulling one dress after another from her closet, she tossed them aside before she finally decided upon a soft pink chiffon. She put it on along with matching pink kid slippers and the flesh-colored silk stockings that had become so popular in Europe. She added a bit more coloring to her eyes to enhance their wideness and their deep blue color.

Looking at herself in the mirror, she felt dissatisfied. The refection she saw was not at all the slender, boyish silhouette that had become fashionable since the war. She tended a bit too much toward voluptuousness in the hips and in the generous curve of the bosom, and the folds of pink chiffon only exaggerated it.

Her tailored blue serge was much more flattering, but Ivy and Diana would be dressed in soft feminine attire, and the pink chiffon would be less offensive to them, less a signal of their differences and her rebellion. With a sigh of resignation, she turned her back on the hateful mirror and made her way downstairs.

She could hear the giggles of little Vanessa, Diana's two-year-old, as she approached the double doors leading into the drawing room. Intermixed with the tinkling bell-like sound of childish laughter were the rich melodious strums of Diana's harp.

Alexis moved closer to the open doorway and stopped, observing the other females of her family. How relaxed they looked! They had not yet dressed for dinner, but were still in day dresses. Vanessa was sprawled across her grandmother's knees, and they both laughed at some pleasure they shared. Even the baby, Lacey, who was not quite a year old, appeared happy as she crawled about the floor gurgling. And there was Diana—beautiful, talented Diana—strumming the harp Langdon had bought for her in Italy. Actually, he had bought it for Diana and Alexis, but it was only Diana who had the talent to play. She also played the violin, which gave her papa special pleasure. Alexis had never had either the talent or the patience to practice.

She could still hear Ivy saying to visitors, "Our Ali is too high-spirited for the discipline a musician must have, but she has a very quick mind." It always sounded as if Ivy and Langdon had to make excuses for her. The "quick mind" never filled them with pleasure or pride the way Diana's talents or Miller's affable, easy-going personality did.

But she was past brooding over it now. She no longer envied Diana her beauty and talent, or Miller his charm. Still, she held back, trying to summon the courage to walk into the room and destroy the perfect domestic scene. Diana spotted her before her courage was forthcoming.

"Hi, Ali." Diana dropped her hands from the harp and stood. She moved toward the baby, and her loose auburn hair, which she usually kept in braids wound close to her head, swayed behind her like a silken veil. When she stooped to pick up the baby, the hair fell across her shoulders, shimmering in the light. "You look great," she said, straightening and glancing at Alexis over the top of the baby's head.

Alexis managed a smile, although she knew she did not look great. She was beginning to worry now that the midcalf length of her dress was too short and the flesh-colored stockings too daring. It was all very fashionable in New York, but Houston lagged behind in fashion trends. She went to the bar to help herself to a glass of Langdon's bootleg gin. "Go on with your playing. Don't let me interrupt you."

"Oh, no," Diana said with a strained laugh. "The girls make too much noise for me to concentrate, anyway."

"That is indeed a lovely dress," Ivy said. Her voice had the same ring of false gaiety to it. Their efforts to appear relaxed when it was obvious they weren't gave Alexis even more the feeling of odd woman out. "You're putting us all to shame," Ivy continued. "Now Diana and I will have to change to—"

Alexis turned toward them a little too quickly, spilling her drink over the rim of the glass. "Oh no, not if you weren't going to anyway. You always used to dress when the family—I mean, I could change—"

"Of course not," Ivy said. "And you're right. All the family will be here. It's a festive occasion." She glanced at Diana. "We'll dress, of course. I only meant we'd have to go some lengths to look as nice as you. I—oh, Vanessa, do stop squirming all over Grandma." She lifted the child from her lap, and Vanessa immediately began to cry. At the sound of her sister's wailing, Lacey started to whine. Alexis fought back an urge to run from the room while Diana and Ivy comforted the children and tried to repair the horrible, confusing damage she had done.

"The children are so tired and fussy after their walk!" Diana exclaimed as she bounced Lacey in her arms, trying to soothe her.

"What's going on in here? Somebody let loose the bogeyman or something?"

Alexis turned toward the doorway to see Clay, Diana's husband, ambling in, his hands stuck casually into the pockets of his smart tweed trousers and a cigarette dangling from his lips, giving him a debonair appearance and much more the look of a college student than the assistant professor he was.

"Clay," Diana said, turning to him, "please take the girls to Marie and have her feed them and put them to bed. We could use some peace and quiet."

"Whatever the little woman says," Clay answered, with a wink aimed at both Ivy and Diana. "Come to Daddy," he said, holding out his arms to receive both his daughters. By the time he reached the large double doors, both children were clinging to their father's neck and giggling with delight. He walked away to look for Marie.

"I was going to ask Clay if he would pick up Miller at the train station," Ivy said. "Do you think he'll mind, Diana? I know it will cut the time short before dinner."

"Of course he won't mind," Diana said. She had begun to braid her hair.

"Why don't you just send Walter?" Alexis asked.

"Then Clay won't have to worry about being late for dinner."

"Send Walter when we could go ourselves?" Diana asked with a laugh. "Oh, Ali, you're always surprising us. I thought you would say that was too bourgeois. What happened to our socialist bluestocking?"

"Alexis is not a socialist, Diana," Ivy said, not so much in her defense, Alexis thought, but more to keep the waters smooth. "That was just a stage she went through when she was younger." As she spoke, she stood and began helping Diana braid her hair.

Alexis was struck with how much alike her mother and sister looked. Both had the same thick, luxurious hair, and neither of them had given in to current fashion and had it bobbed. Ivy's had faded somewhat and was streaked with gray, but there was still evidence of the burnished auburn it had once been. Even their faces were remarkably alike, with the same high cheekbones and the same elegant forehead. Ivy's, rather than wrinkling, had simply relaxed and softened with age.

"I know, Mother," Diana said, winking at Alexis. "I was only teasing Ali. And I'm sure Clay won't mind meeting Miller at his train. They'll have a wonderful time fighting the old Yale-Harvard battle."

"We all must hurry if we're going to get dressed in time," Ivy said. She wound a ribbon around the end of Diana's braid, so that she looked very young. And in spite of the fact that Diana was now the mother of two, Alexis still thought of her sister as something of a little girl.

Diana, three years Alexis's junior, had met Clay Brandywine, a graduate student in engineering, during her freshman year at the University of Texas. She was married at eighteen and a mother at nineteen. Alexis had thought it a waste that she had dropped out of college and not pursued a serious career in music.

"Mama," Alexis said, "I'll go to the train station to meet Miller if you like, so Clay can get dressed. But I still don't see why you can't send Walter if it's going to rush us all to—"

"Oh no, dear," Ivy said, touching Alexis's face with her hand. "Of course you can't go in your lovely dress. And besides, Clay and Miller do love their banter."

"Grandma! Grandma!" The tiny voice called from the top of the stairs, squealing with delight. "Come look! Look at Grandpa!"

"Oh, what is Grandpa up to now with that child?" Ivy said with a laugh. She hurried away with Diana following her to share their delight. "Excuse us, Ali," Ivy said, turning back. "We'll be right with you again as soon as we're dressed."

Alexis raised her gin glass to their backs in a mock toast, then looked around the empty room, feeling as if she had just been rendered invisible. It was not a feeling that was new to her. Whenever she was home, there were dozens of little incidents throughout the day, little acts of erasure brought about by her family's denial of her, or at least their protest of her ideas or maybe even her very existence.

She walked slowly toward the harp. Setting her drink down beside it, she assumed the classic position of the harpist, legs apart, harp resting on her shoulder, and plucked at the strings. The best she could do was pull out a simple melody. The sweeping harmony that

Diana produced eluded her. She dropped her hands suddenly from the instrument, knowing that when she tried to be Diana, she virtually guaranteed her own disappearance.

It didn't matter that she couldn't play, she told herself. It was an instrument for angels like Diana, not for women like her. Bad girls like her, she thought, and a smile fluttered at her mouth. That was what Zane had called her. His beautiful bad girl. He was teasing her that night in Paris the first time he had ever said it, but she had liked the way it had made both of them laugh. How they had laughed! How gay and happy they were until they had managed, each in his and her own way, to obliterate the other.

A gray, menacing pain throbbed in her head. She mustn't think of Paris or Zane or the war or any of that. She dropped her head to rest it for a moment on the frame of the harp, willing herself not to think at all.

"An angel in distress?"

Alexis jerked her head up suddenly to see Jon Calahan standing in the doorway. As he walked toward her, a smile played across his face, but it was not the smile that captured and held her. It was his eyes. They were an uncommon green and illuminated now, as if charged by some hidden source of power.

"Hardly," she said with a casualness that belied her shock at suddenly having been rendered visible again.

"Hardly an angel or hardly in distress?" he asked. He spoke with a slight Texas brogue, but it was overlaid with a veneer of education. She saw now that his face was much more attractive, in a rough and weathered way, than she had first realized. His age, she noted, showed in his graying temples and in the deepened crevices around his eyes, as if he'd had too long and intimate an acquaintanceship with the sun. A slightly crooked smile that showed brilliant white teeth gave him a reckless look.

"Neither." She stood and retrieved her drink. "I'm afraid it's my father's bootleg gin making me a little dizzy." She glanced at him again. He was indeed, quite attractive. Enough so to be vain about it, she guessed.

"Name's Jon Calahan," he said, offering her his hand. "Didn't mean to scare you. Ought not to be wandering through the house like this, I reckon, but I left my host with an important telephone call, and I just drifted away. Then I saw you there sort of slumped over that harp, and I thought maybe I ought to see if you were all right." The flat Texas twang in his voice was more pronounced than she'd realized. Had it not been for that, he could have passed for an easterner, smartly dressed in his black suit and white spats.

"Nice of you to be concerned, Mr. Calahan," she said. "Can I pour you a drink?"

"Maybe I shouldn't if that gin affects you the way you said it did. Might do the same to me."

She laughed and walked to the bar. "It's all right," she said, filling a glass for him as well as another for herself, which she mixed with tonic water. "You get numb after the second glass."

"But not blind, I hope," he said, accepting the glass. "I don't want to miss the view. There's quite a houseful of lovely ladies here."

"You've met my sister and mother, then."

"Mrs. Brandywine and Mrs. Runnels? Your sister and mother?"

"Well, stepsister and stepmother to be exact. Remarkable how much alike they look, isn't it?"

"Stepmother? Then that explains your blond, fair looks."

"My looks need explaining?"

"I'm sorry, I didn't mean—"

"Oh, you haven't offended me, Mr. Calahan. I wondered myself, for a long time, why I looked so different. I'm afraid I learned about my parentage rather embarrassingly late in life. Ivy and Langdon had this old-fashioned idea that my knowing I was their adopted daughter would somehow damage me." She walked to a sofa and sat down, leaving him leaning against the bar.

"But they changed their minds, obviously."

"They had no choice." She gave him a smile with her eyes as she looked at him over the top of her glass. She took another sip of the gin, remembering how reluctant they had been to tell her even after she had accidentally stumbled upon the truth. "It turned out I had a much more interesting background than I could ever have imagined. My real father is my mother's first husband, and my real mother was his mistress, who died when I was born."

Mr. Calahan laughed. "Sounds to me like you're rattling the bones of some family skeleton everybody else would just as soon keep in the closet, Miss Runnels."

"Alexis."

"So that's your name. I was beginning to wonder why you were keeping it from me."

She laughed. "Was I being rude?"

"Only charming."

"Ooh!" she said with a slight tilt of her head. "And so are you."

"I'm afraid your father doesn't think so."

"Papa can be difficult, can't he?" she said, running her finger along the rim of her glass. "Oh, but don't get the wrong idea about those skeletons in our family closet. The skeletons belong to my real father, not Ivy and Langdon. They are perfectly respectable and upstanding citizens. Very admirable, in fact, wouldn't you say? After all, they took me in."

"You sound resentful."

"Don't be ridiculous. I'm grateful."

"Of course."

She tried not to think of it now, tried not to remember how she'd found the letter on her mother's desk when she was sixteen. It had been the name on the return address—Alex, so similar to Alexis—that had compelled her to slip it from its envelope and read it. If she had been more like Diana, proper and mannerly, she would never have opened it and never have known the truth. The letter had been written to her mother from Alex Barton, her real father, in which he had pled with her to allow him to see Alexis, his daughter. Ivy had come into the room and caught her reading it, and then had reluctantly told her the truth.

"Tell me about yourself," Alexis said, eager to change the subject. Mr. Calahan was sitting next to her now, and she turned to face him, tucking her feet under her in a gesture she was very aware was seductive. "How long have you lived in Houston?"

"I've never lived in Houston. Beaumont for awhile, but lately I've been living in West Texas. Little place called Coyote Flats."

"You lived in Beaumont? Then you're in the oil business. That explains why you were here to see Papa. You are, no doubt, one of my father's rich, powerful friends. Is there oil in—what was it? Coyote Flats?" Her voice had taken on a coy tone. She was quite blatantly flirting with him.

"Oh there's oil all right. Just hasn't been much pumped out yet. I expect you've heard, folks are saying the next boom is going to be in West Texas."

"I'm afraid I don't keep up with all that," she said with a careless wave of her hand. "The things that interest my father and mother aren't usually the same things that interest me."

"And what does interest you, Alexis?"

"Right now, you do," she said, leaning toward him slightly. "Why don't you tell me what you and oil and West Texas have to do with Langdon. I suppose he's buying up leases out there."

"He's tried," Jon said. He pulled a pack of cigarettes from his pocket and lit one. "I've just bought up some leases your father wanted. In his opinion I've pulled the rug out from under him."

Alexis sat up straighter. "So you and Papa are business rivals?"

"Maybe a better description is mortal enemies. Your stepfather hates my guts."

"But he invited you to stay for dinner."

"Of course not."

"How rude."

"Rude not to eat with your enemy? I'm damned lucky he doesn't shoot me. This is Texas, remember?"

"How could I forget?"

They both laughed, and Alexis took another sip of her gin. "So you'll be drilling in the West Texas fields soon?"

"As soon as I find somebody with a rig who wants to contract for the drilling, I'm going out there as a wildcatter."

Alexis gave him her best smile. "I've always liked that term, 'wildcatter.' So colorful and so American, don't you think?"

"Well, at least it takes less time to say than 'independent oil speculator.'"

She got up to add more gin to her glass. "Mind if I have one of your cigarettes?" She caught the look he gave her and made a wry face. "Oh, now don't tell me you disapprove of women smoking."

"Would it matter if I did?" he asked, reaching into his pocket. He stood and offered her one, then lit it for her. She inhaled deeply and coughed, choking on the smoke. She was acutely embarrassed, and even more so when he began to pat her on the back, and then offered her his glass of gin. "Want me to open a window?" he asked.

She shook her head, afraid to speak for fear she would cough again. Besides, she wasn't certain whether his offer was out of genuine concern or a means of teasing her. In spite of the fact that she had tried the dreadful things before, she'd never mastered the art of smoking. She managed a swallow of gin, though, and it had a cauterizing affect on her throat. She turned away from Jon, toward the bar, hoping he wouldn't see that she was embarrassed.

"Papa brought you here so he could try to buy the oil leases from you?" she asked casually, holding the cigarette a safe distance away so she wouldn't have to inhale the smoke.

"No, I invited myself here, as a matter of fact. I wanted to make him a business partner. I wanted to offer him the opportunity for joint control of the West Texas fields."

"That means you want him to finance something for you. Or you want to borrow money from him."

There was a moment while he looked at her, studied her, with a slight smile on his face. She couldn't tell whether he was annoyed with her or merely surprised that she had been so blunt.

"I forgot for a minute there that I'm in enemy territory."

"Oh, come now, Jon, I'm not—"

"You're a very interesting woman." His hand was very close to hers where they both rested on the bar, and he reached an index finger to stroke her thumb.

She hesitated a moment then moved away. "That contractor you're looking for, got anybody in mind?"

"Oh, I'll know him when I see him. He'll be a little wild. A little reckless. Hungry, maybe. That's what he'll have to be to make it in West Texas where the land and climate are hostile to everything but rattlesnakes."

"Is that what you are, Jon? Hungry and a little wild and reckless?" The way he looked at her had given her the confidence to flirt again.

"I'm too old to be wild and reckless, my dear. But I'm smart enough to have replaced it with shrewdness, enough so that I'll know the right man when I see him."

"And what do you have to offer this man when you find him?"

"Why, the gamble, of course. The prospect of making it big and having a hell of an exciting time while he's gambling. Everything a man needs to satisfy his hunger."

"And how are you proposing to do this?" She toyed with the cigarette, twisting it in the ash tray, but never once bringing it to her lips again.

"I'm offering a ten percent share of the profits."

The amount surprised her. She had expected it to be more, but she didn't look up. If she met his eyes again, he might see her inexperience. "What do they cost? One of these drilling rigs, I mean?"

"Four or five thousand dollars for a good one."

"Four or five thousand buys a rig and the chance to make millions, I suppose."

He gave her another grin. "That's the idea behind it. No guarantees, of course."

"Of course."

"Somebody will take the bait. Somebody with all the brashness and guts your papa used to have before money and a beautiful wife and two beautiful daughters softened his edges."

"No doubt." She hated the throwaway insincerity of his linking her with Diana's beauty.

"But why am I telling you this?" he said with a laugh. He put his cigarette out and leaned back against the bar. "Why don't we talk about something more pleasant—your children, maybe? Do you live in Houston? Or in Austin like your sister?"

"I live in New York. I have no children. As a matter of fact, I'm not married, and if you dare ask me something clichéd like why is a nice girl like me not married at my age, I'll be very disappointed."

"I try never to disappoint a lady," he said with a grin.

"I'm sure you don't," she said, not daring to speculate on the nuance of his remark. She was, however, secretly pleased that he had gone to the trouble to find out whether she was married. The evening wasn't going to be such a disaster after all, it seemed.

The door opened suddenly and Langdon walked in. "Your car's here, Calahan. Walter will show you to the door. Oh, hello, Ali. I've been looking for you. Your mother said you wanted to talk to me about some scheme you've dreamed up to—What the devil are you doing with that cigarette?"

2

Obviously Ivy had mentioned something to Langdon after all. Now Alexis wondered if it had been a good idea. In spite of the fact that she had at one point wanted to have the talk with Papa soon, it couldn't have come at a worse time. She certainly hadn't planned on it being at a time when she'd had too much to drink and when she'd just been caught sharing a cigarette with his worst enemy.

But it was like Langdon Runnels to choose to do business at a time when everyone but he was at a disadvantage. And come to think of it, it hadn't been a request to talk, but a decree that now was the time he'd chosen to have the discussion.

"Papa, it could wait until later. Maybe tomorrow when we both—"

"I'm going out to the Desdemona field tomorrow, Ali, sorry. Besides, there's plenty of time tonight before supper. You'll excuse us, Calahan."

Jon gave him a nod, but Alexis saw that his face,

like his eyes, had become as hard as granite. When she glanced at Langdon, she saw his cold blue gaze meet the other man's before he turned and left the room, obviously expecting her to follow. She gave Jon a resigned shrug before she exited to follow Langdon, the gin making her weave slightly in spite of her efforts not to.

Before she reached his office at the end of the hall, she excused herself and slipped into the bathroom to splash water on her face in an attempt to clear her mind. Spying a bottle of cologne on the table next to the sink, she uncapped it and swished some of the liquid around in her mouth. With a quick pat of the towel to her lips, she left the bathroom and prepared to face Langdon.

He was seated behind his huge mahogany desk, puffing on one of his expensive cigars and looking like a monarch. His graying hair made his appearance all the more regal. He had kept a trim physique in spite of his more than sixty years, and that intense blue stare was as intimidating as she ever remembered it.

"Come in, Ali," Langdon said.

Alexis tried to read his expression, but his face was like a blank page. His poker face, Ivy called it. The term always made the two of them laugh, as if they shared some intimate secret relating to that. Alexis saw nothing to laugh at now, though. His nondescript expression made her uneasy. She felt an uncomfortable void in her stomach as she moved into the room.

"Your mother told me you wanted to talk to me. She says you want your share of the inheritance now."

"Yes," Alexis managed to say. Her head was spinning. She knew she should be happy that her mother had relented and spoken to Langdon, but somehow it had all turned out to be to her disadvantage. It was no accident, she knew. Langdon Runnels knew how to keep a person unbalanced. He hadn't gotten where he was by pulling punches.

"Why did you go to your mother first? Do you feel uncomfortable talking to me?"

"Who doesn't, Papa?" she said with a lightheartedness she didn't feel. "You're pretty intimidating, you know."

He shook his head. "I don't want you to feel intimidated by me. I want you to feel you can talk to me anytime."

"Really?" She hadn't meant to sound quite so cynical.

He gave her a scrutinizing look. "I mean what I say, Ali. Tell me what you have in mind."

She blurted it out. "A nightclub."

He didn't react. Didn't even move a muscle. He was waiting for her to say more, to defend her position, and that, she realized, was part of his intimidation.

"There's one for sale in New York," she added. "A friend of mine knows the owner, and he says it's quite profitable. I've been there myself. Only the best class of person goes there. No low life. No sleazy—"

"You'd be dealing with bootleggers, of course. To supply you with booze."

"Isn't that what you do? The only difference is that you only deal with them for your own personal use."

"As have you, I have no doubt. But my livelihood doesn't depend on it. That's risky business."

A BAD GIRL'S MONEY

"You're the world's greatest risk taker, Papa. Why should it surprise you that I would follow in your footsteps? Or Mama's? If she could run that saloon back in Colorado, why can't I do it too?" The words tumbled out of her mouth in a breathless blur. "Or do you expect me to be more like Diana and just want to have babies?"

"We're not talking about Diana, and we're not talking about me or your mother. We're talking about you, Ali."

She realized that she should never have made her last statement. It only sounded petty, and she had allowed herself to become too obviously defensive.

"Have you seen a profit and loss statement from this place? Found out why the owner is selling?" he asked.

She hesitated. Things were going even worse than she'd feared. "No, but I know the business is sound."

"How do you know that?"

"Why, because it's always full."

"Full of the best class of people, of course."

"You're being condescending, Papa."

"Am I? Those are your words, not mine."

"Papa—"

"Ali, you haven't done your homework. You have no idea whether this place is making money or not, do you? Or how much work it will be to keep it going even if it is making money. It's not going to be the same thing as running a soldiers' canteen owned by the government. Ask your mother what kind of hard work it is—"

"You've never forgiven me, have you?" she said suddenly, interrupting him. "For running off to the war like that to be a canteen worker. You said I was being wild and reckless then, and you've never forgiven me, have you?"

"Stop digging up old bones!" he said, slamming his palm against the desk with such force it made her jump. "Of course I've forgiven you. What kind of an ogre do you think I am?"

"You tried to—"

"I was wrong to try to stop you, in spite of the fact that I thought it would be dangerous. And hell yes, I thought you were wild and reckless. I hoped you'd get it out of your system, so you'd want to—"

"To what? Settle down? Get married? Have babies?"

"There's nothing wrong with that, Alexis."

"And there's nothing wrong with what I want to do, either. But you're not going to let me do it, are you?"

"Of course I'm going to let you."

"What?" She was stunned. "You mean—"

"I mean I'm not going to stop you. You're right. If your mother could do it, so can you. But if you do it, you're going to do it the same way she did. On your own. Your inheritance will come the same way Diana's and Miller's will. After I'm dead."

"But—"

"You've spent every penny I've ever given you, and maybe that's my fault. I've made it too easy for you. Never given you a chance to learn the value of a dollar."

"Papa, that's unfair. It's my own money I'll be risking. You have nothing to lose!"

Langdon stood, walked around his enormous desk, and took her arm. "Shall we go down to supper, Ali?"

She found she could only stare at him, speechless.

He had won, just as he always did. He had won by making her feel she couldn't do it, because she knew—they both knew—that she was nothing like Ivy. Or anyone else in this family.

They descended the stairs together, Langdon still holding her arm, but neither of them speaking. Alexis felt far too angry to utter a word, and Langdon, she knew, didn't have to say anything. He could crow in silence.

They had not yet reached the bottom of the stairs when they both saw Jon Calahan seated on one of the Louis XIV chairs in the entry hall, his hat and coat resting on his arm as if he was still waiting for the car to drive him home. He stood as soon as he saw Alexis.

"What are you—" Langdon began.

"Some kind of motor trouble with the taxi you called," Jon said. "Walter was just trying to find another one."

Walter walked into the hall, shaking his head. "Can't find a taxi nowhere this time of night."

"I'll drive you home," Alexis said quickly. She was in no way eager to sit through dinner with the family now, and she didn't feel like eating anyway. The gin had made her queasy.

"No," Jon protested. "I won't spoil the family gathering. I'm sure Mrs. Runnels was looking forward to having you all together."

"You wouldn't be spoiling—"

Langdon interrupted her plea. "Hell, Calahan. Stay for supper. Walter can drive you home after that."

His motive for asking his enemy for supper was transparent to everyone, Alexis thought. He didn't want her alone with Jon Calahan. Jon knew that as well. He had an amused look on his face as he said, "I'll be happy to stay."

Alexis sulked in silence during dinner, while everyone else chatted happily. Even the presence of Jon Calahan hadn't caused the discomfort among them she had expected.

She was seated next to Miller, who had arrived with Clay just minutes before. He had not taken time to change from his traveling clothes, but was, nevertheless, quite handsome in his dapper college-boy tweeds. He had the same strong square jaw as Langdon and the same intensely blue eyes, but his thick dark hair, which he wore parted in the middle, was obviously inherited from his mother.

"It was just great!" Miller was saying. "A bunch of us went down from Harvard to see the fight. Dempsey took him in the second round with a left jab," he said, demonstrating the punch.

"I don't understand your fascination with such a violent sport," Diana said. "You're a paradox! You write such beautiful poetry. A regular Carl Sandburg. Very sensitive, isn't he, Mother? And yet you harbor such a plebeian fascination for pugilistics."

Diana was showing off, but everyone seemed to be enjoying it. She leaned across the table to make her point to Miller. "You're a walking contradiction, baby brother."

"No contradiction, sis." Miller cut his roast beef with youthful gusto. "Dempsey's poetry in motion."

Everyone laughed again at his cleverness, and Alexis couldn't keep a smile from her lips either, in spite of her sour mood. She had always loved her charming, affable little brother with a special tenderness.

"What have you been up to besides watching boxing matches?" Langdon asked him.

"Not much," Miller said, winking at Alexis. "Prelaw keeps a man busy."

"Bullshit!" Langdon said.

His coarse remark caused Ivy to hesitate a moment as she was about to bring a morsel of food to her mouth, but she didn't speak.

"Well, I have been thinking of taking up flying," Miller said with a sheepish grin. He glanced toward Ivy as if he were anticipating her disapproval, but she only smiled as if everything he did was wonderful. "Just wish I'd been born a few years earlier so I could have flown in the Great War. Downed a few Germans, you know. You get all the breaks, Ali. Now the world's tamed down so there's nothing left but a few mail runs."

Alexis glanced at Miller, but she couldn't manage a smile this time. He was, she thought, the eternal child.

"You were in the war?" Jon asked with obvious surprise.

"Oh, our Ali's very brave and very modern," Diana said.

"Nonsense, I was just a canteen worker." Ali hoped to end the discussion there.

"But at least she was there," Miller said. "Actually got to fly in an aeroplane, didn't you, Ali? And there was that barnstormer you—"

"That was a long time ago, Miller," Alexis said, cutting him off.

"How about you, Mr. Calahan?" Miller asked. "Ever flown in an aeroplane?"

"Afraid not. Like your father, I've been busy with other things."

Alexis saw the cold look that passed between Langdon and Jon before Langdon directed his attention back to Miller. "There are plenty of other places to find excitement besides aeroplanes, my boy," Langdon said. "And knowing you, I'm sure you'll find them."

"Sure thing, Pop. A chip off the old block, eh?"

Clay joined in the conversation with Miller and Langdon then, bringing in his engineer's perspective of how future designs might affect flying craft. Ivy and Diana made small talk with Jon, and Alexis began to feel oddly disconnected, as if she had somehow managed to become transparent while she sat at her place in the old-fashioned gilded dining room.

She began to see herself the way she imagined the others saw her—irresponsible, hedonistic, and as self-centered as Miller but without his charm. There was no comparing her to the sweet, congenial Diana. Langdon would have moved heaven and earth for Diana, and Miller would move it himself, just with his affability. Alexis on the other hand, would remain invisible.

"Alexis has seen all the moving pictures, of course," Ivy was saying for Jon's benefit. "They're quite the thing in New York."

"Don't know what she sees in that place," Langdon said. "Nothing but a lot of noise. I couldn't wait to get out of there when I was her age."

"I couldn't wait to get out this time myself, Papa," Alexis said. She wondered vaguely if her reply had been appropriate. Langdon had, after all, been speaking about her, not to her, speaking as if she weren't there.

"Really?" Miller said. "What are you up to now?"

"I'm going into business," she heard herself saying. Everyone was looking at her now. At last.

"Business?" Miller seemed intrigued. Ivy glanced at Langdon, but Langdon's eyes never left Alexis.

"Yes, I've decided to become a wildcatter. I'm going into business with Mr. Calahan."

Ivy dropped her fork, and then there was nothing but an appalled silence. Until Jon finally spoke.

"It seems the young lady is following in the footsteps of both of you," he said, glancing at Ivy and Langdon. His eyes twinkled with amusement. "I reckon everybody in the business had heard that Runnels enterprises was built on sheer—intestinal fortitude."

"I wonder if intestinal fortitude, as you call it, is what drives Alexis," Langdon said stiffly. He had gone white around the mouth.

"A wildcatter, Alexis?" Ivy said, ignoring Walter's hovering ministrations as he replaced her fork with a clean one. "But I thought you said something about a nightclub."

"I decided you were right, Mama. With a little advice from Papa, of course," she added with as sweet a smile as she could manage. "Considering Prohibition, it would be poor timing. Besides, it would be ridiculous for me to try to follow in your footsteps. After all, as you said, our motivations are vastly different." As she spoke she was acutely aware that her acquired New York accent was in sharp contrast to the speech of everyone else at the table.

"But Ali, a wildcatter? Looking for oil fields? Do you realize the kind of men who hang around oil fields? It's certainly no place for a young woman." Ivy seemed to have forgotten that there was a guest at the table until she glanced quickly at Jon Calahan. Then she was quite obviously embarrassed that she had brought up such a delicate subject in the presence of someone other than family.

Alexis laughed. "Mama, you certainly don't think all of those soldiers I met during the war were perfect gentlemen, do you? I know how to handle situations."

"Ali—" Ivy said, growing more embarrassed.

"We'll discuss this later," Langdon said, giving Alexis a cold look.

Diana reached a hand to where Langdon's rested on the table and covered it reassuringly. Miller, who was used to being the center of attention, raised his glass.

"To family tradition. Money and guts." He grinned while everyone else stared at him in silence until Langdon laughed softly and raised his own glass in compliance.

His gesture was followed by Ivy, who exchanged a fleeting glance with Langdon. Jon followed by holding his glass up, and then, reluctantly, Diana and Clay joined in.

After he'd drunk the toast, Miller set his glass down. "Speaking of tradition," he said, "I gotta tell you about the tradition the Sigmas nearly destroyed." He launched into a description of some comic boating mishap he and his fraternity brothers had, comparing the comedy of errors to the antics of the Keystone Kops and himself to Charlie Chaplin.

He had used his usual boyish cleverness and easy charm to save the evening, and Alexis was almost glad that she could retreat into invisibility again. It was Jon Calahan who brought a convenient end to the evening by pleading a need to get to his hotel, since he had to get up early the next morning to board a train to Beaumont. Langdon was about to summon Walter.

"Why not let me drive Mr. Calahan to his hotel, Papa?" Alexis said. She knew she was about to upset the easy peace, but she was desperate to talk to Jon again.

"Alexis," Langdon began, "at this late hour, I don't think—"

"Nonsense," she said, cutting him off before he could say more. "I don't mind the late hour at all, and I'm sure Walter is tired after a long day. And I'm sure it's obvious Mr. Calahan and I have things to discuss. That is, unless Mr. Calahan objects."

She had put him on the spot, she knew. He had no choice but to agree to her proposal as graciously as possible.

The green velvet of a Houston night had just begun to spread across the landscape as Jon took the seat next to Alexis in the Cadillac. She was aware of his scrutiny as she maneuvered the car out of the garage and onto the street. It was not common for women to drive even in New York, much less Houston, but she had learned to drive in Paris out of necessity. There weren't always enough men to drive the supply trucks from the loading docks to the canteen.

"I've never ridden in an automobile when a woman was driving," Jon said.

"Are you frightened?" she asked without looking at him.

"I don't scare easy, Ali."

"I trust that the idea of doing business with a woman doesn't frighten you either."

"It doesn't frighten me."

She cast a furtive glance in his direction. "But what? I know there's a but. You were dying to contradict my statement at dinner."

"Alexis, you're wasting your time with me. I do not intend to get involved with you in some cockamamy wildcatting scheme you've cooked up on the spur of the moment."

"Then who do you intend to get involved with?" Without giving him a chance to answer she added, "You all but admitted to me that you're having some problems finding a drilling contractor because the country is unproven. Didn't you just say you needed somebody young and willing to gamble? And don't talk to me about experience. I can get that, or I can hire somebody who has it. Now are we going to do business or not?"

To her astonishment and chagrin, Jon laughed.

"I see nothing funny in this, Mr. Calahan," Alexis said, losing a little of her bravado. "I believe it's only polite of you to answer my question."

"You may be right, but politeness is not necessarily one of my virtues." He gave her a long look, the hint of a smile still on his hard, attractive mouth. "All right," he said finally, "We'll meet tomorrow night to talk about it. That'll give you one day to see if you can come up with the money you'll need to buy a rig and hire a crew."

"One day! I'll need more time than that."

"I'm going to Beaumont tomorrow. Already have a lead on a man with a cable rig there, and he's expecting me."

She felt a moment of mental paralysis. She had let him force her into a corner, and she didn't like the feeling, but she was uncertain of how to counter him. "All right, you see this man in Beaumont, and we'll meet tomorrow night for dinner. Shall I pick you up at your hotel at say—"

"I'll pick you up, my dear. At your father's house. Times may have changed to the point that I have agreed to talk about doing business with a young woman, but I'll be damned if I'm going to change to the point of having one pick me up for dinner."

Alexis laughed. She pulled up to the curb and turned to him. "You're incredibly old-fashioned, Jon."

He smiled at her, then, to her surprise, reached for her hand and kissed it. "And you're incredibly young and naive, little girl," he said, opening the door and letting himself out.

"Where are you going?" she called. "Aren't you going to invite me—"

"Good night," he said as he walked away.

She watched his square, solid form move away from her, wondering how he managed to look so arrogant even from the back, and how it was that she could feel a strong attraction for him and an overpowering dislike at the same time.

It had not gone well with him. Certainly not as she had planned. Instead of convincing him that she could be the wise and efficient person he needed, she had managed to come across as—How had he put it? Incredibly young and naive! She would have to remedy that. If she was lacking in experience, she at least could surround herself with people who were not. That is, if she could come up with the money.

By the time she returned to Green Leaves, Ivy and Langdon had retired to their room, and Diana was with her children, helping Marie bed them down for the night. Clay and Miller had settled into the library, smoking and talking and looking very much as if they did not want to be disturbed. All of this gave Alexis the perfect excuse not to speak to anyone. There would be no escaping it tomorrow, though, she was certain. Langdon would have plenty to say about her brash insistence at going off with Jon Calahan as well as her announcement that she was going into business with him. He'd see it as another example of her irresponsibility.

She went up to her room, removed the pink chiffon dress, and tossed it across the bed. Then she reached for her dressing gown, still thinking about how awkward the evening had been. It must have been awkward for Jon, too, but he had come through it admirably, and he'd seemed more the amused observer than the embarrassed guest. She always mistrusted those cool characters who could stand back laughing at the rest of the world.

Jon certainly hadn't turned out to be the hick she had expected. He was provincial maybe, but too clever to be a hick. Clever. Was that why she was wary of him? Or was it because she had found herself pouring out her life's story to him when she had no business doing such a thing? She was embarrassed that she had told him so much about her parentage. It was something she'd never done before. It must have been the gin. She'd have to watch that.

She drank too much whenever she felt terribly out of place, as she had tonight. She'd managed to upset and turn to disaster every tranquil domestic scene she encountered. Would that have happened with Alex, her real father? Or with the even more shadowy woman whose name she didn't even know, but who was her mother? Or would she have felt at ease with them?

It was ridiculous, she told herself, to be thinking such things. She had long since gotten over the childish notion that her real parents were a knight in shining armor and a queen on a throne. She was silly to have ever had such romantic notions—and silly, too, to have kept the letter, retrieved from the wastebasket after her mother had thrown it away.

Her hand trembled slightly as she opened the bureau drawer now and pulled out the small cedar box in which she had kept her childhood treasures. There, along with an odd collection of seashells, lucky pennies, and notes from girlhood beaus, was the letter, beginning to tear along the folds now as a result of all the times she had unfolded and refolded it as a young girl.

She opened it one more time and noticed that the ink had begun to fade.

My Dear Ivy, the letter began, and continued in an old-fashioned Victorian tone

> *I am writing to you to appeal to your sweet nature in asking you to allow me to see my*

daughter, Alexis, who will have now entered upon the threshold of womanhood. I have longed for these many years to see her, but have refrained, knowing she is by far better off with you, where she not only will receive all that she deserves, but will never guess the truth.

However, as I have now entered the fifth decade of life and as a consequence have become sorely aware of my mortality, the chance to see my only surviving relative before I pass on to the next realm has become of the greatest importance to me. It is my hope that some of the closeness we once felt will be rekindled in you, and you will relent in the punishment I so justly deserve. If you would but consent, I would come, posing as a distant uncle, on a brief visit. I would have my opportunity to gaze into a face that reflects the last vestiges of childhood, hear her young voice, see her lovely smile, and then I would return to the obscurity to which I have rightfully been banished. I am still at the old Golden Palace in Eagleton. I eagerly await your reply, and I remain,

*Your Faithful Servant,
Alex Barton*

The first time she had read the letter, she had felt stunned. She had been still holding it in her hands, incapable of moving, when Ivy came back to her studio. Ivy had seen immediately what she had done, and neither of them had spoken for several seconds.

"I never wanted you to know," Ivy said at last.

When she spoke those words, something of Alexis' world shattered. Until that moment she had secretly hoped that it wasn't true.

"We thought it best that you not know," Ivy had continued, "That you believe that your father and I—that Langdon and I—were your parents, that . . ."

It had all been very confusing after that. At first, Alexis had thought that Ivy was trying to tell her she had been indiscreet when she was younger. That this unknown Alex Barton was someone by whom she'd gotten pregnant, and that she, Alexis, was the result. But Ivy said this Alex was her husband, not just her lover. Her husband! Alexis was aghast to hear that her mother had been married before she met Papa. That meant she was divorced, which was almost as shocking and provocative as conceiving out of wedlock. But the truth, it turned out, was not so simple.

"Your mother," Ivy said, "was your father's mistress. She died when you were born. She was weakened by burns from the fire that destroyed the town. Then your father was—unable to care for you. . . ."

Unable to care for you. What did that mean? Did it mean he didn't choose to care for her? That he didn't want her? Did Ivy not want her either? Did she take her only out of some twisted sense of duty? It was at that very moment, it seemed to her now, that she had begun to feel invisible, to feel herself slipping away, to feel the need to assert herself so that she would not slip into obscurity. All she could do, though, was have a ridiculous tantrum.

"You're lying to me!" she had cried. "You're lying to me because you don't want me. You don't want me to be your daughter."

Ivy had run to her and taken her in her arms, but

she'd pushed her away. After that, neither of them had wanted to look at each other for a while, and the truth was slow in coming out. Ivy hadn't wanted to speak of it, but Langdon had persuaded her.

"Can't you see the agony the girl is in?" he said, days later. "We've got to tell her everything."

Then they told her. Alex had kept the birth a secret and had placed her in an orphanage. Ivy learned of it at about the same time she decided to leave Alex, and, horrified at what he had done, took her out of the orphanage and brought her to Texas, where she'd married Langdon. Alexis hadn't been born to them in the first year of their marriage, as she had always been led to believe. In fact, their marriage had taken place three years after her birth.

The story at least clarified some aspects of her life—the shadowy memories of a nun in what must have been the orphanage, the unspoken questions as to why she did not look like any of the family. It made other aspects of her life more confused and troubled, however. Who was her mother? What was she like? Ivy and Langdon were both very closemouthed on that subject, except to say that she was a dance-hall girl and she was Alex's mistress. Did she have other lovers as well? Did that mean she was a prostitute? Was she pretty? Did she, too, have blond hair and fair skin? Why hadn't her real father wanted her after her mother died? Was there something terribly wrong with her?

Alexis had been tormented by these questions at first, but after a while, she'd had to push them aside, to force them from her conscious thoughts, most of the time at least. It was only at night sometimes, or at times when she felt utterly alone, or utterly invisible, that the doubts and questions came back to haunt her.

Alex had not been invited to come. "It will only wound you," Ivy had said. "I will not let him harm you." But Alexis had been wounded anyway, and she'd had to learn to keep pushing the unanswered questions further and further back. It was silly to become emotional over the past, she told herself now as she stuffed the letter back into the box and pulled a nightgown from the bureau.

She prepared for bed, feeling the heavy weight of the night. Moisture was so thick in the air she could almost taste the gulf. Later, in bed, she couldn't sleep even when she tossed the sheet back and removed her gown to lie naked on the bed.

Memories of the day washed over her. It had all gone wrong, terribly wrong. If she had ever hoped to do business with Jon Calahan, she had ruined her chances now. When she had tried to appear confident, she had succeeded merely in looking like a fool.

But she couldn't give up. If he was right, if there was plenty of oil in West Texas and potential for success, she would have it. She would show them all—Ivy, Langdon, Diana, Miller, the father who didn't want her, the mother whose death she'd caused—that she could make it. Somehow, she would find the money she needed to get started.

Restless, she rose from her bed, went to the window, and stared out into the thick black night until a cloud pulled away from the moon. Then the pale light, shining through her window, turned her naked skin silver. As if on cue, a band of cicadas rioted out of surprise that she was there.

3

Jon Calahan had known all along that it would be hard to find a drilling contractor for his wildcat exploration in West Texas. Like the one he had just talked to in Beaumont, they would all want to stay in East Texas where there were proven reserves. A great black ocean beneath the marshy soil was making men rich and giving them no reason to risk time and capital in West Texas. There, the main thing that had been proven was that nature could be cruel and unrelenting. Months could pass when not even a drop of rain fell. The dry, scorching heat would wither grass and cattle as well as the men and women who were crazy enough to go there.

He'd hoped to get Langdon's backing because the support of Runnels Oil might encourage someone to take the risk. Runnels Oil was synonymous with success. Langdon Runnels had turned him down flat, though. Jon hadn't been entirely surprised, but he had hoped Runnels would suspend his hard feelings of the past for the sake of an investment.

Jon had discounted Alexis' brash offer immediately, in spite of the fact that he'd agreed to have dinner with her. She was a kid, and it was obvious that she was just trying to get back at her father. Now, however, he was beginning to imagine the satisfaction of getting back at Langdon Runnels by doing business with his daughter. He and Runnels had been rivals since the early days of the east Texas oil boom set off by the Spindletop well in 1901. Both had vied for the same scarce capital to develop their oil leases.

Runnels had a bigger cushion than he'd ever had, though, since Runnels had made a fortune in the Colorado gold fields before he ever came to Texas to look for oil. In fact, he had practically pushed Jon out of the market in the past with his financial clout. Jon had bested Runnels on a lease last year, though, and their enmity had deepened when Runnels accused him of using his position as a county commissioner to force a farmer who was behind on his taxes to sell leases to him, blocking Runnels out. Langdon Runnels was no paragon of ethics himself, however, from all that he'd heard. Rumor had it that he'd blackmailed his way into a lucrative business deal back in Colorado that had given him his start toward building his empire.

Jon swore he was going to beat Runnels this time no matter what it took. He was going to move in first and fast, and he was going to build his own empire. He had entrenched himself in the area already—bought up a number of leases and had even moved his wife and son there. Part of his plan was to present himself as a stable resident of the area, hoping it would influence some banker who might agree to lend him the capital he was going to need later to explore and develop.

Eleanor had not been eager to go at first. She didn't want to move so far away from Beaumont, where she had established herself in local society and enjoyed her position as the wife of a local government leader. But, because she saw it as her duty to follow her husband, she had acquiesced.

She was a loyal, dutiful, and ambitious wife—ambitious in that she considered it her duty and calling to see that his career was furthered. And his career, in her mind, had nothing to do with the oil business. That was merely a means of fueling them with the money they needed for what she saw as his true career—politics. She had even used the term statesman, which he found alternately ludicrous and embarrassing. She was the daughter of a county judge, and she'd cut her teeth on politics. She'd been the one who'd encouraged his entry into the political game and helped get him elected to the county commission.

He couldn't deny that he enjoyed the prestige and power. He'd been unprepared for her suggestion that he run for Congress, however. The leap from the board of commissioners of a backwater Texas county to the United States House of Representatives was beyond his imagination until she pointed out that West Texas was a frontier in more ways than one. There would be few qualified candidates in such a sparsely populated area, she said. As far as she was concerned he was already running, and she was convinced he would win.

Eleanor's sense of duty toward him did not, to any great extent, include sharing his bed. What he had originally mistaken for Victorian shyness had turned out to be something more difficult to overcome. It was more than shyness. It was a lack of interest bordering on outright disdain for anything sexual. There had been a series of miscarriages before their son, David, was conceived, and the birth had been difficult. Following that, Jon had detected an enormous sense of relief on Eleanor's part, along with even less interest in marital relations.

He had long since taken a mistress. There had been one in Beaumont and later one in Houston. He had never spoken of them to Eleanor, yet he was confident that she knew. After twenty years of marriage, much that remained unspoken did not necessarily remain uncommunicated. She recognized his need and accepted that he had found a way to satisfy it, just as he recognized that her need for him was something other than physical.

He was haunted, though, by all those miscarriages. He knew what his father would say. Beaty Calahan, the dour Scotsman, would claim that if his seed had been strong, if he had been more of a man, then all those miscarriages could have been avoided. Never mind that other men might blame the woman for such misfortune. Beaty Calahan was always looking for ways his son might have failed to live up to expectations.

Jon tried not to think about any of that now, though, but to focus instead on his new venture. The excitement of a new enterprise was as invigorating to him as a woman. This one wasn't going to be easy, and that in many ways made it all the more exciting. He'd seen the potential early. When one or two of the water wells they had dug in the great expanse around the town of Midland produced a thin film of oil mixed with the water, he'd had the first twinge of excitement, along with an uncanny sense that this was the land that would change his life.

After word got around about the oil film, a handful of wildcatters showed up to spud a few wells, hoping for a strike. Every one of them had turned up dry, but Jon's dream had caught fire. He wanted to build an empire as big as or bigger than Langdon Runnels's. He needed a little capital, though, and a drilling rig.

As he prepared for dinner with Alexis Runnels, he smiled, remembering her brash enthusiasm. She certainly had the guts he was looking for in a business partner. It was too bad she was a woman. He did find her amusing, though, and that youthful, impudent flirtatiousness was attractive, so why not spend a few hours with her?

He leaned closer to the mirror and ran his fingers through the front of his hair. He worried that it was beginning to thin a little, and he was concerned about the graying at his temples. He dampened his comb and ran it through his hair, darkening it with water. But the water would dry, of course. Maybe a little pomade . . . He touched just a little to his hair, and combed it in, then stared at himself in the mirror, wondering what the hell he was doing. The girl had to be twenty years younger than he was—young enough to be his daughter. He had no interest in women that young, and even if he did, he would be a fool to choose Alexis Runnels.

In spite of himself, he smiled as he thought about her. Maybe if he could talk her out of that crazy wildcatting scheme, Langdon Runnels would thank him for that. Fat chance. Runnels wouldn't thank him for pulling him out of a pile of shit.

He dressed in a dark wool suit and changed into

his black patent leather shoes with spats, the ones Eleanor had picked out for him. They were fashionable, Eleanor said, but they made him feel naked. He missed his boots.

He glanced at his reflection one more time and smiled to himself at the irony of taking Langdon Runnels's daughter to dinner. Maybe, he thought, noting that the pomade had darkened his hair quite nicely, maybe he would even take Ali Runnels dancing. Now that would chap Langdon Runnels's ass.

Jon found, to his dismay, that his palms were perspiring by the time the taxi stopped in front of the graceful house known as Green Leaves. He started to get out of the car, but hesitated, trying to collect himself. The pause was long enough to attract the attention of the driver who turned around in his seat to look at him, puzzled.

"Ain't this the place?" the driver asked.

"Sure," Jon said coming out of his stupor. "Sure, this is the place. You wait here. I'll be right back." He opened the door and got out, then walked with quick, determined steps to the front door and rang the bell.

By the time he heard footsteps coming toward the door from the inside, he had regained a measure of confidence. When the door opened, he expected to be greeted by Walter, but it was Alexis who stood in front of him, smiling and looking even more striking than she had the night before when he'd seen her in her swirl of pink chiffon.

She wore a black dress now that made her fair skin and hair look all the more fair and that hugged her figure in a very interesting way. Glittering sequins on the top of the dress were matched by the sparkle of jewels cascading from her ears, which her swept-back bobbed hair revealed in a way that seemed erotic to him. Her cheeks were rouged, and he detected a touch of unnatural pink at her mouth. He was not used to seeing women with painted faces, and he might have protested had it been Eleanor. He could think of no protest now, however. The only thing that entered his mind was a quote from *Henry VI* that his mother had taught him.

She's beautiful and therefore to be woo'd,
She is a woman, therefore to be won.

Beaty Calahan had protested that his wife, Hester, was making Jon "womanish" by teaching him poetry. She had taught him more than poetry, though. She had taught him to love it, and especially the works of Shakespeare. He knew now that in spite of his father's words of scorn ringing in his head, his thoughts were far from womanly as Alexis smiled and reached a hand toward him.

"Jon, how handsome you look!" she said in her crisp New York diction. "So refreshing to see something besides a cowboy."

"What am I supposed to infer by that?" He offered her his arm and led her toward the waiting cab.

She laughed. "I just meant that so many of Langdon's associates are so—well—provincial." He was amused at her habit of calling her father by his first name, but he tried not to let her see him smile. He sensed that she was nervous and didn't want to make her even more so. Her laugh was a little too high-pitched, and her hand trembled slightly upon his arm. Was she nervous about being near him? He doubted that was the case. More than likely she'd had a row with her father over her wildcatter scheme.

"I'm afraid I may disappoint you, Alexis," he said. "I'm as provincial as they come."

She waved a hand. *"A man of neither wit, nor words, nor worth?"*

"That's right. Like Mark Antony, *a plain, blunt man.*"

She stopped and turned to him, obviously surprised that he had recognized her quote from *Julius Caesar.* "Oh, my," she said. Her voice was breathy, sexy. "Not Mark Antony, but Caesar. *This was a man!*"

He knew then that she was more dangerous to him than he had ever realized.

The taxi dropped them off at the hotel. As they entered the dining room, she walked ahead of him and greeted the maître d'.

"George! How nice to see you!"

"Welcome back, Miss Alexis," the man said, giving her a broad smile. They clasped hands, and Jon saw the bill that had passed from one palm to another. Within minutes they were seated in a curtained booth and a bottle of liquor was brought to their table.

"Sorry it's not champagne," Alexis said, "but they never heard of it in Texas, you know."

"Never heard of what?"

They both laughed, and she raised her glass. "To Caesar," she said.

At first he thought it was clever sophistication that led her to try to seduce him by directing the conversation to a discussion of Shakespeare. During dinner she argued, with youthful conviction, Mark Antony's lack of statesmanship compared to Brutus's. Slowly, however, he began to realize that it was merely her lack of self-confidence that had led her to Shakespeare. She'd had no idea of his passion for the subject but was using it as a means of stalling for time—as a way of avoiding the true subject she wanted to talk about until she gathered up her courage.

He toyed with the idea of taking charge and asking her outright if she had gotten the money she needed from her father. Maybe it would end her agony if she could get to the point. Ultimately, he decided against it, as it would most likely bring the evening to an abrupt end, and he was going to enjoy it at least through dessert.

Alexis refused dessert.

"Are you sure?" he asked, trying, he realized, to prolong the encounter. "The 'old-fashioned peach cobbler' looks good."

"And it's just the thing to make my figure all the more unfashionable," she said. "No thanks."

"Then I'll ask for the check, and then I'll see you home."

"Oh no!" she said suddenly. "We haven't—I mean, I was going to—"

"To pay the check?" he teased.

"No, that's not what I meant. I mean, yes. Yes, of course."

"No you're not!" he said firmly. "It's not a woman's place."

She gave him a languid, sexy smile. "You're one of those horrible old-fashioned men who's going to treat me like a shrinking violet and consider me the weaker sex."

"I had no idea that good manners made me either horrible or old-fashioned." He pulled a few bills from his wallet and placed them on the table with the check. "And I had no idea that you could have come up with any kind of an opinion about anyone except Brutus or Antony or Caesar."

"Oh, dear. Have I been that much of a bore?"

He hesitated a moment, allowing his eyes to sweep over her. "I would never call you a bore."

Again, the seductive smile. "And just what would you call me?" Her flirting was becoming a bit too obvious.

"I would call you an attractive, charming young woman who is pretty damned scared because she's pretty damned unsure of herself."

She sat back in her chair, wearing a petulant look now. "You warned me, didn't you?" she asked, "that you were a plain, blunt man?"

He laughed. "That I did."

"And what makes you so sure that I'm damned scared and damned unsure of myself?"

"The way you've been skirting the issue. Your papa didn't turn loose of the money, did he? You want me to finance your scheme."

"Am I always so transparent?"

"I wouldn't know, Miss Runnels. I only met you yesterday. But I'd be willing to bet the answer is no. I'd wager you're complicated as hell."

"Well, you're wrong on one count. I'm not unsure of myself. I know I can—"

"Aren't you?"

"What do you mean?"

"Judging from what you told me yesterday, I think you feel cheated because you're not Langdon Runnels's blood daughter, and you're trying to prove something to somebody. Yourself, maybe. That you're good as anybody else even if you're not blood kin to all that money and power."

She laughed. "You're wrong." She took a quick sip of her drink and leaned across the table. "I told you I got over that shock a long time ago, and I don't believe in wallowing in the past. I believe in the future and in the here and now. In reality. And I have nothing to prove. What I have is pure and simple ambition and a conviction that I can make it on my own."

He tried to speak, but she never gave him a chance. "But you're right about one thing," she said. "Langdon turned me down. So now I have the chance to see if I can really make it on my own."

She paused, giving him a moment to take it in, an all-too-clever smile still on her lips. "See," she said, leaning back in her chair again, "I can play the plain, blunt man, too."

"The plain, blunt truth is you're a woman, not a man."

"What are you getting at?"

"I'm not sure I can do business with a woman."

Anger flared in her eyes, and she sat bolt upright so quickly he thought for a moment she would come flying across the table at him. "But you said yesterday that wouldn't stop you."

"What I said was I'm not frightened of doing business with a woman. And fear has nothing to do with it. I just know it doesn't make sense."

"Why doesn't it make sense? I have everything you want. The guts, the intelligence, the access to the expertise. All I want from you is—"

"Wait a minute." His hand reached across the table and covered hers. "You don't have to convince me of all your assets. This has nothing to do with doubting your abilities. It has to do with practicality. A woman in the oil fields would never be accepted. The men would never cooperate. They'd laugh you out of the business, and you'd be lucky if that's all they did."

"But that's ridiculous. There's no practical reason—"

"You're looking for practical reasons? It takes brute strength to run that machinery, and that's something that, for all your intelligence and charm, you don't have."

"My intelligence, and if need be, my charm, is exactly what I intend to use. I can hire the brute strength. And besides, *think you I am no stronger than my sex?*" She laughed in an effort to appear confident, but he sensed she knew it had failed.

"I think it's time I took you home." He stood and offered a hand to help her from the booth.

She looked up at him but didn't move. "But you can't. You haven't given me an answer."

"I have, my dear. I'm sorry."

Her eyes held his for a moment. Like a little girl's, he thought, staring up at him while she begged for candy, and then her expression changed, to what? Resignation? "All right," she said at last. "You've ruined my hopes for doing business with you, but I won't let you ruin my evening." She stood and took his arm and parted the curtains to their booth. "I want to take you someplace," she said. "We'll take the cab back to Green Leaves to pick up the car."

"Your father's car?"

"Of course. He has two, you know.

He laughed. "Of course."

When they arrived at the mansion, she went straight to the garage and backed the car out. Then she reached across the front seat and opened the door for him.

"Where are we going?" he asked, as he slid in beside her.

She laughed and made the tires squeal as she careened around a corner. He glanced at her, and he knew she sensed it.

"Relax!" she said. "I'm an excellent driver."

"I have no doubt that you are. When you're sober."

She laughed again and made another turn too fast. He saw that they were headed toward Liberty Road.

"You're taking me to French Town."

"Um-hmm."

"A bootlegger."

She turned toward him, a small smile flickering across a mouth that seemed utterly sensuous. "Oh, my," she said in a sultry voice. "You must think I'm really a bad girl."

"Are you?"

She gave him another smile and shrugged. He watched her maneuvering the car through the narrow streets of French Town, a section of Houston populated by black people who had moved in from Louisiana, bringing their Cajun and Creole cultures with them. She parked the car in front of a weathered one-story building that was throbbing with the sounds of a saxophone and a piano and laughter.

He felt decidedly uncomfortable knowing how, being the only white people in the room and by far the best dressed, they stood out as oddities, possibly as suspect. Ali seemed oblivious to that fact, though. She took his hand and pulled him toward a table. In a little while she had lost herself in the music.

Somehow a bottle showed up at their table, along

with two glasses. Jon poured drinks for the two of them, but Ali barely touched hers. She was still enthralled with the music, which, by now, Jon found, was giving him a headache. He still felt hundreds of eyes watching them, and he was growing more and more uncomfortable by the minute. When the tempo of the music changed and several couples began to dance together in the small square near the front, Ali pulled him toward them.

"Let's go," he said, resisting. This was not what he'd had in mind when he'd thought of taking her dancing. Come to think of it, he wasn't sure what he'd had in mind. Maybe it was just that he wanted to be the one who was in charge.

She gave him a questioning look, and then her now-familiar shrug and let him lead her out the door.

"Didn't you like it?" she asked when they were in the car again.

"The music? Why do you ask?"

"Why were you so eager to leave?"

"We were outsiders. It could have been dangerous."

There was her laugh again. "Not in this sleepy little southern town."

She was not as worldly-wise as he'd thought, perhaps, but he wouldn't let her know he suspected that. "You miss the big city." He phrased it as a statement more than a question.

"Of course," she said. "I love cities. New York. London. Paris."

"And you want to come to West Texas? Where there's not a city within five hundred miles?"

She glanced at him. "I want it very badly," she said, holding his eyes with her own.

"You are an interesting young woman, Alexis, and

I tell you honestly, I'm sorry it couldn't have worked out, but I'm sure you realize I can't afford to take a chance on someone who's—"

"Oh, for God's sake, Jon," she said, cutting him off. "Let's not go over that again. I told you I wasn't going to let you ruin my evening." When they reached the hotel, she got out of the car and walked toward the entrance.

"Where are you going?" He opened the door and had to hurry to catch up with her.

"To your room, of course," she said, over her shoulder. "I assumed you'd invite me up for a nightcap."

He took her shoulder and turned her around to face him. "Little lady, I think you've had quite enough tonight without a nightcap."

She met his eyes with an arrogance that he might have thought chilling if she hadn't looked so young. She replied, "I'm certainly old enough and perfectly capable of deciding for myself when I've had enough to drink. And I would appreciate it if you would refrain from calling me either 'little lady' or 'my dear.' They're both so condescending. My name is Alexis."

She pulled herself away from his grip, and he watched her march through the double doors and into the lobby. With a half-perplexed, half-amused shake of his head, he started after her. He caught up with her just as she approached the elevator. Taking her arm, he pulled her back. "If you insist on doing this, take the stairs," he whispered. "No sense in advertising your foolishness to the elevator operator. This is Houston, remember? Not Paris or New York. You could get me arrested."

"How perfectly ridiculous. I'm a grown woman

accountable for my own actions. It needn't be you who takes the responsibility," she said. He saw she was bluffing when she glanced around uneasily. "But you're right, of course," she said. "Let's take the stairs. You go first. I'll follow shortly."

"Third floor. Room three-oh-nine," he whispered.

He felt a foolish pride in being able to climb the three flights with ease and appear perfectly relaxed with no flushed face and no hard breathing when he opened the door to her a few minutes later.

"Here," he said, handing her a watered-down glass of whiskey. He'd poured it from the flask he carried in his suitcase and used tap water to weaken it. The whiskey in his own glass was straight.

She accepted the drink and sat on the edge of the bed. When she took her first taste of the whiskey and water, she grimaced. "God, what I wouldn't give for a glass of champagne or something else equally civilized."

"Sorry," he said. "It's the best I can do." He was standing across the room from her, leaning casually against the bureau. She was dangerous, he thought, but he was too wise, too old to fall into the trap.

"I don't mean to discredit your hospitality. After all, I invited myself up. Besides, it's not your fault. It's this damnable Prohibition law we're forced to live under."

"I would say you've done a pretty good job of ignoring the law tonight."

"Are you moralizing, Mr. Calahan?"

"No, just observing." He set his glass aside and tried not to smile, but he was finding it impossible not to be amused.

"Please don't laugh at me, Jon." The remark surprised him. He had thought she was too tipsy to be so perceptive.

"I would never laugh at you, my dear. Oops! Sorry about that," he added, realizing how he'd addressed her.

She giggled, easing the tension, then seemed to be looking around for a place for her glass. He took it from her and placed it on the nightstand. Before he could move away again, she reached for his hand and pulled him toward her.

"Please do sit down, Jon. You're making me nervous standing like that."

He allowed himself to be pulled to her side. She did not let go of his hand, and as he sat, he sensed her tension again. They were very close. He found himself looking into her eyes and felt her fingers curling around his. An inexplicable magnetism seemed to be pulling him to her. She moved closer, placing a hand on his face, caressing it, then she moved her hands to his shoulders and around his neck.

"I want you to kiss me," she said.

He reached up and placed his hands over hers, as if to remove them. "Alexis." He was fighting to keep his voice firm. "However much I would like to do that, and I can tell you that's a hell of a lot, I don't think it would be fair to you."

"Nonsense," she said, leaning closer.

"I'm married, Alexis."

He felt her reaction—a minute tensing of the muscles in her arms—and felt her pull back slightly. He removed them from around his neck and held her hands in his.

"I'm not trying to play holier-than-thou and tell you I've never had a woman since I've been married, but I can assure you I've always been very discreet and very careful in my choice."

"But I—I don't understand. What's wrong with me?"

He was taken aback at the forlorn, little-girl sound of her voice, and he saw that she looked pale and very frightened.

"There's nothing wrong with you," he said, standing and pacing about the room. "You're bright, attractive, intelligent, witty. Everything a man could want—"

"Oh, Lord!"

"I'm not in the habit of robbing the cradle, Alexis."

"What are you talking about?" she asked in the voice of chagrin. "I'm almost twenty-five years old, and I—"

"That means you're twenty-four. I'm forty-five. Old enough to be your father," he said, with his back to her.

She was silent for what seemed like a very long time, and when he turned around, she stood abruptly and gathered up her shawl and handbag, which she'd thrown on the bed. "I like you, Jon, and I thought you liked me. Perhaps I was wrong." She'd lost her forlorn, frightened tone, and was putting on a front. "I'm very sorry to have embarrassed you or inconvenienced you," she said, moving with rapid steps toward the door.

Quickly, he crossed the room, grabbed her arm and spun her around to face him. "Just a minute," he snapped. "You don't know what the hell you're talking about." She tried to wrench her arm free, but he held it fast. "The only one who ought to be embarrassed is you, coming on like a tramp that way."

"I've had quite enough of your moralizing," she said, trying again to wrest herself free of him.

"No you haven't, damn it!" He took both of her arms and forced her to face him. "Do you see what you're doing? Trying to use your sexual charms to get what you want in a business deal? Don't cheapen yourself, Alexis. You're too fine a woman for that, and—"

"Who do you think you are, telling me when and how to use my sexual charms?" she cried. This time she succeeded in pulling herself free. "It's the only power a woman has. But you know that, don't you? Of course you do. All men do. That's why you try to make us feel ashamed for using it. Men have all the other kinds of power. Especially men like you—physical, political, social. There's nothing left except sex, and you want us to be completely powerless, so you try to make us feel ashamed when we use it."

"Alexis, for God's sake listen to me. I don't want—"

"No! You listen to me." Her chin jutted forward, reminding him of a defiant child. "I thought you were different. I thought you would understand how I—I mean that there could be a remote possibility that you would like me, but—Oh, what the hell! Go ahead! Praise virginity and raise it to a pedestal. Raise it to divinity! Create virgin goddesses for all of us to worship. Try everything you can to make me ashamed. But I won't be! I won't be shamed out of using the only power a woman possesses. My only regret is that it didn't work!"

She rushed out of the room, slamming the door in his face.

For a minute, Jon was too astonished to move. Then he laughed quietly to himself. She was a scared kid, but damn, she had guts! He hoped to God he would be able to hold on to his resolve to leave her alone.

"I'll go back to New York, of course, and I'll get a job," Alexis said in answer to Ivy's question about her immediate plans. She had awakened that morning with a horrible headache as a result of the liquor the night before, but also, she knew, as a result of the unpleasant scene with Jon. Her headache had passed, but she still felt unwell. She had agreed to a walk through the garden with Diana and Ivy in the hope that the fresh air would revive her. Ivy knew nothing about the previous evening with Jon, but she did know that Langdon had turned her down on the investment, and now she was trying to act as a mediator.

"I still think you should consider the compromise I suggested," Ivy said. They were walking through the garden and her eyes were on Vanessa, who had run ahead of them, and who had now stopped to examine something in the grass. Diana walked on the other side of Ivy, pushing Lacey in a carriage.

"I told you, Mama. I want to go into the oil business, not into some dreadful dress shop or hat shop or whatever you think you can convince Papa is suitable. I'll get a job until I can make the money to do what I want."

"What kind of a job?" Ivy asked. "There isn't a lot available to a young woman." She waved away an expected protest with her delicate hand. "Oh I know you've got that degree in literature from Sarah Lawrence, but when it comes right down to it, you're not much better off than I was when I had to go to work."

"You made it, didn't you? Are you saying you could do it and I can't?"

"Oh, Ali." Ivy sounded genuinely distressed. "You know that's not what I meant. Why are you always twisting things that I say? I only meant—"

She was interrupted by a howl from Lacey, who had managed to fling her nursing bottle over the side of the carriage. Diana stopped the entourage in order to retrieve it for her. "I don't know why you don't just get married," Diana said, bending over the carriage to comfort the baby. "You don't have to get some horrible job. You know Papa has a generous dowry for you."

"It just doesn't make sense that I have to be married to get the money I want."

"Your father's old-fashioned, Ali, I admit that," Ivy said. "But he only wants the best for you. If he could, he'd protect you from what he knows can be a very difficult life. But since you're so dead set on trying your wings . . . Well, in his mind there's no other choice but to—There, there, Lacey." Ivy pulled the baby from the carriage and held her close. Lacey immediately stopped her whimpering.

"Oh, Mama, you'll spoil her," Diana protested.

"Impossible," Ivy said. "You can't spoil a child with too much love. Give Grandma a kiss, darling."

"Mama, the modern way is to allow the child to cry. All the books say that a child most certainly must not be coddled and handled by an adult any more than an hour each day. It's a sure way to rob them of independence."

"Phooey on what the books say," Ivy said, bouncing the baby in her arms.

"Mama . . ."

Ivy and Diana went on with their bantering for a

few minutes longer until Diana finally gave in and began playing with her two daughters, too. It annoyed Alexis that Diana couldn't stick to her convictions, and it annoyed her that they seemed to have forgotten she was there. Finally, she slipped away unnoticed.

Alone in her room, Alexis went about the business of repacking her clothes for the trip back to New York, feeling no better than she had before the walk. In fact, she felt worse. She couldn't help remembering what a fool she'd made of herself with Jon. She liked him. She liked him very much. And she really did wish he had kissed her.

She couldn't dwell on that, though. She'd have to forget the entire evening, and she'd have to forget Jon Calahan, but she wasn't going to forget about going into wildcatting. It was just that now she felt uncertain and almost desperate.

She was momentarily shaken out of her mood by the sound of someone knocking, and she opened the door to Marie.

"I just took a telephone call for you, Miss Ali."

"I can't take any telephone calls now, Marie. I have to finish packing."

"Oh, Mr. Calahan didn't stay on the line. He wants you to call him back. Said he wants you to let him know how soon you can be in Midland."

4

"I'll buy the rig, of course, but I want fifty percent of the profits, not ten percent. That's out of the question. I expect no less than the usual business arrangement." Alexis pushed her plate of oysters back and picked up her water glass. For once she could think of Prohibition as a blessing. She might otherwise have ordered wine with her meal, and it was becoming obvious to her that she didn't need even the remotest possibility of not having a clear mind, since she was dealing with Jon Calahan. Her initial euphoria at having him agree to accept her as a business partner was fading quickly.

He gave her an easy, self-assured smile. "But this isn't the usual business arrangement," he said.

"There's nothing particularly unusual about it. It's to be a partnership. They're formed all the time." Her voice was terse and her words clipped.

"But not with women wildcatters."

"What are you getting at?"

"Financing, my dear."

"That has nothing to do with my sex, and I asked you not to call me—"

"It has everything to do with your sex, especially since you told me your father isn't going to finance you."

"I don't see that you need to concern yourself with that, as long as I come up with the money and the equipment."

"You're going to borrow from a bank, of course. If you try to borrow it from a Houston bank, they'll check with your father." He looked up from his plate and gave her his most charming smile. "I believe he's made it pretty clear that he doesn't like me. He can keep you from going into business with me."

"The Houston banks aren't the only banks in the country."

"Of course not, but let me remind you again, little lady, that you're a woman."

The bastard had done it again. He'd used a condescending expression, and it hadn't been a slip this time. It just served to drive home his damnable point even harder. He was right; it wouldn't be easy. In fact it could be next to impossible for a woman to get a business loan for a drilling rig.

"All right," she said, throwing her napkin on the table. "Let's get to the point. What are you proposing?"

"I can help you out. I'll help you borrow the money from a bank in Beaumont. They know your daddy there, too, of course, but they also know me, so it'll be easier to keep him out of it. And I'll cosign the note for you."

"You're not afraid to do that? For a woman, I mean?" She made no attempt to keep the sarcasm out of her voice.

"Let's just say I've decided to trust you."

"If you trust me, then that means you know you won't have to make good on that note. I want forty percent."

"All right, fifteen."

"Thirty-five."

He studied her a moment, then smiled. "Twenty-five, and that's my final offer."

"You're using me."

"And you're using me, Alexis. To show your father you're big enough to do anything you want. I could become the victim of your failure."

She slammed her hand down hard on the table, attracting the attention of all those around them. "But you know you won't be a victim. You know I'm determined to succeed."

"You've got guts. I'll admit that, and I admire you for it. But you've got to look at my side, too. You're inexperienced. I'm taking a risk."

"It's only the risk takers who succeed, Jon. You know that. And besides if you're willing to gamble on finding oil some place that's unproven, why not gamble on me, too?"

"I didn't say I wasn't willing to gamble, but you've heard my terms."

She bit her lip to keep from cursing him. He had the upper hand and was taking full advantage of it. "I want this chance," she said. "I don't want you or anyone else to take it away from me."

He glanced up from his plate. "Why, I wouldn't want to take it away from you, ma'am. In fact, I'm giving you the chance nobody else will give you. The chance of a lifetime."

She clenched her hands in her lap under the table.

"You're not giving me anything," she said evenly. "I'm paying dearly for it, and you damn well know it."

His smile broadened. "I believe you're trying to tell me we've got a deal."

She paused a moment, trying to tame her fury. "We've got a deal."

"We'll form the company as Calahan and Runnels West Texas Oil Company. C and R West Texas. Has a nice ring, don't you think?"

"When do we start?" she asked, ignoring his statement.

"It's got to be soon. I filed a hundred and fifty-one applications for drilling rights in two counties over about four hundred thousand acres, and I've filed for drilling permits in Austin. That means I've got to pay the ten cents per acre fee in thirty days. I've raised most of it. If you get the loan for twenty thousand, you'll have enough to buy the rig and put up the rest."

"Twenty thousand! That's more than twenty-five percent."

"But don't forget, I'm taking all the risks by cosigning. And anyway, part of the money is going to buy a rig, which you will own. It won't all be invested in the drilling permits."

She looked down at her plate, but her stomach was churning. There was no point in trying to eat and no point in sitting across from him and being humiliated any longer. She slid out of the seat and stood, hoping she could manage to take her leave with some dignity. In the next instant, he stood, too, and she found herself having to look up at him.

"I'll meet you at the bank as soon as you can make

the appointment." She kept her tone brusque, but his stature, towering over her, robbed her of some of her confidence. "You can trust me to find a rig, and I'll find a way to get it to Coyote Flats. I think you'll find I'm capable of handling any part of this business venture you can handle."

"If you could make a banker believe that, then you wouldn't need me, would you?" His smile was as charming as ever, and it galled her.

Unable to think of a suitable reply, she turned and walked away. She stopped when he called her name, and, in spite of herself, turned to face him.

"I'll hire a crew," he said. He was fishing in his pocket, tossing a few bills on the table. "It will save you having to go into the oil fields. It can be a little rough for a woman, and I know a driller who can contact some men."

"How very generous of you, and how kind to be so solicitous of the little lady."

She saw his eyes change, become less hard. Yet that only heightened the tension she was feeling until he spoke, softly. "I've been a little tough on you. I apologize for that."

His words surprised her, unnerved her, and once again she could think of nothing to say in reply. The best she could do was shrug and start to walk away again—an immature gesture, she thought with chagrin, but it was too late to change it. Once again he stopped her, this time by walking to her side and touching her arm.

"I meant the apology," he said. "Maybe I was hitting below the belt. Let me make it up to you."

She gave a little laugh. She'd thought it would cover her nervousness, but it only served to emphasize it.

"Please," he said.
"You've been *cruel only to be kind?*"
It was his turn to laugh. "*King Lear?*"
"*Hamlet.*"
"Of course. Well, I never meant to be cruel. Only to be honest. Now I want to be kind. I want to take you dancing."

Her eyes widened in surprise. "Really?"
"And buy you dinner and flowers and—"
"And that will cure the insult? Make up for the shitty business deal you've forced me into?"

His hand tightened on her arm, and with gentle force he edged her toward the door. "You ought to have your mouth washed out with soap," he said, keeping his voice low.

Her laugh sounded young, careless.

She wondered later if she'd displeased him too much. It was one thing to be modern, but another to be crass. It was just that he infuriated her by always being right, always gaining the upper hand. Nevertheless, it wouldn't do to give the appearance of a silly, vulgar child. For that reason, she dressed with care in an ivory silk creation she'd bought in Paris. It was the nearest thing to understated she owned and the kind of thing Ivy might have worn. In fact, Alexis sensed her mother's approval when she came down the stairs that evening and happened upon her in the hall.

"Oh, Ali, you look so pretty," Ivy said, stopping to admire her.

"Thank you, Mother."

"You're going out?"

"Yes." She didn't dare say more. She half expected Ivy to ask with whom, but she didn't. She merely looked at her, an odd expression on her face, leading Alexis to think she didn't have to ask because she already knew the answer.

"Perhaps we should talk sometime," Ivy said.

"About what?"

"About what you're doing."

"I don't know what—"

"About this wildcatting business you mentioned. About Jon Calahan."

"Really, Mama, I don't see that there's anything to talk about. Just because Papa doesn't happen to approve of Mr. Calahan doesn't mean I can't see him."

"He's married, Ali."

There was a moment of tense silence. "I'm a big girl," Alexis said finally. "I know what I'm doing."

"Do you?"

"I've made a business proposal. That's all."

"I see."

"Cripes, Mother," Alexis said, throwing up her hands and turning away from her. "When you say that. When you say 'I see' the way you do, I know what it means."

"Ali—"

"I do! I know it means you don't approve. Can't you just say it? Can't you just come out and say 'I don't approve of you, Alexis. I don't approve of anything you do? Of anything you are?'"

"But that's not true, darling. Of course I . . ." Ivy shook her head and frowned. "Oh, look at what I've done! I've made a mess of this. I wanted to have a quiet talk with you, not an argument on the fly."

"I don't want to argue either, Mama," Alexis said tersely. She knew her outburst had sounded childish, but knowing that only added to her chagrin.

"I haven't had much time with you since you got back from New York," Ivy said. "Couldn't we spend the day together maybe and—"

"Sure." Alexis picked up a shawl she'd left on a hall table. "We'll have lunch sometime at one of those new places down by the university. And we'll talk."

"Ali, I—"

"I'm late, Mother." She gave Ivy a quick kiss on the cheek. "Tell Papa I'm taking the Cadillac again." She hurried out the door to the garage before Ivy could respond.

Alexis felt a moment of discomfort remembering the look on Ivy's face as she'd left. Had it truly been disappointment that they'd not spent more time together? Or merely disapproval that she was seeing Jon Calahan and that she had gone against Langdon's wishes by going into the oil business? Ivy was terribly loyal to Langdon and therefore would not be likely to understand anyone who would challenge him, she thought.

Langdon knew how to wield power, and Jon had been right when he had suggested that Langdon had enough influence to stop a bank loan to her if he wished. That was why they'd agreed that Jon would not pick her up at Green Leaves, but that she would instead, meet him at his hotel. From there, they would drive to a roadhouse he knew about.

The roadhouse was a low, rambling building crouching along the side of Buffalo Bayou with a collection of buggies, automobiles, and wagons parked in the front. Moisture from the gulf layered itself on the windows and played tricks with the light coming from the inside. Made it dance, and made the building look, Alexis thought, as if it were slightly tipsy. Raucous sounds—laughter, whoops, screeches, shouts—spilled out into the steamy night, and along with those sounds was the honky-tonk rhythm of a fiddle, a bass guitar, and a piano.

As they stepped inside Alexis was momentarily disoriented by the crowd, the noise, the heat. She felt Jon's hand move protectively to her waist and felt the pressure of his palm guiding her through the room. She glanced around and thought at first that they were out of place—she in her expensive silk dress, Jon in his dapper suit and tie and spats on his shoes—but she soon saw that there was as much a mix of dress styles as there were ages and genders and levels of affluence. Bottles of liquor were everywhere, as if no one had ever heard of Prohibition.

"How did you know about this place?" she asked when they were finally seated at a table. She found she had to shout to be heard above the noise. At the table next to them, a girl, who could have been no more than seventeen, threw her head back and laughed at something the man on whose lap she was sitting had just said. Alexis saw the man's hand slide up the girl's leg, under her dress.

"A county judge told me about it, friend of my father-in-law's," Jon shouted above the sound of her laughter and the other noise in the room. "That's him, over there." He gestured with his eyes toward a man seated at a table in the corner who was cutting his way through a large steak and obviously enjoying himself.

A waiter came up to their table and leaned close to Jon to speak to him, his voice inaudible to Alexis. Jon made a reply, and the waiter disappeared only to reappear a few minutes later with a bottle and two shot glasses along with a plate of fresh limes.

"It's not champagne," Jon said, leaning across the table to make himself heard. "But it's the best I could do."

"What is it?"

"Tequila."

"Oh, Lord! I always heard that stuff would make you go blind."

Jon laughed and uncorked the bottle. He poured the shot glasses full and shoved one toward Alexis. "Wait!" he said when she picked up the glass. "Let me show you how to do it. There's a little ritual to it." He made a fist and licked the base of his thumb to moisten it, then sprinkled it with salt and licked it off. Next he downed the shot of tequila and quickly sucked the juice from a lime. "Now try it," he said with a nod toward her shot glass. "Salt first, to make you thirsty, then the tequila, and then the lime to kill the bite."

"Whoo! That stuff burns!" she said.

Jon laughed. "It's made of cactus, and they leave the thorns in. The second shot's not so bad."

"Why would anyone want a second shot? It tastes horrible."

Jon had already poured second shots for both of them. "To our partnership," he said, raising the glass to her.

Alexis gave a little shrug and raised her own glass, then drank it without benefit of the lime and salt. She sat the glass down and exhaled, feeling as if she were breathing fire. "You're right. The second one's not so bad," she said.

Jon stood up and pulled her to her feet and led her to the dance floor.

"Let's dance," he said, his mouth close to her ear. "While we wait for our steaks."

"Steaks?"

"I took the liberty of calling ahead and ordering for you."

"You're trying to buy me off, aren't you?" she asked, as he took her into his arms.

"I don't know what you're talking about."

"Yes, you do. And so do I. Don't think I didn't know when I agreed to go out with you that's what you would do. You're trying to buy me off by wining and dining me so I won't complain about the unfair arrangement you forced me into."

"I don't have to buy you off. We've already made a deal."

She giggled. "You're an overbearing ogre."

He looked down at her and smiled.

"My, but you are a good dancer," she said, thinking how quickly the tequila had gone to her head. She felt just a little dizzy and very relaxed. And it was true, he really was a good dancer. She felt as if she were floating, as if she could dance with him all night.

As it turned out, she did. By three in the morning they had danced the fox-trot, the two-step, the turkey trot, and perhaps even the minuet as far as Alexis knew. Jon was the best dancer she'd ever met, and certainly more fun than anyone she'd met recently. She lost count of the number of shots of tequila she'd had, although she did remember distinctly that she hadn't meant to have more than two. It was just that the little ritual seemed so much fun, and Jon had been right. The taste wasn't so bad after a while. In fact, it was rather pleasant.

They'd also had a steak dinner as well as a ham and egg breakfast, and then more tequila. She was finding it hard to remember just what she had drunk or eaten. She only knew that it had all been great fun until she found herself throwing up in the parking lot.

The next thing she knew he had his arms around her, guiding her back to the car, and she felt too woozy to be embarrassed. They drove for awhile, and then he was helping her out of the car.

"Where are we going?"

"To my hotel room."

"Now, wait just a minute. You're not going to take advantage of me when I'm—"

"It seems to me, my dear, that you were not so reluctant to be in my hotel room a few days ago, when you thought you could use it to *your* advantage."

"That's different. I had a clear head then." She was having a little difficulty making her words come out right. "And whatever I was doing then, I want you to know I do not go around in'scriminately . . ."

"Indiscriminately what?"

"You know."

He laughed. "I never thought I'd see you embarrassed. Liquor is supposed to make you lose your inhibitions."

"I'm not going up those stairs."

"Oh, yes you are." He swooped her up in his arms and bounded up the stairs, taking them two at a time, ignoring her continued protest. When he had her inside, he threw her, none too delicately, on the bed and then turned away to the closet.

She sat up and tried to stand, but when she felt a wave of nausea pass over her, she sat down again quickly. "If you think you're goin' to get away with—"

"Here." He flung something at her. "Put that on. Sorry I don't have pajamas."

"I certainly will not! I'm goin' home!"

"I don't think your parents should see you like this."

"I'm not a child, and I can decide for myself how I'll be seen and by who—whom." In spite of herself she giggled at her grammatical slip.

"You're in no condition to drive, and you know it. I'd drive you there, but I can't get a taxi back to the hotel this late, and I don't want to have to explain to Langdon Runnels why I'm driving his car back to his house in the morning."

She leaned toward him and stuck a finger in his chest. "But you don't mind explaining why his daughter spent the night with you?"

"I'll leave that to you."

"You bas—" Before she could complete the insult she had to rush to the bathroom. She emerged several minutes later feeling weak and embarrassed.

Jon, it appeared, could not have cared less, however. He was asleep, or at least pretending to be asleep, on the small sofa, his solid body wrapped in a plaid blanket. His head was turned away so that the thin spot near the crown was for the first time obvious to her. For some reason, seeing that made her want to cry.

She couldn't remember for sure what happened next,

but when she awoke she was on the bed, lying on her stomach, one arm dangling limp and lifeless over the edge, and her head feeling as if someone had pounded it mercilessly for hours. She tried to pull her arm up, but found she couldn't. It had no feeling, and for one horrifying moment, she thought she had no arm.

What had happened the night before? Hadn't she gone out with Jon Calahan? Hadn't she had more than a little to drink? Was she in his bed? Surely she wasn't. Surely she had only dreamed she'd been with him. But this wasn't her bed. Maybe the dream wasn't over.

She tried to roll over, but a pounding, immobilizing pain shot into her head and stayed there. Closing her eyes, she slowly inched her one good arm under her chest until she could grasp the forearm of her limp dangling limb. She flexed her hand and caused her lifeless arm to flop up on the bed.

She opened one eye and managed to focus enough to get her bearings. It was Jon Calahan's hotel room. She was in his bed. She eased herself up, trying to ignore the pain in her head, and when she looked down she saw that she was wearing only a slip. One of his shirts was crumpled beside her. How had that happened? What had she done? She shot a glance to the opposite side of the bed. There was no one there. The bathroom door was open, and there was no one in there either.

At least it would save her the embarrassment of having to face him after her decidedly irresponsible behavior. Still trying to ignore her headache, she got out of bed and made her way to the bathroom. After a shower she felt only a little better, but she knew she had at least to attempt to drive home.

When she pulled up to Green Leaves and unlocked the front door, she silently prayed that she could slip in unnoticed. Walter, however, was standing in the hall when she opened the door. He was dressed in work clothes and holding a garden spade, apparently just on his way out. Marie was a few feet behind him vigorously rubbing the top of a cherry table with a dust cloth. They both stopped what they were doing and stared, first with looks of surprise and then, Alexis could swear, disappointment.

"Miss Ali," Walter said. "What are you—"

"Shhh!" Marie cautioned, gesturing with her head toward the parlor. Then with a silent movement of her hand, shooed Alexis upstairs. "Hurry up, child," she whispered. Alexis did her bidding and hurried up the stairs.

She had not managed to hide a thing, though. Ivy knew. Alexis sensed it with certainty when she went downstairs for lunch. Yet her mother never mentioned it. Instead, she kept the conversation light, giving herself away only with her eyes, which held what—sadness? Disappointment? Contempt? Alexis couldn't read them, except to know that Ivy knew she had not been home all night. It was obvious, of course, since the car had been gone. Langdon would know that, too, and there would be hell to pay later.

She would wait until dinner when he came home to pay her dues, though. In the meantime she had work to do. She still had to locate a rig she could buy, and she had to find a way to finance it without Jon Calahan's help. In spite of his offer to cosign the note for her, she was even more determined not to have to rely on him now because she'd made such a fool of herself last night by showing him she couldn't hold her liquor. Just like a child. Of course that was the way he thought of her, anyway, and he seemed determined to prove his point. What other reason would he have for getting her drunk last night? Just to show that he could? That she was a foolish girl? Not a woman with a head for business, but a silly girl.

How was she ever going to be able to do business with him now that she'd obviously made such a fool of herself? How, in fact, was she ever going to be able to face him? How could she find the courage to speak to him, even?

As it turned out, it didn't take courage to speak to him. It merely took picking up the phone later in the afternoon when Walter told her she had a call.

"Hello, Alexis. Just calling to see how you're feeling," the voice on the other end of the line said.

"I feel quite well, thank you," she replied stiffly. Could he tell by the sound of her voice that she was lying?

"Glad to hear it. Would you like to have supper with me tonight?"

"How kind of you to ask. But I've promised to have dinner with Mama and Papa."

"All right, then, we'll have lunch tomorrow. I've arranged for us to sign the papers at the bank in Beaumont. We can have lunch after that. You like barbecue? I know a little place there in Beaumont that's hard to beat."

She took a moment to answer while her anger seethed. "You've arranged everything it seems, then."

"If you have some objection—"

"Objection? Of course not." She used a voice dripping with sweetness and sarcasm. "Barbecue's fine. Good-bye, Jon."

She slammed the receiver down and whirled around in time to see Walter trying to pretend he hadn't seen her angry reaction.

"I believe the term is railroaded," she said as she sat across from him the next day, a checkered tablecloth separating them.

"Railroaded? Miss Runnels, I have just done you a favor."

"Done me a favor? Ha! I was treated like some sort of idiot by that damnable banker. He actually said I was cute to want to try my hand at the oil business. Cute! He gave me no respect as a businesswoman."

"Good God, you sound like a suffragette."

"Don't put labels on me, Jon. I have as much right to demand respect as you do." Now was not the time to admit to him that she actually had marched for women's suffrage.

"Everyone has to earn respect, my dear. You played up to that banker. You played the cute little darling."

"I had to do that to get what I wanted. I want this chance; I don't want to lose it. I had to make him think you were going to be able to shape me and mold me and that you would make all the decisions. Otherwise he would never have given me the loan."

"You played the game and you got what you played for. You played for money, not respect."

"You bastard—"

"I know for certain I'm going to wash your mouth out with soap."

"Stop treating me like a child."

"Stop acting like a child."

She looked at him over a long silence while she fought back her tears. She fought hard. To shed tears now would only add to her humiliation, only make her look more like a child. He really was a bastard for putting her in such a position, though. And he was a bastard for being so obvious about not mentioning the fiasco of the night before.

She gave him her most charming smile. "I'm playing the game, Jon, but I haven't even come close to getting what I want yet."

He looked at her, his expression grave, unsmiling. She felt a knot in her stomach. Perhaps she'd overdone the coyness. He pushed back in his chair, positioning himself in an arrogant sprawl while his eyes never left her. Then a slight smile crept to his lips and with a shake of his head, he said, "You're going to be one hell of a woman some day."

5

Jon stared into the mirror as he lathered his face, only dimly aware of Eleanor's reflection behind him. She had brought in his coffee on this, his first morning back home in Coyote Flats, and was now making the bed. But he wasn't thinking of Eleanor, he was thinking of Alexis. It had been a week since they'd reached their agreement that day in the restaurant, and he'd thought of her almost every day since then.

He thought of the way she had said, "I want this chance." She seemed so young, so vulnerable. She was almost pleading, and in the next instant she was defiant, daring him to take the chance away from her. He wondered if she knew how hard it had been for him at that moment to keep from taking her in his arms. He'd felt like comforting the poor kid, but it was more than her childlike manner that appealed to him. He had to be careful. She had danger written all over her.

It was one thing to have an occasional discreet dalliance, but it was something else to screw around with Alexis Runnels. She was a member of one of the wealthiest families in Texas, so she would attract attention. It would be political suicide if he got himself publicly entangled with Miss Runnels. It would be a coup, though, to have her as a business partner. The name alone would carry some weight, and he was still reveling in the thought of how old man Runnels must be choking on his own spit to have his daughter linked up with him.

She could be here any day now. She had asked for a month to find and purchase the equipment. It had now been more than three weeks.

As he picked up his razor and began to sharpen it on the strop he kept hanging next to the washstand, he couldn't help remembering the way Alexis had touched his face, then put her arms around him and said she wanted him to kiss her. In spite of himself, he also couldn't help wondering what would have happened if he had. What was that she had said about men inventing shame for a woman who used her sex as power? She said it was because men were afraid of women with power. Was that what he was afraid of? The power she might hold over him? He smiled to himself. Of course he wasn't afraid. He had a feeling she was the one who was afraid.

"Pleasant thoughts, Jon?" Eleanor's reflection suddenly came into sharp focus, and he was aware of the beautiful high cheekboned face framed by thick dark hair pulled back in a chignon, and of her remarkable brown eyes. "You were smiling." She gathered up damp towels and the work shirt he had worn the day before. "What were you thinking?"

"Nothing in particular." He felt the edge of his razor with his thumb and at the same time dropped his gaze from the mirror.

"Jon?"

"Yes?" He pulled the razor across his face, then rinsed it in the basin in front of him.

"It's something to do with the drilling contractor, isn't it?"

He paused briefly, his razor poised near his chin. "What makes you ask that?"

"Don't try to fool me," Eleanor said with a little laugh. "I know what you're thinking. You can hardly wait for the rig to get here and the drilling to start."

"I've got a lot of money at stake, Eleanor." Jon said, plowing wide furrows in the lather. "So yeah, I guess it's been on my mind."

"If only it will work! If you are the one who starts this area developing with oil, you'll win that election for certain."

He rinsed his razor again and spoke to her reflection. "Eleanor, nothing's certain when it comes to politics. You know that."

"There's nobody else in this district who can even touch you, and you know that."

He wiped his face with a towel and kissed her cheek. "You'll have me running for president if I don't watch you," he said.

She laughed. "Why not?" She took the towel from him to wipe away the residue of lather he'd left on her face. "He will be here soon, won't he? The drilling contractor, I mean."

"She said to give her three or four weeks."

"She?"

He felt a sudden hollowness in his stomach. He had

meant to tell Eleanor before now that the drilling contractor was Alexis Runnels, but somehow he had found it difficult to bring up the subject. He knew now what an error he had made. He should have mentioned it straight off, should have made a point of telling her that using the Runnels name was part of the reason he had linked up with Alexis. He had been leery, though, that Eleanor would see through him and discover another, far more dangerous reason for wanting Alexis out here.

"I told you, didn't I? I'm sure I did. The drilling contractor I hired is Alexis Runnels."

"Alexis Runnels? No you didn't mention it." Eleanor's face was expressionless, but somehow he didn't find that particularly comforting. "Do I know her?"

"Langdon Runnels's daughter," he said, buttoning his shirt.

"Really? The one they say lived in Paris or somewhere for awhile?"

"Yes. I'm sure the old goat's livid."

Eleanor's mouth was a thin line. "Does she know who you are? About those awful things Runnels accused you of?"

"I have no idea what she knows. But she's not interested in politics. Politics has nothing to do with this." He was annoyed that he had allowed Eleanor to put him on the defensive.

"It has everything to do with it. He could have put her up to this. It may be a way to spy on you, or worse yet to get you to—that is, to manipulate you to find a way to discredit you."

Jon laughed. "I'm afraid, dear, that her motive is much more childish. She was just looking for a way to get back at her father. She's using me."

There was a silence that seemed to stretch interminably while he combed his hair. "It could backfire," Eleanor said finally. "She could turn on you. Blood is thicker than water."

He thought of revealing the irony to her—that Alexis was Langdon Runnels's stepdaughter and they, in fact, shared no common blood, but all he said was, "Charming expression."

Her eyes flashed with anger. "Jon! Don't belittle me. I'm serious about this. You've done a foolish thing, and you—"

He whirled suddenly to face her. "Don't you belittle me, damn it! I know what I'm doing. I'm no fool." He regretted his outburst immediately, and he could think of no sound reason for his reaction except that he hated being thought a fool.

Eleanor had gone pale. "Of course you're not, darling. It was thoughtless of me to say such a thing."

Before Jon could respond she switched to another topic. "She has money, of course," she said.

The sudden switch reminded Jon of how much he admired her. She wouldn't flinch in the face of his anger. She would keep her dignity, and she would never lose sight of her goal—to make him all that she thought he could be. Obviously, now she was thinking that some of the Runnels money could come in handy for that.

"Did you ever see a Runnels who didn't have money?" he asked evasively. It wouldn't do to admit to Eleanor that Alexis had been cut off by her father. That would only raise unwarranted suspicion. It would be difficult to explain that, aside from his undeniable attraction to her, there was a more realistic if inexplicable reason for wanting to work with her.

She had what he'd been looking for in a partner—a hunger that was both ruthless and reckless.

"But that's not the only reason you hired her, is it?"

Eleanor's question startled him. "I don't know what you mean."

"You're using her, too, aren't you?"

"What do you mean?"

"To get back at him. Her father."

He gave a short derisive laugh. "What do you think I am?"

"I know what you are, dear. You are a clever, ruthless man." She gave him a smile he couldn't read and walked away toward the kitchen.

By the time he had put on his shoes and entered the kitchen, Eleanor had breakfast waiting for him. David was already at the table eating his eggs. Jon felt a surge of emotions—pride mixed with anxiety—whenever he was in his son's presence. That damned uneasy feeling was ridiculous, he knew. Dave was just a kid. The boy glanced up quickly as Jon entered and then just as quickly brought his eyes back to his plate. It all took place in a fraction of a second, so quick that Jon wasn't sure it had happened at all.

"Good morning, Dave."

"Mornin'," he said. The word was hardly more than a grunt. Jon let his eyes linger on his son a moment, wondering what he was thinking, wondering when this unacknowledged gulf between them had been created.

"Glad to see me back, are you?" Jon made no attempt to keep the sarcasm out of his voice as he sat down across from the boy. His tone made Dave look up and then cut a nervous glance at his mother. "Oh, don't let me stop you," Jon said. "Obviously you were too hungry to wait for me. Go ahead. Finish your breakfast."

"It's my fault, Jon," Eleanor said. "I told him to go ahead and eat. He has to go to school."

"It's not your fault," Dave said. "I'm just not used to him being here." Jon noticed how deep his voice sounded, how there were no breaks and squeaks as there had been when he'd heard it only a few months ago, before he left for Houston to look for a drilling contractor.

"Well, I am here," Jon said. "And I'm going to stay for a while."

Dave looked at him for a moment, shoulders slumped, hands in his lap. "I'd like to be excused," he said finally.

"You haven't eaten all your eggs."

"I'm not very hungry."

"You looked hungry when I came in. Do I spoil your appetite?"

Another pause before he spoke. "No, sir."

Jon stared at his son, wondering what the expression on his face meant. Was it contempt? And what had he done in the fifteen years of his son's life to deserve that? How could he tell him that he wanted only his love?

"I have to go to school," Dave said with some impatience after another stretch of silence.

Jon peppered his eggs until they were black and asked without looking up, "How is school?"

"I hate it."

The answer surprised Jon. He glanced up quickly and saw that the boy meant it. "You'd just as well make up your mind to like it, because you need an education."

"I'll get an education. I just don't want to go to school here. I want to go back to Beaumont. That's where my friends are."

"You don't go to school to be with your friends." Jon used one of Eleanor's tough biscuits to help scoop some of his eggs onto his fork, then tasted both. "You go to school to learn. You're too old to be worrying about foolin' around with your playmates."

Dave stood up and moved toward the door, his sudden movement knocking over one of the chairs.

"I'm talking to you, Dave! Don't you know it's bad manners to leave in the middle of a conversation?"

"This is no goddamned conversation. This is just a chance for you to order me around, and I ain't puttin' up with it."

Jon stood up abruptly and for a moment was shocked that he had to look up to meet his son's eyes. "You watch your language in front of your mother, boy, and you have time if I tell you—" He never finished the sentence before Dave left, slamming the door.

Dead silence.

Then Eleanor stirred, bringing the coffeepot to the table to refill his cup. Jon noticed that her hand shook as she poured the coffee.

"Will you be out all day?" In spite of her trembling hands, her voice was calm. It was as if the scene with Dave had never happened.

"Yes," he said, struggling to maintain his own calm. "I have work to do." Better to think of work than to think of Dave, he thought. Better not to think of how his heart ached because of the vast wasteland of misunderstanding that had developed between them and how his heart ached all the more because he didn't understand how it had happened.

"I was wondering," Eleanor said, her back to him as she replaced the coffeepot on the stove, "if I might have a word with you before you go."

He glanced at her, momentarily startled. It wouldn't be like her to want to go over the row with Dave, but he had seen her hand shaking and knew she'd been upset. He wasn't in the mood to talk about their son now, though, or about any mistakes Jon might have made with him, or about anything for that matter. But when he saw how she looked at him so pleadingly, he felt a heavy burden of responsibility for her, along with a great need not to disappoint her.

"Of course," he said.

When she moved toward him, her fragility seemed to disappear in her ice blue gaze. In those eyes, shrewd and bright, and in the firm set of her mouth, he recognized the resilience he'd come to rely upon.

"It's just that I want to remind you of the church supper tomorrow night." She brought her coffee cup to the table and sat down in the chair Dave had occupied. "I have the feeling you've forgotten."

"Tomorrow night? I—"

"You had forgotten." The look she gave him seemed to say she was not surprised he had been so irresponsible. She pushed Dave's soiled plate aside as if she were pushing away everything except her thoughts of the church supper. "It's important, Jon. You can't afford to miss it. There will be a lot of people there. Important people."

A church supper was the last thing he wanted to think about now. He wanted only to find Dave and find some way to make amends, or to tell him to straighten up and quit acting like a snot-nosed little shit. Or he wanted to find some way to forget it entirely.

"I expected to work late tomorrow night," he found himself saying. "I need to go over the lease agreements. I can't imagine who of any importance would be there anyway."

"Everyone's important when they have a vote."

"Eleanor, look, I—"

"Gordon Witherspoon is a member of that church." Eleanor set her coffee cup down with a feathery light grace that belied the look of cold steel in her eyes. "The banker, Jon." He thought he detected the slightest hint of impatient sarcasm in her voice. "You're going to need money for the fall campaign. He knows how to raise it. This is a congressional race, darling. It'll be more expensive than running for the county commission."

"I've also got a living to make," he said, making no attempt to hide the impatience in his own voice as he moved toward the door. He was thinking about Gordon Witherspoon. It wouldn't hurt to be friendly with him in any event. It was going to take money to develop a new oil field, and he might have to borrow from Mr. Witherspoon's Coyote Flats bank.

"Of course you do, darling, but you can't let this—Jon, aren't you going to finish your coffee?"

She watched him go, then stared at the closed door for a few seconds without really seeing it. His attitude surprised her. Of course she'd known he'd be upset after a run-in with Dave. He always was. She hadn't expected the confrontation, though. Dave had seemed so eager to see him, she'd expected things to run smoothly. Jon had been in a good mood when he'd returned home, too. He'd gotten the partner and the financing he'd needed to develop the field, and he'd obviously enjoyed his stay in Houston. With both of them in such a high spirits, she'd thought things would run smoothly.

But Jon had been edgy. He'd picked that fight with Dave. She'd seen him act the same way around his father before he died, seen that same chip on his shoulder. She'd never been able to figure out why he carried it around when he had so much talent, so much untapped strength and power.

He was ambitious, she knew, and there was a ruthless streak in him that she both feared and admired. It was that raw ambition that had attracted her to him to begin with. Her own father had possessed the same traits, only more refined perhaps, less untamed. But he had not had Jon's brains and cunning, and so he'd risen only to a minor position of power as a county judge. He had recognized the potential in Jon, though, just as she had, and together they had groomed him and refined him, given the ruthlessness direction. Now Jon was ready. She knew he was ready. She had felt it in her soul.

She remembered how she had considered not moving to West Texas with him, but she'd known there was the risk of rumor if she didn't. She knew a person couldn't afford scandal in politics, and she was certain Jon wasn't through with politics. She'd made the move hoping he would come back to Beaumont eventually and hoping that with luck maybe he could pick up his career then.

Her ideas changed soon after they'd moved. West Texas was new country, sparsely populated with people to whom Jon, with his folksy manner, could relate. She had seen quickly that the area was tailor-made to further his political career, and she had gone to work immediately to build the base. Jon had not stopped her but had let her lead him. They both knew that he needed her.

Jon always came back from one of his trips full of energy and vitality, and she had been prepared to take advantage of it. She had no illusions about why he came back so revitalized. There was a woman, of course. Eleanor couldn't deny that his dalliances had bothered her at first. She would have liked to have been his only need, just as he was hers, but she had learned to put it into perspective. Jon's women meant no more to him than other men's horse racing or golf games or motor cars. It was a diversion that satisfied a need that had nothing to do with not loving his wife and family. He loved her as much as she loved him and needed her more than he realized.

She had seen the look in Jon's eyes when he had mentioned Alexis Runnels and had surmised that she had been the woman this time. Ordinarily Eleanor preferred to be kept ignorant of names and details, but if she had guessed the truth this time, she wouldn't let it bother her, since, of course, it was obviously over. Otherwise Jon wouldn't have Alexis coming out here. He was, if nothing else, always discreet.

It could be a problem if the young woman fancied herself in love with Jon, of course, but from what she had heard of Alexis Runnels, that wasn't likely to happen. The elder daughter of the Runnels family had the reputation of being the family black sheep— the naughty little rich girl who had defied convention and her respectable Texas family by running with a fast crowd on the East Coast, traipsing off to Europe during the war, driving her own car, and drinking gin. It was even rumored that she'd had a lover. She wasn't likely to be the type to take a little fling too seriously or to fancy herself in love with any one man for too long.

Miss Runnels's reputation could be bad for Jon's career if she became too closely linked with him, of course. Rich and powerful families such as the Runnelses, even without a black sheep, were always fair game for wagging tongues. There was no need to worry yet, though, Eleanor decided. Alexis Runnels was coming to Coyote Flats as a wildcatter just for a lark, no doubt. In time she would become restless and move on to a new adventure. Eleanor knew she had only to bide her time.

The first thing Eleanor noticed when she first saw Alexis was that she looked so young, and it occurred to her that she might have been wrong about Jon having had an affair with her. He'd never in the past been attracted to someone young enough to be his daughter.

She was standing in the doorway of the house looking windblown, blond, slightly plump, and only mildly pretty. Yet there was something about her that made her attractive. Her eyes were intensely blue and large and there was a pampered, well-cared-for look to her skin, but it was her mouth, Eleanor thought, that gave her the allure. It was a mouth that she had no doubt could pout and laugh and purse with pleasure. Yet there was hardness there too, the look of knowing too much too soon.

"You must be Mrs. Calahan," the girl said in her eastern accent. She put out her hand and flashed a smile. "I'm—"

"Alexis!" Jon said, coming in from the other room. "You got here sooner than I expected. What did you do, sprout wings on that Cadillac? I see you've met my wife."

Eleanor was a little taken aback at his exuberance as well as by the way he had draped his arm over her shoulder while he looked at Miss Runnels. He rarely did that and certainly not in the presence of strangers. It made her feel odd and a little suspicious.

"We were just about to introduce ourselves." The young woman's voice was low and throaty and her tone slightly reproachful. She put out her hand again and said, "Alexis Runnels, Mrs. Calahan. I'm Jon's new partner."

Eleanor met her eyes. "Yes, so he told me." He had slept with her, she thought. She could tell by the way they avoided each other's eyes.

"Well, come in!" Jon said. His enthusiastic manner made it obvious he had something to hide. "You must be tired after such a long trip. Even in a Cadillac. Eleanor can get you a glass of tea. Sorry there's no gin."

"I didn't come in the Cadillac. That belongs to Papa. I bought a car of my own, a Stutz." Eleanor saw that the girl's eyes were flashing white fire.

"Well, sure, I just thought he might—"

"Papa's not involved in this. I thought I made that clear from the beginning. And I don't need gin. Or tea either, for that matter. I just stopped to let you know I'm here, and the drilling rig will follow. It's coming by train."

"Good," Jon said. It was impossible for Eleanor to tell by his tone whether he was chastened or amused.

"I'll have to find some way to get the rig to the drill site. Could we hire a truck?" Miss Runnels's mouth was tight with some secret anger and her words clipped.

"We can hire a wagon and some mules to pull it. Don't know that we can find one of those newfangled trucks." Jon said. His tone had sharpened and cooled to match hers.

"It won't arrive until the end of the week. In the meantime I'll be staying at the hotel. I'd like to meet with the geologist if that's possible. Perhaps you could ask him to meet me at the hotel for breakfast."

"If you think it's necessary."

"I do think it's necessary, Jon. I want to learn as much about this as possible. I don't intend to fail."

"Then I'll arrange for you to meet him at the drill site tomorrow. I'll write down directions for you."

Eleanor sensed the tension between them increasing by the second. When Jon had finished writing the directions for Miss Runnels, he handed the paper to her, and she saw the look that passed between them. Alexis Runnels turned away.

"Happy to have met you, Mrs. Calahan."

Eleanor knew without a doubt that the affair had not ended.

6

Alexis pulled one of her dresses out of the bag and hung it on a wire hanger on the single rod that served as a closet in the only hotel in Coyote Flats, then threw some underwear in a drawer and slammed it shut a little too hard, venting an aggression she didn't understand.

It could have something to do with the fact that she'd seen a flyer on the registration desk urging people to vote for Jon Calahan for Congress, she thought. Why had he failed to mention that he was running for Congress? What did it matter that he hadn't? She'd gotten what she wanted out of him. That was all that mattered. She only wanted a chance to prove herself in the new fields, a chance to make money that was all her own and in no way controlled by anyone else. She only wanted to prove to Papa she could do it.

She had no reason to care what Jon Calahan did. She hadn't had any reason to be nervous about seeing him again, either. Yet she had been apprehensive since she left Houston, and the feeling had intensified as she had driven up to his house. It bothered her that the reunion with him had fallen short of her expectations.

What had she expected, anyway? To be greeted with open arms and a kiss? Not likely. The only thing they'd shared had been a discreet flirtation that was all part of going after what each of them wanted. She knew she should have notified him somehow ahead of time of the day she expected to arrive in Coyote Flats. That way, they could have met someplace to go over the details of the arrival of the drilling rig. As it was, it had been awkward walking in cold and meeting his wife. Alexis had anticipated that she would be there, of course, but when Mrs. Calahan opened the door, she'd had a mild shock. She hadn't expected her to be so attractive, so self-assured.

Nevertheless, Eleanor Calahan had been wary, Alexis knew from the silent warning she had seen in her eyes. Eleanor needn't worry, though. Jon wasn't going to risk being indiscreet, and she, herself, wasn't going to risk falling in love again. She'd been foolishly in love with Zane Lawrence, and it had almost destroyed her.

Well, she wasn't going to think about that now, Alexis told herself. She was going to have an early dinner and a hot bath to get the kinks out of her back after the long drive, and then she was going to bed. She wanted an early start in the morning to the drilling site. Jon had said the geologist would be there, and she wanted a chance to talk with him. She wanted to understand as much as possible about this new venture.

The hotel offered no dining facilities, but she found a small place a few blocks down the dusty street. A sign in front read "Club Cafe" with "Blackie Stephanopolis, Proprietor," in small letters beneath the name. The food was fried and heavy with grease, and by the time she'd gotten into bed, it seemed to have formed a lump in her stomach, keeping her awake. It was Jon whose face and voice filled her mind as she lay in bed.

She rolled over to her side and pulled the spare pillow over her head as if to force him from her thoughts. It did no good. She could see him standing in front of her, his arm draped across his wife's shoulders in an unbearably natural way—as if it belonged there, had always been there. As if he wanted her to see that theirs was the perfect comfortable, middle-aged relationship.

Well let it be perfect, damn him. Let it be as perfect as he wanted her to believe. Let him become a congressman if that's what he wanted. She wouldn't embarrass him by hinting there had been anything between them or by mentioning the night she'd spent in his hotel room.

It wasn't going to be hard to put that out of her mind, she told herself, because, after all, he had warned her that nothing was going to come of their relationship. As he had pointed out, they only wanted to use each other.

The bastard! The cool, calculating, manipulative, self-serving bastard. It was clear that a woman would be a fool to get mixed up with a damned politician like Jon Calahan.

She let the pillow drop and rolled over on her back, staring into the darkness that filled the room, willing herself not to think of him. She would think instead about her plan for the next day. She would get up early and head for the drilling site to talk to the geologist. It was important to learn as much as possible as quickly as possible, because she knew without a doubt that in order to survive, she was going to have to stay one jump ahead of Jon Calahan.

Shadowy thoughts of him—his smile, the feel of his arms around her when they'd danced, the creases at the corners of his eyes when he laughed, the thin spot in his hair when his back was to her as he slept—all came back to her, but she fought them away vigorously until at last she fell into an exhausted slumber.

She was still sleeping deeply when the alarm clock she had placed beside her bed snatched her into a startled wakefulness.

A hint of him lingered still in her brain—enough that she remembered her resolve immediately. Flinging the covers back, she got out of bed and dressed quickly in men's flannel trousers and a cotton shirtwaist with leather boots. She'd begun wearing trousers in France during the war when she'd found it necessary to help load and unload supplies for the canteen, and she'd found them comfortable and practical.

She brushed her bobbed hair quickly and picked up the wide-brimmed felt hat she'd bought before she left Houston. It had leather trim around the crown and a braided leather chin strap. Not fashionable, perhaps, but she needed something to protect her fair skin from the late spring sun. Looping the leather strap over her head, she left the hat lying flat against her shoulder blades and picked up the books and papers on geological formations she brought along to study.

She had just entered the tiny lobby of the hotel on her way to her car, which she'd parked at curbside in front of the hotel, when she saw him. He was standing near the desk, hat in hand and grinning broadly as if he had been waiting for her. She was struck by how handsome he looked—maybe the word was dashing—with his trousers tucked into high leather boots, somewhat splattered with mud as if he'd just come in from a drilling site, and his white shirt open at the collar. It was a calculated casual elegance, she thought, noting how the shirt was starched and impeccably pressed. Jon Calahan, the politician, knew how to create an image.

"Good morning, Alexis."

"Why, Jon, what a pleasant surprise." She gave him a frosty smile. "I had no idea Mrs. Calahan would let you out of the house so early."

He laughed. "In your usual naughty-little-girl form, I see."

He had cut her down to size by making her feel like a spoiled child again. "No, just surprised. I really didn't expect you to be here so soon. I thought your domestic ritual might take a little more time. You know. Say good morning to the kids. A nice chatty breakfast. How's school? Did you do your homework? Brush your teeth? Kiss Daddy goodbye. That kind of thing."

He walked toward the door and opened it, then turned back to look at her. "Are you coming?" he asked.

She didn't move at first and didn't speak. She was, she realized, unused to being ignored. "Coming where?" she asked finally.

"I've decided to go with you to the drilling site."

She moved past him, pulling on her driving gloves as she did. "Of course. I'll drive."

"You'd better let me do the driving."

She turned toward him. "Do you think I'm incompetent?"

"I have no reason whatsoever to think you are incompetent," he said, taking her arm and leading her with a firmness toward his car. "You are spoiled, pampered, headstrong, and a pain in the ass." He opened the door to his Oldsmobile and urged her with the same firmness into the seat. Closing the door, he leaned both hands on the window to look down at her better, then said with a teasing smile, "But you're from a rich family, so I put up with it."

The word "bastard" came to her mind again, but she said nothing. She merely gave him an icy glance and turned her face in stony profile to him. She was aware of his arrogant chuckle as he straightened and moved around the car to the driver's side.

"Why didn't you tell me you were running for Congress?" she asked as he started the car.

"Does it matter?"

"It could, if you're too busy with politics to take care of our business."

He turned to her and smiled broadly. "I have you for that, my dear." She had no way of knowing whether he was being sincere or sarcastic.

They rode in silence for several minutes while Alexis watched the countryside through the windows of Jon's car. The land was flat with occasional low rock ledges slicing through the prairie. Lavender-tipped grass spread itself in a thin blanket across the land and rippled lavishly in the wind. Silvery toothed sagebrush and mesquite with feathery, fragile leaves sprang up now and then, as did cactus, emerging full of thorns and defiance. The soil was pale, even chalky white in places, and it looked dry. Yet there was a faint hint of sticky moisture and the smell and feel of salt in the air from the distant gulf. Or maybe, Alexis thought, it was a reminder that the huge dusty expanse they were driving through had once been a sea, according to the geology books she'd read.

Finally Jon broke the silence. "What are you thinking?" he asked just as her eyes fell upon another ledge of rocks.

"Geological formations," she said. From the corner of her eye she caught the hint of surprise on his face, the slightly widened eyes and raised brow.

"Oh, really?"

It galled her that he had expected her to enter into an investment without having any idea of what it was all about. Well, she'd learned not to do that in one uncomfortable session with Langdon.

"Your geologist has tested some of these rocks turned up when the road was cut though, I assume," she said.

"Of course."

"Sandstone? Limestone?"

"Both."

"And he thinks it's promising?"

"He does or we wouldn't be here."

"Of course."

"What's eating you?"

"I don't know what you mean," she said without emotion and still not looking at him.

"When my love swears that she is made of truth, I do believe her, though I know she lies."

"I'm not your love."

"You really are put out."

"Stop treating me like a child, Jon. And don't give me your standard retort that I should stop acting like one. I'm doing nothing of the kind. And you can stop being afraid of me."

A derisive laugh erupted suddenly. "Afraid of you? Of course I'm not—"

"Oh, yes you are. You're afraid I'm going to betray you somehow. Kiss and tell? Is that the expression? I'm not going to ruin your political career by telling anyone I spent the night in your hotel room, so you can stop worrying. We both know nothing happened."

"I'm not afraid of what you will say, Alexis. You have as much to lose as I do."

She turned suddenly to face him. "I have nothing to lose," she said, "and that's what makes you afraid of me."

He answered her with a silent look, and she was certain she saw fear in his eyes. Until he spoke. "My dear, one of the reasons I've survived and prospered, at least modestly, is because I've learned everybody has something to lose."

She met his eyes for a moment, and she saw that the hint of a confident grin was still lingering on his lips. She decided that he was indeed ruthless and possibly dangerous. Finally she spoke with utter clarity. "I knew you were the right one to teach me what I need to know."

The squatting hulk of the wooden-sided tent with a canvas top, which Alexis recognized as Army surplus, was visible long before Jon turned his car off the rough road that cut through the prairie and headed it down two deep ruts that led to the tent. Alexis had not thought anything could be rougher than the rock-and-pothole-infested path they had just traveled, but the bone-jarring and bouncing she was subjected to now proved her wrong. She had to hang on to the dashboard and the side of the door to keep from being thrown to the floor, and if the jolting and shaking weren't enough to make conversation impossible, the cloud of dust that billowed in through the canvas-curtained windows was.

By the time Jon finally brought the car to a halt in front of the tent, steam was hissing from the radiator. Alexis loosened the scarf she wore around her neck and used it to wipe away the sticky mask of sweat and dust from her face. In the same instant a man emerged from the tent. He looked to be several years older than Jon, possibly in his early sixties. His hat was pushed back to reveal a balding head, and he wore round wire-rimmed spectacles. A square jaw and a firm mouth gave him a look of shrewdness. Jon opened the door on his side of the car and got out to greet him.

"You got here earlier than I thought you would," the man said, ignoring the noisy radiator as if it were an occurrence to be expected, and ignoring Alexis as if she weren't there. The two men shook hands heartily. Did you bring any word on the rig?"

"Be here by the end of the week."

"Good. How about the crew for the derrick?"

"All hired. Ready when you are."

"I think we're ready. Come on, I'll show you this formation over here where I think . . ."

He stopped in midsentence, since he could no longer easily overlook Alexis. She had moved beside him and was blocking his path as he swung around. His eyes registered first surprise and then a detached curiosity.

"Alexis Runnels," Jon said, as if it were important to make the introduction as short as possible. "Ali, this is Don Roth, the geologist."

"Runnels?" Roth said, curiosity and surprise still mingling. "Any kin to Lang—"

"His daughter," Alexis said.

Roth glanced quickly toward Jon.

"Remember," said Jon, "I told you I'd found a coinvestor."

Roth laughed. "By God, you're a sly one, Calahan. Langdon Runnels's daughter?" He laughed again, and then, suddenly remembering his manners, turned back to Alexis. "Pleasure, ma'am," he said, touching his hat.

"It's my pleasure," Alexis said. "I've read some of your reports."

He looked at her with even greater surprise. "You what?"

"The report on lithographic and stratigraphic formations you submitted to the University of Texas on the holdings they have here in the west. You were contracted to make that report, I believe?"

"Yes, but how did you—"

"How did I get access to them? Through the library, of course. There," she said, pointing to the distance. "That's the Comanchean limestone you mentioned, isn't it? The potential drilling site must be there at the top of that anticline. Oil and gas are possibly trapped in formations like that, according to your writings. Isn't that right, Mr. Roth?"

"That's right. There's some sign of an ancient mountain uplift there. Part of it's exposed and runs to the northwest, and there are known sulphur deposits there," he said pointing to the slight incline in the terrain. He had easily lapsed into a scientific mode with her, and she could tell he was enthusiastic about the subject.

"Let's have a look," she said. She was already walking away from the two men. "How about seismography?" she asked, over her shoulder. "I've read it could be used to find oil as well as measure earthquakes."

"Unproven," Roth said. "But I think it's promising. Give it three or four more years for us geologists to learn how to use it."

"How long will it take that crew you hired to erect a derrick?" she asked, directing her question at Jon without looking at him.

"At least a week," he answered.

"The rig will be here in a week. We ought to get them started so there won't be any wasted time," she said.

She walked ahead, and both men had to hurry to catch up with her, but she never slowed her pace.

It was Eleanor who invited her to the church social when Jon stopped by the house to pick up some additional geology reports before he took her back to her hotel. Alexis had asked to see the reports, and now, she thought, the need to read them gave her the perfect excuse not to attend the social.

"Oh, don't be misled by the fact that it's a church social," Eleanor said when Alexis declined the invitation. "It will be plenty lively." The way Eleanor looked at her had said more than words—as if she had known her tastes ran to something racier than religion. "And of course Jon will be speaking," she'd said, slipping her arm possessively through his.

It was then that Alexis got a glimmer of Eleanor Calahan's true self. She was ambitious. For her husband, perhaps, which gave it a respectable veneer, but nevertheless ambitious. She wanted bodies at the gathering because the bigger the crowd, the better it would look for Jon.

Alexis had declined again, however, as politely as possible. Jon hadn't mentioned it at all as he drove her to the hotel. The conversation had been confined to geology reports and construction schedules. His arrogantly intimate demeanor of the morning was gone, erased perhaps by her own show of intellect and bravado. Or perhaps it was just that he was tired. After all, it had been a full day, and she certainly was in no mood for banter or flirtation or anything other than supper and then a hot bath and bed.

She took a few minutes to comb her hair and wash her face before she left the hotel and headed for the café. A swarm of stars in a clear night sky greeted her as she stepped outside. They seemed to have almost frightened away a young moon that hung shyly over the row of flat-roofed buildings lining the town's dusty main street.

She'd gone only a short distance when she heard the sound of piano music hammering away the stillness. When she got to the intersection of another street, she saw the yellow glow of lights from inside the white church and saw the congregation of cars and horse-drawn wagons and buggies in front. It looked as if Jon, or the Lord, or maybe hand-cranked ice cream, was drawing a good crowd.

A BAD GIRL'S MONEY 109

She stood for a moment, staring at the scene, then turned back toward the café. It was still open. She could see a dull rainbow of light seeping through the building's grease-filmed window.

"Oh, what the hell," she said aloud. The heels of her boots made soft crunching sounds as she turned and walked swiftly toward the church.

The piano music was still going full tilt, and she could hear singing as well. It was hard to tell whether the songs were hymns or secular music, only that it all had an unsophisticated country sound. How would Jon with his Shakespeare-quoting style fit in? No doubt he would fit in well. He'd exchange Shakespeare for the Bible when the need arose. She remembered him relaxed and laughing, holding her close while he danced with her at the roadhouse in Houston, and then changing like a chameleon when he was in front of Eleanor. She could imagine him spewing forth country-boy homespun banalities in order to charm the home folks into voting for him.

Before she reached the door to the church hall, she heard a male voice coming from the darkness.

"Hey! Look at that!"

Suddenly a flood of light blinded her, and she heard another voice call, "Wow! What a wiggle!"

"Hey, cut it out," another voice said. "That's a lady."

"Hell, that ain't no lady. Look, she's wearin' trousers. You can see her ass, plain as day."

With no hesitation in her step, Alexis turned toward the flood of lights and kept walking until she could make out the hulk of an automobile behind the glaring beams and three figures standing next to it.

"She's comin' over here!"

"I told you to shut up. Now see what you done."

"You shut up, Dave. You ain't nothin' but a baby anyway. You ought to be home suckin' your mama's tit instead o' drinkin' beer. She's just comin' over here to get a little—"

"Get a little what?" Alexis asked, stepping suddenly out of the beam of the light and appearing in front of them. "Why, it's just a bunch of little boys! What do you think you have that I would want?"

She saw the surprised looks on all of their young faces. None of them seemed able to speak now. They could only stare at her with gaping mouths and try to conceal the beer bottles they each held.

The one in the middle seemed less eager to hide his bottle. Or perhaps, she thought, when she saw how he couldn't seem to control the weight of his head, he was too drunk to care.

"You come a little closer and I'll show you what I got you might want," he said.

"Leave her alone!" another one said. "We're sorry, ma'am, Billy didn't mean no harm. He just—"

"Shut up, Dave, you jackass," the drunk one said, taking a swing at the one he'd called Dave.

"Yeah, Davy, you goddamned sissy."

"Dave? Is that you?" Alexis asked, stepping a little closer to peer at him though the darkness. "Why, I've been looking all over for you! Come on," she said, extending a hand toward him. "Let's get out of here."

Before the astonished boy could respond, she had his hand and was pulling him toward the church. He glanced back over his shoulder at his companions and then asked under his breath, "Who are you?"

"Alexis Runnels," she said, dragging him along.

"I don't know you," he said, resisting her pull just a little now.

"I don't know you, either. I just wanted to thank you for trying to protect me from those jackasses."

"How'd you know my name?"

"Dave? Isn't that what your friends back there were calling you?"

"Oh." There was a pause, and then he asked, "Why'd you say you been lookin' for me?" She could see by the lights from the church that his eyes were bleary, and he looked a little tipsy.

"I was trying to do you a favor, Dave. You were decent to me, and I appreciate that, and I didn't like the way your friends were treating you for trying to be nice to me."

"Yeah, but—"

"And I figured your parents wouldn't like the idea of you being out there drinking anyway."

He stopped suddenly and looked at her. "You know my folks?" He kicked the ground with the toe of his boot. "You know my dad, I guess. Ever'body knows my dad."

"I have no idea who your dad is, Dave. I just figured that any mother and father wouldn't want their young son drinking booze."

He gave her a defiant look. "I ain't so young I have to have my folks tellin' me what to do."

She could see, now that the light from the church was falling on his face, that he was fair-skinned and had remarkably green intelligent eyes that were clouded with just a little fear and uncertainty. He had an angular face and a head of thick blond hair. In a few years, he would be a handsome man. She gave him a smile. "Well, then," she said. "In that case, would you honor a lady's request and escort me inside?"

He hesitated a moment, then he shrugged. "Okay. I guess."

She moved toward the door, and he followed behind. She sensed his unease, but just as she reached the doorway, he scurried in front of her and held the screen open in an awkwardly chivalrous gesture.

The big room that was the church social hall danced with laughter and light and was choked with the heat generated by at least fifty bodies. Women in cotton dresses and men in freshly laundered white shirts stood around the edges of the room or sat at tables eating plates of fried chicken. Alexis sensed eyes turning toward her as soon as she entered and felt them scrutinizing her and the trousers she wore. The attention seemed to make Dave uncomfortable, and without realizing she was going to do it, she put an arm protectively around his shoulders. He was startled and almost jerked away from her, but she caught his eye and smiled. He hesitated a moment, then smiled in return and seemed to relax a little.

In the next instant the glances of the small crowd around them was drawn away, however, and, along with the rest of the people in the room, focused on a podium at the opposite end.

"Oh, no!" Dave said. "He's gonna do it."

Alexis removed her arm from his shoulder and gave him a questioning look.

"My dad. He's gonna make a speech."

"*That's* your father?" she asked, surprised.

"Yeah. I'm surprised you don't know him. Everybody else does."

"I take it you don't like him? Or at least you don't like his speeches."

Dave shrugged. "They're just a bunch of politician bullshit. I mean—Gosh, ma'am, I didn't mean that, I—"

"If it's just bullshit I don't want to listen to it," she said, trying to put him at ease. "Let's go sit outside where it's cool."

Dave gave her an uncertain look that broke into a nervous grin. "Yeah, sure. Why not?" he said. He seemed unsure about what to do next, though, so Alexis walked ahead of him and pushed the screen door open, holding it for him. She gave him a smile, and he ducked his head to cover his own self-conscious grin as he walked out ahead of her.

Once they were outside, though, there seemed to be no place to go. There were no trees to sit under, only sparse mesquite scrub in the flat expanse behind the church. And there was no lawn, only chalky ground where the meager prairie grass had been chewed away by rubber tires and wooden wagon wheels. The only invitation came from the back of one of the trucks that had been parked there. Alexis made her way to it and climbed up to sit down, then gestured for Dave to sit next to her.

She leaned her head against the back of the truck and breathed a sigh. "It's been a long day for me," she said. "I don't suppose your friends have any of that beer left, do they?"

"You want a beer?" he asked incredulously.

"Well, sure. Is there something wrong with that?"

"No, I guess not. I mean no! I mean, sure, I can find you a beer."

He made a flying leap out of the pickup and

bounded across the parking lot to the car he'd been in before. Opening the door, he reached under the front seat for a bottle, then uncapped it with a key he produced from somewhere before he raced back to the truck.

"There wasn't but one," he said. "We'll have to share." He took a long swallow from the bottle then handed it to her.

Alexis laughed, and at the same time they heard applause coming from inside the church hall. "What do you mean, share?" she asked, taking the bottle from him. "You're too young for this."

"I'm not as young as you think."

Alexis ignored his halfhearted defiance and took a sip of the warm beer, then leaned her head against the cab of the truck again. "Tell me about your father," she said.

"Didn't you see him? He's a big shot. What else does anybody need to know?"

"What else is there?"

"I don't know. He's smart, I guess. At least he's good at making people think he is."

"Good at bullshit, you mean?"

Dave snickered. "You can say that again."

"Does he bullshit you?"

Dave waited a long time to answer before he said, with a note of sadness in his voice, "No."

"He's honest with you?"

"I think he makes it pretty plain he doesn't like me."

"What makes you think that?"

He gave a short, derisive laugh. "I don't ever do anything to please him. He thinks I'm dumb. He thinks I'm lazy. He thinks I'm everything he's not."

"And are you?"

Again another pause. "It's not my fault I wasn't born poor like him, so I can't claw my way up the way he did. But I could work if he'd give me the chance. I could work in the oil fields. Maybe I couldn't wheel and deal and con people outta their money the way he does. But I could work on the rigs if he'd just give me the chance."

More applause came from inside the building.

"But he won't give you the chance?" she asked.

"No. He wants me to be like him."

"Able to bullshit people."

"Well, yeah, I guess. But I don't know how to be like him." Before she could stop him, he took the bottle from her hand and took another swallow of beer.

"Have you ever told him that?" Alexis asked, taking the bottle back with decided firmness.

Dave snickered and raised both arms to rest them on the sideboards of the truck bed. He looked relaxed, as if the beer had begun to have some effect. "I've tried. But it don't do no—I mean it doesn't do no good. He has a way of gettin' hold of a person and bendin' 'em into what he wants. He uses people. Even Mama. People think she's had so much to do with where he is. They don't know him, though. Mama can only push him so far. He's smart, I'll give him that, but I ain't nothing like him." He snickered again. "He don't like it when I say ain't. But I ain't. I ain't nothin' he wants. So I just make him mad all the time. Gimme another swalla o' that beer."

"No. I'm not going to give you anymore beer. How many have you had, anyway?"

He shrugged. "Just a couple besides this one."

"Well that's more than enough, because you're not

used to drinking it. Anyway, I don't want you any drunker because I want you to hear something I have to tell you."

"What?" A look of anticipation spread across his face in a grin.

She leaned toward him and whispered, "I'm one of the people your daddy has conned out of their money."

He looked at her with beer-blurred astonishment. "You?"

She nodded.

"But I thought you didn't know him."

"I didn't know he was your father."

"So the son of a bitch got to you, huh? 'Scuse me. I shouldn't say son of a bitch in front of a lady."

"He made me his business partner."

"Well, I'll swear! You're a woman!"

"So they tell me."

They both laughed, and Alexis stood up and brushed her trousers. "You know, we really ought to go back in—"

"I see you've met David." Alexis turned suddenly at the sound of the voice and saw Jon standing next to the truck. Even in the semidarkness she could see the anger on his face and sense it from his stance. "And given him something of an initiation, I see," he added, his eye on the beer bottle that was empty and rolling around the bed of the truck.

7

Dave stood up in the back of the truck, weaving slightly. "She didn't do anything, Papa. She was just—"

Alexis put a hand on his arm. "It's all right."

"Go get in the car, David." Jon's voice was frighteningly steady. "Wait for your mother and me."

"But Papa, I—"

"Now, goddamn it!"

Dave cowered and eased himself out of the back of the truck, then made his way through the parking lot, stumbling once as he walked.

Alexis turned toward Jon with a streak of rage in her eyes. "Did you have to humiliate him that way?"

"Get down out of that truck. I want to talk to you."

Alexis put a hand on the sideboards of the truck bed to aid her as she vaulted to the ground. "No," she said, facing him squarely. "I want to talk to you."

He took her arm roughly, forcing her to walk

with him while he spoke in a low, angry tone. "You're going to listen first, because I'm telling you to stay away from my son! You can play around with your spoiled rich girl loose morals all you want in New York or Paris or Houston, but by God, not with David. You're not going to harm him with your disgusting—"

"Wait a minute!" She jerked her arm free and spun around to face him. "Just what are you accusing me of?"

"For God's sake, you were in the back of a truck, drinking with him. You shouldn't have to ask what I'm accusing you of. And keep your voice down." He looked around the empty parking lot nervously.

"You're damned right, I shouldn't have to ask, because nothing was going on." Alexis let her voice rise defiantly higher. "You're the one who's disgusting. I was having a beer, sure, but I didn't do a damned thing to your son except talk to him, which is something you obviously never do."

Jon pulled her farther away from the building and spoke in a hushed but angry tone. "David was so drunk he could hardly walk. You saw him."

"Dave wasn't drunk. Just had a little buzz. And he was that way when I first met him tonight. Get your hand off of my arm! And for your information, he would have been even drunker if I hadn't gotten him away from that crowd of boys."

Jon dropped his hand from her arm and looked at her with a confused and troubled expression. "David was drinking with those boys again? Larry Tedford and Billy Whitner? A tall, skinny kid and a redhead?"

Alexis's only answer was an angry glance over her shoulder as she walked away.

"What made you pick David to save instead of one of the other two?" Jon called after her.

She stopped, but kept her back to him. She felt anger seething inside her. He was still doubting her, still obliquely accusing. "Because," she said, finally, turning around to face him, "he was decent to me. Tried to keep the other two horny little bastards from insulting me. He's right, you know. He's not at all like you."

She turned and walked away from him, fighting back tears of hurt and anger.

Jon watched her go, feeling miserable. She was undoubtedly right about the two boys and about David drinking with them. He'd done it once before. He could believe David had tried to defend her, as well. He was that kind of kid. In fact, he could believe the entire story, and now he was angry at himself for accusing her. But he was also angry at David for having the beer and angry at her for being so young and reckless and vulnerable—and for making him want to take her in his arms. He started once to call to her, at least to apologize, and even took a step toward her, but no words came from his dry, aching throat. He watched mutely while she disappeared into the silky folds of darkness.

When he got back to the church hall, Eleanor was waiting for him.

"Did you find him?" she asked.

"He's all right. He's in the car. Asleep by now, probably."

"He wasn't with those hoodlums? Wasn't getting into trouble?"

"He's fine."

"Jon, are you all right?"

"Of course," he said without looking at her. He moved into the crowd to shake hands and to smile and to eat more of the fried chicken and hand-cranked ice cream.

He found he couldn't eat, though, and couldn't focus on what people said to him or remember names that he should have remembered. He could only think of Alexis and of the things he had said to her and the way she had looked walking away from him. He thought of making some excuse to Eleanor about meeting with a possible financial donor for his campaign and then going to the hotel to find Alexis, but he discounted that. What good would it do? She would no doubt just refuse to see him. Instead, he told Eleanor he wanted to go home.

"I've got a god-awful headache."

"But Jon," she protested, "you can't just leave. All these people expect you to stay. Here," she said, reaching into her purse and producing a bottle. "Take some of my headache powders. It'll get you through the night."

"I don't want any of your headache powders. They never do me any good, and besides, we need to get David home."

"But you just said David is sleeping, and—"

"I'm leaving, Eleanor. Would you like to come with me?"

He had spoken with a sharpness that he knew she saw as dangerous. She wouldn't risk a scene, he thought, and he was right. She slipped her arm through his and let him lead her toward the door. She was smiling graciously and telling everyone they passed how happy she was to see them and how necessary it was to have their son home so he could get a good night's rest before school the next day. She was, Jon realized, the perfect wife.

David, to Jon's great relief, was indeed asleep in the back of the car. There would be no need to speak to Eleanor of the beer he'd consumed, and certainly no need to mention the encounter with Alexis Runnels. There was not even a problem getting him into the house. He was, after all, only tipsy, just as Alexis had said.

Eleanor showed no signs of suspecting anything was amiss with the boy. It was impossible to tell whether she was being discreetly silent or totally unaware. She was still thinking about the gathering.

"It went rather well, I thought," she said as she hung her dress in the closet. She was standing in front of him in her slip, the white flesh of her arms and shoulders a dramatic contrast to the dark hair she had unpinned and let fall across that whiteness.

"I'm not so sure," he said. He had removed his coat and was now loosening his tie. "I'm not sure anyone understood what I was saying about the League of Nations or even cared."

"You ought not to spend so much time on that issue anyway. It doesn't matter whether they understand or care about it. What matters is what they think of you. And they love you. Try to remember that. And they'll love you even more if you concentrate on lower taxes, instead of something remote like the League of Nations." She was seated in front of her dressing table now, brushing her hair. There was a brief moment of silence before she spoke again. "Was Miss Runnels all right?"

"What?" The question, the sudden change of subject had caught him off guard.

"Miss Runnels. I saw you speaking to her out on the parking lot."

"Of course she was all right."

"Not just speaking, really," she said. "You seemed to be arguing."

"Arguing? Of course not. I was just asking her if she'd seen David."

"Had she?"

"As a matter of fact, she had. It seems they introduced themselves and hit it off pretty well."

"Mmm," Eleanor said. She put the hairbrush down and disappeared into the bathroom. "It could be they hit it off because she's so young. She can't be more than three years older than he is," she said, calling to him from behind the half-closed door.

"That would make her only eighteen. She's older than that."

Eleanor emerged wearing her nightgown. "Are you sleeping with her, Jon?"

Jon felt his chest tighten and the blood drain from his face. "My God, Eleanor, of course not."

She looked at him for a moment, her expression saying she didn't believe him, then without a word she moved to the bed and threw back the covers. Jon tossed his shirt on a chair and sat down to unlace his shoes, angry with himself for letting her put him on the defensive when he had nothing to be defensive about. Any attraction he'd felt for the spoiled little brat had been nothing more than a passing thing—a moment of fascination because she'd proved to be interesting and tantalizingly intelligent, in spite of her immaturity.

"Why did you ask such a thing?" he asked finally.

Eleanor didn't answer. She lay with her back to

him, so still that he thought for a moment that she was asleep, but then she turned over to face him. "It isn't as if you've never—"

"She's young enough to be my daughter, for God's sake," he said, interrupting her.

"Of course," she said, pulling herself up to a sitting position. "I shouldn't have brought it up." She switched on the light on a table next to the bed and reached for a book. There had been no humility in her statement, just a matter-of-fact admission that she'd made a slip.

He knew that they both understood what she had meant—that it was best for both of them and for their marriage that his liaisons remain undiscussed. He refused to think of them as infidelities. His fidelity to Eleanor in the sense of commitment and loyalty was and always had been beyond question.

Jon got into bed beside her and picked up his own book. He found it next to impossible to concentrate, however. He kept seeing, in his mind's eye, Alexis turning away from him, hurt and angry by his accusations, and he kept remembering the way she smelled, the way she laughed, the sound of her voice. He willed himself not to think of any of that, though, and to concentrate instead on the words he was reading.

He was reading only words, though, words with no meaning. Glancing at Eleanor, he was struck once again by her beauty—white skin, dark hair, finely drawn aristocratic profile. He could still be moved by her looks, if not to passion, at least to desire and an indefinable yearning.

Reaching across the bed, he ran a finger down the length of her arm. She flinched at his touch at first, and then, as if she had been caught in an improper act, glanced at him and gave him a smile that he could only think of as apologetic. He had not moved his hand; it rested still on her arm. He moved it to her breast, and she closed her book and put it aside, very carefully, very precisely, then turned toward him again. He had not been surprised at her action. It had all been repeated so many times before, and they both knew all the movements now by rote.

He kissed her, and she responded by opening her mouth to him slightly, in just the way he knew she would. She let him, without resistance, pull her down into the bed until they were lying together, facing each other, his arms around her, her hands resting lightly on his chest. He caressed her, and she was warm and pliable and unresisting. His physical response to her was slow. He felt a stab of worry, but he forced himself to cast the worry aside and to hold her closer, kiss her with more fervor, to think of her beauty, her intelligence, her devotion to him and his career. He forced himself to remember that she was everything a man could want.

But he could not concentrate on any of that. All he could think of now was his physical failure, which was becoming more and more apparent and more and more disquieting. He rolled away from her, and she spoke his name.

"Jon?"

He made no response, and instead groped in the darkness for his shirt to find the cigarettes he'd left in the pocket. In the brief flowering of the match he saw her sitting up in bed, reaching for the lamp.

"Don't put too much importance on this," she said in the sudden flood of light.

"What do you mean?" He drew deeply on the

cigarette, letting the smoke roll through his chest to wash away, at least temporarily, the ache.

"It's not as important as you seem to make it. Please, Jon, you mustn't take it so hard. We have David, and we have your career. The congressional seat is almost in our grasp. That's all that matters, isn't it? As long as we're happy, your little failure shouldn't matter."

There was a long silence in which he heard nothing except the word "failure" resounding over and over, and his father's mocking voice telling him he was womanish.

"Has it—happened with—with the others?" Eleanor asked in a small voice.

He jerked his head toward her. "My God, Eleanor!"

"Forgive me. I should not have—"

"Go to sleep," he said sharply, reaching for his shirt and trousers. "You must be tired."

"Where are you going?"

He was still buttoning his trousers on his way out the door and he didn't bother to answer her.

He found his way in the dark to the kitchen and reached for the whiskey bottle he kept behind the Hoosier cabinet. He hoped there was enough left in the bottle to lull him into gray unfeeling. He poured all of it into a glass and took the first taste without pleasure. Eleanor's words were still reverberating in his mind. *Your little failure.*

She had never spoken to him of failure before. But it had always been different in the past. It was more that he simply seldom felt a true desire for her. She had never seemed to mind that and certainly had never thought of it as a failure. Why had she used that word? And why had she asked about the others? It was so unlike her to cross over that line of silent, unspoken agreement between them.

He'd wanted to tell her that it had not happened before. But how could he have done that? It would have destroyed the delicate structure of their relationship, which was based on discretion and prudence and maybe even denial. He would have been lying, anyway. It had happened before, once, when he'd had too much to drink. But that was the liquor, of course. Everyone knew it had that effect, so it meant nothing, he told himself.

He downed the last of the whiskey and pushed the glass back, staring at its emptiness, waiting for the grayness to overtake his senses, but it was slow in coming. He couldn't help thinking that maybe things would have been different tonight if it hadn't been for that scene with Alexis. He hadn't yet gotten her out of his mind. He couldn't help thinking how he'd hurt her. It was precisely that memory that had precipitated his failure with Eleanor, he thought, but his mind was clouded enough now that he couldn't quite analyze it, couldn't quite think it through.

He could think of nothing, in fact, except Alexis. Was she reliving that scene, too? Were those tears he'd seen in her eyes as she'd turned away? Was she crying now? Or laughing? Or sleeping and not thinking of him at all? He couldn't believe that was the case—that she had been completely unmoved by their relationship. She had stirred him, both sexually and intellectually. She had made him laugh, made him angry, made him feel. Wasn't that better than this state of near paralysis? God, no, it was worse. Yet, in spite of that, he knew he had to see her again.

Tonight, he thought, with a jolt of clarity that came to him like an epiphany, cutting through the numbing effect of the alcohol. He had to see her tonight.

Eleanor was asleep when he went back into the bedroom for his boots. She looked peaceful, unperturbed, but that was part of her strength, to be able to put failure behind her and go on. Neither of them, he knew, would ever mention tonight again.

He saw the light from one window on the second floor of the hotel as he parked the car, and he knew, without a doubt, that it had to be Alexis's room. It gave him confidence. He would not have to feel embarrassed about waking her. It could be, he thought through the residue of a rather pleasant fog that remained in his mind, that she was even expecting him.

It seemed an eternity that he stood in the hallway before the door opened and she was standing there in front of him in an ivory satin robe, her short golden hair like a disheveled halo around her head. She was clutching a book to her chest like a schoolgirl. She wore a surprised look, and then something he thought might have been anger flickered in her eyes. For a moment he feared she was going to close the door in his face.

"Jon? What—"

"Can I come in?" he asked, relieved that what he had thought was anger was merely surprise.

"What do you want?"

"I want to come in—to apologize."

She looked at him for a moment, and he saw, in

spite of the firm set of her mouth, something fragile in her eyes. She stepped aside and waved him in with the hand holding the book.

"This seems a momentous occasion. An apology from the patriarch."

"Don't rub it in. I mean it."

"Well, then we ought to celebrate. I'd offer you something to drink, except that in this godforsaken place I have no idea where to go to get some." She closed the door and leaned against it. "But from the smell of you, I'd say you've already had your nightcap."

"I'm not drunk, if that's what you're getting at." He sat down on the bed, and she sat across the room from him in a flimsy-looking ladderback chair, her legs crossed so that her robe parted slightly and he saw that she was wearing satin pajamas that matched her robe. "I don't want you getting the idea that I had to drink to get up my courage to come here." The liquor was beginning to wear off somewhat, leaving him edgy. He reached into his pocket for a cigarette only to find he'd failed to put them back in his shirt.

"Didn't you?"

"No, I'll admit I'd had a stiff shot, but I had a completely different reason for . . . I mean . . . Do you have a cigarette?"

"No. I don't smoke. They make me cough." Her expression was deadpan. Torturing.

"Alexis . . ." He looked at her, feeling confused again. "You are a remarkable young woman. I suppose I don't quite know how to take you."

"You mean you don't know whether to think of me as a woman or as merely young."

"No, of course not, I . . . I mean yes, maybe you're right. What I'm trying to say is, I've been too quick to judge you. Especially tonight. I should have given you a chance to explain yourself at least, and I apologize for that."

She smiled and managed a languid, very alluring slouch in the chair. "It did look rather incriminating, I guess, and given my bad-girl reputation, I suppose it's understandable, what you did. But not acceptable," she added in a way that let him know she was enjoying his discomfort.

"No, it wasn't acceptable, and I hope you understand that I . . ."

"Jon, are you all right?"

"Except for the fact that I seem to be having a hell of a time saying I'm sorry, I'm fine."

"No, it's more than that. You look so distraught, so . . . There's something wrong."

He wished to hell he had a cigarette. "Why in the world would you think that?"

She clamped her gaze on him as if she were staring into his soul, and several seconds passed while he wondered what she was seeing. "Why don't you just tell him how you feel?" she said finally.

"What?"

"You love your son very much, don't you? That's what this is all about. Why don't you just tell him and stop being so hard on him and on yourself?"

"I don't know where you get the idea that I'm hard on him. He's got everything he could possibly want."

"He wants to know you love him."

He laughed, a short derisive sound. "He's my son. Of course he knows I love him, but two males don't go around telling each other."

There was another long pause before she said quietly, "Why not?"

He was stunned. "What do you mean, why not?"

"Didn't you want to know your father loved you?"

"That has nothing to do with this."

She stood up and walked toward the window. "It's what we all want," she said, staring into the darkness. "We all want to know for sure." She turned around to face him, her eyes glistening.

At first he thought there were tears, but in the next moment he wasn't sure. It could have been nothing more than the light, he thought, now that she was standing in front of him, looking him squarely in the eye.

"Your son wants your approval, Jon. I think he would give anything he had to be like you so he could earn that approval," she said, as she sat down beside him.

"You don't know what the hell you're talking about. The kid's got a smart mouth. The last thing in the world he cares about is my approval."

"That's not true. It's just that you make him feel like a failure."

He felt a wrenching tightness at the bottom of his heart, and for a moment he felt as if he had crawled into Beaty Calahan's skin. Had he made David feel as if he didn't measure up, the way his own father had made him feel?

"All of a sudden you're an authority on my son just because you spend a few minutes boozing it up in the back of a truck!" he said, lashing out at her. He felt sick even before the words were out of his mouth, before she turned away from him again, angry and hurt. He reached for her. "Alexis . . ." She tried to jerk away as she had earlier that night, but he held her firmly, forced her to look at him. "I'm sorry. God,

I'm sorry. Maybe—maybe it's because you're hitting too close to home. I don't know, I . . ."

For a moment the anger in her eyes wouldn't die, and he couldn't go on. She must have read something in his face, though. He felt the tension drain from her, felt her arms relax under his grip. "Lord, you do love him, don't you?" she whispered.

"More than life itself." He found that he could hardly speak.

"Then tell him." She touched his face with just the tip of her finger. "Tell him it's okay if he makes a mistake now and then. That it's okay if he's not like you."

"But he should know. . . ."

She dropped her hand, started to turn away. "People need to be told, damn it. You have to find the words to tell him."

"Where art thou, Muse, that thou forget'st so long?"

She turned back to him and gave a short little laugh—the nicest, most appealing sound. "Why did you say that?"

He found himself smiling. "I'm just saying I don't always have the words I need."

"You're the strangest man."

"And why do you say that?"

"You're clever. But you're not always smart. Don't you know how important love is?"

She was all seriousness again, and he found himself getting lost in her eyes. He also found himself unable to answer her. The truth was, maybe he didn't know what love was—had never known, until this moment at least. But that was ridiculous, of course. She was just a kid. No, she was very much a woman, sitting there with ivory satin clinging to her arms, her shoulders, her calves, the soft little mounds that were her breasts.

She leaned toward him. Or had he leaned toward her?

His lips met hers. Soft, pliable. A small opening, a hungry response, and then she turned away. Stood. Walked to the window.

"You'd better leave," she said. "Your wife . . ."

"Yes," he said. "I'd better."

He saw himself to the door, leaving her staring out the window into the night again. It felt to him as if nothing had been resolved. He wasn't even certain she'd accepted his apology. The only thing he was certain of was that he need no longer be concerned that his earlier physical failure might be permanent.

8

He was ruthless, hungry for power, egotistical, and capable of incredible charm to mask it all, she thought, as she watched him from her upstairs window getting into his car. She had known that from the beginning, of course. Those were exactly all the reasons she had chosen him. She needed someone like that to help her launch her independence. She had made no secret of the fact that she was willing to use any means she had to get what she wanted. Did that make her ruthless as well? Power mad? Did it make her like Jon Calahan?

She didn't like being so attracted to him. He was supposed to be a means to an end, that was all. Of course he hadn't meant for it to go beyond a harmless flirtation either. He had made that clear that night in the hotel in Houston when he had scolded her for being so forward. She still blushed when she thought of that. She had acted impulsively. How young and foolish it must have made her look to him.

The fact that he had come to her tonight with some strange unsettled air about him, and she had sensed his need for her had only confused her further. She touched her lips with one finger as she remembered the kiss. The sensation had been warm and deep so that she felt like a schoolgirl, tingling all the way down to her toes. What did it mean that he had kissed her? That he had decided he could risk a little more than a flirtation?

She shivered and turned away from the window, then closed the shade so that the heavy weight of darkness would not burden her. Her thoughts were burden enough. Of course she wasn't going to get involved with him, she told herself. And she would forget about his kiss soon enough.

In spite of that resolve, she found it difficult to sleep. He wouldn't leave her mind, and in the close, thick black of the night, she could feel him thinking about her as well.

It was very late when she finally fell asleep, and when she awoke, a brazen young pink dawn was filtering through the shade. She glanced at her clock and saw that it was only 5:00 A.M. Abominable time to be waking, she thought. It had been much more common in the past for her to be just getting into bed at this hour. Now, though, in spite of her restless night, she had no inclination to try to go back to sleep. She was eager to drive to the drilling site.

She dressed quickly and left the hotel before anyone was stirring. The morning air, cool and tart as white wine, invigorated her. She breathed deeply, and it made her slightly tipsy with anticipation as she drove toward the site. The open stretches of pastel prairie, mother-of-pearl-colored earth dotted with pale green cactus and mesquite and capped by a sky still lavender-tinged with morning, now seemed delicately beautiful in contrast to the way she had perceived it a few days ago.

To her surprise, Jon was already there when she arrived. He was helping two men unload lumber from a wagon pulled by six mules. Another man had already begun constructing the base for the derrick that would support the cable drilling rig she had bought. She knew that a water well was ordinarily drilled first, and then a windmill erected in order to supply the water necessary for the crew so that it wouldn't have to be hauled to the site in barrels, as was obviously being done now.

She got out of her car and ran toward Jon. "Why didn't you tell me you were going to start this today?" she called brightly.

He glanced up and she saw surprise in his eyes. She felt a surge of warmth and felt for a moment like Venus walking toward Adonis.

He sees her coming, and begins to glow,
Even as a dying coal revives with wind.

For one ridiculous moment she thought he might be thinking of the same lines, but in the next moment she saw his eyes change.

"I didn't see any reason for you to be here. In fact, I didn't think you'd be interested in coming out so early. You're used to sleeping late."

The coldness in his voice made her stop, dead still. For a moment neither of them spoke. She saw then that what was in his eyes was something akin to fear. No, not quite fear, but some cautionary reflex. He was thinking of his political future, she thought, thinking that she could easily ruin it if she appeared too eager to see him, if they let their relationship go too far. She felt her intoxicating exuberance going flat as champagne diluted with water.

"Whether or not I like to sleep late has nothing to do with it. I should have been told you were starting this." She fought to keep her tone measured and even. She would show him that he had nothing to worry about as far as any relationship between them was concerned. She would show him that she was competent and professional.

She saw the surreptitious glances of the workers. They had heard the ice in her voice, and she could sense them straining to hear, over the sounds of their work, what was coming next.

"Sorry, my dear," Jon said. "I didn't think you'd be interested in the preliminary work."

"Why shouldn't I be interested? I'm your partner. I expect to be here for every phase of this, from construction to drilling."

One of the men dropped a piece of lumber at those words, and the other two exchanged quick glances. Jon, obviously uncomfortable with the attention they were getting, put down the board he'd been holding and said, "There's some coffee in the tent. Let's go get you some, then maybe you'll feel better."

"I feel fine, and I don't want any coffee."

"Then why don't you tell me what you do want so I can get back to work. I've got a job to do here."

"What I want is to be told about every aspect of this investment," she said. "I want to be consulted about every step." She hadn't meant to sound so shrewish, but it was too late to take it back.

"If it'll keep that damn burr out of your saddle, hell yes, I'll even have the men ask your permission before they take a piss if that'll make you happy."

"Do they ask you before they take a piss?" she asked sweetly.

"Watch your language or I'll—"

"You'll what? Turn me over your knee?"

He looked at her for a moment as if he couldn't think of words that were vile enough. The color of anger touched his face and he turned away. "I've got work to do," he said.

"We both do," she said.

She followed him to the truck and pulled a long board from the back, just as he had done. It was awkward and almost impossible to handle, and when she dropped it, he turned back and gave her a scowl. Then he helped her pick it up.

"Let's call a truce," he said.

She stared at him a moment, feeling as if he'd just scolded her, and wishing she had been the one who had offered to make peace. Lord, he was impossible! Always one jump ahead of her.

"All right," she said. She wiped her hand on the seat of her trousers and extended it to him.

He was caught off guard for a moment, then he encircled her small hand with his and smiled, but the guarded look was still in his eyes.

By the end of the day she was exhausted, and she was late getting to the drill site the next morning, a fact that caused her much chagrin and embarrassment. Jon did not mention it. In fact, she wasn't certain he had even noticed it. He seemed intent upon ignoring her, except when it was necessary to discuss some aspect of the construction or to get her opinion for some decision. That little kiss obviously had embarrassed him. She resolved to put him at ease by assuring him that she attached no significance to it. But she never got the chance. He avoided her with great care.

By the end of the week the derrick had risen like the skeleton of some prehistoric giant. The cable tool had arrived and was transported to the site by the mule teamsters. Then it had been threaded into its arms and braces so that it hung from the middle, looking vaguely dangerous and obscene, ready to penetrate the earth. By then, Alexis felt that she had slid into a state of peaceful animosity with Jon. They both worked diligently at staying out of each other's way and at being painfully polite when it was impossible to avoid each other.

"I've hired the crew," Jon said one morning when they had just arrived at the drilling site. "I got the best I know. The best I ever worked with." They were in the makeshift office they'd set up in the tent. There was little room, and their desks had to be pushed flush together so that they faced each other when they were both seated.

"I wasn't given the opportunity to interview anyone," she said in an icy voice.

He gave her a look of impatience and of irritation bordering on anger. "We agreed on this from the first. You buy the rig. I hire the crew. You had a crew in mind, maybe?"

"Of course not. I just thought you would at least discuss this with me. I told you I wanted to be consulted."

"Alexis, this is one of those times when there is nothing to discuss. You need only be informed, which is what I am doing now."

"I see."

"Look, I didn't mean any disrespect. I sent a wire to Buck Simpson, the best damned driller I know. I told him to get me a crew. I told him I wanted enough for three tours, so we can work around the clock." She noticed he had pronounced the word *towers* the way a seasoned oil man would, the way she'd heard Langdon and his cohorts pronounce it. "I did it to save time. We have to get this well spudded soon, otherwise we lose our drilling rights. We got into this to make money, not to waste time."

"Of course."

"Hell, there may come a time when a decision has to be made that you know more about than I do. If it does, I expect you to go ahead and do it. Just like I did."

"Do you?"

"Alexis, believe me, I acted in the interest of both of us. I'm afraid we're going to have to let some of these old boys get used to the idea of working for a woman. You know, let them ease into it," Jon said.

She knew she was in no position to argue with him. Like it or not, he was undoubtedly right. But she gave no response. She merely looked at him, sitting back in her chair, arms folded in front of her, eyes trained intently on his face.

"And if you do come around, I wouldn't try to be too, well, elitist—highfalutin, as they say."

"Are you telling me not to be a snob? Or not to be myself?"

"I'm just telling you this is going to be a precarious situation. You can't be too friendly, of course, being a woman. They'll get the wrong idea, but still—"

"I'm not a total idiot, Jon."

He looked at her a moment, as if what she had

said somehow troubled him. "Of course you're not," he said quietly. "That's one of the reasons I love you."

Alexis felt her heart skip a beat, and she stared at him, stunned. He was gathering up papers from his desk as if he were totally unaware that he had spoken the words. "I've got to get that cable hanger fixed today if I can," he said, still in a matter-of-fact tone. "If I don't, it'll delay the spudding. Also, I meant to tell you, I think I found an old army truck we can buy. If we get it, I might have to send you in it to Midland for some casing. Think you can handle the truck?"

He looked at her, calmly, blandly, as if he couldn't hear the rushing of her blood that reverberated so loudly in her own ears. She managed to nod her head and to say, in a strange voice that seemed to come from somewhere outside of her, "Of course." Then, forcing herself to try to think rationally, added, "I can pay for it with a bank draft from the Coyote Flats Bank, I assume." He hadn't meant the words, "I love you," of course. They were throwaway lines, something akin to his condescending "my dear" or "little lady."

"Shouldn't be a problem," he said on his way out the door.

She watched him leave, wondering what had just happened.

It was three days later that a roadster pulled up to the drilling site and a stocky, compact man got out. He walked with a hint of a swagger toward the office and stopped when he saw Alexis standing in the door way. He pushed his wide-brimmed hat back on his head to reveal a receding hairline and a forehead kept white by the hat, in contrast to the reddened and weathered look of his face. Reaching into a breast pocket for a cigarette, he continued to scrutinize her.

"Afternoon, ma'am." He squinted against the sun, deepening the wrinkles around his eyes, then he lit the cigarette, blew out a plume of smoke, coughed, and said, "I'm lookin' for Jon Calahan. He around?"

"He's around," Alexis said cautiously. Her attention was drawn to the roadster again. A tall, dark-haired man had unfolded a lanky frame to get out of the car. He was a good twenty years younger than the first man, and he was smiling while he looked at her, letting his eyes travel quickly up and down the length of her body.

"Buck Simpson! I see you made it!" Jon was striding across the expanse between the rig and the office shack. He extended his hand toward the older man. They shook hands vigorously, and all the while Alexis was aware that the younger man's eyes remained on her.

"Well, I got your wire, and I thought, what the hell. I ain't never been to West Texas. . . ."

While the two of them talked, the younger man sauntered toward Alexis, slow, languid, his thumbs hooked in his front pockets. "My name's Nick Bodine. You his daughter?" He gestured toward Jon with a slight jerk of his head.

"No."

"Wife?"

"I'm his business partner."

He grinned at her. "The hell you are."

"The hell I am."

"Well, now, this is goin' to be interesting," he said, pronouncing the last word *enter-resting.*

Alexis caught his dark-eyed gaze once again, briefly, before Jon introduced her to Buck Simpson. Jon told Buck she was his partner, and Buck responded formally and politely, but Alexis saw the look of surprise and suspicion in his eyes. Then he walked away with Jon, toward the rig, discussing the rest of the crew, who, Buck said, would arrive by morning. Nick Bodine followed along with only one backward glance toward her.

Alexis thought of joining them, but she couldn't think of a way to do it without appearing as if she were an eager, juvenile tagalong. She might have risked it anyway, except for the leer on Nick's handsome face, coupled with the fact that being miserable—sunburned and covered with sweat—did nothing for her self-confidence.

Later, she drove back to the hotel and went to bed early so she could awaken early the next morning and get to the well site by the time Jon and the new crew were there.

Dawn had not yet made its appearance through the shade in her room when she was awakened, not by the alarm, but by a knock on the door. When she opened the door into the darkened hallway it took her a moment to realize that it was Dave who was standing there, waiting to be asked in.

"Good heavens, Dave," she said, in a hoarse, groggy voice. "If your daddy finds you here . . ."

"He don't know."

There was another moment of uncertainty. "Well, come on in," she said finally. She stood aside, pulling her satin robe together. He walked in and glanced around the room uneasily, then looked at her, giving her a slight, embarrassed shrug and a self conscious smile. Alexis ran her fingers through her hair. "To what do I owe the pleasure of this visit?" she asked.

"I want you to take me out to the well. I want to be there when it's spudded."

"Couldn't your father do that?" She walked to the dresser and picked up her brush and pulled it in quick, short strokes through her hair.

"Aw, hell, you know what he'd say."

"Watch your language, young man."

"Don't treat me like a kid."

She turned around and grinned at him. "Okay," she said. She wasn't about to give him the same response Jon had given her when she'd demanded the same thing—that he wouldn't be treated like a child if he didn't act like one. She put the hairbrush down and sat on the edge of the dresser. "So your father wouldn't want you to go. What would he want you to do? Stay in school?"

"He just wouldn't want me to be there. He wants me to be interested in other things, he says. He doesn't want me working on the rigs."

"And you?"

"I'd love it. There's this one guy, Nick Bodine? You haven't met him yet, but he worked on some of the other wells Papa has wildcatted. He says there's nothin' like the feel of that iron in his hands. He says it's almost as good as feelin' a—What I mean is, he says there just ain't nothin' like it."

"Ain't nothin'?"

"Don't you go correctin' my language. I get enough of that from Mama and Papa. Nick says I sound like a college boy anyhow."

"Is there something wrong with that?"

He shrugged. "He says those college boy geologists

don't know sh—don't know anything at all about the oil business. He says all they do is guess at where to drill a hole, and he's as good at guessin' as they are."

"So he doesn't have much use for college boys?"

"No, I guess not."

"Like your father."

Dave shrugged. "Papa's out of touch with what's really goin' on. He doesn't understand anything. I guess he wants me to be like him. And I can't make him see I'm not him, I'm not smart like him."

Alexis studied his face a moment, the look of youthful defiance barely masking something deeper and sadder in his eyes. "You want this pretty bad, I guess. To be there when the drilling starts."

"I sure do!" The way he said it, with such enthusiasm, reminded her of Miller, and of how much she missed her brother. Dave lacked Miller's self-assurance, but he had a charm of his own and the mark of a misfit on his soul that made her see him as a brother in spirit.

"Your papa's going to hit the ceiling when he sees me driving up with you."

"No. Once I'm there, and we're in front of all those people, he'll overlook it."

She laughed. "What makes you think so?"

"He won't want to make a scene. He won't do anything to put himself in a bad light."

She stood up and walked to her closet. "That's a fine attitude to have toward your father." She pulled a pair of trousers and a shirt from the closet and inspected them. "I've got to get dressed and get out of here, or they'll start without me. You be a good boy and go home. Your father thinks you're too smart for the oil fields, and I think he's right."

"But what about you? Aren't you smart? And you're in the oil business."

"Don't confuse me, kid. Just go home."

He hesitated a moment, giving her a look—a mixture of anger and disappointment—before he stormed out, muttering under his breath.

She laughed as he left, and then was surprised to find him waiting for her in the car. She looked at him, started to reprimand him, but she saw that kinship again, the defiant soul brother, and she knew he sensed the same thing, even if he couldn't identify it. She sighed and slid into the seat beside him.

"You're determined to get me in trouble, aren't you?" she said, as she pressed the starter button on the car. He didn't answer, except to give her an uneasy glance. "Well, I guess it doesn't matter," she said with a laugh. "If you didn't do it, I'd find a way to do it myself. I always do."

"You do?"

"Well, you know. The black sheep. Every family has to have one."

Dave gave a short laugh. "Try and tell that to my father."

"It's hard to tell your father anything."

Dave laughed again, with more ease this time. "I guess we both know that, don't we? Does he still think it's your fault I got drunk last weekend?"

"I told him you were defending my honor, and I was trying to keep you sober. But neither of us has exactly sterling reputations, so I'm not sure he believed me."

"You got a reputation?"

She glanced at him and grinned. "You've heard of

girls like me. The kind your mama warns you to stay away from."

Dave grinned, intrigued. "Does Papa know?"

"Your papa doesn't care. He's just after my money."

"Well, he was sure mad at me last weekend. He was still remembering the one other time I got drunk, and I threw up in his hat."

"You what?"

"I had to pass through the living room on my way to the bathroom. I sort of bumped into the lamp table and his hat was on it, and it fell off, and then it happened. I didn't mean to. It just happened."

Alexis roared with laughter.

"I tried to wash it," Dave said, laughing with her so hard he could hardly speak. "But felt don't wash too good. He was madder 'n hell the next morning."

"That reminds me of the time my brother and I tried to smoke our papa's cigars. We couldn't get the darned things lit, so we soaked the ends in kerosene. Every cigar in the box."

"What happened?"

"They exploded. The whole box. Spontaneous combustion, I think it's called. Anyway, after we soaked 'em, we heard Mama coming, so we never got to try lighting them. We just left them in the box on Papa's desk. Then it got hot inside that box and all that heat made the kerosene burn. Exploded on Papa's desk when he was talking to somebody important."

They were still laughing at each other's stories when they drove up to the well site. Alexis's laughter died as she got out of the car and she saw the look in Jon's eyes. Her prediction that he would be angry was correct. It was obvious that for one reason or another, he did not want Dave there.

He said nothing, though, and instead simply turned away and directed his attention to the derrick. Alexis felt a knot tighten in her stomach. Dave was right. He wouldn't do anything to put himself in a bad light in spite of the fact that he was angry. He was the perfect politician. He could speak of love carelessly when it served him and swallow his anger when need be. She would leave him to his little charades. There were certainly plenty of other things to think about now, anyway.

The crew had begun to assemble the cable. A blazing fire in a forge next to the cable assembly competed with the sun's warmth that had already begun to gather in the early morning hours. The heat was borne on a vast, bone-dry wind that swept across the openness, sucking at the fire and at the breath of all who stood in its presence.

Nick Bodine worked over the fire, lifting a heavy oval bit from the yellow flames with massive tongs. Alexis saw the ripple of muscles in his arms as he placed the bit on a table and then swung a hammer in a perfect rounded and sensuous rhythm to shape it. The floor of the derrick was strewn with iron shafts and lines made of hemp and linked metal as well as massive tools Alexis couldn't identify. She sensed Dave's excitement as he moved nearer the derrick until the fire from the forge reflected in his eyes.

It was only moments later that Nick and Buck Simpson attached the bit to the cable and with one long, unceremonious thrust, it penetrated the maidenhead of the earth's crust.

9

Jon was aware of the exhilaration she felt when the drill bit slipped into the casing to take its first bite out of the earth. It was a palpable thing, that excitement emanating from her. He could feel it on his skin, hear it ringing in his ears. It began to mingle with his own, and when she glanced at him and their eyes held for a moment, he could see the little laugh that bubbled from her involuntarily, although he couldn't hear it over the roar of the machinery. She looked so young, so exhilaratingly charming, that he found himself returning her smile in spite of himself. His anger with her for bringing Dave along had evaporated in the emotion of the moment.

Dave, standing beside her, touched her arm, and said something to her. She grinned and put an arm around his shoulders. It surprised Jon that the gesture didn't appear to embarrass the boy. He seemed completely comfortable with her. It struck him then how seldom he had seen his son look so relaxed, or how seldom he had seen him laugh, as he had been doing when the two of them first drove up. Jon had felt a moment of envy that she could provoke that laughter and that sense of ease, when he could not.

Of course she would be able to make Dave laugh and feel at ease. She didn't have the responsibility of raising him, of seeing to it that he made something of himself. The boy sure as hell wasn't going to do that by skipping school and coming out to the oil fields. Jon felt anger rising within himself again at the thought of how the boy had defied him, and at Alexis, too, for being a part of it and for not needing to give a damn.

He turned away suddenly and headed for the tent to look at a new geology report he'd gotten from the University of Texas. Inside the makeshift office, he tried not to think of her again, but to concentrate instead upon the reports. He did a reasonable job of doing just that, for a little while at least, but eventually he was compelled to glance out at the rig again.

What he saw momentarily shocked him. Dave and Alexis both were on the platform, and Dave was helping Buck direct the drill pipe into the casing. Alexis stood nearby smiling broadly, encouraging him. Jon threw down his pencil in a pique of anger and burst from the door of the tent. He was about to storm toward the well when he stopped suddenly. This was no time to make a scene, he knew. He would wait until he was at home with Dave to remind him that he had been told he would not work on the rigs, and that he would be severely disciplined for defying that order as well as for skipping school. As for Alexis, he would have to find a way to deal with her as well. She would have to be told what her limits were as far as Dave was concerned.

There was more she would have to be told. The cost of drilling was going to be more expensive than he had anticipated. He couldn't convince Buck and his crew to take the work as a "bean job" whereby they worked just for food and a place to stay, with a promise of a small interest in the well if it came in. A "bean job" meant that if there was no oil, there was no pay, and Buck and his crew didn't want to take that chance in an unproven field. C and R West Texas was going to have to pay them fifty dollars a month and provide them with tents to sleep in at the drilling site. With a driller and a tool dresser each on the two tours, that was two hundred a month in wages.

It was expensive, but he'd had to entice the crew somehow to come to the powder-dry, windswept prairies of West Texas where the towns were fewer and farther apart than they were in East Texas. That meant less excitement and social life for the men. It certainly meant fewer women. The only way to compensate for that, if only temporarily, was with money.

He would wait until later to break that news to Alexis, though. Tonight maybe. She would be too preoccupied now with the excitement of the first day of drilling. It occurred to him that he might be only looking for an excuse to see her again alone. He would have to be careful about being alone with her. He couldn't afford a scandal or even a rumor now that he was running for Congress.

For now, he had to concentrate on his work. He studied his geology reports with an eye toward moving to another site if this one proved to be a dry hole. He'd start looking at core samples before too long. If the samples didn't look promising, then they'd have to reconsider whether to drill deeper or find another spot. The sooner they could discount the possibility of oil, the less money they would lose.

He ran his fingers through his hair and mentally chided himself for having such negative thoughts. It was unlike him to do that. He had not gotten where he was by looking on the dark side of everything or by thinking about how much money there was to lose. He had gained a foothold by thinking of the money and power there was for the taking.

He hoped it would be only a temporary thing, this strange upheaval that had come into his life, this unhealthy focus on losing and on failing as well as the physical failure he'd experienced. He'd hoped he'd proved that was only temporary by just being around Alexis, but it had happened again with Eleanor. She had been even more kind and understanding than she had been the first time. Lord, it was hell to get old, he thought.

But he wasn't old, he told himself. He certainly didn't feel that way around Alexis, in spite of the fact that she only added to the upheaval in his life. He was having a hard time denying that his attraction to her was only temporary. He'd even told her he loved her, but that had been a slip of the tongue. Or a slip of the heart? Was he really falling in love with her? He wished he could get her out of his head. Out of his life. He wished, sometimes, that he'd never met her.

Pushing away from his desk, he went to a cabinet he'd brought into the office to hold his supplies and his own collection of geology books. Behind one of the books was a bottle and a glass he'd stashed there.

He poured himself a generous portion and studied it a moment, swirling it around. He refused to drink his liquor straight from the bottle as his father had done. It was one small way of reaffirming to himself that he was not Beaty Calahan—he was not crude, unpolished, and unforgiving. He downed the liquor in one throat-scalding gulp, hoping it would ease his tension somewhat.

He tried once again to focus on the geology reports in front of him, but in a little while he found himself wondering what a spoiled little rich girl like Alexis thought she was proving by working on an oil rig platform. He stood up and walked to the window again. She was standing on the platform watching the work, her hands on her hips. The curve of those hips was accentuated by the fit of the men's trousers she wore. Her short blond hair was blowing all across her face, obscuring it, but making her look, somehow, even younger than she was—a little like a mischievous boy, except for those lovely curves.

His gaze followed hers to the platform where Dave still stood beside Buck. They both had their hands on the cable, and Dave was listening with rapt attention to something Buck was telling him. Coaching him to judge the type of formation by the vibration of the cable, maybe. They said a good driller could do that. Dave's face, shirt, and trousers, Jon could see, were streaked with grease. He looked like a goddamned driller or tool dresser, and he had a ridiculous grin on his face as if he was enjoying it. The thought of that made Jon angry.

What the kid was enjoying was his rebellion. He was reveling in the fact that he was doing something he thought his old man didn't want him to do. David was still insisting that he wanted to be an oil-field worker and showing no interest in a college education. Jon had half a mind to give him what he wanted, in fact, to insist that he work on the oil rigs, just to show him how hard the work was, to show him how he would be wasting his mind to settle for that kind of work. But he was afraid the kid would be seduced by the romance and the quick money and would forget about his education until it was too late. Jon knew he couldn't risk that. Dave had the potential to be everything a man could be—physically, mentally, and financially. He would be the kind of man who could have put Beaty Calahan in the shade in any respect, and Jon knew he wasn't about to let him mess up that chance.

He started to turn away from his vantage point at the window to return to his desk when he saw the beam mounted high on the derrick shudder and then suddenly fling itself like a giant arrow toward the derrick floor. He saw, in the blink of an eye, that it was headed straight for Alexis, and at the same moment he burst out of the tent, shouting a warning. There was a flash of fear on Alexis' face, the sound of the beam hitting the floor, a blur as Alexis fell before he could reach her.

For one frightening moment he was paralyzed, unsure of what had happened. Then he saw her raise herself to a sitting position with the help of Nick Bodine, and he knew that it was Nick who had saved her by knocking her out of the way.

In one leap Jon was on the derrick platform. "Ali, are you all right?"

"I'm fine," she said, appearing embarrassed by the attention.

"Goddamned carpenters," Nick said. "Don't they know how to put one o' these things together?"

"Woman on a rig," Buck Simpson said. "It's bad luck."

"Shut your damned mouth," Nick said, helping Alexis to her feet. Dave, his face so white Jon thought he might be about to faint, moved closer to Alexis to give her a hand as well.

"Ali," Jon said, "come into the tent. Sit down for a while until—"

"I said I'm all right," she responded, but he could see that she was shaking. "Get that beam back in place," she said, turning back to the crew. "Nick, see if you can't get it done right."

"I'm givin' it one more chance," Buck said. "But if anything else happens, then I ain't workin' on no rig where a woman—"

"You can leave any time you want," Jon said angrily.

Buck held his gaze for a tense moment. "Ah, hell," he said, turning away to help Nick lift the heavy beam.

"Ali," Jon began, "are you sure you don't want to—"

"Haven't you got work to do in your office?" she snapped. She was busy picking up the debris the beam had scattered when it hit the platform.

He watched her for a moment and saw how she was making a point of ignoring him. "Just be careful. We can't afford any delays." Reluctantly he went back to the tent, but he still couldn't keep either Alexis or David out of his mind. Again and again he glanced out the window to reassure himself they were safe. It took several more shots of the whiskey to calm his nerves so he could stay seated at his desk long enough to get even a little work done.

He was surprised when she came into the tent just as the crew was quitting for the day. Her face was streaked with grease, as were her trousers, and her hair was windblown and tattered. It made her look all the more like a naughty child.

"I just wanted to tell you I'm leaving with this tour," she said.

For the moment he was caught off guard that she had picked up the lingo so quickly. She'd even pronounced the word *tower* in the oil-field dialect. "All right," he said, without looking at her. "Are you sure you're—"

"I'm fine," she said, then moved quickly toward the door.

"Alexis!"

She turned to look at him.

"I don't want you bringing my son out again on a school day." He hadn't planned to say that. It was just that it was the first thing that came to his mind as a way to keep her with him longer. He didn't know what was wrong with him.

"He only wanted to be with you," she said, and he saw that the look around her mouth had softened a little. "He would have asked you to drive him, except he knew you'd turn him down."

For the briefest moment he wanted to believe that she had spoken the truth, but in reality he knew she didn't know what she was talking about. David had never wanted to be with him. "Leave my relationship with my son up to me, Alexis," he said with cold finality.

She left without another word, and he felt her absence, heavy and oppressive, all around him.

* * *

"I've got to go over some of these reports with Miss Runnels after supper," Jon said as he gathered up all the papers he'd brought home with him and stacked them carefully on the desk he kept in the living room of their small house.

Eleanor was busy setting the table, and he could sense her turning to look at him through the archway that separated the dining room from the living room. "Didn't you see her today?" she asked.

"Of course."

"Couldn't you have gone over all of that earlier, then?"

"There wasn't time. You know how it is when a well is spudded. There's core samples to look at, new machinery to be tested, breakdowns to deal with."

She had asked how the first day of drilling went when he'd first come home. She always asked, and he knew she was genuinely interested, but only in an indirect way. The close call Alexis had experienced would be of no importance to her. She would only want to know that things looked good for their success. It was never far from her mind, he knew, that the sooner they became financially secure, the more time he could devote to his political career. He was grateful to her for her support and encouragement, just as he knew he should be.

"David came home with Miss Runnels today," she said in a tone of voice she might have used to comment on the weather.

Jon felt an iron grip of emotion in his throat for a moment. "Yes," he managed to say, finally, so calmly it surprised even him. "He skipped school. I plan to have a talk with him about that."

"Why didn't you tell me he was at the drilling site?"

"I've hardly been home long enough, Eleanor." He slammed the geology book he'd been perusing down on the table harder than he had meant.

"I suppose he got her to take him. He must have walked over to her hotel. I would have thought you'd mention that as soon as you got home, since you're so against him—"

"I said I plan to have a talk with him. Now what else can I say?" Again he had spoken more sharply than he intended to.

"She upsets you, doesn't she?"

"What are you talking about?"

"Miss Runnels. There's something about her that sets you off. Is it because she's so young and flirtatious?"

"Good Lord, Eleanor, what are you getting at?"

"Nothing. I'm sorry."

"She's just a kid in a lot of ways. Got a lot to learn."

"I suppose so." She was silent for a moment before she added, "David seems to have a crush on her, too."

He didn't miss the implication that *too* meant she was lumping him in with David in that regard. He didn't comment, though, and neither of them mentioned either Alexis or David until they sat down at the table.

"Where's David?" Jon asked.

"In his room," Eleanor answered without looking up from the piece of meat she was cutting.

"He's not eating?

"He said he ate in town with Miss Runnels."

"I see."

"I told him that was improper. Maybe you could speak to her as well."

"I will, yes."

There was a silence that seemed awkward to Jon before Eleanor resumed the conversation by telling him about the campaign schedule he would need to follow. Jon responded with a protest that he couldn't leave the drilling site for long periods.

"Of course I know it's important for you to succeed at this," Eleanor said. "It can only help your political standing to be successful. We'll just have to work out a reasonable schedule."

Jon didn't answer, and as they came nearer to the end of the meal, he found he could think of nothing except the prospect of seeing Alexis again soon.

He knocked on the door to her hotel room several times before he finally gave up and walked down the hall, feeling a mixture of disappointment and anger. Where could she be? She knew no one in the town, no one to go visit, except him and Eleanor.

It occurred to him then that she would never be the type to "go visiting" anyway as some small-town girl might. She was a city girl, used to excitement. She would go looking for a way to celebrate the fact that she had just spudded her first oil well, and maybe that she had escaped that near accident.

He wasn't going to chase after her, he told himself. She could celebrate to her heart's content. He was going home, and he'd talk to her tomorrow. Through the opened curtain of the Oldsmobile's window, he could hear the shouts and laughter and the sound of a piano coming from Blackie's, and he could see the café's yellow lights sending out their dingy invitation into the night. In spite of his resolve, he drove toward the café. As he drew near, he slowed down. She was in there somewhere, part of that teeming mass.

He parked the car and got out. When he stepped inside he felt the weight of the air, heavy and thick and human-scented, a shocking contrast to the delicately thin night air, spiced with mesquite and creosote. Blackie was sitting in front of the piano pounding out "Yama Yama Blues."

He scanned the room until he saw her sitting at one of the tables near the back. Several bottles of what he knew to be Mexican beer sat on the table. Alexis was one of the few women in the room, but there was another woman at the table with her. Buck Simpson had his arm around the other woman's neck and a bottle of beer in his hand, so that when he took a swallow, he had to move the woman's painted face very close to his. Jon had seen that type of woman in every oil town he'd been in—oil-field hookers who hung out in sleazy honky-tonks. It angered him to think that Alexis was risking being branded as the same kind of trash by what she was doing now.

It looked as if the rift that had begun between her and Buck over his superstition about a woman on the rig was well on the way to being healed. He saw her throw her head back and laugh at something Buck said, a silvery tinkle of sound that made the thick air sparkle, and then when the man next to her said something, it grew into a bawdy whoop. She reached for one of the beer bottles and took a gulp. She seemed about to spew it out as another laugh came bubbling up, but she swallowed hard and wiped her mouth with the sleeve of her forearm. Her hair clung to her forehead and temples in damp question marks, and her face was flushed with excitement and youth and alcohol.

Jon felt an emptiness—an acknowledgement of the gulf that separated them. He started to move toward her, unsure of what he would do. Perhaps he meant to jerk her up from the table and take her away where he would have her to himself. Perhaps he only wanted to narrow the physical distance between them. He wasn't sure of the reason; he wasn't thinking clearly. After only a few steps, he stopped as he saw Nick swagger up to the table and pull her to her feet, then take her in his arms and whirl her around in time to the music. Alexis moved with him, graceful, unperturbed. She said something Jon couldn't hear, leaning down, still in Nick's arms, to address the crowd at another table, and it brought a lusty laugh from all of them. He saw then, that when she was free of whatever doubts and fears had haunted her, she could live her life on wings and lift others to soar with her into the bawdiness of carefree youth.

Nick spun her around clumsily and pulled her closer. Jon saw her try to resist, saw her turn her face when Nick tried to kiss her. Others had joined them on the dance floor now, and the piano music seemed to have grown even louder. Jon saw Alexis move her hands to Nick's chest and try to push him away. No one on the dance floor seemed to notice. Everyone was too drunk on the Mexican beer and the thick air and the loud plinkity-plink of the piano. Jon tried again to move toward her, but the crowd was in the way. He pushed and elbowed and shoved his way through until he was standing in front of her. Nick was holding her a little apart from his body now, looking at her with bleary, drunken eyes.

Jon reached for her wrist to pull her away. He heard her gasp, felt her resist, heard her swear. "What the hell . . . ?" But he didn't stop. He pulled her roughly through the crowd until they were outside in the gossamer night.

"Just what do you think you're doing?" she asked, jerking her arm free.

"I'm taking you back to the hotel," he said, angry that she was being defiant. "Or do you enjoy being pawed at like the rest of those women in there?"

"It's none of your business what I enjoy, and anyway, I can take care of myself."

"You're drunk. Get in the car."

"So what if I am? It's none of your—"

He grabbed her arm again and jerked her hard toward the car. He opened the door and almost shoved her inside. He had expected her to open the door on her side and let herself out when he went around to the driver's side, but when he got in the car, she had made no attempt to leave. She merely glared at him angrily without saying a word.

As soon as he stopped the car in front of her hotel, she got out, slamming the door as she walked toward the entrance. When he caught up with her, she turned to face him abruptly.

"You have humiliated me. Isn't that enough? Must you dog me by following me to my room?"

"I meant no humiliation, Alexis, I—"

"You meant to save my honor," she said sarcastically as she walked up the stairs. "You meant to see that I *rode forth, clothed on with chastity.*"

"You know Keats as well as Shakespeare."

"That's not Keats, it's Tennyson." She inserted her key and unlocked the door. He expected her to slam the door in his face, but she merely stepped inside, threw her handbag on the bed and began unbuttoning the cuffs of her sleeves and rolling them to her elbows. "Are you going to stand in the hallway all night?" she snapped, glancing over her shoulder.

He stepped inside, near dumbfounded that she had, in a manner of speaking, invited him in. She sat down on the bed and unlaced her shoes. "You came to chew me out about something you've had stuck in your craw all day. Get it over with so I can go to bed."

"That was not my purpose. I came to discuss—"

"Don't think I didn't see you pacing back and forth in that tent, looking out the window. You were so damned mad you couldn't see straight. And don't tell me to watch my language!" she said, tugging at her boots with a vengeance. "You were madder than hell because I brought David out."

"That is certainly something we have to talk about."

"There's plenty we have to talk about."

"We do. You're right. But maybe now's not the best time after all. You've been drinking, and—"

"So what if I've been drinking." One of her boots hit the floor with a thud. "Not that it's any of your business, but I only had one beer. At least I don't take it to work and hide it in the bookcase."

He was stunned and embarrassed, and even more so when she looked up at him with a grin. No, not a grin, a smirk.

"I found it one day when I was trying to educate myself on the Delaware formation that's supposed to be a good oil repository. It's behind Caraway's *Ameri-*

can Geology. Not bad stuff. I could smell it on your breath when I came in the office."

"What do my drinking habits have to do with this?"

She stood up abruptly, wearing only one boot, and pointed a finger in his face. "You have the nerve to ask me that? Well, I'll tell you what it has to do with this. Exactly the same thing my drinking habits have to do with this." She glared at him a moment, then she backed up and stood on one foot while she pulled her other boot off, along with the stocking.

Jon found himself preoccupied with the sight of her toes, small and pink, tapering off to a delicate slender nub that was somehow erotic. He was jolted to attention by the sound of her other boot hitting the floor. She was looking at him now, hands on her hips.

"All right, let's get it over with. Tell me I was wrong to bring David out there. Tell me what an idiot I am."

"You're not an idiot, my dear, but it's obvious you don't understand the responsibilities of parenthood. The boy was skipping school."

"I would never assume that I understand anything with the clarity you do, because you possess such unfathomable wisdom."

"Don't be a smart aleck."

She threw up her hands and turned away from him. "God, Jon, you can be such a condescending pedantic snob."

She was right, he thought. He was making an ass of himself. "I don't mean to be a snob, Ali."

"Don't you? Then why did you come here except to make me feel—"

"I'm here because I find it hard to stay away from you. Because I've fallen in love with you," he said, blurting it out.

She looked at him, stunned. "Jon, don't . . ."

"Don't what? Don't say it? Why not?"

"Because it complicates things."

"No, the fact that it's true complicates things. Saying it makes no difference. When I saw that beam falling toward you today, I knew I couldn't bear it if anything happened to you. I knew—"

"Stop!" She moved to the other side of the room, as if trying to distance herself from him and from the truth as well. "Oh, God," she whispered.

He got up and walked over to her. "Do you know how long I've wanted to hold you in my arms? Tell you I love you? I've wanted to tell you how hard it was for me to stay away from you that night in the hotel in Houston, and I've wanted to make sure you know that kiss that night here in your room was not just a lecherous old man making a pass. I want you to know, Alexis, that I love you more than—more than I should."

He saw that she had tears in her eyes, and he wiped one away, gently, with his thumb. She slipped her arms around his waist and put her head on his chest. It was such a gentle gesture, so much like a child might have done, that he was, for a moment, disarmed. He felt awkward, unsure of what he should do with his own arms, but they had moved automatically to hold her close, and then his hand was stroking her hair.

She raised her head and looked up at him. She was about to speak, but he stopped her with his mouth on hers. He felt her lips open slightly to him, respond with eager, hungry little pulls.

Then suddenly she tried to turn away, and she whispered, "No," but he grasped her wrist and pulled her back to him and led her toward the bed, kissing her again and pulling her down until they were both seated on the edge.

10

She only wanted him to hold her, to help her push away the memory of the heavy iron shaft hurling from the heavens ready to crush the life from her body. She had been more frightened than she had wanted to admit. More than anything, she hadn't wanted any of the men to see her fear as weakness, and she certainly couldn't admit it to Jon. But she could let him hold her, let herself feel the reassuring comfort of another human body.

She clung to Jon and let herself feel the sweetness of being in his arms, another small reassurance that she was still alive, that she had survived one more possible erasure. She felt the warmth of his lips at her temples, moving along her jawline, seeking out her lips. She didn't try to stop him, not even when his lips found hers. When his mouth became more demanding, she responded to his demands as if it were the natural, the right thing to do. How could it be wrong when it felt so right? It was not until he pulled her down with him on the bed that some sense of what they were doing touched her conscience.

"Jon, we have to stop this!" she whispered.

"Why?" His hand had moved to her breast, and he was caressing it through the soft fabric of her shirt. She felt her nipples tingle under his touch, and for a moment she couldn't think of how to answer his question or even what he was asking. She moved her hands to his back, and when he began to caress her ear with his tongue and then to invade it seductively, she clung to him.

His mouth found hers again, and for a moment, the briefest moment, she let him kiss her, and she kissed him back. Then she pushed him away and sat up, breathing heavily.

"This is crazy," she said.

"Crazy?" he asked, pulling himself up to face her. "This is what you had in mind, wasn't it? When you tried to seduce me in Houston."

"That was different. I—"

"What was different about it?"

"I didn't know your wife then."

He laughed—not unkindly, but softly, indulgently. "You knew I had a wife."

"But—"

"But you were just being daring?" He smiled at her, making her feel like a foolish child. "Just being a naughty little girl who was going to do what ever it took to get what she wanted?"

"I suppose I was," she said, buttoning her shirt and making a show of calm sophistication that she didn't feel. "You were the old wise one. You kept me honest, and for that I suppose I should be grateful."

He placed his hand over hers. "Let me be honest now. I want to make love to you."

She looked at him for a moment, uncertain how she should respond. "Nothing has changed."

"Yes, it has. You know it has."

"You still have a wife."

"I've fallen in love with you."

"You still have a wife."

"That doesn't matter, Alexis. No, wait," he said, grasping her hand with more firmness when she went back to her buttoning with a swift, defiant movement. "I want you to understand. Eleanor and I have a very comfortable and intelligent relationship. She has never had the same needs I have, yet she has never denied me the right to acknowledge and indulge my own."

"You're saying she lets you play around because she doesn't like to do it."

For a moment his expression was grave. Whether he was angry or merely embarrassed, she couldn't tell. Then he laughed. "Are you always so blunt?"

"Are you always so equivocal?"

"All right, I'll be frank. I have kept a mistress from time to time, but I don't play around. There's a difference."

"Of course." Her tone was sarcastic. Then there was a long silence while their gazes locked, and there was a breathlessness between them, as if each knew the brink they had happened upon. She spoke again, quietly. "Am I to be your mistress?"

He held her eyes with his a moment longer, as if he was contemplating it. "My lover," he said finally.

"There is a difference?"

"I have never been in love with a mistress."

"I want no strings attached. I want you to know that I don't wish to marry."

"I am already married."

"It will get complicated, nevertheless."

"It need not. If we are discreet."

"And I will regret it, of course."

He touched her hand gently. "Never."

"Oh yes," she said, "I will most certainly regret it." She began to unbutton his shirt.

"Alexis, I want you to be sure."

"No, don't stop me. It's too late."

"I want no regrets, I want this to be—"

"To be what? Perfect? It won't be." She slipped her hands inside his shirt and felt the tangle of hair across his chest and the rapid pounding of his heart beneath her palms.

He laughed softly. "All right, the old wise one will concede. It won't be perfect."

"But it can be heavenly."

He held her face with both his hands and brought his own face very close. *"Then come kiss me, sweet and twenty."*

"Ah yes," she said, her lips on his, moving softly, seductively as she encircled him with her arms and quoted the rhyming line, *"In delay there lies no plenty."*

She felt the blood warm inside her body, and for that moment, at least, she could believe that life was eternal, death impossible, and invisibility forever forgotten.

He stayed for a while afterward, holding her in his arms, neither of them speaking. She would not break the silence; she would savor it, and she would not let herself think of what they had just done except in the context of pleasure. And love? She didn't know. She was afraid to think that she might actually love him. Wasn't it enough to *make* love? To love someone was another matter, and far more risky. The risk of loss. The emptiness, the miniature death that came with grief.

The harsh truth was that she wouldn't love Jon Calahan because she had lost him before she ever had him. He belonged to his wife, his son, his career. He could say he loved her because he had all those riches. She had only herself and a terrible fear of loss. She had given herself, physically and emotionally, to Zane Lawrence. She had loved him unconditionally and wholly, but she had lost him anyway, first to another woman and then to the war.

She had broken it off with him when she found out about the woman, in spite of his contrite apology, in spite of his confession of weakness and his vow that he loved her. It had been a bitter quarrel, a bitter parting, and then he had died the next day, his plane downed by German guns before they'd had time to let the wounds heal, to find out if a reconciliation was even possible. It was all somehow unresolved, except the loss, which was final and undeniable, and it had left her unwilling to risk loss again.

Because of that, she would be Jon Calahan's lover, and she would make love with him, but she would not love him. There would be no strings attached.

"What are you thinking?" he asked.

She smiled and shook her head. "You mustn't ask."

"Why not?"

"You don't want to know."

He pulled her close and nuzzled her neck. "Of course I do."

She shrieked at his nibbling. He seemed in a particularly playful mood, as if the lovemaking had revived something in him.

"Then I was thinking that I want to make love to you again," she said. "And I don't think you want to hear that just yet, because—"

"What makes you think I don't?" he asked, throwing the covers back to show her his erection. He pulled her close again, and then rolled her over, teasing her with his tongue and with all of his body until she cried out for him.

It was very late when he left, well past midnight, but she lay in bed where the scent of him lingered and the memory of him was still very much a presence. "Oh, Lord," she said aloud to the darkness, "what have I become?"

She fell asleep knowing the answer. She had become, at long last, alive.

Eleanor awakened when he came into the bedroom, although she knew he was trying to be quiet. It annoyed her a little that she was such a light sleeper and so easily disturbed. It made her long for the big house in Beaumont where there were five bedrooms and she was able to have private sleeping quarters of her own. But she couldn't stay in Beaumont, of course. Jon needed her with him to run his campaign, and besides, even if he'd been able to run it by himself, it wouldn't have looked right for his wife to be all the way across the state. It was important to project the image of a solid, traditional family life.

It was inconvenient, though, to be awakened so late at night. She lay there for a moment, half afraid that he would know she was awake and would want the "act of darkness," as she had come to think of it. It was Jon who had first used that expression, one of his tedious quotes from Shakespeare, it seemed. She'd never been able to plow through the heavy, ancient language of the old bore, but she had to admit that turn of phrase at least seemed fitting. When Jon made no move toward her, she felt a fleeting moment of groggy gratitude before she drifted easily into sleep.

When, by the end of the second week, she was still free of any responsibility for sex, she knew that he had found another mistress. She supposed it to be Alexis Runnels. She had never met any of Jon's women before, and she preferred it that way. Her concern was that the women would not be so indiscreet as to ruin his career, but she had learned she could trust Jon to see to that.

Alexis Runnels was a bit of a surprise, because she was not what Eleanor had considered to be Jon's type. For one thing, she wasn't strikingly beautiful. Eleanor knew that she herself was, in her own mature way, more beautiful than Miss Runnels. For another thing, she'd always known Jon was attracted to a certain type of intelligence—quiet and introspective, which Miss Runnels certainly was not. Jon would eventually find Miss Runnels's aggressive intellect tiresome, she assumed.

He had never shown signs of being attracted to such youth before, either. She could brush aside his attraction to such a young woman this time as no more than a middle-age folly that would pass soon enough, but it could be dangerous, nevertheless. She feared that Miss Runnels's youthfulness might make her indiscreet. She would have to watch her carefully.

It was David who, several weeks later, alerted her to the fact that she needed to act quickly.

"You're up early, son," she said, as he came into the kitchen where she was preparing breakfast.

"I'm goin' out to the rig. Ali's pickin' me up."

"Who?"

"Ali. You know, Papa's partner."

"Oh, you mean Miss Runnels."

"Ow, that's hot!"

"What are you doing with that coffee?"

"Drinking it."

"Coffee? You never used to drink it before."

"Ali got me started. She keeps a pot in the tent all the time. Heats it with a little gasoline burner."

"You've been out to the rig a lot lately, it seems."

"Sure. Lots of times. Ali picks me up after school sometimes."

"After school? I thought you were with that Whitner boy."

"Naw, he just hangs around with a buncha kids. I like it out at the rig. Ali's taking me today, too. For the whole day, since it's Saturday. She said she'd come by here to pick me up on her way out."

Eleanor felt her unease growing. "How does your father feel about you spending all this time at the rig?" she asked, her back to David while she finished cooking his breakfast. "I hope you're not having those constant arguments over it. It won't do to have him upset all the time. He needs to keep his mind on the campaign, not family squabbles."

"Ah, he's not mad anymore. Ali worked him over."

She turned toward the table carrying a plate of eggs and bacon for David. "Worked him over? What do you mean?"

David laughed. "She's got him wrapped around her little finger."

Eleanor hesitated midway between the stove and the table, forgetting for a moment that she was carrying the plates. David didn't notice. He was busy stirring sugar into his coffee. She moved toward the table and set the plates down. "Why do you say that?" she asked, trying to sound casual.

"Well, that's what Nick says. And he's right. She can get the old geezer to do anything she wants."

"David! I will not have you referring to your father that way."

"All right, sorry."

"Who is Nick?"

"Nick Bodine. He's a tool dresser."

"I see," she said, thinking the name sounded vaguely familiar. "And you say he mentioned this— change in your father?"

David shrugged. "I guess so." He was playing with his food, not eating much. Eleanor was well aware that the eggs were undercooked and the bacon burned, but cooking was not her strong suit. She'd always had a Negro woman in Beaumont to do the cooking, just as all the better families did. But here, even if a person could find one, it would look as if she was putting on airs. She had to project the right image for the sake of Jon's career.

"Has anyone else commented on this to you?" Eleanor poured herself a cup of coffee and sat down across from David, trying harder than ever not to sound concerned. "On the fact that Miss Runnels seemed to be having an effect on your father, I mean."

"I don't know. Maybe. They don't talk about it much. Just Nick. I guess maybe 'cause he's kinda sweet on her. But she won't hardly give him the time of day." He laughed again. "You shoulda seen him Tuesday. Papa and Ali went in the office to work on some kind of report and Nick nearly broke his neck tryin' to stretch it far enough to see what she was doin' in there. He's sweet on her all right. Can't keep his eyes off of her."

"Really?"

"Yeah, he's even made up some excuse to go in the office and see her, and—"

"Tuesday?" Eleanor interrupted. "You say this happened Tuesday?"

"Yeah, that's right."

"That was the day of the rally in Midland. Jon was supposed to be there."

"Maybe he forgot."

"How could he forget? The party chairman was supposed to be there, too. I knew I should have gone with him! Are you sure it was Tuesday?"

"Yeah, I think so. Anyway, he didn't go to any political rally. He's been at the rig with me and Ali every day. I guess maybe he figured it wasn't so important."

Eleanor felt as if she'd been hit in the stomach. "He knows it was," she said, barely above a whisper.

She saw Jon coming into the kitchen, and she saw the look on his face—a distant smile as if he was thinking of something else, and she had no doubt what, or rather who, that was. She would have confronted him then about missing the rally, but that, of course, was out of the question with David present. She simply greeted him with a pleasant "Good morning" and got up to fix his eggs.

Perhaps it was best that she wait anyway, she thought, breaking the eggs into a skillet. She had to think this through. One thing was crystal clear, though, and that was that Miss Alexis Runnels knew a good thing when she saw it. She was the type to be attracted to a man of power such as Jon was obviously destined to be. Sleeping with him wouldn't be enough, of course. She would want control of him somehow, and it was obvious to Eleanor that David was the means by which she meant to gain that control.

Miss Runnels was no fool. She must have seen how badly Jon wanted to be close to his son, and it was an old trick for a woman to use a man's children in order to get even closer to him. Even if it didn't work, and it very well might not, she thought, since Jon was no fool either, there was still a danger in what was happening. If this Nick that David had mentioned could see that Alexis had Jon under her spell, then others would most certainly see it too, and that would start tongues to wagging.

A sex scandal or even the hint of one could ruin Jon's chances. Even if that didn't happen, his foolish preoccupation with her had already caused him to miss an important political meeting. It was obvious that something had to be done, Eleanor thought, as she scooped the eggs up out of the grease. And it had to be done quickly.

Eleanor picked up a biscuit and put it on the plate with the eggs. She failed to notice that one of the yolks had broken and cooked to the consistency of rubber. She only knew she was about to work herself into a headache that could keep her bedridden for days. She knew, too, that she couldn't afford that. It was important for her to stay well so she could manage Jon's campaign for him. He might be a clever and even brilliant man, perhaps even with the qualities to be a statesman, but he was, nevertheless, completely unaware of the finesse and organization and attention to detail it took to run a campaign. He was too wrapped up in his business, and now, it seemed, in Miss Runnels as well.

She became vaguely aware that Jon was speaking to her. "I'm sorry, dear, what did you say?" She unconsciously placed her fingertips at the back of her skull where the headache was beginning.

"I said I'm afraid I'm not going to have time to eat this," Jon said, smiling at her apologetically. "I didn't realize how late it is. One of the crew will be here in a few minutes. Nick Bodine. Do you remember him? He used to work for me in Beaumont."

"The one who's sweet on Miss Runnels," she said.

"What?" There was a surprised look on his face.

"David told me," she said and noticed Jon's quick, uneasy glance at David.

"This has nothing to do with Nick being sweet on anybody," Jon snapped. "It's about a truck Nick knows about that's for sale."

"A truck? You're gonna buy a truck?" David asked enthusiastically.

"You may remember Nick," Jon said, ignoring David and attempting to appear nonchalant. "A tool dresser. Worked for me on a well in Beaumont. I don't think you ever liked him. Kind of a ladies' man, so I don't wonder that David thinks he's sweet on

Ali. But he's a good worker, and he told me he heard about this truck we could use to move the rig when we..."

"Ali learned how to drive a truck in the war," David said at the same time Jon was speaking. "That's how come she can drive so good now. Good as any man."

"... need to drill another well on one of those leases," Jon continued.

"Miss Runnels was in the war?" Eleanor asked, turning to David.

"Sure. She told me all about it. In France. She was a canteen worker, and sometimes she had to haul supplies when they—"

"David, please don't interrupt when I'm trying to talk to your mother."

"Jon, dear, I think you're overly agitated," Eleanor said with a little laugh. "Anyway, what does it matter what I think about this Nick? If he's a good worker, that's all that's important, isn't it?"

She was remembering Nick Bodine now—handsome, young, devil-may-care. The more she remembered, the more the sickening pain in her head subsided. All the young women were quite taken with him. He could have had his pick of any of them, and she recalled that he thoroughly enjoyed the picking. It could be, she thought, smiling, that with just the right amount of finesse, her problems could be solved.

"You said he was a bad influence on David, if I remember," Jon was saying, but she hardly heard him.

"We must ask him to come for supper."

"You want to ask Nick Bodine for supper?"

"Of course. Wouldn't that be the neighborly thing to

do? I bet that young man doesn't know many people here yet and would appreciate—"

Jon gave a hoot. "Nick Bodine never had any trouble getting acquainted with people. You don't need to worry about that."

"We'll invite Miss Runnels, too," Eleanor said, ignoring him. "I have a feeling she doesn't know enough people either."

"Eleanor, that's not necessary. These people are out here to do a job. To make money. They don't need you to see after their social life."

"Nonsense. Everybody enjoys a civilized meal with good company now and then. I'll invite Mr. Bodine myself when he shows up. David, you see that your papa invites Miss Runnels if I miss her."

"Eleanor, I insist that you not—"

"Too bad there's not a decent place to shop for groceries. I wonder if I could get that Mexican woman who works at Blackie's Café to help with the cooking. Oh, never mind, isn't that a car I hear? He must be here. Now don't spoil things, Jon. I'll take care of everything and make sure everyone has a good time."

As soon as she opened the door Eleanor remembered that she had, indeed seen Nick Bodine before, and she had forgotten until now how handsome he was.

"Miz Calahan," he said, giving her a dazzling smile. "It's mighty nice to see you. How do you manage to look so pretty? Any other woman would be shriveled to a prune livin' out here in this dry hole."

"It's nice to see you, too, Nick. Please come in. We were just talking about you."

Jon stood up hurriedly. "I'll just get my hat, and we can be on our way."

"Talking about me?" He was still smiling at Eleanor and looking at her as if he found it impossible to keep his eyes off of her. "Well, now I don't know whether that's good or bad. Hey! Dave!" he said, glancing beyond her. "No wonder you've growed a foot since I seen you in Beaumont. Look at that breakfast you're puttin' away. Your mama takes good care o' you, I see."

"Aw, she don't do no such of a thing," Dave said, embarrassed.

"I'm surprised you left East Texas, Nick," Eleanor said. She poured a cup of coffee to hand him.

"Eleanor, we don't have time for—"

"Surprised?" Nick chuckled as he accepted the cup. "I don't know why. I'm always looking for new opportunities."

"Of course," Eleanor said with a secret smile.

"Do you really know where there's a truck?" Dave asked.

"Sure do, son. She's a Mack some old boy over at Midland wants to—"

"David, Nick can tell you all about the truck later," Jon said. "We've got work to do."

"Yes, David," Eleanor said, "maybe when we have Mr. Bodine over for supper tomorrow night. You will come for supper, won't you, Mr. Bodine? We're having Miss Runnels come too." She could almost feel the weight of Jon's dismay. She wanted to tell him that she understood that he was worried about the awkwardness having his mistress for supper might cause. She wanted to tell him not to worry because she was confident that he would see, eventually, that she was doing the right thing.

"Come for supper?" Nick asked. "Why I'd be

pleased to, Miz Calahan. And ya'll are havin' Ali come too?" he asked, directing his question to Jon.

Jon glowered but didn't answer.

"She's right charming," Eleanor said. "As a matter of fact, she'll be here in a few minutes if you care to wait."

"Ali's coming here?" Jon asked, unable to conceal his alarm.

"To pick up David. She's taking him out to the rig," Eleanor said with deceptive calmness.

"I told you not to skip school any more to go out there, David," Jon said sharply.

"There's no school on Saturday," David said in a tone of voice that seemed to indicate that Jon was mentally inadequate.

"Jon, stop fretting, for heaven' sake. Everything is going to be all right," Eleanor said.

When he turned to look at her, and she saw his flushed face and his furrowed brow, her chagrin was replaced with a moment of compassion. Nevertheless, she couldn't let him ruin his career. If he was going to keep a mistress, it was going to have to be someone with whom he could be more discreet.

"Please trust me, Jon. It will be good for Miss Runnels to be in the company of someone her own age."

His expression changed. To rage, she thought, because of the veiled reference to the difference in their ages. For a moment she was frightened. Then the look was gone, replaced with something she didn't understand before he turned and was gone.

11

The dinner invitation had come as a surprise to Alexis, and the idea of dinner with Jon and his family made her uncomfortable. She'd done her best to decline, but Eleanor had insisted and was so persistent Alexis had given in out of weariness. Now she wished she'd been stronger and stuck to her resolve. David was pleased, though.

"It'll be fun having both of you there. You and Nick. Nick's a swell guy," David said. "You do like him, don't you, Ali?" David's face was covered with dust that was rising up all around the car and sifting in through the opened window as they made their way across the flat, mesquite-dotted expanse. She had been teaching him to drive over the past few weeks, and he was driving now, smoothly, showing his natural ability for things mechanical.

Alexis glanced at him and smiled, thinking how like a little boy he looked with that dirty face, so much like Miller had looked when he was young. "I guess I like Nick well enough," she said.

"He's sweet on you, you know."

"Nick likes anything in a skirt."

"That ought to let you out, then," David said with a snicker as he glanced at Alexis's trousers.

She reached across and ruffled his hair. "Don't make fun of the way people dress, David," she teased. "It isn't polite."

"You know how come Mama invited Nick to supper, don't you?" David asked.

Alexis stretched out on the seat, her head back, her eyes closed as she let the warm, dry summer breeze drifting through the windows caress her face. "I can't even imagine why she invited me," she said. "She must be desperate for company."

"She's trying to set you up with him."

Alexis opened her eyes and glanced at David. "She's what?"

"She's trying to be a matchmaker. I heard Papa tell her he's not your type. They got into a big argument over it."

Alexis sat up straight, her full attention on David. "Over what? The fact that I'm not his type or that I'm coming to supper?"

David shrugged. "I just heard part of it. It was late at night when they thought I was asleep. Mama said you ought to have somebody your own age to hang around. Papa told Mama she was buttin' in where she didn't have any business. Said you and Nick could manage your own lives. Then Mama said something about Papa's political career, and their voices got real low, but I could tell they were still arguin'."

When she didn't answer, David shot a glance in

her direction. "Hey, it ain't nothin' to worry about," he said. "You don't have to hook up with Nick if you don't want to. Mama's always tryin' to run people's lives for 'em. It's just her way."

Alexis still didn't respond. She was lost in her thoughts. Was Eleanor trying to steer her toward someone else in order to end the affair? Was she jealous after all, in spite of what Jon had said? Alexis had tried to convince herself that there was nothing wrong with the arrangement she had with Jon Calahan, since there was no one to be hurt, yet she had known all along it was not so simple. There was plenty of potential for hurt. Eleanor, perhaps, could be hurt after all. And Alexis knew, in spite of her wish to deny it, that she, too, could be hurt again.

She had been a fool, she thought, to have placed herself once again into a situation where she was the misfit, the odd one out. She could end up with no choice but to disappear from Jon's life.

"Oh, don't look so gloomy, Ali," David said. "You can get through one evening with Nick. I like him. I think he's the bee's knees."

She gave him a grin. "What kind of language is that?"

"Now, don't go sounding like Mama."

Alexis tried to force away her blues. "Why? Ain't she the cat's pajamas?"

They both laughed. "You're the cat's pajamas *and* the bee's knees," David said. "You think I don't know how you stuck your neck out for me?"

Alexis shrugged. "Well . . ."

"I mean it. Bringing me out here, getting Nick and Buck to let me help 'em on the rig. I know Papa musta given you hell. Oh, gosh, I'm sorry, Ali," he

Discover a World of Timeless Romance Without Leaving Home

Get
4 FREE
Historical Romances from Harper Monogram.

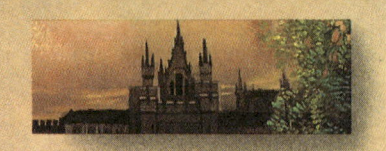

JOIN THE TIMELESS ROMANCE READER SERVICE AND GET FOUR OF TODAY'S MOST EXCITING HISTORICAL ROMANCES FREE, WITHOUT OBLIGATION!

Imagine getting today's very best historical romances sent directly to your home – at a total savings of at least $2.00 a month. Now you can be among the first to be swept away by the latest from Candace Camp, Constance O'Banyon, Patricia Hagan, Parris Afton Bonds or Susan Wiggs. You get all that – and that's just the beginning.

PREVIEW AT HOME WITHOUT OBLIGATION AND SAVE.

Each month, you'll receive four new romances to preview without obligation for 10 days. You'll pay the low subscriber price of just $4.00 per title – a total savings of at least $2.00 a month!

Postage and handling is absolutely free and there is no minimum number of books you must buy. You may cancel your subscription at any time with no obligation.

GET YOUR FOUR FREE BOOKS TODAY ($20.49 VALUE)

FILL IN THE ORDER FORM BELOW NOW!

YES! *I want to join the Timeless Romance Reader Service. Please send me my 4 FREE HarperMonogram historical romances. Then each month send me 4 new historical romances to preview without obligation for 10 days. I'll pay the low subscription price of $4.00 for every book I choose to keep – a total savings of at least $2.00 each month – and home delivery is free! I understand that I may return any title within 10 days without obligation and I may cancel this subscription at any time without obligation. There is no minimum number of books to purchase.*

NAME_____

ADDRESS_____

CITY_____STATE____ZIP_____

TELEPHONE_____

SIGNATURE_____

(If under 18 parent or guardian must sign. Program, price, terms, and conditions subject to cancellation and change. Orders subject to acceptance by HarperMonogram.)

GET 4 FREE BOOKS
(A $20.49 VALUE)

TIMELESS ROMANCE READER SERVICE

120 Brighton Road
P.O. Box 5069
Clifton, NJ 07015-5069

AFFIX STAMP HERE

said, blushing. "I didn't mean to say that. I know I'm not supposed to cuss in front of a woman. It's just that I don't hardly think of you as a woman."

"Gee, kid, thanks."

"That's not what I mean," he said uncomfortably. "I just mean, well . . . you . . . you mean a lot to me, Ali. If anything ever happened to you . . . I mean like that time you nearly got hurt when that beam fell, I don't know what I'd do."

Alexis glanced at him and saw the subdued expression on his face. "Now don't go getting sappy on me," she said.

David grinned sheepishly. "Don't tell Nick I'm a sap," he said. "He'll throw me off the rig."

"Your papa wouldn't let him."

"What are you talkin' about?"

"Jon. I don't think he'd let Nick keep you off the rig now. I think he likes having you around."

Dave snorted. "Who are you trying to kid?"

"He loves you."

He glanced at her quickly, uneasily. "Now who's gettin' sappy?"

"He does, David. I think he just has a hard time showing it."

"You can say that again."

"You love him, too, don't you?"

There was a tense silence, and she saw David grip the steering wheel until his knuckles turned white. Finally he burst irreverently into "Sipping Cider Thru' a Straw." He was still singing at the top of his voice when they drove up to the rig.

Alexis had expected to find Nick and Jon at the rig, since Eleanor had said they had left more than an hour before she came to pick up David. She was even more shocked to see the crew had not even begun to work. The forge was cold and the rig silent while Buck Simpson and Billy Tyson, the tool dresser from the second tour, sat smoking and passing a bottle of bootleg whiskey between them.

"What's the meaning of this?" Alexis asked angrily, walking up to Buck. "Why aren't you working? You're being paid good wages to—"

"Now hold on just a minute, lady," Buck said, pointing at her with a lighted cigarette between his fingers. "I was out here at dawn, before you ever opened your pretty little eyes this morning. Then Calahan come out and shut us down."

"What do you mean, shut you down?" She'd made an uneasy peace with Buck, but she knew he still was not entirely comfortable with the idea of a woman at the drilling site.

"He done it after he looked at the core samples," Buck said. "Had some smarty college boy geologist with him that didn't seem to like what he seen in them samples."

"Was Nick with him? Did they come out here in a truck?" David asked eagerly.

"Yeah, he was in a truck," Buck said. "Nick was driving it. That's why he traded tours with Billy here, to help Calahan get that truck. I tell you, the son of a bitch don't care how much dirt he throws in your face with them big old wheels on that thang. Noisy damned contraption damned near—"

"What was it Jon didn't like about what he saw?" Alexis asked, interrupting Buck's tirade. It was obvious he didn't have David's reluctance to swear around women. That was of little concern to her now, though, since she could think of a few choice words to apply to Jon. She should have been told about a geologist coming to inspect core samples.

"Damned if I know what the college boy didn't like," Buck said. "Something about the looks of the sand. Damned if I know what it was. If you ask me he was just showing off. Them core samples don't mean nothin'. I say there's oil here. You go to huntin' another site, it's going to cost you money."

"Another site? Is that what the geologist recommended?"

"Best I could tell that's what they was talkin' about," Buck said.

"It's goin' to cost plenty to cap this hole and spud another one," Billy said. "But, hell, what do we care? We just work for wages and do what the boss says."

"Hey, you two, there's a lady present!" David said, speaking up for the first time.

"It's all right," Alexis said quietly to David, but Buck also came to her defense.

"The kid's right, there's a lady present. Watch your goddamned mouth in front of a lady, Billy."

"What kind of a job is this?" Billy asked. "We got some old fart for a boss and he's got to have a college boy and a dame to tell him what to do."

"Well, the old fart's not here, now," Alexis said, "so the dame is telling you what to do. Let's get to work. We can drill through some more of that sand today, and we'll have more core samples for the college boy to look at."

"You want us to drill?" Buck asked, surprised.

"That's what we pay you for."

"But the boss said—"

"I'm the boss, Buck. I've got money invested in this hole just like Jon Calahan, and since I haven't heard anything to lead me to believe it's the wrong hole, I say drill."

"But, Miss Ali—"

"None of us is making any money when we're all sitting on our . . . butts," she said, stumbling over the last word, which she knew was still far too descriptive to be considered ladylike. It did, however, have the effect she had hoped for.

After an awkward silence Buck laughed uneasily. "You're sure as hell right about that," he said. "Let's get to work, Billy."

The work continued throughout the day, and with no more problems than usual, Alexis was pleased to see. She did find, however, that she, along with David, kept watching the horizon for signs of the truck, but there was nothing except the relentless blue of the sky and the unyielding flatness of the prairie. And there was the wind, hot, dry, and furious because it had no trees to sing to, no oceans or mountains to flirt with. It could only sweep across the prairie with a vengeance that was both surly and sorrowful. Alexis found it exhausting to contend with its eternal push that robbed her eyes and skin and sometimes, it seemed, even her very breath of vital moisture.

By the end of the day, neither she nor David was inclined to talk. Besides the wind to battle, there had also been a broken drill bit and a long delay while Billy, who was not as adept as Nick, tried to repair it. Alexis slid into the passenger side of the car, leaving Dave to steer it across the rough expanse that passed for a road. She tried to rest her head against the back of the seat, but the constant jarring caused by the rough terrain made it difficult.

"Hell of a day, wasn't it?" David said, his voice flat from weariness.

"Watch your language."

"Why do you keep saying that to me? You don't seem to mind when the other men cuss, and you even cuss yourself when you're—"

"The other men aren't Jon Calahan's son."

"So what? Does that make me special?"

She sat up straighter and looked at him. "Yes, Dave, it does. It makes a difference who your father is. Believe me, I know."

"What are you talking about? It don't make any— no difference. It don't make *no* difference," he said defiantly. "All that matters is who you are. And I'm going to be who I want to be."

"Yeah, well you ought to set your sights a little higher than Nick Bodine."

"Are you going to start in on me too? Just like my old man? What are you taking his part for? You're put out at him."

Alexis shot a glance at him. "For heaven's sake, Dave."

"Well, you are! And I don't blame you. He ought to have told you what was going on today. It's like you told Buck, you got money in that hole too."

"David . . ."

"Come on, Ali, admit it. You're sore at the old man."

It was true, she was angry at Jon for not communicating with her, for acting with such little regard for their relationship, both personal and business. She glanced at David again and was struck by his face, streaked with grease and dirt, and his eyes, the same alarming green as Jon's, but with less of the world in them. He turned toward her, taking his eyes for a moment off the road, and his youthful intensity, his absolute guilelessness warmed her.

"All right," she said, unable to contain her smile. "Yes, I'm sore. I'm damned sore."

David laughed and broke into "Sipping Cider Thru' A Straw" again, and this time she joined him.

Alexis took special care in dressing for her evening at the Calahans', choosing a dress of blue silk that clung to her body and ended in a flounce halfway to her knees, revealing her flesh-colored silk stockings and her white pumps with the fashionable high heels. She had washed her hair, taking advantage of the fact that it would dry quickly in the arid climate, and she'd brushed it until it shone like a golden halo. She'd added subtle color to her cheeks and lips and enhanced her eyes with a little mascara. She lamented the fact, still, that she was not beautiful like her sister, Diana, but she would try to use everything she had to her best advantage. And she knew as soon as she walked into the door of Jon's house that she had the advantage.

She saw the look in Jon's eyes when he saw her. Was he pleased or merely shocked? It didn't matter, she thought. At least she had his attention. She had the attention of Nick, as well, who was smiling at her and moving toward her. His smile never faded the whole time Jon was taking the silky shawl she removed from around her shoulders.

She looked around for David, but he had been banished to his room, apparently. It was a shame. She knew how he had been looking forward to this, and she had the feeling she might need an ally.

Nick looked more handsome than ever in a clean white shirt, with his dark hair slicked back in a dapper style. "Wow!" he mouthed for her benefit only, flashing his dazzling smile. "Shoulda took her with us today when we bought the truck," he said aloud to Jon, but still without taking his eyes off Alexis. "Mighta got a better deal. Woman looks like that can have anything she wants. Excuse me, Miz Calahan," he added with a quick, embarrassed glance toward Eleanor, as if he had forgotten she was there and was afraid he'd gone beyond the acceptable in polite company.

Eleanor laughed. "No need to apologize," she said with a forced brightness. "And anyway, I expect you're right." She sent a benevolent smile in Alexis's direction. "Miss Runnels does seem accustomed to having anything she wants." Her eyes held Alexis's, coldly conveying some hidden message beneath her words.

Alexis was taken aback by Eleanor's ruthlessness, but it served to awaken her. It was more obvious than ever that Jon had misled her. Eleanor was not understanding about their relationship. She had invited her here to humiliate her and to let her know she was protecting her turf. Why had Jon allowed this evening to happen? Why had she herself allowed it to happen? Perhaps she'd been caught off guard, since her previous brief encounters with Eleanor when she'd stopped by to pick up David had been, if not cordial, at least benign. It was too late now to think about all those things, of course. All she could do now was smile and pretend to be charmed by Eleanor's insults.

Since she had no comeback, what followed was an embarrassed silence in which Eleanor's remark lingered like a bad smell until Jon stepped forward and said, not without some awkwardness, "Let's all have a drink. I managed to dredge up something besides Mexican beer. Gin, Ali, your favorite."

"Why, aren't you thoughtful, Jon?" Eleanor said, as if she was trying to ignore the insinuation that Jon knew too much about Alexis's intimate preferences. Jon glanced at her before he left the room to get the drinks. Eleanor excused herself to check the dinner.

"I'm told you found a truck," Alexis said, turning to Nick. "War surplus?"

She saw the grin on Nick's face and knew that he knew precisely what had just transpired between her and Eleanor. "Nope. A Mack. Used, but in good shape. Expensive," he said in a tone that might have suggested he was not talking about a truck.

Alexis tried to force away her discomfort. "You know what they say. You get what you pay for, and quality is expensive."

"You know what they say. You get what you deserve," he added, grinning.

"Oh, I do hope you're right, Nick," she said sweetly.

Nick laughed. "This is going to be one hell of a night," he said. "You're one smart-aleck little gal."

She gave him a smile that melted the heavy aspic of the evening for the two of them. "I'm tired, Nick. Don't mean to take it out on you. Just drop the dirty innuendos, okay?" She slumped into the sofa.

"The dirty what?"

"Just talk nice to me, okay?"

"Sure thing, baby."

"And don't call me baby."

"Damn! You are touchy."

"We've got to pretend we like each other, Nick. Otherwise our hostess will think we're rude."

"I do like you, honey. And you're gonna love me once you get to know me."

"Tell me about the truck. How much?"

"A thousand dollars."

"My God! I wonder if we can borrow that much."

"You're going to have to talk to Jon about that."

"There's a lot I'm going to have to talk to Jon about."

"Now don't get me in the middle of what ever this is between y'all."

Alexis glanced at him as if his words had brought her to her senses. "Okay, Nick. I won't. I promise. Let's talk about something else. Tell me about yourself. Where are you from?"

"Oklahoma."

Eleanor had returned and was, Alexis knew, looking on with interest. She seemed to be moving nervously between satisfaction that her matchmaking had worked and suspicion that it had been too easy. Jon entered with the drinks and was clearly annoyed. Alexis did her best to ignore him and instead continued to amuse Nick, who was openly willing to allow himself to be seduced.

It was by chance that she found herself alone with Eleanor in the living room after dinner when Nick had excused himself to find the toilet and Jon had gone to find another bottle of gin.

"I'm glad you came, Miss Runnels," Eleanor said. She was seated in an overstuffed chair opposite her.

"It was kind of you to invite me."

"I want you to know I have nothing against you."

Alexis raised an eyebrow that conveyed a desire to

understand what Eleanor had meant but also masked a sudden alarm that something unpleasant was coming.

"Nothing at all," Eleanor continued. "It is just that the campaign makes Jon particularly vulnerable. I only want to make sure you don't hurt him. I know you're fond of David, and I expect you know that if you hurt Jon, David will be hurt as well."

Alexis was surprised at Eleanor's candor, and she felt her alarm growing, a storm roiling in her stomach, yet she spoke with absolute calm. "I have no intention of hurting anyone, Eleanor. You can be assured of that."

"Thank you, Miss Runnels," Eleanor said and gave her a cordial smile just as Jon reappeared.

Toward the end of the evening, Alexis was riding an incandescent crest of brash ebullience that was part gin, part pain, and part denial. She could look at Jon and see that he was jealous of the attention she was giving Nick. Worse, though, she could feel in his glance that he loved her. Worse yet, she knew that she loved him, although she knew she must never tell him. Her love was a warm and living thing, like an ovum inside her. Yet she would turn away from the thought of their love having warmth and life and substance, and Jon must do the same.

The evening had shown her something with utter clarity—that she was not meant to be a mistress. She did not know how to keep from hurting others— Eleanor, whose ruthlessness was no more than protectiveness, or David, whom she loved as much as Miller or Diana or perhaps more, because he clearly needed her when no one else had. She could not allow herself to destroy Jon's family. But most of all she could not destroy herself.

When she left that evening, mercifully early, it was with Nick. He had slid under the wheel of her car automatically, as if there would be no question as to his proprietary right to steer the direction of the evening and probably even the direction of their relationship.

"What the hell was that all about?" he asked as they drove away.

"What was what all about?"

"You know what. Eleanor was protecting her flank like a doughboy. I think she thinks you've been sleeping with him."

Alexis shot him a quick glance and felt as if her heart and breath had suddenly vacated her chest.

Nick was silent for a few seconds longer before he asked, "Have you?"

"I can't imagine that would be any of your business."

Nick laughed. "Maybe it is. That's the reason she threw us together, you know. I'm a deecon. To get you away from Jon."

"Decoy, you mean."

"Well, anyway, she wants to keep you away from her man."

"I know. But she needn't have troubled herself. I'm not sleeping with him."

She was aware of Nick's sideways look in her direction, but she ignored it and stared straight ahead into the star-struck hollowness of the prairie night. It wasn't a lie she'd just told, she thought. It was true. From now on she wasn't sleeping with him.

"But you'd like to," Nick said. "Or at least he'd like to," he added quickly when he saw, or sensed the sudden turn of her head in the darkness. "Look, I don't blame him. Who could blame a guy married to a cold fish like Eleanor, especially when a red-hot and feisty little number like you comes along."

"Can the flattery, Nick."

"No, I mean it. You're quite a gal. I mean, even old Jon thinks so. And he ought to know. When he's not making money he's laying some good-looking woman, so he's had the experience to be a good judge of—What I mean is, a guy would have to be out of his mind not to want to—well—hell, I'm trying to give you a compliment."

"In that case, thank you," she said, feeling sick and near tears. She fought the urge to tell him to shut up because she didn't want to hear any more about all the women Jon had laid. "Now will you take me home?"

"Home? I thought we'd look for a little action. Want to go to Blackie's?"

"I'm tired, Nick, and we'll have to be out at the rig early in the morning."

"Hey, are you kidding me? I thought you were a slick city gal. You know, all New Yorky."

"A slick city gal? No, you thought of me more like a slab of meat. Some choice cut to be picked out of the butcher's case by the likes of you or Jon."

He gave her a surprised look. "What are you talking about? I never meant . . ." She glanced at him and saw, by the dim light of one of the few street lights, that he wore an expression of distress. "Look," he added. "I just thought we could get something decent to eat. Besides being a cold fish, Eleanor's a lousy cook. Let me make it up to you for whatever insults I've heaped on you tonight. I'll buy you a chicken fried steak at Blackie's."

The thought of Blackie's chicken fried steak was by no means enticing to Alexis, but the idea of a lonely hotel room suddenly seemed even less so. "Okay. How can I pass up an offer like that?"

He was a perfect gentleman all through the second dreadful meal she'd had that night, then she took him back to pick up the truck he'd left at the Calahans', and then he followed her to the hotel. She was surprised when he got out of the truck and walked with her to the front door.

"I got me a room in the hotel for the night just down the hall," he said. "Decided I didn't want to drive that truck all the way out to the tent. You can call me if you need me," he added, but he was careful not to press her. He was still being the perfect gentleman.

He showed up early the next morning at her door. She was cooking her breakfast eggs on the little gasoline burner she'd found and persuaded the hotel manager to let her keep in her room. She invited Nick in to share breakfast with her, then she drove to the rig with him in the truck. As they approached, she saw Jon coming out of the tent, hand shading his eyes against the sun that was still morning-fresh, not yet the cruel hammer it would be by noon. The crew was not out yet.

Jon greeted them with a detached cordiality. "Have you noticed that anticline to the north?" he asked, addressing her as they walked toward the tent. Nick was busy looking under the hood of the truck. "A geologist I hired showed it to me yesterday. Said the geography and surface formations look favorable."

"I've noticed the anticline," she said. "Why didn't

you tell me you were going to hire a geologist again?"

"There wasn't time. I heard about him in town yesterday late and contacted him. I wanted him to have a look at the samples, because they didn't look good to me."

He was pulling away cautiously, she sensed, because they both knew it had gone too far and was not going to work. A rush of thoughts crowded her mind—things she could or could not say. Should she tell him that she loved him? Or just that it had to end? Before she could decide, he spoke again.

"Why the hell did you tell the crew to drill yesterday? Are you trying to bankrupt us?"

"I told the crew to drill because that's what they're paid to do," she said.

"Goddamn it, Alexis, I told them to stop for a good reason. We're just throwing money down that hole."

"Why wasn't I told that when you found out about it?" In spite of her quick retort, she had no sense of being able to recover fully and hold her ground. The angry look in his eyes was giving him an advantage.

"It's like I said, there wasn't time. I had to talk to the geologist. So I told the crew to hold off."

"I'm a partner in this venture. I should be told what's going on."

"You were told what's going on. Through the crew. I told them about the core samples. This is no time for female petulance."

"Female petulance has nothing to do with this. You would have expected the same courtesy had I been the one to consult with a geologist. In fact, I would not have consulted him without your being present, and I have a right to expect the same consideration from you. Where's the crew this morning?" she asked with a sweeping gesture of her hand toward the silent rig.

"I dismissed them."

"You what!"

"I told you, we're throwing money down a dry hole."

"You sent them back to Beaumont?"

"Not yet. We'll wait for the tests on the new core samples. If the geologist thinks we should drill deeper—"

"I should have been told, Jon. I should have been told everything. I should have had the right to know where I stand." She had blurted out that last sentence recklessly, out of anger, out of deep hurt, not knowing if he would understand her impulsive double meaning.

His eyes locked with hers, and she knew that he understood. There was a long silence while she tried to subdue the ache she felt inside, knowing it had to end between them. Finally she spoke softly, in a voice that belied her turmoil and pain. "It's not going to work, is it?" They both knew she wasn't talking about the drilling, and they both knew their argument had been brought about because their feelings were on edge.

Jon tried to speak, but seemed to have difficulty. Finally he said, "I didn't expect Eleanor to—"

"It's all right," Alexis interrupted because the sound of his voice made her heart break with love for him. "There's too much at stake," she said. "Too much for you to lose. And you were wrong about her. She does care."

"Alexis . . ."

She managed a laugh, a show of bravado that sickened her with its dishonesty. She wanted to cry, not laugh, or more than that, she wanted to tell him how much she loved him, how much she wanted and needed him, how much she was hurting inside. "We both said no strings, didn't we? So now there's nothing to untangle," she said instead. "Nobody's hurt."

"Sure," he said. "Nobody's hurt."

12

"You look sizzling!" Nick said when she opened the door to her room to him. He had promised to take her to Midland for supper. She had dressed to the nines in a soft gabardine dress with a long waist and a flounced skirt in a mustard color that showed off the soft gold of her hair. She wore ropes of pearls around her neck and a perky evening hat set at a jaunty angle atop her head.

"You, too," she said, giving him her best smile. He looked like a dandy in his dark striped suit with its tight-fitting waistcoat and the impeccable white spats that covered the gleaming black patent leather of his shoes. He carried a carefully creased light tan felt hat in his hand.

"Do I look like a politician, maybe? Like I could run for Congress or something?"

"Why would you even want to?" she asked, amused as she turned back to pick up the handbag that matched her chocolate brown high-heeled shoes.

"Well, you know. Jon Calahan's the big shot around here. Who could blame me for wanting to dress like him? Especially when he gets all the attention from the ladies."

"Does he?"

"Don't he?" Nick had stepped into the room and closed the door behind him. He was looking at her with a crooked, knowing grin on his handsome face.

"I hardly see him. He's quite busy with the campaign recently."

"And leaving the business for you to run."

"That seems to be working out rather well. Shall we go?"

She moved toward the door and started to open it, but Nick closed it with his hand just over her shoulder. She turned around suddenly, surprised, and his other hand, still holding his hat, went up over her other shoulder, trapping her.

"You're going broke, Alexis," he said. His face was very close to hers and the cocky grin still on his lips. "You shoulda listened to Jon and give up on that hole when he first said to, 'stead of waitin' so long."

"I can tell this is going to be a pleasant evening," she said, meeting his eyes with a cool gaze.

"God, you're a smart-ass," he said. He buzzed her on the cheek and dropped his hands, allowing her to turn around quickly and open the door. "Did old Jon know what he was getting into when he took you on as his partner?" he asked, following her out.

"Are we going to spend the entire evening talking about Jon Calahan and the fact that I'm going broke?" she asked without looking back. Her high heels clicked a sharp staccato on the linoleum-covered floor of the hallway. She heard his amused chuckle as he walked behind her, and she felt his eyes on her body, which was covered by the soft, clinging fabric of her dress.

They had to leave Coyote Flats early in order to drive the distance to Midland and back and still leave enough time for a few hours sleep. Alexis had been there once in the truck to pick up a drill bit, and she knew the town to be only little bigger than Coyote Flats. It had a few more cafés, if no fancy restaurants to choose from.

Alexis expected no more than the fried, greasy fare she'd grown used to in Coyote Flats, but at least it would be a diversion, another way to try to keep her mind off of Jon, and Nick wasn't such bad company, really. She'd gotten accustomed to his brashness and grown rather fond of him. He was sweet and caring in his impertinent way. She had come to think of him as a close friend, or perhaps as a big brother, in much the same way she thought of David as a younger brother. If Nick had a completely different attitude toward her, she couldn't let it concern her. She had made it clear that companionship was all she wanted or needed from him.

"Want to drive?" Nick asked when they reached the car, which she kept parked in the lot at the side of the hotel.

"Why not? Since it's my car," Alexis said with a laugh. She noticed that Nick had already placed a package in the back seat. Something he'd gotten from a bootlegger, no doubt. She slid under the wheel, barely giving Nick time to get in before she spun out of the lot, leaving a spray of pale sand and fine pebbles in her wake.

They drove down the unpaved streets, plunged down a steep hill on the outskirts of town, and leveled off momentarily before they began the gentle climb of another one, the Stutz bobbing along in the gossamer dust like a tiny canoe amidst the swells and spray of a great sea.

Nick moved closer to Alexis and slipped an arm around her shoulders. "To tell you the truth, I can't blame old Jon for taking you on as a partner. I'd like to merge with you myself."

"You're unbelievable, Nick."

"You're unbelievably beautiful. Hey! Do you have to take them curves so fast?"

"If we're going to get there before dark."

"What's the rush to get there before dark? We've got a battery on this thing. We can turn the lights on. And don't give me any of that crap about needing to be back to get out to the rig tomorrow. Jon will be there. No campaign speeches anywhere. Eleanor gave him time off for good behavior."

"Still, if I'm losing money as you seem to think I am, I need to be there to protect my interest."

"What do you mean as I seem to think?" Nick asked. "You know damn well you're losing money, but hey, baby, no reason to get touchy about it. I never seen no wildcatter yet that didn't go bust at least twice before he made it."

"I don't intend to go bust."

"Nobody ever does. But I know it's costing you like hell to keep drilling, 'specially after you had to pay to move the rig to that new site."

"We had to move, Nick. You just reminded me of that. It was your opinion that we should have moved sooner. I admit you're right. I ought to trust your opinion. And Jon's. All right?" She made no attempt to hide her irritation.

"And it's my opinion you're going broke."

"Damn it, do you have to keep rubbing it in?"

"I'd like to."

"Jesus, Nick!"

He laughed and moved his arm, settling back with his head against the back of the seat. "All right, I'll try not to rub it in. I'm just trying to wake you up. I hate to see you have to quit. I know there's oil there."

"I'm not going to quit."

"You're going to have to because you're running out of money, and old Jon is too busy with his politicking to go after anymore."

"Then I'll just have to go after it myself."

"Why don't you ask your daddy? Langdon Runnels has got to be one of the richest men in the state. Hell, maybe in the whole country."

"I can't do that."

"Why not?"

"I just can't, that's all."

He sat up and looked at her. "Oh, I see. The family's black sheep, huh?" When she didn't answer, he went on. "Why don't you ask some of your rich friends, then?"

"What do you think I am? A common beggar with no pride?"

"I'm not talking about begging. I'm talking about finding investors. That's the way it's done, baby. That's the way old Calahan would do it if he wasn't up to his ass in politics."

"Investors?"

"Sure. I'll bet even your old man does it that way. Even with as much money as he has. You just go out to all your rich friends and you touch 'em for a little cash. You show 'em the good news. You know, all those newspaper stories about oil strikes. You impress 'em with some o' them geological reports, then you put the make on 'em."

Alexis was silent for a moment, thinking about what Nick had just said. "How many do you think I'd need?" she asked finally.

Nick shrugged. "Not many, if you get the right ones."

"And you really think it's there, Nick? You don't think this is another dry hole?"

Nick grinned. "I don't think this is no dry hole, baby. There's oil down there. It's just gonna take the right man with the right tool."

Alexis let the innuendo go by with no reaction. She was thinking that what he had said about investors made sense. She was still thinking of potential investors when they arrived in Midland and when they found the café next to the hotel and ordered their meals.

Where might she find those investors? Not Houston, certainly. She didn't know enough of the town and its people, and those she did know would give her the same response she'd encountered when she'd tried to get financing for the venture to begin with. Word would get back to Papa. It would be like having to get permission from him, and she wanted none of that. She was going to do this on her own. But where else could she go? Her friends in New York? It was every bit as inbred as Houston, of course, but at least there were no real family ties to hold her back. In fact, when she had lived there, she'd had free rein to be as bold and eccentric as she dared.

That could be part of the problem, though. She'd garnered the reputation of being impetuous and reckless and maybe even slightly naughty—the fun-loving and rich bad girl from Texas.

Jon could project the right image, with his maturity and that solid, experienced manner that provoked trust. Yet he was a stranger, and in an inbred setting that was always suspect. The ideal plan, of course, would be for the two of them to work together on the likes of the VanLureses and the Woolforths and the Winninghams. But that was out of the question, of course. Jon was too busy with his campaign.

"Penny for your thoughts." Nick's voice startled her for a moment, and she found herself looking at him and feeling slightly disoriented, as if she hadn't expected him to be there, sitting across from her with a plate of fried catfish in front of him. He gave her his boyish grin again. "Hell, baby, for your thoughts, I'd give a hundred bucks."

She laughed, slipping back into her crisp, indifferent demeanor. "You'd feel cheated. I was thinking about finding some investors."

"No, you weren't. You were thinking about Jon."

Alexis felt her carefully constructed mask slip. She couldn't even manage a smile, much less a careless laugh. She could only look at him, caught in his beautiful chocolate brown gaze, as guileless as David's.

"You're in love with him."

She forced her eyes away, picked up her fork and pretended to be interested in the food. "Don't be ridiculous."

"Don't try to lie to me, baby. This is old Nicky you're talking to. Hell, I ought to know it when I see it. I been there myself—hung up on some broad that's married. And it's not like you or me was the first, either. Happens all the time."

The thought sickened her—the idea that the moments she and Jon had had together, the times they'd made love, were no more than a cheap adulterous pattern that had been and would be repeated over and over again by other couples who thought they were just as desperately in need of each other.

She put down her fork and caught Nick's gaze again. "I'm certainly not hung up on Jon Calahan," she said evenly. "I'd be a fool not to admit I find him attractive, of course. Obviously, many women do. Didn't you just tell me earlier he spent a lot of time laying women?"

"Hey, look, I didn't mean for that to upset you. Maybe I shouldn't have even said it. I just—"

"Why should it upset me?" she asked, with a little laugh and a nonchalant wave of her hand. "After all, I'm not his wife, or even his mistress." She'd managed to regain some of the sound of cynical detachment. "And, really, do we have to talk about him? I came here to have a good time."

She saw the look on Nick's face, and for a moment it troubled her. It was as if he could see through to her soul and tell that she was lying, but in the next instant his charming grin returned.

"Then you came with the right fella, baby."

"I was counting on that."

"I want to take you to a picture show," he said. "It's Mary Pickford. I think it's called *Daddy Long Legs*."

"Oh, Lord, that sounds wonderful," she said, beaming. She didn't dare tell him she'd seen it a year ago in New York.

"And besides that, I got a little surprise." He gave a quick, surreptitious glance around the room, then winked at her.

"A surprise?"

"I know Jon said you like gin. . . ."

"Jon told you that?" she asked, wondering why the conversation couldn't stay away from him and wondering why the aching longing wouldn't stop.

"Sure. At his house that night, remember? He said he bought the gin just for you. 'Cause you like it."

"So he did."

"It's harder'n hell to get ahold of. I couldn't find any, but I got Brinninstool."

"What?"

"Brinninstool whiskey. It's made in Mexico."

"How sweet of you, Nick," she said, feeling suddenly as if she wanted to cry. Nick was being so thoughtful, but it wasn't enough, somehow, to fill the emptiness where Jon belonged in her heart.

A deep rumbling drew her out of her melancholia, and she was aware of a sudden hush in the room. It was as if each patron in the restaurant had been summoned by the sound, like the call of a mighty god. Every eye turned toward the window to glance at the clouds that had begun to gather into folds of royal purple in the twilight.

The storm had come up suddenly, as was usual in the arid west. It hadn't taken all day to fume and fuss with imposing heaviness as it might have in Houston or along the eastern seaboard. Instead it had made its entrance dramatically, leaping with the flair of a flamboyant actor whose aim was to startle or sometimes just to tease before it disappeared behind the black curtain of the night horizon.

A few splatters hit the plate glass window and inched downward, plowing furrows through a film of dust. There was a rumble of pleasure in the room, a kind of symphonic answer to the thunder. Rain was rare enough in that area to be a novelty.

Nick, who was from the soggy east side of the state, seemed indifferent until the drama got his attention with a slashing fiery crack that caused even the dishes on the table to rattle.

"God a' mighty!" he said, his eyes as wide and electrified as the sky.

Alexis laughed. "It's going to be a perfect night," she said. "It's even going to rain."

It had barely begun to sprinkle when they left the restaurant and made their way to the car, although the lightning still danced its dangerous and elaborate prelude. Nick took her arm and tried to hurry her through the gathering storm, but Alexis found she didn't want to rush out of it. She had been in the arid west long enough now to want to savor each drop, to let the moisture replenish her. Before they reached the car, though, the measure of the storm had quickened, and she had to make a dash for the Stutz to keep from ruining her hat and dress.

Nick took the time to pull a fruit jar from the package he'd thrown into the back seat before he ducked inside. He took the top off and poured a little in the lid, then set it afire with a match he struck with the nail of his thumb.

"What in the world are you doing?"

"Testin' it. If the flame burns blue it's ok. If it's yellow, then it's got some kinda poison oil in it. Could kill you. Make you go blind. You gotta test this Mexican stuff." He blew out the blue flame and took a long drink from the jar before handing it to Alexis.

She hesitated a moment at the idea of such lack of grace, then with a shrug took the jar and brought it to her lips. The liquid burned, but it tasted remarkably good. After a few minutes, though, instead of the warm, mellow feeling she'd hoped for, she felt only a renewed sense of empty longing. She waved away his offer of a second drink. "Let's go see little Mary," she said with a ring of false gaiety.

"Sure thing, baby," Nick answered. He drove to the front of the theater to drop her off, and when he joined her inside, she saw the bulge in his jacket where he was concealing the jar. He took surreptitious nips from it all through the show, but she refused each time he offered it to her, deciding to forgo the burning taste for the equally numbing effects of seeing *Daddy Long Legs* for the second time.

When the celluloid drama ended, they walked out of the theater into a night as thin and delicate as lace. It had been rendered that way by the rain, and Alexis was immediately saddened that they had missed it. They had now only its aftereffects. Drops of water fell intermittently from the bottom of the marquee and the tops of street lights and the roofs of buildings. Wide murky puddles dotted the street in front of the theater. The unpaved side streets, Alexis could see, had been thickened with the mix of rain and dirt and crisscrossed with webs of deep ruts that held vehicles like trapped insects.

Nick was weaving from the effects of the liquor and had to steady himself against the side of the box office.

"I'll get the car," Alexis said. "You wait here."

Nick's answer was a drunken salute.

At least he was happy, she thought. He sang boisterously as they drove through the rain-soaked town. His mood was contagious and Alexis found herself singing with him. They laughed and sang and then laughed some more when Nick spilled some of the whiskey on her dress as he was waving the jar around like a conductor's baton. It was ridiculous, she knew, but anything was better than wallowing in self-pity.

Her singing stopped when she reached the edge of town and drove into the morass that was supposed to be the road to Coyote Flats. She felt the car slip and careen, and she slowed to correct it. Then when she tried to move forward again, she found she could not. The engine would only grind and strain.

"We're stuck!"

"We damned sure are," Nick said, sobering slightly.

"What are we going to do?"

"I could walk back to town. Get us some help."

"Lord, in this mud? You'd sink up to your knees."

"Then there's not much we can do except wait 'til morning and hope somebody comes by to get us out."

She breathed a heavy sigh and let her head fall against the back of the seat.

Nick opened the door and took a cautious look out into the night. "Mud or no mud, there's a little matter I've got to take care of," he said. He got out of the car carefully, bracing himself against the sides and walking with slow, slogging steps through the mud. Alexis knew he was relieving himself, and she was grateful she had at least taken the precaution of that before they left the theater. While he was out of the car, she took the opportunity to crawl over the seats to the backseat. If she was going to have to spend the night, she would at least make herself as comfortable as possible.

A BAD GIRL'S MONEY

In a little while Nick opened the door and stuck his head in. He saw her lying cramped in the back seat and grinned, then opened the back door and stepped in. Alexis sat up, surprised.

"I thought you could take the front," she said.

"Just wanted a good-night kiss," he said, giving her a gentle buss on the forehead.

She looked at him. "You're sweet, Nick. And thanks for wanting to do this for me."

"Do what?" he asked with a laugh. "Get you stuck in the mud in the middle of nowhere?"

"Of course not. You know what I mean. I enjoyed myself."

He had moved very close so that she could smell his boozy breath. "I'm enjoying myself now," he said, and he kissed her, full on the lips. She didn't stop him. Wasn't this a way to forget? To fill the emptiness? She responded at first, but it was no good. She turned her face away, but Nick's arms were still around her. He pushed her downward until she was on her back, and he was on top of her, kissing her still.

She pushed against his chest. "Nick . . ." He didn't move away, but tried to kiss her again. She was about to resist harder when he sat up.

"Christ!" he said, throwing his head against the back of the seat for a moment, and then she sensed him looking at her. "Can you beat this? I finally get you alone in the back seat, and I'm too damned drunk to get it up."

"Oh, Nick . . ." She knew he was lying. She had felt his erection through the thin fabric of their clothes. He was making an awkward attempt to ease out of the situation.

"But it wouldn't matter, anyway," he said, sounding remarkably gentle. "It's like he was back here with us. No, don't try to say that ain't so, Ali. It's okay. I told you, I know how it is. I been there myself. He's never very far away in your mind."

"Oh, Lord," she whispered and tried not to cry. He pulled her toward him and held her gently, letting her tears dampen his shoulder until they both fell asleep.

Early the next morning a farmer came along with a wagon and four mules. He unhitched two of the mules from the wagon and hitched them to the car to pull it out of the mud. Much later they made their way through a treacherous muddy stretch until the road began to look drier. By the time they reached Coyote Flats there was very little sign of rain. The storm and flooding had been localized, a typical phenomenon of the great stretches of the Permian Basin. It was as if nature was judicious in meting out her moisture to such a voraciously thirsty land.

Jon was standing in front of the hotel when he saw Nick drive up in the Stutz. He and Alexis both got out of the car.

"Hello, Jon, sorry we're late," Nick said. "Hit some bad roads between here and Midland." He'd left the door open behind him and the jar that had held the whiskey rolled out, spilling the last remains of its odoriferous liquid and coming to rest at Jon's feet.

Jon raised his eyes from the jar to the two standing in front of him. They were both disheveled and wrinkled. It was apparent that they'd had one hell of a night. Alexis met his glance, but her eyes revealed nothing.

"I stopped by to tell you we're meeting with the banker this morning," he said to her. "He's waiting for us. If you're interested, meet us there." He clamped his hat on his head and started to walk away.

She moved toward him, headed for the hotel entrance at the same time, her eyes on the door, refusing to look at him. But he had seen something flare in her eyes—something he hadn't expected. Anger, maybe. He had expected embarrassment. When they met, their shoulders touched briefly, inadvertently, and he could tell that she reeked of liquor. Still she didn't look at him, and she ignored the touch as if it had been no more than a brush with a stranger in a crowd.

In less than twenty minutes she was ushered into bank president Gordon Witherspoon's office by his secretary. Alexis had changed into a dark blue dress with a conservative white collar that made her look for all the world like a schoolgirl. The smell of liquor was gone, but the telltale circles under her eyes were still there.

"Please don't get up," she said in her crisp eastern voice when Gordon and Jon, along with Cyrus Mahon, who was sitting in the chair next to him, made a move as if to stand when she entered. She walked briskly to the other empty chair and sat down. When she passed by he noted that there was the faint smell of talcum he knew she used after her bath. He had, in fact, dusted it on her body himself once or twice.

He found himself wondering if Nick Bodine had done the same. Nick said they'd been to Midland. He didn't like the idea of her going that far off with him and spending the night. But the truth was, whatever they'd done, they could have been doing it every night in Alexis's room. Or Nick's room even, since he'd taken to staying at the hotel. The thought of that made him angry, and he let the anger wash over him along with the sound of the voices—hers clear and with a slightly high youthful pitch, Gordon's slower and measured as he introduced Cyrus as a potential investor.

Jon glanced at Alexis and saw that she was sitting with her hands in her lap, but there was no tremor to them that might have suggested any discomfort. She turned her cold gaze toward him, and it was a moment before he realized they were waiting for him to speak.

"I . . . I beg your pardon," he said, acutely embarrassed.

"The lady just asked what the chances are of you gettin' the legislature to extend the time before you have to start drilling," Gordon said in his easy drawl.

"I would hope the chances are good. This is university land we'll be drilling on. The state will share in the revenue."

"And I suggest you get the drilling permits combined into sixteen-section units," Alexis said, her tone still showing no emotion.

"Sixteen-section units?"

"It would make it easier to interest investors to have one drilling permit for the entire unit. Mr. Mahon here just agreed."

She was right, of course, and he silently chastised himself for not thinking of that himself. "Of course," he said. "I'll work on it."

"You got a smart partner here," Mahon said. There was a nasal twang to his voice that made him sound as if he was whining. "I'll sure think about this investment. Just give me a little time." His chair made a scraping noise on the floor as he stood up. He extended his hand to Jon, and Jon shook it, managing a smile. He was thinking, though, that time was running out. The legislature might not extend that drilling time, and Gordon, along with the bank in Houston, was going to be demanding payment on the notes they were holding.

When Cyrus had made his slight bow to Alexis and left the room, Gordon confirmed his fears. "I reckon you better do what you can to snare him and as many like him as you can," he said. "You got a note that's overdue now. I can't keep carryin' you, Jon. Beg pardon, Miss Runnels, but that goes for both of you."

Jon stood up quickly to keep from letting his humiliation show. Alexis, he noticed, had stood, too.

"You'll get your money, Mr. Witherspoon. Soon. Thank you for your patience." She turned and left the room without giving Gordon Witherspoon a chance to reply.

Jon picked up his hat and followed her out. When they were outside she turned to face him so abruptly he almost ran over her. "When did you set up this meeting with the investor?"

"Alexis, I didn't know about it until late yesterday when Gordon told me."

"You could have told me then."

"I tried to. I called you, but that damn hotel telephone was out of order, so I came to your hotel and you were gone." He saw her expression change from angry defiance to something else. Was it shame? "So I came back early this morning, hoping to have time to talk to you before the meeting," he said, driving home his advantage.

Their eyes locked for a moment. "I'm sorry I missed you," she said finally, still very cool, but he had seen her look soften. "I . . . we went to Midland to the picture show, and we got stuck in the mud. I didn't think it ever rained enough here to make mud."

"I saw the cloud," he said, not knowing whether to feel relieved or not. Stuck in the mud? All night alone together in that car? Doing what? Not sleeping, from the looks of her eyes.

She seemed about to say more, but she hesitated.

"You're too tired to discuss this, since you were up all night," he said. "And if you have a hangover, then we can wait until—"

"I don't have a hangover," she snapped. "Nick did all the drinking, and what he didn't drink he spilled on my dress, so there's no need to assume I can't function."

He was silent a moment, wondering what she was trying to tell him. That nothing had happened? It shouldn't matter, of course. Hadn't they agreed it wasn't going to work between them? Wasn't she free to do as she pleased?

"Would you like some coffee?" he asked, finally, wanting desperately to ask more.

"Yes," she said, "but none of that black tar that passes for coffee at Blackie's. I'll put a pot on the hot plate in my room." She had caught him by surprise, and his heart leapt at the thought of being alone with her again in her room. She had already started to walk away, but she turned back to him and said in a tone that was mildly sarcastic, "That is, if you're sure you want to risk it."

"I'll risk it."

"Good, because I have something I want to discuss with you. It's strictly business, of course."

When they reached her room he saw the clothes she had thrown carelessly around the room when she changed to meet him at the bank. She scooped them up in a flurry and tossed them in the closet, then grabbed the coffeepot and filled it with water.

"How are David and Eleanor?" she asked.

"They're well."

"I haven't seen Dave in a while. I miss him."

"He's busy with school."

"I know, but I still miss him."

"I'm sure he misses you as well."

"He reminds me of my brother."

"Mmm."

"We're in a hell of a mess, Jon."

"Yes."

"We've got to do better than Cyrus Mahon."

He had managed to follow the abrupt change of subject without losing his balance, but now he had to keep his balance by not showing how scared he was they were going to lose everything. "Cyrus is a start, and once we get him interested, then others will come along."

"The first thing we're going to have to do is buy up some leases that have some producing wells on them so we can show investors that our properties are worthwhile. Maybe some of those around Wichita Falls. I'll sell my rig and we'll buy them, then buy another rig when we get the investors' money."

"Good Lord, that's crazy. Everybody out here is going to know there's a difference in Coyote Flats and Wichita Falls."

"In New York it's all the same. Just somewhere out West."

"What?"

She set the pot down, forgetting to light the flame. "We need big money, Jon, and quick. New York is a better place for big, quick money. I know people. I know we could interest them. But I can't do it by myself. I need you to go with me."

For a moment he couldn't speak. She wanted the two of them to travel together to New York? Finally he said simply and with deceptive calm, "Of course."

13

"You'll be making the trip together, then?" Eleanor sat in front of the small Queen Anne desk she'd brought with her from Beaumont. She'd been editing the speech he was scheduled to make the following month at a barbecue in Midland, but she had put the pen aside now and turned her chair to face Jon, her hands folded demurely in her lap. Her voice was calm, but he could see the tension in those hands, in the way one grasped the other a little too tightly. Even though her face remained as composed as ever, there was something flickering far back in those wise gray eyes.

"Of course not, Eleanor. Traveling together would not be prudent," he said with an equanimity that matched Eleanor's and that masked completely the exploding anticipation he felt inside.

"No." The single word was part affirmation, part invitation for him to say more.

"No need to worry. I'm as anxious to avoid an

appearance of impropriety as you are. More so, probably."

"Of course. But will that be possible?"

"I don't see why not. I just told you. We're not traveling together."

"But you'll be there together."

"Of course we will. To find investors. She knows the people, and I know how to sell the idea to them. But that doesn't mean we'll be doing anything improper."

"Others may assume—"

"Eleanor, I am taking precautions so that others won't assume anything. Miss Runnels is leaving a full week before I do, and we won't be returning at the same time. No one here need know we've gone to the same place. Even the drilling crew thinks we're going different places to look for investors."

Eleanor stood and walked nervously toward the window to stare out at the stark expanse of earth and sky outside. "This wasn't a good idea, taking on a woman as a business partner. It can harm your political career if talk gets started."

"If any harm was going to be done, then it's already done. But I don't think there's been any. In fact, it may win me a few votes. Don't forget, you women get to vote this year."

"Is that what you were thinking when you enlisted her as a partner?"

He did not fail to catch the slight edge of sarcasm in her voice. Once again he was surprised at her reaction. He had thought he'd seen the last of this uncharacteristic behavior, particularly since his own behavior with Alexis recently had been nothing but exemplary.

"What are you getting at?" he asked.

"You have been unwise, Jon. You've never done this before. You've always been—detached."

"Never done what before, Eleanor? I swear I don't understand your concern."

She turned to face him. "You've never—brought one of them home before."

He felt as if he'd been punched hard in the stomach, and he found it impossible to respond.

"I know what you're thinking. That you didn't actually bring her home. That I was the one who invited her to our house. But don't you see? She was already in our home because you encouraged it by making her your partner and getting her out here. She has David wrapped around her little finger. He's as charmed as you are. She's very clever. She knows the way to a man's heart is through his children."

"Eleanor! I won't have you insinuating—"

"She's toying with you, Jon. I had to invite her to our home so I could learn the truth for myself. And then when I saw it, I didn't want to humiliate you by telling you this, but the truth is, you were flattered by her attention because she's young enough to be your daughter."

"Do you think I'm such an old fool, for Christ's sake?"

"I have never thought of you as a fool, Jon. I admire you more than any man I've ever known."

He saw in her eyes that she meant it, and at that moment he felt great devotion to her. "Eleanor, we've been over this before," he said, calmer now. "And I assured you that you have nothing to worry about. I have not been seeing Miss Runnels except on a business basis. And anyway, I expect you know, she's far more interested in Nick Bodine at the moment."

She looked away briefly, then turned back to him and said, "You've got to be careful, Jon." Deep worry lines creased her face. "If you make a mistake now, there won't be time to recover. The election is only a few months away."

He gave her a smile. "Don't worry. I'm not going to make any mistakes."

"Jon . . ."

"Yes."

She raised her face to meet his and kissed him full on the lips. Her hand lingered for a moment on his arm, then she turned away and left the room, leaving him to stare after her, even more surprised and not a little confused.

His stupor was shattered when David burst into the room. "Hey, Papa, is it true? Ali's going to New York, and you're going with her?"

"Who told you that?"

"She did."

"Alexis told you we're going to New York?" He was surprised she'd mentioned it. He'd thought she would be as eager as he was not to divulge that they would be together.

"Yeah. Only she's going first, she said. To line up a few millionaires so you can put the touch on them for some dough." He threw his books on the sofa and sprawled on it, his legs extended in front of him while he munched on an apple.

"And I'm sure she told you in just such colorful language." Jon noted that his legs extended almost to the center of the small room. He must have grown a foot since they'd left Beaumont.

"Well, that's not her exact words exactly, but . . ."

"English will do fine from now on, if you don't mind. No more of that—" He stopped, realizing what he was doing. Just as Alexis had said, he was alienating himself by constantly showing his disapproval. He laughed a little uneasily. "No more of that unless you teach me to speak it, too. I suppose Ali understands it like a native."

"Ali's okay. Bee's knees."

"I'm sure she is. What else did she tell you?"

"About going to New York, you mean? Nothing. But it would be great to go there with her."

"Great?"

"Yeah, sure. Terrific. I'll bet she knows every nook and cranny. All the gin joints and speakeasies and everything."

"I'm sure she does."

"Well, and I mean all the other stuff too. You know, the buildings—the Plaza Hotel, Saint Patrick's Cathedral. She says it's Gothic. And the piers. Ships from everywhere, she says. And every language on the face of the earth. All those immigrants. Think how interesting it would be to talk to those people that came from someplace across the ocean. Bet you could learn a lot."

Jon looked at his son in surprise. He hadn't known he knew so much about New York. That he knew what "Gothic" meant, that he had a longing to learn about people who came from somewhere else. Had Alexis created this hunger in him? Or had it been there all along, and she had simply exposed it? "Maybe someday I can take you with me," Jon said a little uneasily.

"It would be great to go with Alexis. She would

know so much about it. And to go to Europe with her, too. She's been there, you know."

"So I've heard."

"She's terrific. She's done everything. All the things I want to do someday. Travel. Live in New York. Fly an aeroplane. You're lucky, Pa."

"Lucky?"

"Yeah. Gettin' to be there with her."

Their eyes held for the briefest moment, and Jon felt his heartbeat accelerate and his blood warm on his face first and then all over his body. "I meant what I said," his voice quivering slightly. "I'd like to take you sometime."

"Yeah, sure, Pa." He stood up, leaving the apple core on a table and wiping his hands on the seat of his pants as he left the room.

Jon stared after him, feeling an emptiness, an uneasiness that he had somehow said the wrong thing, or failed to say the right thing. And then it occurred to him that for once there had been no argument.

He noticed the buildings first, rising like gods into a misty morning sky as the train approached the station. His first feeling was one of alienation. These were gods he did not know. Even their slender, towering shapes were foreign to him. He was a man who knew the earth and lived close to it, whose life and interests and pleasure were to invade its depths, not to send concrete and steel soaring above its surface.

An electric excitement ran through the passengers as the train slowed, reaching a peak when it stopped and people crowded the aisles and the doorway. Jon remained seated a moment, watching them, and felt a strange reluctance to join them in their trancelike movement toward the doorway and into the teeming sea of bodies outside. His instinct was to stay on the train and to will it back to Texas, where there was earth and sky, and most of all, where there were fewer people.

But then he turned toward the window again, and he saw her. She spotted him at almost the same instant. A smile illuminated her face as she waved excitedly. He waved back, and she mouthed something to him he couldn't interpret. But she was there, waiting for him, and he forgot completely about his earlier instinct to turn around and go back. He stood up and moved toward the door.

When he stepped from the train, she was lost again in the crush of people. He stood alone in the crowd, searching for her, wishing he were taller so he could see above the heads. He felt a moment of irrational distress that she might have been swallowed up by the crowd, which seemed to have a squirming, wriggling life of its own. Then he saw her again, pushing her way through the mob, and he heard her calling his name. He reached for her, touched her hand, then lost contact when she was pushed aside, but the throng had fueled his own aggression, and he used his shoulders, his arms, his willpower to force his way toward her until suddenly she was in front of him.

"Oh, Jon, I'm so glad you're here." She looked up at him, and they were very close. Her mouth was so inviting, her breath so warm and sweet on his face. His arm went around her, and he knew he was about to kiss her, but she turned away quickly, holding his hand and pulling him with her through the crowd.

"We'll get your luggage and take a taxi to the hotel. I have a room for you in the Plaza."

"The Plaza? My God, Alexis, even a rube like me knows that's the most expensive place in town. Couldn't you have gotten something cheaper?"

"Of course it's expensive. That's part of the plan. We need to put on a show of prosperity if we're going to interest the right people. We need a place to invite them for meetings, and believe me, they're used to the best. I'm staying with friends, of course, but I'll be just a short distance away on Fifth Avenue."

"They're not giving rooms away, I'm sure. Somebody's going to have to pay for it."

She turned to face him. "Why, Jon, that's not like you. I thought you were the high roller. The hell-bent Texan."

"A high roller has to have something to roll. We're almost broke, you know."

She didn't flinch. "Our investors will pay the bill, of course," she said, with absolute calm.

He gazed into her eyes for a moment, knowing that icy blue clarity masked a little fear, but she wore the mask well. "By God," he said, grinning, "if you're not Langdon Runnels's blood daughter you should have been."

He saw the mask slip for a moment, but she averted her eyes and pointed toward the baggage car. "Over there," she said, pointing to the collection of trunks and suitcases. "You get your luggage, and I'll hail a taxi."

He was amazed at her resourcefulness and her unabashed aggressiveness. Within minutes they were in the taxi, and she was giving the driver instructions.

"I want you to see a little of the city," she said, her

eyes bright with excitement, "so we're not going straight to the hotel just yet." They maneuvered their way through streets completely unfamiliar to him while Alexis pointed out buildings and recited little bits of information. "Fifty-seventh street is the center of trade now, of course, but Wall Street is where we'll find the money. I want you to see that. And Fifth Avenue, of course."

The trip was a winding, confusing, circuitous route to Jon, and before long he'd lost all sense of direction. They passed under railways, down narrow side streets, and through wide straight boulevards, all of which were choked with traffic, both horse-drawn and motor-driven. Tall, grand buildings lined all the streets, more than he thought could ever have existed on the face of the earth. Alexis kept up her litany of information, and he found himself turning his head this way and that to take it all in. He sensed her enthusiasm and knew that she was as infatuated with the city as a young girl might have been with a daring, brash lover.

"This is Trinity Church," she said, pointing to an old building surrounded by what looked like a large pasture to him, but he soon saw it was a graveyard. The driver turned onto another street, and suddenly they were in a shadowed canyon of even grander buildings. Alexis named them all to him—banks, investment houses, more banks that looked like white palaces or temples where gods dwelled. "And there's the stock exchange," she said, "and over there, see? That beautiful building? That's the Sub-Treasury. And that one with the columns, that's the House of VanLures, my friend's father's bank, and that one . . ." She went on, pointing out building after building, and he was struck once again at how brash and daring and totally unpredictable the city was. He could see why she loved it.

There was power here, and it was as raw and throbbing and alluring as the oil fields. He felt a rush of excitement because he knew that the power of these gods, like all other gods, lay in the hands and hearts of men. He had only to find the key to using it and the power would be his.

He was still flushed and exhilarated when the taxi left the street and plunged into another sea of noisy traffic. There was more blaring of horns, more tire-screeching turns, more loss of a sense of direction.

They drove past an incredibly tall tower, which Alexis said was the Metropolitan Life building, some massive department stores, a library guarded by stone lions, the ornate cathedral David had mentioned, until finally the taxi came to a halt on a street in between a castle and a grandiose fountain. It took him a moment to realize that it was not a castle but a hotel, and beyond it was Central Park.

Alexis leaned forward and pressed several bills into the driver's hand. The fare had to be enormous, Jon thought, since it seemed they had driven all over the city. Alexis opened her own door and slid out of the taxi. Jon followed her out and looked around him.

"God almighty," he said under his breath.

She laughed and took his arm. "Come on," she said. "Let's look at your room." They were already being welcomed by a bowing doorman, and someone else was unloading the luggage from the taxi. Alexis walked straight to the elevator and gave a number to the impeccably uniformed attendant who conveyed them upstairs on silent cables. Alexis stepped out in front of him and started down the hall.

"It's not the fanciest room in the hotel," she said, "but it's respectable, and it will serve our purpose. I think you'll be comfortable."

"Respectable, hell!" he said, as she opened the door. He glanced at the gilded sitting room full of ornate furniture. It was something Eleanor had said was named for some French king whose number he could never remember. Gold velvet drapes covered one entire wall and gold carpet, thicker than marsh grass, covered the floor. An enormous vase of fresh flowers sat atop a delicately carved chest, and opposite that was an elaborate fireplace. Luggage was being moved into the room, and Alexis was busy handing out more bills. Jon left her to the unquestionably urban chore and walked into the adjoining bedroom.

There was more of the French furniture, including a bed covered with rich gold and white brocade, and through an open doorway he could see the bath, gleaming white and gold. All he could think was that it was going to take a hell of a lot of fast talking so they wouldn't end up in debt for all this luxury.

"Beautiful, isn't it?"

He turned to see that Alexis had finished with the ritual of dispensing money and had come into the bedroom. She had removed her prim hat and jacket and stood before him now in a figure-hugging straight skirt and a silk blouse that matched exactly the startling blue of her eyes.

"Yes," he said, "beautiful." His eyes were on her, and they both knew that he wasn't talking about the decor. He glanced at the bed, and then back at her, but she had dropped her eyes and made a move to turn away. He grasped her arm, stopping her, and she met his gaze again.

"I'm staying with Stella VanLures," she said with quiet firmness.

"We can keep it discreet, of course, and if you're doing it to save money, two of us can stay—"

"It has nothing to do with money," she said, "or with the need to be discreet. At least not for the sake of my reputation." She pulled herself free of his grip and walked out of the bedroom. She was now standing in front of the long chest, gazing out the window behind it. "A bad girl's reputation is actually envied in my circle of friends here," she said over her shoulder with a little false laugh.

"Are you a bad girl, Alexis?" he asked, moving toward her. He stopped when he saw her back stiffen. She was toying with one of the delicate, feathery flowers that sprawled, spiderlike, from the vase. She dropped her hands when one of the petals broke and turned toward him.

"Perhaps I'm not." She drew a shuddering breath, and he thought he saw tears in her eyes, but he didn't move any closer. There was still some invisible barrier between them. "At least I'm not bad enough to want to continue an affair with a married man. Not even here, where no one will know."

He felt a tightness in his chest when she turned away from him again. "I was an immature fool to have started this," she added.

"I don't understand," he said, feeling helpless. "We have to be careful in Coyote Flats, but—"

"No, you don't understand. You just don't get it, do you?"

"Guilt? Is that it? I told you, there was no need for you to feel you were betraying anyone. I told you, Eleanor and I have an understanding, and I can assure you that her primary concern is for my political career. She doesn't feel—"

"To hell with your understandings!" she said whirling suddenly to face him, her eyes blazing. "You understand nothing. Especially not what Eleanor feels. Open your eyes, Jon. Open your eyes and see that she loves you."

"Our relationship is one of mutual respect. You are too young to realize that such a thing is possible, of course, that romantic love is not always the most important emotion between a husband and wife."

He saw her blanch. "Bullshit!" she said, spitting the obscenity at him in a way that only reminded him of how young she was. "She doesn't want to share you. It's as simple as that, and your political career has nothing to do with it. Why do you think she threw Nick at my feet? Or, more precisely, threw me at his? She was trying to save you from me. And not because of your damned political career."

"It didn't seem to me it was Eleanor who was throwing anybody at anybody else's feet. You took to it like a duck to water. Running off to Midland to spend the night together, sodden with bootleg gin and—"

"Oh, God, spare me the self-righteous ranting," she said. "What difference does it make to you, anyway?"

For a moment there was absolute silence except for the thudding of his heart. "The difference," he said finally and with grave softness, "is that I love you. I don't want to share you."

"Jon," she whispered, as if she was beginning some protest. He moved toward her, but she stopped him with a hand on his chest. "Nothing's changed," she said. "There's still Eleanor and David. There's still—"

He took her in his arms and kissed her, but her mouth was tight and hard. He felt her entire body resist, felt resentment in her rigid back and in her thighs when he ran his hand down her body. But he placed his hand in the small of her back and pulled her closer to him and kissed her again. She raised her hand to his face as if to push him away, but it lingered there and he felt her lips soften. She dropped her hand to the back of his collar and, reluctantly at first, gave him more access to her warm, moist mouth. The kiss deepened, and he began to invade her with his tongue, to explore and fill her.

She made a move as if to pull away, but when his hand went to the top button of her blouse and unfastened it, she did not stop him. Neither did she stop him when he unfastened the next, and then the next, nor when he bent to kiss her breasts where they blossomed softly over the top of her lacy chemise. He heard her small gasp when his mouth went back to hers, while at the same time he cupped a breast with one hand and used the other to grasp her buttocks and pull her against his groin. He would have lowered her to the floor and taken her there had she not stiffened and pulled away when there was a soft knock at the door.

They looked at each other for a moment, mildly startled, and then she went into the bedroom, buttoning her blouse. He adjusted his trousers to try to conceal his erection, then squared his shoulders and walked to the door. He opened it to a bellboy who pushed a cart holding dishes covered with silver warmers into the room. He tipped the boy generously, hoping to get him out as quickly as possible, and started for the bedroom. But it was too late. Alexis was just emerging, looking fully buttoned up and composed. She went straight to the sofa where she had left her hat, jacket, and handbag.

"I took the liberty of ordering brunch for you," she said, setting the hat on her head and securing it with a pin. "I wasn't sure you would have eaten on the train, and I thought you'd be too tired to go out."

"You're leaving?"

"Yes. I had a late breakfast with Stella, so I'm not hungry."

"But you'll be back later, of course."

He saw the slight, all-but-imperceptible flicker of her glance toward the bedroom, and then she said quietly but firmly, "No. Not until morning."

Damn him! she thought, tears welling in her eyes as she hurried down the hallway toward the elevator. What right did he have to make her love him? What right to seduce her with his love? She brushed the tears aside and thought about Eleanor while she waited for the elevator. Their conversation had been remarkably frank, yet there had been no anger or sorrow in Eleanor. Only fear. Could that mean that Jon was right? That Eleanor's only concern was that his association with her would ruin his political career?

But what difference did it make if that were true? she thought. He was still a married man, and she could not come to terms with that, in spite of what she had thought earlier. She had to purge him from her mind and concentrate on the business. She would concentrate on making the right contacts and getting the investors they needed, and she would concentrate on having a good time with her old friends while she was in New York. There were plenty of them still around to keep her busy so that she would not have to see Jon at all, except on a purely professional basis. He would have to look elsewhere for a mistress.

"Is he really terribly experienced?" Stella asked as she pulled the sleek satin evening gown up over her small naked breasts. Her voice was low and throaty and somewhat overly cultured.

"Who?" Alexis asked, preoccupied with attaching one of Stella's long diamond earrings to her right lobe. She was sitting in front of the dressing table in Stella's sumptuous bedroom putting on the finishing touches while Stella dressed for the theater.

"You know perfectly well who," Stella said, addressing her reflection in the mirror. "That Texas cowboy you brought here. Your business partner."

"I don't know, really. Why do you ask?"

Stella laughed, a low, syrupy sound, as she pulled a cigarette from a silver case on her bureau and attached it to the long black holder, then lit it with a silver lighter. "Because," she said, blowing out a hazy, fragrant cloud of smoke, "I think you're more than mildly attracted to him."

"Don't be ridiculous," Alexis said with a little laugh. She stood up and looked around for her jeweled evening bag, unable to meet Stella's eyes. She was wearing a pale green satin gown that clung to her body. "He's older, you know, in his forties. And quite married."

"Um-hum." The way Stella lounged against the bureau and held her cigarette in its silver inlaid holder made her look chic and seductive. "What's it like, sleeping with an older man?"

Alexis shot a glance at her and saw the knowing grin on Stella's aristocratic face. "I'm sure I don't know," she said, her voice trembling slightly.

"Of course you do," Stella said. "You were positively glowing when you came back after meeting his train. And besides," she said, blowing a perfect smoke ring into the air, "you had your blouse buttoned wrong." She gave Alexis the merest hint of a sly grin. Alexis met her eyes. She had learned long ago that it was best not to be embarrassed around Stella, since nothing embarrassed her. "I'm terribly jealous, darling. You always have all the fun."

Alexis turned to the mirror and pretended to check her makeup. "You have plenty of fun, and the money to see that the fun never ends."

"Money!" Stella said with surprising disgust. "Money has nothing to do with it, and you know it. It's that naughty streak you have. No, no, don't tell me I'm the naughty one," she said to Alexis's reflection when she saw she was about to protest. "It's not the same thing. I like my comforts too much to be really naughty the way you are. You defy custom, darling. You're the adventuress. Taking off for the wild West to gamble on oil, and before that, France. My God, what a life you've had. I'd give all the money I have for a year like you had in France. But I let that one pass me by because I thought it would be too uncomfortable. Now it's too late. The war's over."

Alexis walked to the window so she wouldn't have to look at Stella.

"What happened there, Ali?"

"A war happened there," she said sharply without looking at her.

"It changed you. Made you even more of an adventuress. No, more than that. It made you ruthless."

"You're being melodramatic. I grew up, that's all. Do you have any gin?" she asked, before Stella could say more. She hated her prying.

"Of course." Stella went to a chest and pulled out a bottle and two glasses. "I must say the new mysterious-lady facade you've developed since the war has made you terribly attractive. All the men were smitten with you at the Thornbergs' party last week. Including Paul."

"Nonsense," Alexis said as she accepted the glass from Stella. "Paul is very securely in your pocket, and you have the ring to prove it."

Stella laughed her throaty laugh again. "He's wonderfully rich, you know. Even more so than Daddy. I can't wait for you to see his yacht. He's having a sailing party next week. He'll invite you, of course."

"It sounds like fun," Alexis said, although she wasn't at all sure it would be. It had taken her only a few days to be reminded of how bored she'd become with the fast crowd she'd associated with before the war. She was glad, however, she'd at least found a way to get Stella's mind off Jon.

Alexis found that although she'd been starved for entertainment and cultural activities in Texas, and although the play was a new one by the emerging playwright Eugene O'Neill, she still could not enjoy the theater. She couldn't stop thinking of Jon and of the way they had parted. It was wrong for them to be lovers, perhaps, but it wasn't right for them to be apart, either. In fact it was miserable, and Stella's fast life and social whirl were no diversion.

She was edgy and in a dark mood when the play ended. She was no better during dinner at Lorbers, which had once been her favorite restaurant. She did, however, do her best to put on a facade of gaiety. Later, as she rode with Stella and Paul in Paul's chauffeur-driven limousine back to the VanLures mansion, she felt exhausted from her charade. She had declined the invitation to accompany them to a chic speakeasy after dinner, and she had been afraid they would not accept her excuse of needing to sleep so she could meet with investors the next day. She soon saw, however, that there would be no protest when, even in the darkness of the Rolls, she could see Stella's practiced fingers unfastening the buttons of Paul's fly.

14

Alexis held her hands clasped in her lap so they wouldn't flutter and give away her nervousness. It was important that William VanLures not guess how desperate she was that the meeting she had arranged between him and Jon be successful. She had approached him when she first arrived in New York, knowing that as one of the country's leading bankers, he'd have contacts that would lead to a number of potential investors. It had proven difficult to convince VanLures that she was a serious oil speculator, however. He still saw her as the spoiled little rich girl who'd been a longtime friend of his own spoiled and rich daughter.

"Oh, yes, the evening was quite pleasant, actually. I enjoyed it very much," she said, in answer to Mr. VanLures's question. She smiled benignly as she rode with him in his limousine to the Plaza.

She was dressed in a new gray suit with a soft white silk blouse, both of which she'd just bought at

Saks. She'd lost weight from skipping meals and working long hours at the rig and had to have something to fit her trimmer figure. Fortunately her past record of purchases at the department store had earned her the privilege of charging the clothes she'd bought. She tried not to think of the enormous bill that would be coming due at the end of the month, however, or of the fact that she was virtually penniless now that Papa had cut off her trust fund allowance and sent her out on her own. Her debts were enormous, since she had not only the rig to pay for now, but the Wichita Falls leases as well.

"But you came home so early," VanLures was saying. He was dressed in a finely tailored pinstripe suit that matched exactly the dark gray-brown of his deep-set eyes and accentuated the solid, stocky proportions of his body. "Wasn't spying on you, of course," he added. "Just happened to be in the library and saw you going upstairs. Expected you to be up all night with Stella and Paul at one of those speakeasies you young people are so fond of."

"Well, of course, a threesome's a bit awkward, you know," she said and gave him a wink, using every advantage she could manage. She wondered if Ivy had ever felt so frightened and desperate when she took her big gamble to form the Sweet Ivy Gold Mining Company. She knew of the reputations of both her parents from their risk taking in the early days. But times were different then, less complicated.

VanLures responded with a delighted chuckle and reached to pat her hand. "Can't imagine you being alone for long, my dear. Beautiful young woman like you. Just give 'em a chance. Don't frighten 'em all away by being all business."

"Frightening is the last thing I want to be."

He gave her a brief look of surprise and laughed, a little uneasily perhaps, as if he wasn't sure whether or not he was being teased. "Ought to take the time to enjoy yourself like other young women," he said, sounding a bit patronizing. "God knows Stella never misses the chance."

"But I do enjoy myself, Mr. VanLures. I enjoy my work. And besides, younger men bore me so."

For several seconds he looked at her, leading her to wonder what he was thinking. She saw that his expression had changed from that of the indulgent if slightly flirtatious older man to something else—something harder.

"You're flirting with me, Alexis," he said finally, a slight smile flickering across his mouth.

She felt her cheeks burn. "Of course I'm not, I—"

"Oh, but you are. But don't look so stricken. I admire ruthless, ambitious people who use everything within their means to get what they want. The kind of people I like to have working with me."

She smiled and relaxed a little.

"But the fact remains, you're a woman."

She stiffened again. "Surely you won't turn down the opportunity for an investment just because of my sex."

"Of course not. If I turn you down it will be because I think you're offering a bad investment. Keep in mind, though, that others may not be so enlightened. It's best that you let the gentleman from Texas do the talking. I pray to God he is a gentleman and not some hayseed in buckskins. And I hope he's every bit as ruthless and ambitious as you are, my dear."

She smiled again and relaxed once more. "I think, Mr. VanLures, that you will find Jon Calahan everything you could hope for."

Jon did not disappoint her. He was dressed impeccably in a dark suit and spats and introduced himself to VanLures before she had the chance, then ushered the two of them into the sitting room of his suite where he had a coffee service with croissants and fresh fruit waiting. He saw the surprised look on her face but merely gave her the slightest smile.

"Coffee?" he asked, pouring it into one of the thin china cups and handing it to her first.

"Two sugars," VanLures said, settling into one of the chairs. Jon poured his coffee as well and used the tongs a bit awkwardly to pick up the sugar cubes. VanLures, Alexis saw, was eyeing him carefully.

Jon didn't seem to notice, or at least pretended not to. He sat down next to Alexis on the sofa facing VanLures and said affably, "Now, let me tell you about one of the sweetest little deals you've ever heard of."

He proceeded to talk about the geological studies that had been done by the University of Texas on the Permian Basin. He showed him the geological reports as well as maps and drilling permits and the company documents that named the two of them owners of C and R West Texas. He told him the company had already begun drilling in order not to forfeit the drilling rights. He scrupulously failed to mention that the effort had produced nothing more than a dry hole.

"Anything promising?" VanLures asked.

"Very promising," Jon said without flinching. "But we're going to need capital to drill further. That's why we're here."

VanLures set his cup down carefully and turned his intense gaze on Jon. "I've looked into your background, Calahan. You've done some oil drilling on the eastern side of Texas, I believe, and you're running for Congress."

"You're very thorough, Mr. VanLures," Jon said, settling back against the sofa. His voice was calm, but Alexis could feel a heightening tension. It emanated from Jon like an invisible electric current.

"Of course. That's how I got where I am," VanLures said. "It pays to have good contacts when one wants something. Particularly information. And good information, I'm sure you know, Mr. Calahan, is vital where investments are concerned."

"Your contacts seem very reliable," Jon said. "So I'm sure you know of my success in the East Texas fields."

VanLures laughed. It was the laugh of a man who knew he was in control. "Of course, but I also know how quickly one can lose everything in that speculative business. It pays to be cautious." He leaned back against the sofa and folded his arms across the front of his chest. "Now tell me," he said. "What has your success been like in West Texas?"

Alexis stood up and retrieved the briefcase she'd left on the chest next to the window. "Here, Mr. Van-Lures," she said, shoving a sheaf of production reports in front of him. "These are reports from our properties in some of the West Texas fields."

VanLures studied the papers from the Wichita Falls leases they'd bought with the last of their capital, and his questions seemed endless. It was almost noon when Jon finally stood and walked to one of the cabinets near the door and produced not only a bottle of gin, but vermouth as well. Alexis raised her eyebrows in surprise when she saw them, but he merely winked at her and turned his attention back to William VanLures.

"Could I interest you in a little refreshment before we continue?"

"Well, I'll be damned," VanLures said, not bothering to hide his surprise. "Hasn't anybody told you about Prohibition? How the hell did you manage that?"

"It pays to have good contacts when one wants something," Jon said, echoing VanLures's earlier words as he mixed the drinks.

VanLures laughed. "Damned resourceful, you Texans," he said accepting the glass. After his second martini he admitted that he'd been looking for a way to invest in oil exploration in the West.

"Potential to make millions," he said. "Need for oil can only increase. Besides that, it's got to be an exciting business. I like excitement, the risk, the gamble. Face it every day in my own business, of course, but it's not the same. Not the same as being out in the trenches, so to speak."

"We can promise you plenty of excitement," Alexis said, handing him his third martini. "But we need your help, of course. We need you to help us contact other investors."

"Oh, I already have," VanLures said, waving away the glass. "You'll have the first meeting with two of them in my office tomorrow afternoon. James Palmer and Peter D'Angelo." He walked to the mirror and straightened his tie. "Got to be going. Busy day, you know." He walked to the door. "By the way, Ali. It was clever of you to buy those properties in the Wichita Falls fields before you came. Damned resourceful, the two of you. Damned resourceful!" he said as he left.

Alexis and Jon stared at each other, too stunned to speak at first. Then they both laughed. "Good Lord, I feel as if we've both just been steamrolled," Alexis said, setting down the martini she had tried to hand VanLures.

"Maybe we have, but we got what we wanted. Maybe we did a little steamrolling too."

"I should say you did," she said, glancing at the liquor. "Where did you get this stuff?"

"Contacts. Just like I said."

"You've been in New York less than twenty-four hours. How could you have contacts?"

"The bellboy."

"Bellboy?" she asked incredulously.

"Sure. And if you want to know a good bookie or get a high-class dame in your room, he can arrange that too."

"You're insufferable," she said with a laugh.

"And you're beautiful."

Their eyes locked for a moment before she looked away. "Jon . . ."

"Don't say it," he said. "Don't tell me it would be wrong."

She walked to the sofa and picked up her handbag. "Let's not talk about it. We'd only disagree. And we've got to save our energies for the—"

"Alexis," he said, grabbing her arm and stopping her before she reached the door. "We've got to talk about it. I love you. I need you. There's nothing standing in our way. Isn't that simple enough?"

"It's not simple, and you know it." She tried to move away from him, but he held her firmly.

"If it's not, then it's only because you're making it that way. I won't force you. You know that. But there is absolutely no reason why we can't be together."

"No, I don't want it this way."

"It's the only way it's ever going to be, and we both know it. We knew it from the start." He hesitated a moment and eyed her cautiously. "You're not telling me you've changed your mind, are you? About marriage. You're not holding out for that?"

"Of course not," she said quickly. "I'll never change my mind about that. I told you, no strings."

"I'm not attaching any strings, and I'm not going to force you, but I am going to go on loving you."

It was so tempting to believe him, to think that their love could actually be possible. It was tempting to believe, too, now that they were thousands of miles away from Eleanor, that she was concerned only about their being discreet, and that all that mattered was that they loved each other. Alexis knew she could no longer deny to herself that she loved him, but she still dared not say the words aloud. VanLures's words echoed in her head. *It pays to be cautious.* She knew that was even more true where her heart was concerned.

"Don't make it so difficult for me," she said finally, turning away from him.

"Hell, you're the one who's making it difficult, I—"

"Let's not go over it again, Jon. We both have other things to think about. The meeting with those investors, for one thing. I have to meet Stella and some old friends for luncheon. I'll try to get away by two-thirty. Then I want to meet with you to talk about Mr. Palmer and Mr. D'Angelo." He tried to interrupt, but she went on, talking fast, not giving him a chance, half afraid of what just the sound of his voice could do to her. "You'll need to know something about them. They're both in manufacturing and both rich, but their personalities are vastly different. You'll need some understanding of that if we're going to get their money. I'll call you later and we'll talk about it."

"Fine." She saw the thin bloodless line of his lips, but she avoided his eyes as she opened the door and left. The words she had wanted to say but had left unsaid burned in her heart. *I'm going to go on loving you, too*, she thought. *Oh, God, forever.*

The meeting was a success. She had coached Jon on the fact that James Palmer would be interested in the financial prospects only, but Peter D'Angelo would be equally intrigued by the romance of the venture. She had made suggestions on what he should wear, discussed what she should wear and how much she should stay in the background. The rehearsal paid off. Within three days they had the backing of both, and they'd been invited to a party at the VanLures mansion during which Jon would be introduced to more prospective investors.

"Darling, he's absolutely breathtaking," Stella said, pulling Alexis aside in the grand ballroom of her father's house after she'd spent considerable time dancing and flirting with Jon. "Not exactly handsome, maybe, but attractive. So mature. Darling, you are sleeping with him, aren't you? Because if you're not, I'm going to seduce him."

"If you want to seduce him, it wouldn't matter who was sleeping with him, Stella."

Stella laughed. "You're right, of course. All's fair in love and war, as they say."

She moved away to dance with Jon. Alexis watched them with a combination of amusement and annoyance. It was so like Stella to want to taste the new elixir and so like Jon to be intrigued with her privileged candor. Neither of them made any attempt at concealing the fact that they were enjoying each other's company. Was that what annoyed her? Was it simple, ridiculous jealousy?

"What's this about oil exploration in Texas I've been hearing about?" a voice behind her asked. She turned to see Martin Graham smiling at her.

"Why, Mr. Graham, how lovely to see you," she said and gave him her best smile. Martin Graham, with drooping sea-colored eyes, hair the color of new pewter, and a mound of a stomach encased in the finest of black worsted wool tuxedo, was one of William VanLures's contemporaries. He was known to have a liking for female company and to be among the wealthiest of the Manhattan elite. He'd made his fortune in real estate as well as a number of other business ventures, one of which, it was rumored, was supplying guns to Pancho Villa's band of marauders in Mexico. "You've heard about our oil exploration?"

"I've heard you've got your pretty little finger into something out West."

"Oh, I have, Martin, I have," she said, linking her arm through his. "Let me tell you about it," she added as she led him toward an adjoining sitting room.

An hour and several glasses of champagne later Martin Graham seemed sufficiently impressed that Alexis thought he might be willing to invest a sizable amount of money. He hadn't made his money by making careless decisions, though, so she couldn't say she had him in the bag. Before he made a commitment, he wanted to see some of the geology reports and other documentation, and Alexis promised to set up a meeting with him the next day. She then introduced him to Jon and left the two of them together while she moved about the room to gather more of the ripe prospects William VanLures had so generously planted at his party.

Within a little while she had spoken with several more potential investors. If Jon was doing as well as she, they should be able to have the money they needed within a few weeks. She looked around the room at the mass of glittering, homogenized pomposity, searching for Jon once again. He would not blend in with this crowd. He would spread his accent on just a little thicker on purpose, and he would, in spite of his acquired urbanity, display an openness unique to a native westerner which, to an easterner, bordered on wildness.

But he was not there. She scanned the room over and over again without seeing him. She had given up and decided to step out into the garden for some fresh air when she spotted him. He was standing half in the shadows near a softly whispering fountain with Stella VanLures. Stella threw her head back and made the throaty, sultry sound that was her laughter and then turned toward him and put both her arms around his neck, coming very close to him in a slithering, boneless movement. She kissed him then, full on the lips, and Alexis saw his hands come up to caress her back. She turned away quickly and fled into the house, outrage howling inside her like a powerful wind. It was not outrage at Jon and Stella she felt, but at the sick, empty feeling in her chest she knew to be the raw vulnerability she had somehow forgotten to disguise and keep at bay.

Inside, the party had suddenly lost all of its glitter and become instead, too fluorescently white and shrill, infected with too many voices, too many bodies thrumming with power and the hunger for it. She ignored an invitation to dance as she hurried for the front door. She asked the butler to get her wrap and call a taxi, and then she stepped out into the strangely pagan purpleness of a Manhattan night, knowing that she could not for one more minute bear to be inside the home of Stella VanLures.

She waited with quivering impatience for the taxi. She was being silly, of course. Stella could do anything she wanted, and so could Jon. She had no expectations for Stella except for her predictability, no claims on Jon except to love him, and no expectations for him at all because that was the way she had chosen it. But she couldn't stay there. Not tonight. She could not stomach Stella's late-night recapitulation of the evening—who had been overheard saying what, who had danced with whom, who was sleeping with whom. She would not want to hear her throwaway comments of how charming she had found Jon to be, or worse, she didn't want to have to face her not mentioning him at all and keeping the secret of their liaison inside the dark womb of her sultry soul.

When at last the taxi came, Alexis stepped forward briskly and reached for the door. She felt the warm and powerful sensation of a presence behind her just as a dark gloved hand materialized on the door handle.

"Where the hell do you think you're going?" Jon asked when she turned to face him.

The question and the angry tone of his voice surprised her, and for a moment she was unable to respond. She could only stare at him in astonished unbalance. She started to speak, but decided it was better not to say anything than to appear a fool. She was about to move around to the other side of the taxi when he stopped her with a firm hand on her shoulder. "I said, where the hell do you think you're going?"

"Are you drunk?"

"What kind of a question is that?"

"Let me go." She pulled free of him, opened the door herself, and got into the taxi. Within the same second he got in, too, and instructed the driver to take them to the Plaza.

"The Barbizon," she said, giving him the name of a less expensive hotel, and one that was for women only.

"The Plaza," Jon repeated firmly. The driver turned around and gave them both a look that was a mixture of puzzlement and disgust. Alexis slunk back into the seat, her arms folded in front of her, and the driver put the car in gear, apparently deciding to follow Jon's instructions.

"Now are you going to tell me what you're up to?" Jon asked.

"Obviously, I'm going to the Plaza."

"Yes, we are, and we're going to have a long talk, and you're going to tell me why you stormed out of that gilded and overfurnished barn we were just in."

"I wanted some time alone," she said stiffly. "I've made a lot of important contacts tonight, and I wanted time to organize my thoughts before we begin meeting with investors later in the week."

"Hell, you could have found a room to be alone in there and they wouldn't find you for a year or two."

"Stella would have come to my room tonight to gossip about the evening, and one has certain obligations, certain conventions to follow when one is a guest in—"

"Cut out the crap, Ali! You turned your tail and ran when you saw her put the make on me out there in the backyard."

She gave him a quick nervous glance and felt as if she wanted to slide under the seat.

"I saw you out there, so don't give me any of your highfalutin speeches about obligations, unless you think your obligations include spying."

"I wasn't spying," she said, staring straight ahead at the back of the taxi driver's head. She was too angry and embarrassed to look at Jon. There was a long silence except for the sounds of the motor and the muted cacophony of the night traffic. As the silence grew, it became intrusive and as nerve-grinding as fingernails on a blackboard. She gave him a surreptitious glance and then turned her head to stare in bewilderment when she saw that he was filled with silent, body-shaking mirth.

She turned away from him, trying to stay angry.

"You're cute," he said, putting his arm around her.

"Don't you dare tell me I'm cute! That's so condescending."

"But you are."

"Then so are you. The way you reacted to Nick."

"We're both being a little ridiculous," he said, still with a little laugh. "Both having a little trouble not being possessive."

"I wasn't being possessive."

"Yes, you were," he said, pulling her closer.

"And were you? With Nick?"

"Of course I was. But it's wrong. We agreed to that, remember? No strings?"

She managed a laugh. "You're right. No strings," she said, turning so that her face was very close to his.

"I shouldn't be blamed for wanting to possess you tonight, though. You were the most beautiful, most desirable woman there." His voice was husky, and she knew he was about to kiss her.

"Jon . . ."

At that moment the cabby pulled the taxi to the curb and called out, "Plaza Hotel."

Jon paid the driver, and she was left wondering whether or not she would have let him kiss her. She had come to her senses now, though, she thought. But the Plaza doorman opening the door and Jon getting out and offering his hand to her blurred her resolve.

"Come on," he urged when he saw her hesitancy. "We need to talk. We'll just have coffee in one of the restaurants if you like. No strings."

She hesitated only a moment longer before she let him help her out and followed her into the lobby. He took her arm amidst the bowing, attentive staff, and led her, not toward the restaurant, but to the elevator.

"I thought you said we'd have coffee in one of the restaurants."

"On second thought, I think it will be better to have coffee sent up. We can relax, think better."

"Jon, all of this can wait until morning. There's really nothing to—"

"I'm wide awake, and so are you. Why waste time until morning?"

She rode up the elevator, wondering why, knowing the answer, wanting to turn and run, wanting to stay, hoping they could both keep up the pretense of doing some serious work.

When he opened the door to his room, she didn't know what to do. "I shouldn't have come," she said.

"Yes, you should. You know you wanted to."

She turned away and moved across the room to the window. "Order the coffee," she said over her shoulder.

"It will keep you awake."

"You are drunk. I could smell it on your breath. Now you've gotten me up here with this ruse."

"I'm only a little drunk, and it was no ruse. You knew what you were doing." He stood in front of her, very close, with his hand braced on the window frame. She leaned against the frame, her hands behind her back, locked together.

"Don't do this, Jon. We haven't resolved anything."

He continued to hover over her a moment, then made a wry face and dropped his arm. He went to the telephone and called room service for the coffee.

Alexis took a deep shuddering breath and moved to the cabinet where Jon had stored the gin and vermouth earlier. She opened it and pulled out both bottles.

"You're a fine one to accuse me of being drunk.

You drink way too much, my dear," he said, putting down the telephone.

She turned quickly toward him, her sudden rush of emotions a mixture of both anger and defensiveness.

"But only when you're trying to hide something. Usually from yourself," he added.

"I'm not hiding anything from myself," she said, pouring the liquor.

"And neither am I." He took the glass and the bottle from her hands and set them on the cabinet. His arm went around her. "I want to kiss you."

"No, please. . . ."

He pulled her close and touched her lips with his, lightly, seductively undemanding. "I'm not going to hide anything. I want more than a kiss. I want you. I want you naked and panting and crying out for me, and I want to be on top of you and inside you, and—"

"Good heavens, Jon." She pulled herself free and turned her back to him, pretending to be busy with the liquor and the glass again. When he placed his hands on her arms and turned her once again to face him, she knew that he was shocked that she was laughing.

"What? You think it's funny?" He sounded hurt.

"No!" she said, unable to stop laughing. "It's not funny."

"Then why . . . ?"

"Because it's . . . I don't know . . . because it's late and I've had a crazy evening, and because we're living on the edge by putting you up in this overdecorated barn with no money to pay for it." She was all but choking on her giddy, nervous laughter. "And because you make me so . . . so damned nervous and because . . . because I wish . . ."

"You wish what?" he asked when she couldn't stop laughing long enough to finish the sentence.

"I wish," she said, sobering, "I wish you didn't want to do all those things to me because I want them, too."

He pulled her close again and she stiffened, but he didn't let it stop him. He kissed her, but the kiss was no good. They were both tense, and after a while she turned her head away.

"We can't . . ."

"We can," he whispered. He used his hand on the back of her neck to turn her to face him again, his thumb on her jaw, massaging it gently. He leaned toward her and kissed her lightly again and then came back for more like a hummingbird who had discovered a sweet elixir. He began to explore her with his tongue, and she tasted the moist yeastiness left by the liquor and let him taste her until she began to relax and to respond, her hands coming up to rest on his chest and then clutching at his shirt when the kiss deepened, became potent, arousing, more than a kiss, an invitation, and an acquiescence.

His hand slid from her back to take possession of one of her breasts, and she could only respond by thrusting it deeper into his palm while her body warmed and her heart thrummed a wild rhythm. His fingers moved to unfasten the tiny buttons at the back of her dress and to pull it free of her shoulders. He kissed her chest above her breasts, her throat all the way up to her chin and her lips and then the full ripeness of her breasts. He returned to her mouth and pulled her closer to him with his hands on her buttocks, and then he began to slide the soft fabric of her dress upward, slowly, inch by inch, until she felt his hands on her hips, moving over the straps of her garter belt, back to her buttocks, up to her waist and inside the waist of her panties.

With his hands on her bare skin he pulled her against him and pressed his body toward her. She felt the hardness of him pressing against her, hurting her slightly where it met bone.

Sensations bombarded her like hundreds of attacking insects, nipping at her, mingling with her blood. Somewhere in her desire-drugged mind she knew she should stop, but the opiate was overpowering, and she could manage only a moan of pleasure.

There was a knock at the door. She was momentarily startled and made a move to pull away, but he held her close, ignoring the knock and the voice calling out, "Room service." He began slowly to pull her dress from her shoulders, past her breasts, over her hips, and with it her panties. He freed her bra next, and it fell to the floor. The continued knocking at the door seemed distant, a part of another world and meaningless.

She stood before him in garter belt and silk hose, and in the next moment she felt pleasure, like water, flow into dark inlets of her being, resting there in eddies, making everything wet and slippery, puffing itself into bubbles that burst into a warm, sensual stream.

She let the waves of pleasure overtake her as he took her with him to the floor, and she felt his hands slide beneath her and lift her to meet him. There was a cry of pleasure, and it was too late, far, far too late to stop.

Later, he lay on top of her for a moment, bracing part of his weight with his hands on the floor above her head. She heard his breath coming in ragged gasps and felt her own breath throbbing in her heaving chest, out of rhythm with the fluttering pulse in her throat. He rolled off of her and she lay very still for a moment—sated, numbed by pleasure. Her only thought was that she loved him.

"God, I've missed you," he said.

She turned toward him and smiled faintly. The sound of his voice had pulled her out of her voluptuous semiconsciousness. She reached for her dress and pulled it over her, covering her nakedness.

"Are you all right?"

"Of course," she said, but she couldn't look at him. The fluttering in her throat had become an ache—a knot of tears. It was not new, she told herself. It had happened before, this postcoital *tristesse*. It meant nothing. But the questions flickered through her mind. What about Eleanor? David?

He had pulled on his trousers and now he was reaching for her chin, turning her face toward him. She tried to resist, but it was only one more battle she lost.

"You're crying. Why . . ."

She tried to laugh. "It's nothing, really. Don't you know women do this sometimes afterward? It's like when we cry when we're happy."

"You're not crying because you're happy, Ali. Don't lie to me."

She stood up, trying to hold the dress over her front with one hand while she picked up her things with the other. "I've got to be going. I ought to get back to—"

"I said don't lie to me. And look at me."

Her eyes met his, reluctantly.

"You're feeling guilty."

She was silent for a moment, weighing whether or not she should deny it. Finally she said softly, "Yes."

"Don't. It was an act of love."

"It was an act of adultery."

"Ali, we've been over this. It's not adultery when there is an understanding. You've misinterpreted Eleanor."

She turned away from him. "Jon, I'm not sure . . ."

"I'm sure. And I'm sure of something else, too. You're not just some quick lay for me. I want you to be a permanent part of my life."

She turned back to face him suddenly. "What are you saying?"

"The same thing I've said over and over again now for months. That I love you. That I want you forever."

"Forever is a long time, Jon, and we promised each other no strings."

"All right. No strings. Just don't leave."

Their eyes held for a long time, and then finally all she could manage to say was, "Oh, Lord!"

But she didn't leave.

15

The next two weeks became to Alexis a heady, pleasure-soaked dream in which she moved about giddy in a gilded world. There were more parties in opulent Fifth Avenue mansions, meetings on Wall Street, evenings at the theater or on someone's yacht. She had done it all before, but this time she was with Jon, and he was reaching for her hand at the theater or under the table at dinner, kissing her in the moonlight aboard the yacht, laughing with her at the sideshows on Coney Island or finding new small and intimate restaurants in out-of-the-way places when they could steal a few hours away to be alone.

She kept up the pretense of staying with the VanLureses, but no one seemed aware of the nights she did not return to the mansion. No one except Stella, who prodded her for details at first, but even she lost interest quickly enough when she was launched headlong into the plans for her wedding at just the same time she began having an affair with a French diplomat she had met at one of her father's parties.

The meetings with potential clients went well. Alexis advised Jon on the personalities and backgrounds of the various investors, and during the meetings, she played the charming hostess and said very little. It was evident to both of them, though, that her behind-the-scenes coaching and Jon's natural salesmanship, along with VanLures's endorsement, paid off. They had the $150,000 they needed within three weeks.

"It's wonderful!" Alexis said. "We're not only going to be able to pay for this god-awful expensive trip, but we're going to make a fortune. I can just feel it."

"Well, at least we have the seeds to plant now," Jon said with a laugh. "A hundred fifty thousand seeds, to be exact." He gave her a quick kiss. "I still have some of the gin left. Want to celebrate?"

"No," she said, "I want to enjoy this. I don't want any liquor to dull the way I feel. It's as if nothing could ever go wrong again, isn't it?"

His response was to encircle her waist and kiss her again before he picked her up and carried her to the bedroom.

"Shouldn't we take separate trains?" Alexis asked the day Jon made reservations for their return.

"There's nothing to worry about," Jon said. "I wired Eleanor that we would be arriving together. I told her it was urgent that we both get back as soon as possible. I think she'll understand that we had to change our plans."

Alexis felt a brief sting of betrayal that he had discussed it at all with Eleanor. She hadn't known when he had wired her, since it hardly seemed he'd been out of her sight long enough to do that. She was determined not to let a moment of petty jealousy ruin their last few days together, though.

They shared the excitement of the passing landscape as they raced like Cupid's arrow through the country's heartland, then clung to each other in the sleeping berth at night, laughing at their attempts to bring their own rhythm into synchronization with that of the rocking, swaying train.

For the three days they were alone together on the train, Alexis shut out the future along with the past. In the future, Jon would go back to being Eleanor's husband and David's father. In the past were Ivy and Langdon and the family in which she had somehow never belonged, and all the mistakes she'd made in attempting to prove herself to them. But in the present were Jon and the tiny kingdom they shared on the train. In the present it was true that nothing could ever go wrong again.

The feeling lasted until the day they arrived in Coyote Flats. Alexis stepped off the train just ahead of Jon and saw Eleanor waiting for them with David standing behind her. She knew then that she had been thrust suddenly into the future.

"Welcome back!" Eleanor said, smiling broadly. She tilted her head to receive Jon's kiss. "It's wonderful that you got the investors, darling." She linked her arm through Jon's and turned to Alexis. "Jon said your contacts were invaluable, and it must have been wonderful for you to see all your old friends again."

Alexis managed only a brief smile in reply and then looked beyond Eleanor at David, still standing in the background. Eleanor's uncharacteristic show of congeniality and enthusiasm was unsettling to her. She wasn't sure what it meant, but David was always a delight to her.

"Hi," he said, grinning shyly. "So you really got the money?"

"We got the money."

"Good! I can't wait to get a rig going again. Nick says he'll teach me even more about it once we get started."

"It won't be long now," Alexis said.

"It must be great knowing all those rich people."

Alexis draped her arm over his shoulder. "Not as great as knowing you."

"Ah, Ali," he said, blushing profusely.

"I mean it. And I brought you something."

"What?" His eyes shone like a ten-year-old's.

"Here," she said, pulling out a stereopticon. "It comes with scenes of the city and the harbor."

"Wow! Thanks, Ali. Do you think I might get to see it for real some day? Will you take me next time? Nick says I ought to go with somebody who knows their way around, and he says he bets there's nobody who knows her way around any better than you."

Alexis laughed. "Of course, Dave, I'd love to take you to New York and show you all of it."

"Don't be ridiculous, David," Eleanor said. "Of course Miss Runnels wouldn't want to be tied down with a boy. A young woman like her moves in a fast circle. I'm sure none of us would fit in."

"Then maybe I'll just go by myself sometime. Nick says he's going someday."

"Nick says, Nick says," Jon said with a little stilted laugh. "Can't you start a sentence any other way?"

David looked suddenly embarrassed and then even more so when Jon clasped his shoulder and said, still in his stilted voice, "Hello, son."

"Hello, Papa," David answered with strained politeness. "Good to have you back."

"Thank you. It's good to be back."

They looked at each other in awkward silence for a moment before Jon spoke again. "I told you, I'll be glad to take you to New York sometime, son."

"Swell," David said without enthusiasm.

"There are a number of good colleges in the area you will want to look into."

Alexis saw the quick flash of emotion in David's eyes. She knew he was about to lash out at his father, but his glance flickered in her direction. "Yeah, sure, Pa," he said, swallowing his anger—for her sake, she thought.

"Have you ever heard of Coney Island, Dave?" she asked, hoping to ease the tension.

"Coney Island? Oh, wow, Nick told me he'd heard about it. Said it ought to be something. Did you go there? Heck, I bet you've been there at least a hundred times."

"Maybe not quite that many. But I did go this time, and look." She rummaged in her bag again. "I brought you this." She produced a postcard with a sepia-colored photograph of a roller coaster.

"Oh, wow!" he said, reacting with all the enthusiasm that had been missing when he spoke with his father. "Did you ride this?"

"Dozens of times," Alexis said, smiling at his exuberance.

"Is it really scary?"

"It scares me to death every time I ride it," she said, not daring to look at Jon because she knew he was remembering, as she was, how she had clung to him, laughing and terrified.

"Scary as an aeroplane?"

"A hundred times worse."

"One day I'll fly over France just like you did."

"I'm sure you will," Alexis said with a little laugh.

"Nick says flying ought to be the closest thing to freedom there is. Do you think he's right? Do you think it's better than—"

"David, I'm sure Miss Runnels is tired after her trip," Eleanor said. "Leave her alone, for heaven's sake, and let her get home where I'm sure she wants to be."

Alexis looked at Eleanor and felt a numbing chill.

"Come on, Dave. Let's get the suitcases in the car," Jon said, sounding distressed.

The drive to her hotel was, thankfully, a short one. Alexis sat in the back seat with David, answering his questions about New York and hearing his enthusiastic account of Nick's teaching him to be a tool dresser. Jon, she saw, sat with his back rigid as he drove, while Eleanor, seated next to him, relayed information on a political rally he would be attending in a few days.

When they reached the hotel, Alexis's luggage was quickly unloaded, and she was bidden a polite and formal goodbye by both Jon and Eleanor while Dave made comic gestures to her behind their backs and mouthed, "I'll see you later."

When, less than half an hour later, she heard a knock at her door, she expected to see David standing there, ready to try to entice her away to Blackie's to tell him more about New York. But it was Eleanor who was standing in the hallway, her expression serious almost to the point of being grim and her astonishing eyes now the deep, dark color of a fire that has burned itself to ashes.

"We need to talk, Alexis," she said.

Alexis held the door open for Eleanor while her mind leapt. What did it mean, she wondered, that Eleanor had, for the first time, used her first name rather than calling her Miss Runnels?

"Sit down, Eleanor," Alexis said, her voice slightly more cynical than congenial. "I'd offer you coffee or something if I had any, but I have a feeling anyway that this isn't a social call."

"Apparently I didn't make myself clear the last time we talked, Alexis," Eleanor said, turning suddenly to face her. Her lips were as bloodless as stone. "So I'm going to be blunt, so that this time there is no mistake. Stay away from my husband."

Alexis' chest felt suddenly heavy, as if something the size and weight of a boulder had been dropped on her.

"Eleanor, I never had any intention of—"

"You are about to destroy him!"

Eleanor had spoken with such hot vehemence Alexis felt as if she'd been forced to swallow fire. "Destroy him?" She found she could barely speak above a whisper. "Destroy him, you say? Neither of us has the power to do that, because he won't allow it. If you knew him at all you would know that. When I'm with him he is—"

"Spare me the juvenile romanticism," Eleanor interrupted. "When you are with him he is more complete? Happier? More himself? Alexis, my dear, you are being foolish. You are one of many, and there will be others after you. Your name is Legion. Oh, don't look so stricken. I can't believe you didn't know it. I've known it for a long time, but I can forgive Jon his little hobby. It's always been harmless enough up to this point. You see, I'm a very modern and enlightened woman," she said, walking away from Alexis, throwing her words over her shoulder. "Just the kind of woman a smart and cunning man like Jon needs, because I know how to see that his needs are satisfied and at the same time appear traditional and devoted." She turned to face Alexis again, making her point with dramatic emphasis. "He has such great potential, Alexis, and he is soon going to be where he can use that potential to the greatest advantage. In the United States Congress."

She paused, but Alexis could not find words to speak. She could only stare, horrified at what was happening, and at the same time, mesmerized by Eleanor's show of power and cunning.

"You are not what he needs, Alexis," Eleanor said, her eyes shooting straight through her. "No matter how much, in the heat of passion, he may claim that you are. You are not what he needs, and we all three know that. He, you, and I."

"Why are you doing this?" Alexis finally managed to say, her voice choked with anger and humiliation and the tiniest spark of defiance.

"Why? I told you why. Because I don't want him destroyed. And that is exactly what you are going to do with your childish indiscretion. You even arrived on the same train, for heaven's sake. Don't you see what that does to his reputation? You could have, at the very least, insisted that one of you take a later train from San Angelo."

"I never wanted to hurt anyone, Eleanor," Alexis said, feeling like a chastened child. "I never meant to humiliate you."

Eleanor laughed cruelly. "The only person you've hurt is Jon. I only hope you kept your little liaison in New York more discreet. Gossip can travel with lightning speed all the way to Texas. If it does, you may have hurt him beyond salvaging. Let's hope you haven't. But in the meantime, I don't want to take any more chances. I'm afraid discretion is not enough, Alexis. We can't afford anything short of innocence. It has to end between you and Jon."

"Why aren't you talking to Jon about this?" Alexis asked. "Isn't it his responsibility, too? Doesn't he at least have some say in the matter?"

Eleanor's laugh was low and throaty, almost a growl. "He would deny any attraction to you, child, much less any affair you might be having. He would think that by denying it he is protecting me. Jon is not a realist, my dear. He is a romantic. Only men are true romantics, you know, and that is why we women must protect them. It's up to us to be the realists, my dear. You will learn that eventually."

Again Alexis found she couldn't speak. Was what Eleanor said true? Was Jon the romantic who was in need of protection and who would deny his love for her to protect his wife?

"You do understand, don't you, Alexis?" Eleanor asked, her eyes dangerous.

There was a sickening silence before Alexis answered in a voice heavy with despair. "Yes, I understand."

"I knew you would," Eleanor said with a self-satisfied smile. "I knew you were smart enough to get my point, and I knew that you fancy yourself in love with him enough to see that he's not hurt." She gathered up her gloves and purse that she had thrown on the bed. "Don't take it personally. You just got the unlucky draw. You happened to come along just when Jon's star is rising. Under previous circumstances, your little affair might have gone completely unnoticed."

She walked out, leaving Alexis drained and utterly numbed. When at last Alexis could think at all, she knew that she had been wrong about Eleanor. It wasn't love for Jon that drove her. It wasn't even jealousy. It was cold ambition. Jon was ambitious, too, and that, no doubt, had kept him with Eleanor. Alexis knew that she could be hurt by that ambition, because she had let herself go too far with Jon. If it had been no more than a flirtation or a sexual fling, she could have survived, but she'd fallen in love, tangled the strings. Now survival would not be so simple. Now there were things that had to be resolved. He would come tonight, she thought, because he would be as eager to see her as she to see him, and when he came, they would try to find a way to straighten things out.

He didn't come that night, and he didn't come the next morning, either. She drove out to the well site late in the day and saw that the crew was already there. They were unloading the rig that Jon had instructed them by wire to buy just before he left New York.

"Buck!" she called, waving to him as she got out of the truck. "I didn't expect to find you here already. Where's Jon? In the tent?"

"Ain't seen him since yesterday," Buck said. "He told us to get out here and get the rig ready. Said to start drilling soon as we could. I figure we'll be at it in the mornin'."

The door to the tent opened and Nick emerged carrying a cup of coffee. "Well, if it ain't the Lady Runnels. What made you decide to get out so damned early?" he asked, grinning.

"Where's Jon?" she asked, ignoring his friendly needling.

"He went to Midland. I figured you knew that." There was a pause while he waited for her to confirm that she'd known, but she said nothing. She merely looked at him with a sense of foreboding.

"He went to buy rope for the cable, I guess," she said when she was finally able to speak. "He did mention we'd need more if we were going to drill deeper."

"Hell, we got the cable," Nick said. "Got that in Coyote Flats. He went off with Eleanor."

"Eleanor?"

"Some political thing, I think. Dave's staying with me after school." He paused a moment then said, "Sorry, sugar."

"Sorry? For what? What he does with Eleanor is none of my business," she said sharply as she turned away.

Nick caught her arm and pulled her back. "Hey, this is Nick you're talking to, baby. Don't try to feed me any bullshit. What he does with Eleanor is killing you."

"You don't know what you're talking about."

"Yes, I do, and so do you. You're in love with him."

"I don't fall in love with married men," she said. "I'm a realist," she added with a wry laugh as she remembered Eleanor's words.

"The hell you are. I'll bet you spent three weeks in bed with him in New York, didn't you? And you thought it meant he loves you too."

She looked at him, horrified that he could make it sound so cheap.

"Don't let him do it to you, Ali. Jon Calahan's a smart man. Maybe even a kind man once in a while and a hell of a politician. He was cut out to be a winner—a success—and he knows it. A man like that can't love nobody but hisself." He let go of her arm, but held her with his eyes, and she saw genuine concern there.

She turned away quickly, before Nick could see her tears.

"Just remember one thing, baby," he called to her. "You deserve better than that. You deserve the best."

His words startled her and she hesitated, almost turned around. Did she? she wondered. Did she really deserve the best? Or had she always gotten what she deserved as the odd one out, the bad girl who got her comeuppance?

Alexis wiped her hands on a greasy rag that hung on a cross beam of the derrick before she picked up the log to study the annotations Buck had made indicating the depth and the formations through which they had drilled. She had been helping Nick shovel coal into the forge to heat one of the drill bits so he could reshape it with his hammer and drill another few feet before the day ended.

Buck's careful and precise markings showed that they had drilled through shale for a week with no signs of anything. There should be sand beneath the shale where, she hoped, oil that had been squeezed from the shale by the powerful forces of the earth would be trapped, along with pockets of gas.

Buck's notations marked each formation carefully. Alexis read them and tried to remember the significance Jon and the geologist had attached to each, but she was having trouble concentrating. She'd arrived at the drilling site by dawn every morning for the past week, and this morning she'd awakened not feeling well. She had, in fact, not been able to eat her breakfast, and now she was feeling weak and light-headed. Behind her the whining and groaning of the cable and motor and the steady pounding of the drill as it chewed at the earth's innards made her head throb and sent pain ricocheting through her skull and down the bones of her neck. Heat from the forge left her sticky and nauseated.

She tried to study the log again, but she wasn't sure of what she was seeing except that there apparently was no more sign of oil than there had been the day before or the day before that.

"Hi, Ali, whatcha doin'?"

She glanced up to see David getting out of Nick's car and walking toward her, a blurry silhouette against a silk banner of sky streaked with pink and gold. The sight of him there with Nick made her angry. Jon and Eleanor should never have left him for this long, she thought, and should never have left a playboy like Nick in charge.

"I'm working," she snapped. "What are you doing here?"

"I came to help. Buck says I'm about ready to start guidin' the drill bit down by myself. He's goin' to show me how to fit it into the casing and—"

"He's not going to do any such thing. You're going back to school. Nick, take him back. Damn it, what do you think you're doing bringing him out here when he ought to be in school?"

"It's Saturday, Ali," they said in unison.

She looked at them both for a moment, silent and frustrated, while something awesome and strange roiled inside her. She threw down the logbook and walked rapidly toward the tent.

By the time she was inside the tent and the door had slammed behind her, she had begun to feel foolish, and because of that she was certain she didn't want any company just now. She hooked the curved end of the slender latch into its eyelet to keep away any solicitous inquiries. She could well imagine David and Nick's reaction to what must, to them, seem to be an illogical feminine temperament. It wasn't illogical, of course. There was good reason for her reaction, although she could admit that perhaps it did appear childish to have stalked off the way she did. It was better than letting them see her tears, though.

She kept her back to the door and sniffed hard, doing her best to keep from crying. Her tears were tears of anger and frustration and had nothing to do with David, she knew, and certainly nothing to do with whether or not he was in school. It was Jon with whom she was angry. Or maybe not Jon at all, but with herself—for getting herself involved in such a hopeless situation.

There was a knock at the door—Nick, of course. She hurriedly wiped the tears off her cheeks and called over her shoulder in a voice edged with the contempt she felt for herself. "What do you want?"

"Are you all right, sugar?"

"Of course."

"Well, you sure seemed pissed about something."

"I'm not pissed, damn it, I'm just busy. We've both got work to do; now leave me alone so I can get it done."

"Hey, darlin', this is old Nick you're talkin' to." She heard him push at the door, trying to open it but meeting resistance from the flimsy latch. "So don't give me any of that bullshit"—he pushed again, and the latch rattled in its hook—"about not being pissed." One final push and the latch broke and fell to the floor, taking pieces of soft wood from the door and door frame with it. "Shit," Nick said as he stepped inside and looked down at the latch on the floor and then at the badly scarred door. "What'd you do that for?"

"God only knows."

"Well, you shouldn't have locked me out, sugar."

"Damn it, Nick!"

"Damn it what?"

She glared at him, unable for the moment to think what to say.

"Okay. I won't call you 'sugar.'"

"Or 'honey' or 'baby' or—"

"I said okay, but that ain't what's wrong with you."

She glared at him again.

"Did the bastard knock you up?"

"*What?*"

"I said did he—"

"I heard what you said. Jesus Christ, Nick."

"Well, you been actin' so touchy lately, and I know women get kinda peevish when they're in a family way. 'Specially when it ain't convenient for them to be that way, so I just thought—"

"I'm not pregnant."

"Then maybe you've got your period. Is that all?"

Alexis sat down and sighed loudly as she propped her elbows on the desk, letting her head fall into her hands.

"Well, I know women get the same way when the monthlies come around." He sounded vaguely apologetic.

"You seem to know a lot about women," she said, still with her head in her hands, her voice muffled.

"Hell, it don't take no genius to see there's something wrong with you. I just hate to see you like this. I wish there was something I could do."

She looked up, touched by his words and the gentle tone of his voice.

"I was hoping maybe everything would be okay after y'all went off to New York together. You know what I mean. Everybody needs a little nooky now and then. That's another thing makes a person crabby. When you don't get it enough. So I thought maybe bein' off away from everybody like that y'all would get the chance to—"

"I get your point, Nick," she said, standing. "Is there anything else you'd like to comment on regarding my private life or my bodily functions?"

"Now, don't get touchy."

She looked at him for a second or two, then shook her head. "Does everybody on the face of the earth assume we were sleeping together in New York?"

"I wouldn't say that. Not everybody knows you're in love with him."

She glanced at him again, and their eyes held for a moment.

"It won't work, Ali. You know that. He's only gonna hurt you more. He's got a family, and he's a goddamned politician. He's not going to give any of that up. Move on to something else." He waited for her to speak, and when she said nothing, he sighed and turned toward the door.

"Nick . . ." He turned to look at her. She paused a moment, not knowing how to say it. "Thanks for caring enough to do that," she said, with a glance toward the splintered door frame.

"Hell, baby, ol' Nick loves you."

16

She knew Nick was right. There was no way she could win. Eleanor had made it clear, and so had Jon. She had not started out to win him, though. Her only purpose had been to use him. How had it happened that she had come to love him? How could she have let herself be so foolish?

She had been foolish before, and she had thought she'd learned her lesson. She had loved Zane Lawrence, but she had not been enough for him, and then his death had robbed her of the chance ever to prove that she could be. Was that what was hurting so much now? The fact that she would never have the chance to prove to Jon that she was all he'd ever need? If that was the case, then she was indeed a fool, she thought. They'd both agreed from the beginning what their relationship would be. Falling in love had complicated things for her, but not for Jon. She had almost made a fool of herself by spinning out a lethal, invisible web of strings for herself. She should be grateful that Jon had kept his head. Now she had to find hers again and to remember her goal was money, not love.

It was not difficult, she discovered, to keep her mind occupied with the drilling. She was at the site early every morning, watching the core samples, going over them with Nick and Buck, running errands when the crew needed some replacement part for the rig. She even found herself doing some of the repairs herself, wielding pliers and wire cutters and heavy wrenches as if she'd done it all her life. By the end of each day she was covered with grease and dust and sweat.

She had taken to spending the night at the rig on the cot in the office tent, washing herself off at the windmill each night, just as the crew did, and sharing the same canned beans and stale bacon cooked on a small kerosene stove that sat under a mesquite bush. At night when the men retired to their tents, they left her to sleep undisturbed on the cot in the office. That was due in part to the fact that they were too tired to do otherwise, but also because she knew Nick had threatened them with severe harm if they came near her.

David came out again on the second weekend and stayed with Nick in one of the tents. By late Sunday afternoon he was still there, still helping Buck and learning how to sense by the vibration of the drilling line, the sound of the motor, and the feeling in his gut when to let the tools down deeper into the hole or pick them up. He was also learning from Nick how to heat the drill bits in the lurid orange of the forge and dress them by pounding them out to a sharp, pointed configuration that could chew into the earth voraciously, looking for the payoff.

Alexis could see that David looked tired from lifting the heavy hammer over his head countless times and from breathing in the heat and sweating it out again. But his eyes glowed with a fierce and terrible and youthful excitement. Her first thought had been to warn him that it was getting late, that it was time to leave for town because he had school the next morning, but seeing his eyes and sensing the excitement that emanated from him, she let it go and instead walked away from the rig toward the windmill. She was too tired to argue with him anyway.

She picked up the dipper and scooped it into the water barrel and tasted the water—hard water, full of minerals and a hint of salt, as if the ancient sea that the geologists said once covered the basin was still lurking beneath the surface. She took another dipper of water and poured it over her head the way she had seen the men do. The evaporation in the sunstruck October was almost instantaneous, and the cooling effect deliciously, if all too briefly, satisfying. She stood, reveling in it for the moment it lasted, then pulled a handkerchief from her pocket and mopped at her forehead, her eyes still on the endless horizon where a gentle undulation flirted with the flatness.

But those soft mounds and the blue ridge on the horizon seemed, when one tried to approach them, always out of reach, like a virgin's kiss. Like a wildcatter's dream, she thought wryly. She had, of late, come to lose her resentment for the starkness of the landscape, though, and to see it instead as refreshing. It was as if her spirit, too, was being pulled toward the limitlessness like a luxurious stretch of arms upon waking in the morning. She had, in fact, come to find that she needed these spirit stretches.

A sudden shout brought her attention back from her mental rambling like a recoiling spring. She saw Buck motioning for her to come to the rig. She dropped the water dipper on the ground and ran when she saw the excitement in his face.

"What is it?" she asked as she clambered over the framework.

"Look." Buck pointed to the casing. Alexis looked closer and saw the bubbles in the water. "I think those are gas bubbles," he said.

"Gas?"

"That means there's oil there, too."

"Bring the bailer up," she ordered. "Let's have a look."

"Nick, give me a hand here," Buck said. But Nick was already there, as was David, all of them hovering as the tools were pulled and the bailer sunk.

There was silence except for the wind moving through the crossbeams of the derrick with a slushing sound, like waves rocking against land, and the clanking of the metal bailer as it hit the sides of the casing. After what seemed an interminable time, Buck brought the bailer to the surface. The excitement and tension in all of them was sharp-edged and quivering. Alexis moved closer to the bailer and looked at its bounty of the earth's innards—solid clumps of sand and rocks, all of it bleeding dark mud. But the mud was darker than usual. Oil?

Nick leaned over the bailer and sniffed, then yanked off his glove and put an index finger into the sludge and tasted it. He glanced at Alexis and nodded. She felt as if her heart had vacated her chest and was vaguely aware that the tension around her had shuddered and cracked.

"Is it enough?" she asked. "An impressive showing?"

"Yeah, I'm pretty sure it is," Nick said. "But we ought to bail a few more times just to make sure."

"How much do you think—" Suddenly the derrick platform began to quake, and Alexis heard a distant roar. At the same time Nick grabbed her arm and pulled her roughly away from the casing. The handkerchief she had tucked up her sleeve fluttered to the floor.

"We got to move!" he said. She noticed Dave and the others had already cleared the derrick. "I think she's about to blow in. She could blow the whole goddamned derrick down."

"David!" she shouted when she saw him turn back to the rig and pick up the handkerchief she'd dropped. He glanced at her and grinned as he plucked the handkerchief from a splintery board. The well began to growl and hiss, and Alexis knew with certainty that hell itself had been disturbed and was coming to the surface for revenge.

Dave jumped off the platform, a gallant knight waving the handkerchief of a lady, and then it happened. A sudden plume of heavy darkness shot upward from the shaft, roaring and snorting, and a heavy liquid night blocked out the sun, snorting again as the weight of it broke the walking beam and soared over the crown block.

Alexis could only stare in utter awe at the spurting artery until she began to laugh, the sound coming up from inside her as bawdy and wild as the blowout. She was aware of David and Nick staring at her, and when she looked at them and saw their faces mottled with great blotches of oil, she laughed even harder. Her own face looked the same, she knew, because she could sense the heavy wetness and smell it and taste it and feel it soaking into her pores.

"It's the Jonali!" David shouted above the roar of the oil.

"The what?" she asked.

"The well! I think we ought to call it the Jonali," he said, "after you and Papa."

"Okay," she said, still shouting above the roar. "The Jonali. But not just the well. The Jonali field. We're going to develop a whole field here!"

"Three thousand feet!" Nick said. He was also shouting, trying to be heard above the raging gusher. "Three thousand goddamned feet!"

"Three thousand goddamned feet and one hundred and fifty thousand goddamned dollars!" Alexis shouted in return.

"You're gonna make it back, honey. Just look at that! You got over a thousand barrels a day there. Five thousand, maybe. Hell! Maybe ten."

Alexis glanced at the leaping oil. "That's not enough."

Nick laughed. "What?"

"I want a hundred thousand."

"You hear that, Nick?" David shouted, excited. "She wants a big one. And she'll get it too. I know she will."

"Hey," Nick protested. "I don't know if you can—"

"Don't tell me it can't be done. I've seen wells produce that much."

"Oh, yeah. Some of your daddy's wells in East Texas. But this ain't a proven field. You might have to have five wells to do what your daddy does with one back there."

"Then that's what I'm going to do, Nick. C and R is going to be the biggest oil company in Texas."

"Didn't I tell you?" David said. "She can do anything she wants, I bet."

"God, baby, you're somethin'," Nick said. "Greedy as hell. All that money your old man's got and it ain't enough."

"Don't judge me, Nick!" she snapped. "I have no claim to Langdon Runnels's money."

"Oh yeah, sure, baby. And I'm the king of Siam. But hey, don't get me wrong. Greed is what made this country great." He walked away, shouting at Buck. "We got to get that flow tamed and into some barrels so we can turn it into greenbacks for the little lady!"

Alexis turned away and put her arm around David. "Come on, Dave," she said, leading him toward the windmill. "Let's get some of this stuff washed off and go to town. I'm going to buy you the biggest steak in Coyote Flats."

"You gonna notify Papa about this?"

She stopped and looked at him, trying not to let her hurt and anger with Jon show. "Now, how can I do that when I don't even know for sure where he is?"

"He'll call you when he can. I just know it. And he'll be back soon. He wouldn't want to be away from you too long. I know that, too."

Alexis glanced at David and their eyes locked for a moment. "Nonsense," she said, trying to keep her voice steady. "He's got a campaign to run, and he knows I can handle this, so there's no reason to hurry back."

"You're the reason."

There was another moment of silence while her heart thudded in her chest, and she fought back a dizzying sickness. "I don't like what you're implying."

"He's in love with you, isn't he? That's why he went away with you to New York."

"Dave . . ."

"Don't worry. I know all about things like that."

"What are you saying? You don't know any such thing."

"Yes I do. I know—"

"David!"

"Don't treat me like a baby, Ali. You said you wouldn't."

She looked at him, her heart pounding harder, her fear mounting—fear that she had gone too far and somehow managed to damage this boy.

"Don't cry, Ali."

"I'm not crying!" she insisted, in spite of the fact that tears had filled her eyes and threatened to spill over. "I just want you to know I'm not a . . . a . . ."

"Oh no, Ali, I didn't mean—"

She shook her head. "Let's drop it, David. I don't want to speak of this ever again."

"But—"

"I mean what I say. You will not mention it again." She turned away from him and pulled out her handkerchief. Dipping it into the water barrel, she began to scrub vigorously at the thick black oil on the back of her hand.

"Out, damned spot."

Her head jerked up suddenly, and she met Dave's gaze, terrible in its youthful gall. "What did you say?"

"It's a quote from Shakespeare. Lady Macbeth said it when she was trying to rub the truth away." There was a pause, and then he added almost apologetically, "Papa taught it to me."

She continued to look at him for a moment longer, and she was struck at how much like Jon he was, in spite of the fact that David tried to deny it. She loved them both beyond reason. "Oh, Dave!" she said, letting the handkerchief fall into the mud around the water barrel. She pulled the boy close to her and hugged him the way she used to do Miller when he needed comforting. Only this time it was she who needed someone to take away her fear and confusion.

"It's all right," Dave said, pushing away, a little embarrassed. "I'd be in love with you too if I was Papa."

She tried to smile as she reached a hand to ruffle David's hair. Behind him she could see hell rising from beneath the earth, thick, rich, and black, and she knew that nothing was all right.

Nick had said it was greed that drove her. Why couldn't he see it as ambition? Wasn't that what he would call it in Jon? The mere fact that her family had money shouldn't make a difference. Why should ambition be admired only in the poor or only in men? It wasn't fair. But she had learned long ago that the most a person could hope for was that life could be interesting, not fair.

A BAD GIRL'S MONEY 287

The Jonali Number One had just made life a little more interesting, and she was going to do all she could to keep it that way by developing an entire field. Work was already under way to spud Number Two. The company owned leases on four hundred thousand acres, part of which was land owned by the University of Texas, but the best prospects for more oil, it now appeared, included an area to the west, which they didn't own. She was already busy trying to secure it for C and R West Texas.

"You the woman in on that well with Mr. Calahan?" Bob Lucas asked. Alexis had driven fifteen miles to get to his ranch house, which sat in the middle of three thousand acres of sparse grass and mesquite.

"Yes. I'm Alexis Runnels. I'm Mr. Calahan's partner in C and R West Texas, and I'm here to talk to you about leasing your mineral rights."

"He's that feller runnin' for office, ain't he?"

"That's right, sir, and since he's busy with the campaign, I'm the one who—"

"Heard him speak week ago Friday in Midland. Had a right smart bit to say about taxes and them damned yeller-bellies that deserted during the war. Wasn't in favor of givin' 'em no pardons, he said. Wasn't in favor of no more tax, either. More or less made sense to me."

"Mr. Calahan has a populist appeal, of course. Now about the leases—"

"No tellin' what his chances are now that women are gonna vote. You just watch. They'll be wantin' to give them yeller-bellies pardons like them Republicans do, and they won't know a thang in the world about taxes. This country's liable to be in a mess now, thanks to the women votin', if you ask me."

Alexis could only stare at him, speechless for the moment.

"You ain't one o' them suffrage women, are you?"

"I'm just here to talk to you about C and R West Texas leasing your mineral rights," Alexis said.

"Uh-huh. I heard about that well y'all brought in. Figure it'll drive up the price a little."

"I'm prepared to make you a fair offer, Mr. Lucas."

"Good. You tell Mr. Calahan I'll be glad to consider a offer. 'Specially if it's fair."

"Mr. Calahan won't be able to contact you. I'm afraid he's busy with the campaign, but I'm prepared to offer you ten cents an acre and the standard one-eighth royalty."

"Well, I'll sure keep that in mind, ma'am. You tell Mr. Calahan I said I'd think about it. Tell him to get in touch with me in a day or two."

"Mr. Calahan is preoccupied with other things. You'll be dealing with me."

"Well now, you're going to have to talk to the boss, ain't you? So we might as well wait until he's free."

"The boss, Mr. Lucas?"

"Would you like a piece of pound cake and a cup o' coffee before you have to go? Mother, get her a piece," Bob Lucas said, calling out to his wife, who had never emerged from the kitchen.

Alexis was obliged to accept the pound cake, and left a little while later, still without the lease and with Bob Lucas insisting he would talk only to Jon. She found a similar reaction at other ranches, and by the end of the week she still did not have a single new lease.

A strong wind had come up during the night Saturday, sweeping out of the panhandle with an icy blast and graybeard skies. By Sunday morning the wind was still blowing, colder and harder than ever. Alexis had caught a glimpse of the skies from her window and felt the wind through the gap-toothed walls of the hotel as she arose from bed. She made up her mind to go to the well site today rather than seek out more leases. No one, it seemed, wanted to deal with a woman, and anyway, it had been several days since she had checked on the well, except to rely on reports from Nick.

A hot bath before she left would be relaxing and warming as well she thought. She spent a long time soaking in the tub before she returned to her room. When she opened the door and saw someone sitting in the chair near the window she was startled at first, but in the next moment she recognized him.

"Hello, my dear," Jon said with a hint of cynicism in his voice that let her know the morning was not going to be smooth. "Why in the hell didn't you let me know?"

There was a long moment of silence while she tried to regain her composure. That would not be easy, she knew, since she was wearing only a bathrobe and a towel around her head. At last she spoke with a calm that surprised even her. "What a surprise to see you, Jon." She pulled the towel from her head and went to the mirror to comb her hair.

"Damn it, Alexis, a whole week ago?"

"Yes, it was lovely. Sorry you missed it," she said without looking at him.

He stood up and grabbed her arm, forcing her to face him. "Nick told me. Left a message for me at the hotel in Midland. You weren't even going to tell me. What kind of silly little-girl game are you playing with me?"

"I had no idea how to reach you," she said with an icy calmness. "I didn't even know you were gone until I learned about it, quite by accident, from Nick after you didn't show up at the rig. Since then, I've been busy. I haven't had time for games."

He sighed—a mild sign of his frustration—and let go of her arm. "Look, Ali," he said, his voice less angry. "I knew you'd be upset, but I didn't even know about the campaign trip until we got back from New York. Eleanor had it planned, and we had to leave early the next morning. There was no way I could let you know. But you must have known I was going to be busy. Hell, the election is in two weeks."

"I should have known. Yes, there are a lot of things I should have known."

"Ali . . ."

"Regardless of the campaign, do I have to remind you that you also have a business to run? You could have at least kept in touch for that reason."

"I left messages for you with the desk clerk, damn it. He said he'd tell you I called. I'd have called more often, but you know the telephones are unreliable. More than half the time I couldn't get through."

Her anger melted, and she looked at him, knowing that what he had just told her was undoubtedly true. "I never got a message," she said, a little contritely.

"It won't always be like this, Ali. The campaign will be over soon."

And then what? she thought, but didn't say it aloud. He was going to win. She knew that. And then he would be in Washington, and she would be in

Texas. They had never talked about that. But what need had there been? Hadn't they agreed that whatever they had together was for the moment with no strings, no ties to the future? There was only the present, she reminded herself again, and she knew at that moment as she looked at him that she loved him. She saw the smile in his eyes and on his lips and knew that the smile was for her, that he was happy to be with her again. In the next moment, though, she heard the silent warning in her heart and forced herself to remember her resolve.

"What are you thinking?" he asked, his eyes searching hers.

She looked away, and walked to the chest to pull out a package of cigarettes Nick had given her. "I'm thinking that I need to talk to you about some oil leases," she said, lighting one of the cigarettes. She inhaled deeply and the smoke burned her lungs, but she managed not to cough, and she found the pain a welcome distraction from the searing pain of her spirit.

"Ali, do we have to talk about that now? Can't we—?"

"No, Jon," she said quickly. "We can't. And we both know that, don't we?"

He gave her a long silent look and then shrugged. "All right. What about those oil leases?"

Within ten days Jon had only a few of the additional leases they needed. He'd had to pay a premium price, though, because word had already begun to spread that the Jonali Number One had come in strong. The country would soon be filling up with drilling rigs and crews representing other companies. C and R was wasting no time either. A new well had already been spudded on one of the old leases, and another one was scheduled within the week.

It was four days after the new leases were secured that the first election in which women had been allowed to vote was held. Alexis cast her ballot for Democrat Jon Calahan. He won the election, and she knew that would change her life far more profoundly than the discovery of oil and the money that had already begun to flow into her bank account.

17

Life, Eleanor thought, was perfect. She was the wife of a United States congressman, and she was well on her way to becoming one of the wealthiest women in the state, if not in the entire country. She would soon be rid of the tacky two-bedroom house she'd been forced to live in for the past several months, and she would have a truly elegant apartment in Washington. How she hated the little wood-frame Coyote Flats house as well as everything else about West Texas! It was all so stark and wild and unrefined. Now, at least, she would only have to make a pretense of liking it when they came back during the congressional recesses. They could at least have a home in Midland, though, a little further removed from the grime and primitiveness of the oil camps.

Now she could truthfully say that all of the sandstorms she had endured, all the ugly landscape, all the primitive living conditions, all the absence of friends had proved worth it. Eleanor knew that she was once again among the socially elite in the state—even more so than when she'd merely been the daughter of a county judge. She knew enough about Washington social politics to know that this was a different game altogether. She would be on the bottom of the social register as the wife of a freshman congressman and one from the hinterlands besides. But she also knew how easily money could raise a person's social standing, and she was going to have money. Plenty of it.

David would attend the best schools and circulate among the best people. Perhaps, in time, he, too would go to Congress—the Senate, perhaps, and she would become a virtual queen mother.

Oh yes, she thought, things were working out well. Even the potentially disastrous situation involving Alexis Runnels had, in the final analysis, been advantageous. She had provided the capital for the initial investment, the family name Jon needed to win the confidence of more investors, and the right contacts for the East Coast money, and she had provided a sufficient diversion for Jon—a means of satisfying his considerable sexual appetite and his need for variety.

Eleanor now realized that she needn't have concerned herself unduly over the fact that he had been in love with Alexis. She should have known she could trust him to let his Scotsman's good sense win out in the end. He had been discreet while in the throes of the affair, and he had, in fact, seemed to lose interest of late. Instead he had concentrated wholeheartedly on the campaign just prior to the election and on the business since then. Perhaps he'd had his fill in New York. She couldn't imagine why she hadn't thought of something like that before—contrived some opportunity for him to be alone with the girl for some extended period of time so he could get all he wanted of her and be done with it.

The little talk she'd had with Alexis had seemed fruitful as well. Or maybe she'd gotten her fill of him, or had found someone else, or had seen that Jon was losing interest. It didn't matter what the reason, the important thing was that everything had worked out splendidly.

She was not so naive to think there wouldn't be other liaisons for Jon, but he had shown her he knew how to keep his little hobby from ruining his political career. Instinct told her, though, that the dalliances should not be with Alexis Runnels. He had fallen in love with her once, and that made her potentially dangerous yet.

She took comfort in the fact that they would be moving to Washington soon and that Jon and Alexis would both be busy with the development of the new oil field until that time. Jon would be even more busy with the plans they had to make for the move and with certain political obligations they had to meet before leaving.

He seemed in no mood to discuss any of it, though, when he returned to the house late that evening. He was eating his supper and seemed distracted. She had hoped to have more of his attention and had even contrived to have David absent so she could go over several important things with Jon.

It had not been difficult to talk David into going with Nick to the well site. The boy was always eager for anything to do with an oil rig, and Nick, as always, was congenial enough to take him along.

David was, in fact, so enamored with the rough and dirty life of the oil field crews that she could envision his balking at leaving it for the more refined atmosphere of Washington just as he had once balked at leaving Beaumont. It could be handled, of course. It was certainly nothing to mar the perfection.

"I don't want to think about any damned reception in Austin right now," Jon was saying, marring the perfection slightly. "I've got to get another crew going. Alexis wants to spud a well with that rotary rig she hired. She's right, a rotary will be faster and more efficient than a cable rig. And we've got a meeting with the university board in a week. We have to negotiate the override with them on that university land."

"But Jon, it's the governor's reception," Eleanor protested, putting emphasis on the word "governor." "We can't miss that. And we're going to have to leave early so we can shop for the proper clothes. Besides that, you know we'll be expected to host something while we're in Austin."

"What do you mean, host something?"

"Well, a reception. At one of the hotels, I reckon. We need to see to that. We don't want it to be tacky, now. They'll remember that in Austin, and you remember, dear, we need Austin."

"It's not Austin that elects me, it's—"

"There's not much time, Jon. Since we'll be leaving for Washington soon."

"Eleanor, I can't take off for Austin! Not with this oil field just developing. And I don't see why we have to leave for Washington until just before Congress convenes."

"Why, we have to find a place to live, Jon. You know that. We can't just wait until the last minute."

"We can stay in a hotel until we find a place to live."

"We don't want to be looking for something after it's all been picked over. I hear the best addresses are in the neighborhood where the vice president lives."

"I don't know, Eleanor—"

"And we'll want to get David in school, of course. The best. It takes time to find out that kind of thing. And another thing, what about furniture?"

"What about it?"

"Well, we'll have to buy new, of course. Nothing we have will do for Washington. Do you think we ought to buy something traditional? Something imported maybe? Or should we try that modern look you see in all of those Hollywood picture shows?"

Jon didn't answer. In fact, she wasn't certain he had even heard her. He stood, tossed his napkin on the table and walked toward the washstand. "Where's David?" he asked, as if he had just that moment realized the boy hadn't eaten with them.

"He's with Nick. They're out at the rig with the second tour. There's always an excuse for him to go out there since you have crews drilling around the clock now."

"Doesn't he ever come home for supper any more?"

"I gave him permission to go, Jon. We have things to discuss, plans to make." He was moving away from her, still giving her the impression that he wasn't listening. "What about the furniture?"

"What?" he asked absently.

"The style, Jon. I need to know what you think would be the most appropriate." She had to shout almost, since he had left the kitchen and disappeared into the living room.

"You decide," he said, walking back through the kitchen. He was wearing his hat and coat.

"You're going out?"

"Yeah. Got to keep this boom rolling in our favor so you'll have money for all that stuff you're talking about." He sounded mildly teasing.

"You're going to the drilling site." It was not a question.

"The drilling site? No. They can handle that without me. I've got to meet with Ali."

Eleanor felt a tightening in her spine. "Jon, do you really think you should—"

"Don't wait up for me," he said on his way out. "I'll probably be pretty late." He turned back to her and said, half apologetically, "We'll discuss all this Austin business tomorrow, I promise. And I mean what I said about the furniture. Whatever you decide is all right with me."

Jon pulled the bottle of gin out from under the seat of his car after he had parked in front of the hotel. He carried it inside, concealed inside his coat, and when Alexis opened the door he looked around cautiously before exposing it.

"I brought you a little present," he said with a broad smile.

"Good Lord, are you trying to ruin your political career before it even gets launched?"

He stepped inside. "No, I just wanted to buy you a present." He went to her small cupboard and pulled out two glasses. "You going to stay in this rattrap forever now that you're about to be rich?"

"Why not? It has all the basic necessities."

He noticed that she was still wearing the trousers and shirt he'd seen her in earlier in the day, and he found that he was disappointed that she had not dressed up for him. They had not seen much of each other at all since the night he'd come to her room after returning from the campaign trip. She hadn't even attended the party to celebrate his election victory. He hadn't pressed the issue. After all, she'd been preoccupied with the business, especially since he hadn't been around much lately to help with the details. He had to admit, though, he'd felt let down when she hadn't shown up.

He handed her a glass. "I thought the idea is to have more than the basic necessities."

She laughed, a little too cynically, he thought. "I've lived all my life with considerably more than the basic necessities. Now that I have my own money, all of a sudden I'm not at all sure that's the idea." She took the glass and set it on the small table, then opened a briefcase lying on the corner and pulled out some papers.

"What's wrong, Ali?"

"What makes you think anything's wrong?" She was shuffling the papers, preoccupied with them.

"Don't give me that bullshit, Alexis. You're pouting about something."

She gave him a look of cold, privileged arrogance. "I hardly have time for bullshit or pouting, Jon. We have work to do. You came here to go over these leases and the geologist's reports so we could make a decision about—"

"I came here to get you drunk so I could get you in the sack."

She looked at him for a long moment. He saw her

waver—a split second of vulnerability—then she turned her gaze away and gathered up the papers. "You can take these with you and study them on your own," she said, placing them inside the briefcase. She closed it and handed it to him. "I'm going to bed—alone."

He took the briefcase and flung it aside, causing it to open and the papers to scatter across the floor. "Damn it, Alexis, let's cut the crap. I know you're still mad because I was gone so long and you didn't hear from me, but I explained that. I'm back now, and I want to be with you. I want—"

"We've been over this, Jon, and you know that whatever it is you want, I want too, but we can't have it!" He saw to his surprise that she was crying. "So why do you keep making it worse? Why don't you just leave?"

"Why can't we have it? I've told you, there's no reason—"

"You told me Eleanor doesn't mind. You told me there would be no strings attached. You told me you loved me. Well, you're wrong about the first two, and if you mean what you said about the last—if you really love me—then for God's sake leave me alone. Leave me in peace!" The tears spilling over her eyes made him feel helpless.

"Ali, darling, I wasn't wrong about Eleanor, you just—"

"God, Jon," she said, turning away from him, "how can you be so blind? She's come to me twice because she's scared she's losing you. I am not going to be a home wrecker, Jon. No!" She held up her hands and backed away from him when he tried to take a step toward her. "Don't try to confuse me. All you'll do if you try to kiss me and make love to me is get the strings tangled. And there are strings, Jon. No matter what you say, there are strings attached. They're attached to my heart, just like they're attached to Eleanor's. If you pull on them too hard, something's going to break."

"Alexis, please, I love you. I don't want—"

"All right. I believe you love me. I believe it because I want to believe it, but I don't want it to be true. I—oh, God, Jon, I don't know what I want except that I want this never to have happened." He tried again to touch her, but she flinched and moved away. "Just leave me alone, please. Can't you see I don't know how to be somebody's mistress? I don't know how to be that bad girl you used to talk about."

"If you would just stop crying . . ."

"I'm going to stop crying," she said, wiping at her eyes with the backs of her hands. "And I'm going to stop loving you. Yes, as soon as I can, I'm going to stop loving you. Now will you please leave?"

"I'm not going to leave. Not when you're like this."

"Yes, you are! You are a United States congressman. A married man. And you don't belong here. I don't want you here." She had opened the door and was standing on the threshold, like a doorman, waiting for him to leave. He stood there for a moment, trying to think what to say to change her mind, worrying that if he said anything, someone in the hallway or behind one of the closed doors would hear. He opened his mouth and was about to speak, but he could think of nothing to say. He could think of nothing to do except leave. He walked away, feeling miserable.

He heard her crying behind the closed door, and he stopped once in the hallway. For a moment, he thought he would turn back, but it wouldn't matter, he knew. She wouldn't let him in. He drove home, wishing he'd retrieved the bottle of gin. Maybe it would help if he could dull his senses.

He left on a day when the wind was screaming, dry and cold, across the alkaline prairie. Alexis saw the crowds gathering at the train station from her upstairs window at the hotel, saw the wind push brittle gray skeletons of tumbleweeds along the street and then lift them into the air like sacrificial offerings in honor of the occasion.

The whole town was at the train station to see him off, with the band from the high school clamoring "America the Beautiful" not quite in unison. David was out there somewhere in that crowd, with Nick, probably. He had persuaded his parents to let him stay in Coyote Flats until the end of the semester, and they had agreed somewhat reluctantly, according to what she had heard from Nick.

Alexis searched the crowd from her high vantage point, trying to get a glimpse of Nick and David, but she couldn't spot them. There was Eleanor, though, looking elegant in a gray fur-trimmed coat and matching hat and Jon near the front of the crowd in a dark suit and a very eastern-looking hat. Alexis turned away when she saw him take Eleanor's elbow to help her up the steps to the Pullman car. She went back to the stack of invoices for drilling equipment she had strewn across the table and did her best to concentrate on them.

When she heard a surge of noise and applause from the crowd, she raised her eyes from her work, but she would not go to the window. The noise of the crowd subsided presently, and there was a long moment during which she heard nothing except the wind. It made her edgy, and she glanced once toward the window. Was he still speaking? Would she have one last glimpse of him if she went to the window again? Still she would not get up. Shuffling the papers, she tried once again to concentrate while the wind, seeping through the walls, made her shiver.

The train whistle howled, long and lonely in two-part harmony with the wind. Alexis put down her pencil and glanced in the direction of the sound. For a moment she felt his thoughts reaching out to touch her, but then he was gone and she was left with nothing except the tears rolling down her face.

"But I don't want to go to Washington for Christmas. I want to stay here," David complained. He was seated at one of the tables at Blackie's with Nick and Alexis.

"Hell, kid, if it was up to me you could stay here forever, but it ain't up to me. Your daddy sent this wire that I was to put you on the train a week from today." Nick waved the yellow telegram at Dave with one hand while he stirred the fourth teaspoonful of sugar into his coffee with the other. He added a splash of thick yellow cream. "Anyway, I don't know why you'd want to spend Christmas in this shit-hole place."

"Well, you and Ali are going to be here, ain't you?"

"Don't say 'ain't,' Dave," Alexis said without looking at him. She was absently fingering the oilcloth table covering.

Nick took a sip of his syrupy coffee and leaned toward Dave. "You can say 'shit' and 'hell' and 'damn' all you want, and it won't bother her, but 'ain't' will get your ass chewed off."

Dave laughed and Nick glanced at Alexis.

"Ain't that right, sugar?"

"You go on to Washington for Christmas, Dave," Alexis said. "It'll do you good to get away from this guy. He's a bad influence."

"But I don't want to go to Washington. Couldn't I stay here with you, Ali? We could all have Christmas together, couldn't we? And New Year's day, too."

"A dingy hotel room is no place for a kid like you to celebrate the holidays," Alexis said.

"I'm not just a kid," he said a little too emphatically to sound grown up. "You know I can do a man's work in the oil fields. Admit it."

"Okay. I'll admit you can do a man's work. Still, families are supposed to be together for the holidays. Your parents love you. That's why they want you with them."

"Yeah, well, I guess that means you're going to Houston then, don't it?" There was a look of challenge in his eyes.

"No, smart-ass," she said with a grin before turning away on the pretext of searching for Betty Jo to refill her coffee cup.

"But you said families are supposed to—"

"I'm busy, David. I've got a business to run. Somebody has to be here, and since half of this partnership is going to be in Washington, that leaves me." She still couldn't look at him. She was afraid that if he saw her eyes he would know that she dreaded going to Houston every bit as much as he dreaded going to Washington. There was, for her, that old feeling of inadequacy, of being the odd woman out, not quite fitting in with and measuring up to the Runnelses, but there was another reason to stay away now, she feared. A reason she didn't want to think about.

"You may just as well face it, kid, you're going to Washington for Christmas," Nick said.

"Ah, shit!"

"David!"

"Well, you said 'ass' awhile ago," David said in response to Alexis' reprimand.

She shook her head in dismay. Nick stood and gave Dave a friendly slap on the shoulder. "Speaking of asses, we got to get ours outta here and get to work. Let's go, Dave."

"What?" Dave asked, surprised.

"You done all that braggin' about holding down a man's job. Let's see if you can live up to it."

"Now, wait a minute. He's going out to the rig on weekends only," Alexis said, standing as well. "He's got to go to school."

"Hell, one day won't hurt. It'll be compensation for him having to go to Washington."

"Come on, Ali," Dave pleaded. "One day won't hurt."

Alexis saw the look of excitement and eagerness in his eyes, and knew she was going to relent. "You're going to have to stop picking up all the filthy language and bad grammar you hear on those rigs."

"Shit yes you are," Nick said with mock solemnity.

Alexis rolled her eyes. "Jon's not going to like this. He'll have my head on a platter."

"Papa won't care. 'Specially if he don't know."

"How can I argue with logic like that?" Alexis asked with a shrug. She put her arm around David's shoulders and walked with him to the truck parked in front of the café.

"You miss him, don't you?" Nick asked as they bumped along in the truck, headed for the new drilling site. David was sprawled in the back, leaving Alexis alone with Nick in the cab of the truck.

Alexis had her eyes on the enormous flatness of the landscape. "Miss who?" she asked, doing her best to keep her emotions and her consciousness flat as well.

"You know who. Jon."

"Don't be ridiculous."

"Don't take me for a fool."

"All right, I miss him. So what. I'll get over it."

"In the meantime it's making you bitchy."

She caught his eye and their gazes locked for a moment. She pursed her lips against the laughter she knew was coming unbidden and illogical, but it burst forth anyway, and Nick laughed with her.

"Sorry, baby," Nick said.

She leaned her head against the back of the seat. "I said I'll get over it." She closed her eyes against the dizziness and the unsettled feeling in her stomach that rivaled that of her mind and heart.

She tried to push away the nausea and the feeling of heavy tiredness when they reached the site, busying herself with watching the drilling, checking on the core samples. In a little while she retreated to the office in the tent to go over invoices and pay records. Concentrating on her work was proving difficult, but she worked hard at it, doing her best to push aside any thoughts of Jon. Some unseen force seemed to be working against her, though. She found the small office alternately too hot and then too cold, and the bleak landscape she could see outside her tiny porthole-sized window seemed oppressive in its openness.

She was only vaguely aware of the voices of the drilling crew outside the shack, and hardly more so when the voices turned to shouts. Then the sudden explosion. It was, for the briefest of moments, a welcome relief from the heavy weight of her mood. She burst out the door of the shack in time to see the fragments of casing flying through the air, borne on a pillar of black smoke that suddenly turned to roiling crimson, horrible yet utterly beautiful against the colorless landscape.

She heard the words shouted by someone—"Gas pocket!" Men were running away from the spectacle. Nick, David—she saw them both and knew they were alive. And then it came down—a black blow from heaven, striking David across the back, sending him sprawling, face down. She screamed and ran toward him, her whole being crying out for him to stand up and run toward her. But he was still, too still and too silent.

She fell to her knees beside him and felt the hot wind from the explosion pushing at her as if to push her away, but she wouldn't go. She gripped his shoulders and called his name.

His eyes opened, wide, frightened, and she saw blood oozing from his mouth, scarlet against the white, white face.

"David!" she said again. "Get up. We have to get you out of here."

He said something she couldn't hear. She put her

ear next to his mouth and heard the whisper. "Can't move. Something broke."

"Nick!" she screamed. But he was already there, kneeling beside them.

"Take it easy, kid. We got to move you. Got to get you away from this goddamned fire."

David's only response was the same wide-eyed look. But there was less fear in his eyes, Alexis thought, and seeing that made her own heart cold with fear. He smiled at her. "Shit!" he said and tried to laugh.

"David, don't . . ."

"Tell Papa I . . ."

He was silent then, only his eyes crying out something she didn't understand, and then they were silent too.

She called his name again. It was an empty sound, but she couldn't stop until Nick came to her and pulled her to her feet and led her away.

18

The funeral was held two weeks before Christmas in the winter-stark Baptist church where Alexis had first seen David in the parking lot next to the fellowship hall. There were no flowers, since they were out of season, and there were no greenhouses within reasonable distance.

The wind was blowing, unseasonably warm for December, and by ten o'clock, just before the service had started, it had blown away the lead-colored curtain of clouds to reveal a startling blue sky. The West Texas sun was not the same butter yellow sun of Houston, but was golden instead, as if it had been touched by Coronado's dreams. The blue and gold made the day overdressed for the occasion, but Alexis found solace in it. David would have reveled in it, would have wanted to skip school to savor it. Could she make herself believe that he was out there somehow enjoying it now on another plane of existence? Perhaps he was even a part of it—a part of the golden sun, the apple-crisp air, the earth hiding for a little while its secret ripeness. It was as if David was doing the same—hiding for a little while, self-conscious and embarrassed over this outrageous trick he had just pulled.

She hadn't cried. She had done nothing more than sit in stunned silence while Nick, equally silent, held her hand. Together they had gone through the motions of all that had to be done, including notifying Jon and Eleanor.

She had hardly seen Jon since he and Eleanor arrived on the train. A crowd of friends and political associates and constituents had been there to meet them and immediately swept them away. She'd caught only a glimpse of them—Jon looking somber and tired and older, and Eleanor, her face covered with a veil, leaning heavily on him.

She'd gone to the house to pay her respects, or to share their grief, or maybe just to look for her own solace in the ritual of it. But she hadn't found it. She had felt once again the odd woman out. Jon was still surrounded by people, and she could only touch his hand and then for a brief moment feel his face next to hers in a formal embrace.

His words had been virtually meaningless. "Thank you for coming, Alexis." She had looked into his eyes and not been able to find him there.

And now the funeral. Alexis sat next to Nick in one of the pews, awaiting the arrival of the family. The church was full, and there was a paradoxical atmosphere of excitement permeating the crowd because the funeral had, in fact, been turned into a state occasion. Governor Hobby was supposed to arrive with Jon and Eleanor, along with Thomas Marshall, the lame-duck Democratic vice president, who was representing the White House. David would have hated it, Alexis thought. He would have called them stuffed shirts or some other descriptive and probably off-color name borrowed from the likes of Nick and Buck and the other oil field workers who sat in the same pew with her now.

A thin, bird-like woman played "Jesus Is Tenderly Calling You Home" on an old upright piano that sounded as if it had been tuned for honky-tonk pieces rather than hymns. Her eyes kept darting toward the back of the church, and eventually a flood of sunlight and the sound of the eternal West Texas wind signaled that the door had opened. The piano music softened, and the entire congregation stood and turned heads around as the family entered—Jon and Eleanor, a woman who was undoubtedly Eleanor's sister, a handful of others who were obviously relatives, the governor and the vice president.

Alexis saw only Jon. She was shocked at the way he looked, at how he had seemed to have aged overnight. His face was drawn and haggard and his shoulders slumped with the heavy weight of grief. Eleanor looked somehow stronger now. Her face was once again covered with a veil, but her body was straight and her movements confident. It was now Jon who seemed to be leaning on her.

Alexis felt the loss and grief and pain and rage building inside her, but she held her tears through all of it—the hymns and the eulogy and the sermon and the solemn procession past the open casket.

Trembling, she walked past the casket and forced herself to look upon David's white face, upon his hands, folded in a ridiculously pious manner on his breast. But she refused to see any of it, and she refused to think of him being in that closed casket during the emotionally charged graveside service beneath a sky that was foolhardy in its cloudless beauty.

She did not go to the wake, held in Jon and Eleanor's bereft little house after the funeral. It would be full of people bringing in food and staying to offer sympathy and support. She wouldn't be missed, she thought, so she went, instead, to her room and wept at last. She cried for the loss she felt in her own heart, and also for the pain she had seen in Jon's face. She cried for the rage she harbored for her carelessness in allowing David to come to the rig that day and for David's carelessness in putting himself in harm's way and subjecting them all to such pain and grief. She wept bitterly as well for the unfinished business between Jon and his son and for the unconditionally unbiased randomness of death.

It was Nick who finally came for her the next day and took her to the café and insisted that she eat something.

"You gotta keep your strength up, baby," he said, pointing to the plate of ham and eggs he had just ordered for her.

Alexis looked at the eggs, flecked with the grease in which they'd been fried, and smelled the thick scent of the sugar-cured ham. She felt her stomach lurch, and she stood up quickly, then raced out the back door, headed for the outhouse behind the café. She didn't make it before her empty stomach convulsed with dry heaves, and she had to lean against the weathered wooden outside wall of the café.

"Good God, Ali!"

She glanced up at Nick's frightened eyes staring at her.

"I'm all right," she managed hoarsely. "It's just that I haven't had anything to eat in the last thirty-six hours, and the sight of greasy ham and eggs—"

"Shit, just look at you! You're too weak to stand up." He wore a frightened look as he placed his arm around her and led her away from the café. "Let's get you back to your room. I'll bring you some soup if you don't want ham and eggs."

"No, Nick, I can't."

"The hell you can't. You got to get your strength back. Got to get you back on your feet." He sounded angry, as if he was mad at himself for allowing her to be sick.

She let him lead her back to her room and help her into bed. He showed up a few minutes later with hot soup and crackers from the café, along with strong black tea. Then he stayed by her side while she ate, watching over her like a mother hen.

"You're takin' this pretty hard, baby. You want to talk about it?" he said finally, when he'd cleared all the dishes away.

She was silent a long time before she said. "I'm going to miss him. That's all."

"It was a goddamned shitty thing to happen."

She looked up at Nick from where she sat propped against the headboard of the bed. He was standing beside the bed, a cigarette he'd forgotten to light dangling from his lips, and there were tears in his eyes.

"Yeah," she said. "It was a goddamned shitty thing to happen." She reached for his hand. He sat on the bed beside her and let her cry for a moment while he held her.

"Shit!" he said in a voice unsteady with unshed tears. "Fuckin' shit!" He wept too, then, his shoulders shaking with sobs while she held him.

In a little while he brought in a bottle of bootleg whiskey from his car and offered her some. She declined, still wary of her queasy stomach, so he drank it all, trying to ease his pain. They talked while he drank. She couldn't remember what they said. Only what they didn't say. They didn't mention Jon. She'd wanted to, wanted to know if he and Eleanor had left on the early train that morning, along with the governor and the vice president. Wanted to ask if Jon had left any instructions for her about running the business. And, damn him, about how she was supposed to go on with her life with both him and David gone.

But she didn't ask. She gave Nick his chance to empty himself of some of his grief, and then she rented a room for him down the hall and put him to bed.

She slept poorly that night, her mind still crowded with images of David alive and dying and dead, and of Jon grief-stricken and aging and then leaving her with no solace. Along with the images was the specter of a new yet familiar fear that haunted her and that she could not yet face.

Nick showed up at her door the next morning, looking haggard and unshaven and smelling decidedly sour.

"Hello, baby," he said weakly when she opened the door to his knock.

"Hello, Nick."

He looked down at his hands for a moment. "I just want to say . . ."

"You don't have to say anything, Nick."

He looked up at her. "I reckon I don't. Hell, what are friends for?"

She shrugged and smiled wanly.

He gave her a nod. "Let's go get 'em, baby. Let's go set the world on fire." His face blanched. He was obviously appalled at the reference he'd just made. "I mean—"

"Let's do it," she said quickly, belying her true feelings. She had no spark left to set the world on fire.

He nodded and stepped into the room. "We got the well capped," he said. "And it's a good thing. It was burning outta control."

"We'll move on to another site. I've got the geologist's studies here." She pointed to a stack of papers on her work table.

"I seen the geology reports. Some of the best sites are the ones we ain't got leases on."

"It can't be helped now. Jon did all he could before he had to leave. He was going to come back to it, but now I don't know if he'll be up to—"

"You gonna let Transcontinental bid 'em out from under you?"

"Nick, I've tried. You know the disadvantage a woman has."

"Shit, baby, you got to make your own advantages. Find a way around it."

She looked at him, letting what he had just said soak in, and slowly she felt some of her strength returning. Giving up must have been just what Langdon had expected of her. He had thought, no doubt, that once she was out on her own she'd never make it as he and Ivy had done. But she could. She would.

She'd find a way around the problem. If leasers wouldn't take a bid from a woman, she'd find a man to do it for her. She'd start with a man the land owners respected—the president of the Coyote Flats Bank.

It was more than a week before she felt up to going to the bank to see Gordon Witherspoon. He was eager to see her, but not for the reason she assumed.

"I want to talk to you about Jon," he said when he had ushered her in to his office at the back of the bank.

"Jon?"

"He's taking the death of his son pretty hard, you know." Alexis could only look at him, too drained of energy, still too full of her own raw grief to know what to say. "It's to be expected, of course, but the way he looked at the funeral, the way he sounded when I talked to him later . . ."

"What are you getting at?"

"I hope you understand, Miss Runnels. I'm only being realistic. Jon Calahan is looked up to in this part of the country. A successful businessman and a savior, so to speak. That's why the district sent him to Washington."

"You're talking about him in the past tense, Mr. Witherspoon. As if he were the one who died."

"Now, don't get me wrong. People are going to be understanding, give him time to grieve. I'm just saying I had a gut feeling this threw him off balance more than ordinary."

"I don't understand."

"Well. This is mighty hard for me to say, and I hope you don't take it the wrong way, but if he looks too weak, it's going to hurt his business and his politics. Nobody's going to want to lease mineral rights to a man that don't seem to have what it takes. I'm right sorry to be saying it. I hope you know that, but it is realistic, Miss Runnels."

She was silent, trying to keep from saying something she would regret. "I can assure you that C and R West Texas will continue to be strong and aggressive," she said evenly.

"I hope you know what you're talking about, ma'am. If Jon Calahan lets his business go down, I reckon it could hurt a lot of people."

"That is precisely why I am here, Mr. Witherspoon. I want to talk to you realistically about C and R West Texas. We're going after more oil leases, but I need your help. Jon's not up to it and we have to act now."

"Very wise," he said, when she had explained her proposal to him. "You're absolutely right. Most of the ranchers won't feel comfortable leasing their rights to a woman. I can arrange to buy the leases through the bank. I don't reckon we need to mention your name as the buyer, do we?"

"That's the whole point, Mr. Witherspoon."

Alexis left, then, feeling somehow dirtied by the experience. Jon was a commodity who was not to be allowed to grieve lest he fail the country or the local bank. And she had played into the idea by telling Gordon Witherspoon things she was not sure she meant. How could she be sure that C and R West Texas would continue to be strong and aggressive? It wasn't only that Jon would not be at the helm because of his grief, but that she had her own grief, too, and along with it, a new worry. With each passing day, a nearly paralyzing fear was being confirmed. She was pregnant with Jon Calahan's child.

Eleanor raised herself from the elegant sofa in the Washington apartment where she had been sitting for the past hour, trying to finish up the thank-you notes to all the people she'd never met who had attended David's funeral or sent their condolences. From time to time she glanced at the door that led to the room they'd set up as Jon's home office. She was listening for some sign that he was working—looking over proposed legislation he needed to familiarize himself with, making telephone calls, anything that would signal he was trying to put David's death behind him and get on with his life.

It had been three weeks since the funeral, and no one expected him to be recovered from his grief, but she could see him sinking deeper and deeper into it, allowing it to consume him. She could see it ruining his career, his life. The thought of it filled her with rage, which she did her best to suppress with the damper of propriety and her sense of her wifely responsibility. The rage was there, nevertheless, seething.

She glanced at the clock and saw that it was almost five. They'd been invited to a reception at six at the home of the Mexican ambassador. No one would be offended if they didn't attend, of course, under the circumstances, but it would not be unseemly if they did at least make an appearance. It would be a small party, since most of Washington was home for the holidays before the inauguration. Jon had not wanted to stay in Texas, though, because the memories of David were too much for him now. The reception, Eleanor thought, had come along at just the right time. It might do Jon good to be with people, might restore some of his old energy and vitality.

She walked toward the study, taking secret pleasure in the spacious living room so beautifully appointed with the new furnishings she'd acquired. She'd decided upon a conservative traditional style of high quality, and she could well imagine the elegance when all of the pieces she'd ordered were in place, with the muted winter sun filtering through the windows as it was now, giving the room the soft, mellow glow of tasteful prosperity. She stopped a moment to savor it, her hand resting gracefully on the satin-like finish of one of the tables.

This quiet elegance was the very thing she'd always dreamed of. She had tried so many times to imagine David here, but she had never been able to do so. It was as if it was never meant to be. The realization left her feeling saddened and painfully empty, but she knew she couldn't allow those feelings to overwhelm her. She had to be strong now, because Jon was not.

When she walked into the study, Jon was sitting at his desk staring out the window. He made no move when she entered, and she wasn't sure if he was unaware that she was there or merely didn't care. Either way she felt shut out.

"Jon . . ."

He turned to look at her with that enormous emptiness in his eyes. It was all too familiar to her now, and she'd come to dread it.

"The reception at the ambassador's this evening . . ."

She hesitated, giving him a chance to protest if he would, already forming her own rebuttal in her mind. He said nothing. "It's only an hour away. Had you forgotten?"

"I'm not going."

"Please, Jon. This could be good for you. We wouldn't have to stay long, of course. Nobody expects that, but—"

"Damn it, Eleanor, I don't want to do this."

He had not raised his voice, but she could sense danger in his silent rage.

"You might feel better if you did. Ever think of that? Ever think that maybe you need to get out? We wouldn't have to stay long, like I said, but we've both got to get on with our lives here."

"You don't understand, Eleanor," he said in his dead man's voice. "I mean I don't want to do this. I don't want to be here."

She felt a sudden emptiness. "Jon," she managed in a voice hoarse with disbelief.

"I'm sorry, Eleanor."

"Give it time, dear," she said, struggling to keep her composure. "I know your grief is heavy. So is mine, but we both have to try to cope."

"I don't think I ever wanted it in the first place," he said as if he hadn't heard her.

"For heaven's sake, Jon, don't be absurd. You're grieving. In time you'll see things differently."

"I've made up my mind, Eleanor. I'm going to resign."

She thought for a moment that she hadn't heard him correctly, and she felt disoriented, as if she were spinning in a vortex. She saw Jon's face, his vacant eyes, and she knew she had heard the words. "But that's ridiculous," she managed to say weakly. "You haven't even begun. And think how awkward it would be to resign now. For both of us."

He turned his empty gaze toward her. "I said I'm sorry."

Suddenly all she could feel was anger. "You're sorry? Is that all you can say? You're sorry for giving up everything? All that you've worked for? Your future?"

"I've lost my son," he said, his eyes flaring in the first show of emotion she'd seen. "Anything else I might be losing is nothing compared to that." He turned away from her, swiveling in his chair into his own private darkness again.

"I've lost a son, too," she said with cold rage. "Don't you think I'm hurting just like you? Oh yes, I'm hurting. Does that surprise you?" she asked when he turned to look at her again. "Don't you think I had hopes and dreams for him, too, just as I have for you?"

"Yes, Eleanor," he said in the voice of agony. "We both had hopes and dreams, and now I can see that we never let him have his own hopes and dreams. And it's too late."

"Stop it!" she cried, making no attempt to stop the tears that choked her voice. "I won't dwell in your self-pity. I won't dredge up all the things we did wrong. And don't think I can't think of plenty. I am his mother. I loved him. I miss him. But I want us to get on with our lives."

For a moment it seemed that she had touched something alive in him. Perhaps, she thought, it was her tears that had awakened him. Perhaps he was truly surprised at her pain. He seemed about to speak, but a gray shadow eclipsed first his eyes and then his face, turning it ashen. She was struck at how old he looked in that moment, but in the next instant she knew nothing but terror when she saw him grip the sides of his chair, as if he were trying to stand, as if he had been struck by an electrical shock. She screamed his name as he clasped his chest and slumped forward, falling to the floor.

"How long have you known?" Nick asked. He had just pulled a cigarette from the pack he kept in his vest pocket. He put it in his mouth, rolling it nervously with his tongue, but not lighting it. His eyes darted to Alexis's still flat stomach under her shirt and then to her face. She was sitting on the bed in her hotel room, looking up at him as he stood near the window.

"For the past two months, at least. Maybe longer. Ever since you asked me that day out at the rig, maybe. At least I was suspicious then." Her voice shook, and she blinked back the tears she had tried to keep from forming.

"Have you told him?"

"Of course I haven't told him. You're the only one I'm going to tell."

"How the hell you think you're going to manage that?" His eyes went to her stomach again.

"I'm going to get an abortion, Nick." Her voice sounded strained as she tried to talk around the painful knot in her throat.

Nick removed the cigarette from his mouth and crumpled it in his hand, allowing the tobacco to sift to the floor. He fished in his pocket for another, but found the pack empty. Alexis tossed him a pack from her bedside table.

"You've got to help me, Nick."

He pulled out one of the cigarettes and stuck it in his mouth, then took it out again. "Shit!" he said. He looked like a frightened child.

"I hate to ask you," she continued, "but you're the only one I felt I could . . ."

He wiped the back of his hand across his white mouth, then moved toward her. "You done the right thing, baby." He sat down beside her and picked up her hand. "Old Nick's gonna help you. We'll figure somethin' out."

She wanted to cry and forced herself not to, but she let her head rest on Nick's chest while he stroked her back.

"Just don't worry about a thing." He pushed her away gently. "I'll marry you," he said. "I know a justice of the peace that can fix things so it looks like we done it, what? Two months ago? Three?"

"Nick, this is not your problem."

"But, sugar—"

"No. I've thought it through. I have to do it this way. Don't you think he'd know if I married you and had the baby? Don't you see how it could ruin him?"

"But you got to think of yourself too, babe, you—"

"I am thinking of myself. This is what I want." She found she couldn't look at him and focused her gaze instead out the window at the distant slender skeleton of a derrick Kansas Transcontinental had erected south of town. There was a long silence. "Can you help me—get it done?" she said, finally, still unable to face him.

"Jesus, baby."

She turned to face him. "Can you?"

She saw the uncertainty on his face. "I heard of somebody," he said after a moment. "A Mexican woman in Midland. Some gal Buck was screwin' said she done it for her once. But hell, Ali, you shouldn't have waited this long."

"What do you mean?"

"Don't you know? The longer you wait, the more dangerous it is for you. Shit, she ain't no doctor."

"A doctor won't do it, Nick."

Nick glared at her, agony distorting his face and burning in his eyes. He pulled the unlighted cigarette from his mouth and threw it on the bedside table. "Damn it, Ali," he said, his head sinking into his hands with a heavy weariness. "Why the hell did you let him knock you up?"

"You know there's no answer to that," she said with no attempt to hide her anger. "It's not like I'm the first person this ever happened to." She could no longer hold her tears back either, and she sobbed uncontrollably.

He stood up quickly and was opening the chest, then the closet door. "Where the hell's that gin you always keep?"

"There isn't any," she said, still crying.

"Shit!" He blundered toward her and took her in his arms again. "It's okay, baby. Don't get mad at me. Just let me worry about you a little bit, okay?"

She nodded her head and tried to smile, and he held her in his arms for a little while and let her cry. He stayed until her tears were gone, and then he left, promising to be back the next morning to drive her to Midland.

She didn't sleep. She lay awake throughout the

night staring into the darkness, trying not to think, yet unable to keep away the vision of Jon and their son. It was a boy, she knew with some knowing she didn't understand, and the two of them, father and son, moved through her mind linked by the same cord to her soul. Their movements, she thought wryly, were the first stirring of life. But it was best not to think that way. Best to think only of what she had to do.

She found now, though, that she could think of David. In some ways he was still alive to her. As much alive to her as the bit of plasma inside her. He would always be, wouldn't he? What would he think of this? He'd have been shocked, of course. Shocked that she was pregnant. Shocked that she was getting rid of it. Mustn't think of that. Mustn't think of any of it. Her head hurt now from too much thinking and too much crying.

She was dressed and waiting for Nick the next morning. When she heard a knock and opened the door, it was not Nick who greeted her, but someone from the railroad station with a telegram. It was from Eleanor. Jon was dying, and it was imperative that she come to Washington immediately.

19

It was three days by train to Washington, during which she sat in agonizing silence, staring at the passing scenery, alternately praying and crying, and three nights during which she had slept virtually not at all. She could eat very little either, since the morning sickness had returned with a taunting vengeance, as if to remind her of Nick's words—that the longer she waited the more dangerous an abortion would become. Nick had wanted to come with her, but she had insisted that he stay with the rig and had tried to assure him that she would be all right by herself.

She had sent a telegram to Eleanor immediately, informing her that she was on her way and instructing her to telegraph her at any of the stations along the way of any change in Jon's condition. She had actually used that term, "change in Jon's condition," because she couldn't bear to have the words "in case of Jon's death" loose and throbbing somewhere in the atmosphere. It did not occur to her to think of her reasoning as uncharacteristically irrational, or to remind herself that Eleanor had already transmitted the words "Jon is dying" to her. She could hardly think at all.

She could not figure out why Eleanor might have asked her to come. Was it some aspect of the business that had to be dealt with? Something that, in her distraught confusion, she couldn't remember? It didn't matter why. She had to be there, oh please, God, before it was too late.

Eleanor was at the station waiting for her. Alexis spotted her almost immediately, and she was struck by how perfectly elegant she looked, her svelte figure wrapped in pearl gray cashmere with a large silver fox collar caressing her aristocratic face and illuminating her deceptively vulnerable-looking eyes. Her appearance, or at least her bearing, along with her expensive clothes, made it impossible not to notice her.

She did not wave when she saw Alexis but raised her chin in a quiet gesture of recognition and moved toward her. They stopped within arm's reach of each other and did not embrace. Alexis tried to speak, but a thousand pulse beats hammering in her throat robbed her of her voice. The sounds of the train station seemed to have amplified beyond tolerance, and she felt a moment of blackening dizziness. She prayed that she would not faint, lest that force her somehow to give away the secret growing inside her. She tried to concentrate on the words Eleanor's delicately tinted lips were now forming.

"He's waiting for you."

Alexis felt weak with relief. He was alive! The world around her began to spin more erratically, but she willed herself to keep her balance and to keep at bay the blackness that was threatening her again.

"Are you all right?" Eleanor's voice was coming to her through a gray fog, and her face, which Alexis could now see had been enhanced by the most delicate and tasteful touches of makeup, showed a concern that bordered on annoyance.

"He's waiting?" Alexis managed to ask, ignoring Eleanor's inquiry about her well-being.

"Yes. In the hospital. He's very weak. It's his heart, I'm afraid."

"Will he . . . ?"

"Will he live? I don't know. But we must believe there is hope, mustn't we? That's why I asked you to come."

Alexis looked at her, still not completely certain what she meant, but Eleanor had already turned away toward a uniformed man who had been waiting behind her. She was giving him instructions about the luggage, and then in a little while they were beside a limousine, and the man, who Alexis now realized was a chauffeur, was helping them in and loading the luggage. It had not taken Eleanor long to acquire the trappings of the wealthy, but she had unmistakably done it with taste and elegance.

"We'll go to the house first. I have a room ready for you. You look as if you could use some rest." She raised a hand in protest to the objection she saw was about to come from Alexis. "I know you want to see him, but we mustn't rush things. You will see him tomorrow. He has been told that is when you will arrive. He mustn't have company this late in the day. I'm afraid he's very weak."

"Eleanor, please tell me why you asked me to—"

"In due course, Alexis." Eleanor's voice was decidedly firm, and she cast a cautious eye on the back of the chauffeur's head. "You must excuse the house. It's only a town house we've rented until—until later, but I think you'll be comfortable."

Alexis knew Eleanor's "later" meant when the profits from the oil were more readily available. It was obvious, though, that Eleanor knew that it would not be long.

The drive to the Calahans' home seemed interminable, and the conversation a tiring facade of inquiries about the state of the exploration back home and the development of the Jonali field as well as meaningless reports of senators and cabinet members who had inquired after Jon. Eleanor told her very little about his actual state—only that he had collapsed at home, but had regained consciousness, and that the doctor was concerned that his heart was weak and that his grief was hampering his recovery.

When at last they reached the town house, Alexis was ushered up to the second floor. A maid opened the door to a large bedroom full of dark, heavy furniture and paintings of eighteenth-century pastoral scenes, overly ornate and sentimental.

"Mrs. Calahan asks that you meet her in the garden room in half an hour," the maid said. "If you would like me to unpack for you while you freshen up . . ."

"No, please. Just leave me alone for a moment," Alexis said with a wave of her hand.

When the maid had left, Alexis sank wearily to the bed, sitting on the edge with her head in her hands. He was alive! She felt enormous, weakening relief and at the same time a grating sense of fear that she might yet be too late. How ill was he? So ill, obviously, that he couldn't stand too much shock or too much anxiety. Could he die in his sleep before she was permitted to see him? She couldn't bear that thought, and vowed that she wouldn't even permit it to cross her mind again. Instead she would concentrate on finding some way to endure the hours until Eleanor deemed it time for her to see him.

She stood and went to the adjoining bathroom to wash her face and prepare herself to meet with Eleanor and to find out exactly why she had been summoned. The nausea and dizziness she'd felt earlier had passed, but when she glanced at herself in the mirror, she saw that her face was pale and drawn and marked by dark circles under her eyes. Her face had also grown thinner and she knew that in spite of her pregnancy, or perhaps at this stage because of it, she had lost weight.

She washed her face and tried to camouflage her wan look with makeup. She brushed her hair and glanced at the watch she had pinned to the lapel of her traveling suit. It had not yet been thirty minutes since the maid had left, but she felt far too restless to wait in her room for the time to pass. She slipped out into the hall and down the wide staircase, hoping to find the maid or someone else to inquire where she might find the garden room.

She saw Eleanor before she found anyone else. She was sitting alone at a table in a room walled by windows and greenery. On the table was a stack of papers, and Eleanor was busy going over them. She had removed her coat and looked very stylish in her dark silk mourning dress. She looked up when Alexis entered.

"Ah, yes," she said, unsmiling. "I suspected you might be down early. Dora," she said, calling over her shoulder to the unseen servant. "Clear these papers, please, and bring some tea. Would you like something to eat as well, Alexis? You look a little pale. Maybe a little nourishment would revive you."

"No, thank you," Alexis said. She sat across from Eleanor in the chair she had indicated with a movement of her graceful hand.

"I trust your room is comfortable."

Alexis managed a nod and a barely audible, "Yes, thank you."

"I thought it best you stay here as my guest in order to minimize any gossip."

"Gossip?"

"Don't be naive. You are an attractive young woman, Alexis. If people thought you came here to see Jon without my knowledge or without my blessing, there would be speculation as to the reason. There is speculation enough just with your being business partners. What we must do now must be done carefully."

"I don't understand."

Eleanor's silence was obvious as the maid Alexis had met earlier returned with a tea service. Eleanor waited until the tea was served before she turned her attention back to Alexis.

"Jon has not been himself since David died." She paused, and Alexis saw something dark behind her eyes. "He has been—severely depressed."

"That's understandable. We've all been—"

"Yes, we've all been saddened," Eleanor said with quick impatience as she picked up her teacup. "But Jon has gone beyond that. He has lost interest in his political career."

Alexis knew then that the darkness Eleanor harbored was desperation and fear that she could lose the life she coveted.

"Perhaps that means nothing to you," Eleanor went on. "After all, I am not so naive as to fail to understand that his political career takes him away from you."

"Why are you telling me this, Eleanor?"

Eleanor set her cup down carefully. "Because I'm afraid it goes beyond even his political career. I'm afraid he has lost his interest in living."

Alexis felt something cold wash over her.

Eleanor's face had taken on a pinched look, and her lips had gone white, but her eyes were fixed on Alexis, dangerous as poison darts. "You are the only one who can help him," she said calmly.

"I don't understand."

"I think you do, Alexis," she said quietly. "You love him, of course."

Alexis stared at her, not knowing what to say.

Eleanor's smile was cold. "You must—make him happy."

There was a long painful silence.

"Do you think this is easy for me?" Eleanor asked finally. Her voice was cold, quiet, full of restrained anger. "It may surprise you how easy it is, actually. You see, I would do anything to save Jon. I refuse to see any of that bright future, none of that wonderful potential wasted. I won't let him die."

"Eleanor, what are you trying to do to me?"

Alexis's voice sounded more pleading, more full of pain than she would have wished.

There was a sudden wildfire in Eleanor's eyes, another show of desperation perhaps. "I'm not trying to do anything except save him, Alexis." The harsh tone hinted that her composure was wearing around the edges. "This has nothing to do with you beyond the fact that you are the only one who can help him now."

There was a moment of hesitation. A fatal moment, Alexis thought. Eleanor saw it too. She folded her hands in front of her, resting them on the tea table, and resumed talking. "You must see him. Talk to him, reaffirm your love. Sex is out of the question for a while, of course, but the doctor assures me that if he recovers, it need not be forever. Within a few weeks—"

Pushing her chair back, Alexis stood and turned away quickly, too appalled and confused to be able to stay in Eleanor's presence.

"Alexis!" Eleanor called in a tone that was stern and dangerously civilized. Alexis stopped, with her back to Eleanor still. "I won't have you playing these silly games," Eleanor said.

Alexis whirled to face her. "My God! Do you think I'm no more than a prostitute? Just a . . . a prosthesis to be used for—"

"I think you love him," Eleanor said sharply. "And if you do, then you will be as desperate to save him as I am."

There was another moment of hesitation before Alexis again turned away toward the French doors leading out of the room.

"The car will be waiting for you early tomorrow

morning," Eleanor said to her back. Alexis paused a moment, but did not turn around. She dared not risk facing her again.

She hurried to her room and flung herself across the bed. She thought of death. Her own. She tried to pray for it, but she seemed to have forgotten how to pray. And anyway, she knew, there would be no such mercy.

Alexis was trembling when the car stopped in front of the hospital the next morning. She had not seen Eleanor again, but the maid had come to her room to bring her breakfast and to tell her the car would be waiting in front in an hour. A note in a small sealed envelope contained the number of Jon's hospital room.

When the chauffeur opened the door and offered his hand to help her out, she saw the concerned look on his face. She had lost another night's sleep, and she had no doubt that she looked even more ill than she had the day before, in spite of the fact that she had done her best to disguise her dark circles and pale skin with makeup.

She was being used. There had been no attempt at deception, and she was not deceiving herself. The realization had kept her awake all night, and she thought of it now as she walked up the front steps and down the long halls to the elevators. The fact that she was being used was immaterial, really, she realized, because she would have come anyway. Eleanor must have known that. She would have known that Alexis would not have risked never seeing him alive again. Jon would have known it too, wouldn't he? Wouldn't he have been expecting her even without Eleanor's having sent for her? He would have known that word of his illness would reach Texas quickly and that she would come as soon as she heard.

Would he be glad to see her? Would his heart be pounding as dangerously as hers was in anticipation of their meeting? Or would he have lost interest in that as well? She was afraid to think of that. Afraid to open the door when at last she had found the room. She hesitated a moment, her hand on the doorknob, heart clamoring recklessly. She would have to distance herself from those fears, perhaps even from her love for him. She had to be strong. Finally she grasped the knob and pushed the door open.

He lay in profile to her, floating on a starched and sterile white cloud of sheets while a nurse fussed at his side. But Alexis hardly saw the nurse. Her eyes were on Jon. He sensed her gaze, and when he turned to face her, the fragile remoteness she had tried to establish shattered. He had never looked his forty-five years before David's death, and now he looked that and more. His skin was pallid, his face thin. But his eyes, she saw, were still magnificent. Still capable of holding her spellbound.

Alexis was vaguely aware of the nurse glancing from one face to another, of perhaps sensing the threads of tension that were taut and quivering. She slipped out of the room, and Alexis took another step forward, and then another and another, slowly, until she was beside his bed. She reached for his hand and held it with both of hers. She didn't dare try to speak. Not yet. It was all she could do to keep from collapsing to her knees or falling across him to hold him against her. She merely stood, praying that he would not sense that her body was trembling.

"Your last respects?" he asked, wryly.

"Oh, God, Jon . . ."

"Eleanor said you arrived yesterday," he said, freeing his hand and making an attempt to sit up. Alexis tried, in a flurry of confusion, first to help him, and then to restrain him.

"Do you think you should—I mean, are you allowed—"

"I'm allowed to do anything I damn well please."

She pulled back, afraid that she would upset him unduly. Was he being stubborn because of an ego that refused to admit he could die? Or resigned because he thought he would?

"What did she tell you?" he asked, staring straight ahead. She couldn't think why he did not wish to look at her.

"She said . . ." Alexis found she couldn't speak, didn't know what to say. She was suddenly angry with him because he could die and because he didn't seem to care how it would hurt her.

He continued to stare straight ahead for several minutes until she began to believe he had forgotten she was there. She couldn't bear being invisible to him, so she turned away and moved quietly toward the door.

"Ali . . ."

She was startled at the sound of his voice calling her name. How she loved the sound! How she wished he would hold her! She turned.

"Ali, I . . ." Suddenly she was at his side again, feeling awkward, not knowing what she should do. He reached for her hand and brought it to his lips. "I'm glad you're here," he whispered.

"Oh Lord! I . . . I was so afraid I'd be too late, that I'd never see you again."

"A part of me is already dead, you know," he said wearily.

"Jon, you can't stop living because David—"

"I lived for him, Ali. He never knew that, I guess. Nobody knew that, but I lived for him. Everything I did was so he would have the best of everything. All that I never had. But I failed him somehow. I saw that, but I saw it too late. And I never figured out how to make it up to him before . . . before he died." He turned to look at her, and she saw the deep, raw pain. "I never ever even told him I loved him. I guess he never knew that I did."

"He knew, Jon. His last words were, 'Tell Papa I love him.'"

He stared at her, his face even more ashen than before, as if he were afraid to believe her. Alexis held his gaze, her chest hurting as if her own heart were somehow about to rob her of life. She had told Jon the truth, she told herself. Those were the words David would have said, had tried to say.

"He said—"

"I wanted to tell you at the funeral, Jon, but I never got the chance. You were surrounded by people—the vice president, the governor, everyone. . . ." She stopped speaking when she saw the tears in his eyes, suddenly frightened that she had upset him.

"I ought to go. I was told not to stay too long. The nurses—"

"To hell with the nurses. I want you to stay. I want

you to talk to me. Tell me everything that happened that day. How he . . . how he died."

"Jon, do you think it's wise?"

"Damn it, Ali, I need to do this."

She looked at him, seeing the pain in his eyes, and she felt his hand grasping hers as if he were groping for understanding, maybe groping for some reason to live.

"He was very happy that day," she began. "He was looking forward to working on the rig. He even mentioned that he was following in your footsteps, that you'd worked in the oil fields when you were his age."

"He said that?"

"Yes. He did. Nick heard him too."

"He never understood that the reason I didn't want him to was—"

"All he understood was that he thought it was important to be like you. He wanted to be the same bullheaded, I'll-do-what-I-please-and-to-hell-with-everybody-else person you are. That's what you have to understand—that he thought you'd had a full and exciting life, and he wanted the same thing. He wanted to follow in your footsteps for a little while before he made his own."

"But he didn't have to follow in my footsteps. I could have made life easier for him."

"No, you couldn't have. He didn't want you to. He wanted to live his own life. To prove to you he could be everything you were. You know how excited he could get about life—about working on the rigs, about going to New York, about flying aeroplanes. He wanted all the adventure. He wanted to learn to be a man, a man like you. He wanted to please you because he loved you."

Jon's eyes burned into hers. "I loved him too. I wanted him to know..."

"He knew, Jon. He knew."

"You have to tell me everything," he said, his eyes so fever-bright it alarmed her. "How it happened. How he came to say all of that."

She told him everything, including the details of the explosion and the casing that flew into the air and the details of all that she knew Jon wanted to hear and that David would someday have said. She repeated again David's last words that now had become reality to her. Jon was weeping when she finished, and she was filled with renewed terror that she had upset him beyond the limits of safety. She wanted to leave to find a nurse, but he clung to her, and she took him in her arms and held him while he wept.

"I love you, Jon," she heard herself saying, and the words she had waited so long to utter lightened her heart, took away all the constricting pain. "I love you more than you can ever know."

Alexis and Jon spent an awkward Christmas together, she leaving early enough to allow Eleanor to come to the hospital to spend part of the day with him. Alexis had wired her family that she would not be home for the holidays due to her business partner's illness. They had responded with a wire conveying their wishes for his recovery and disappointment that she would miss the family holiday, and she had felt a twinge of guilt at not being there along with a secret pain at the formality of their exchange.

Jon was sitting up in a chair when she came for her daily visit two days after Christmas. Now that the holiday was over, Alexis sensed that he was as much relieved at its passing as she. He smiled when he saw her, and it was then that he said the words that struck a chord of fear in her heart. "You look different somehow, Alexis. I can't quite put my finger on it."

Alexis forced a little laugh. "I'm no different, darling. But you are. I'm so relieved that you're improving." He had indeed shown steady improvement since her arrival.

"No, it's you. You looked god-awful when you first came. You still have circles under your eyes. But there's a glow about you, too, that I've never seen before."

"There's a simple explanation, of course. Now that you're feeling better, so am I."

"Take care of yourself, Alexis. I worry about you."

"You're not supposed to worry." She gave him an affectionate kiss on the top of his head. "Bad for the heart. And anyway, there's nothing to worry about. I always take care of myself. You know that."

She was, in truth, feeling somewhat better. The morning sickness had begun to subside in the past week. It had become her daily routine to be awakened by the maid with her breakfast and then to meet the chauffeur soon afterward to be driven to the hospital. The staff apparently thought she went each day to go over business matters with Mr. Calahan, and she went along with the charade by taking a briefcase with her. She spent two hours with him each morning and then returned for an hour in midafternoon.

She was given full run of the house, but saw little of Eleanor, who seemed to have immersed herself in being a congressman's wife and was forever at teas or meetings to plan the social events surrounding the coming inaugural. Eleanor had also arranged her visits with Jon so that they did not coincide with Alexis's visits. Alexis was grateful for her absence, since too much contact with her would have been awkward. Among other things, she had an irrational fear that Eleanor might somehow guess her condition, in spite of the fact that her waist had not yet begun to expand and the swelling in her breasts was still not noticeable to others.

"Alexis . . ." She turned to look at Jon now. "You were someplace else again. What's occupying your thoughts so lately?"

She tried to smile. "Nothing, really. Or maybe everything. Your health, the oil leases . . ."

"Don't think about that now, Alexis. Think about us. I'm glad Eleanor had the forethought to send for you."

She found she had to avert her eyes.

"Please don't let that disturb you. I told you she was understanding."

"No," she said, forcing herself to look at him, "there is so much that neither of you understand."

"Don't be melodramatic, my dear."

She smiled slightly. "You're feeling well enough to insult me?"

"No insult was intended."

"No, I suppose not," she said with a wry laugh. "I'm sure it never occurred to either of you how you're using me." She regretted her words as soon as they were uttered. She hadn't meant to say anything to upset him. "Jon, I'm sorry. Please forget I said that."

"Don't handle me with kid gloves, damn it. I can't stand to be patronized."

She saw that he was flushed. "Jon, please, I—"

"We all use each other in one way or another, my dear. If I remember correctly, you are one of the most adamant advocates of that. It was you, I believe, who said a woman should not be condemned for using her sexual charms to get what she wanted. A woman's power, I believe you called it. And you had no compunction about using that power."

"If you think the only reason I—"

"I think that we both need each other."

"There was no ulterior motive for my coming here, Jon," she said evenly.

"You came because Eleanor sent for you."

"No, I came because I love you, and I was scared I was going to lose you." Her heart was pounding unmercifully, and when he waited so long to reply she felt a white-hot fear that she had gone too far.

"You are not going to lose me," he said at last. "I have decided to live. I have you and Eleanor to thank for that."

"Oh, Jon," she said in a small voice of enormous relief.

"You've given me back something to fill the emptiness that was killing me. You've given me the assurance that my son loved me." He was silent again for a long moment, looking down at his hands. Finally, he raised his eyes slowly. "I owe you both my life. You and Eleanor. I must try to repay you both somehow."

"No . . ."

"Please," he said, raising a hand in protest. "No false modesty. I mean what I say. I'm sure Eleanor is grateful, too. She wouldn't have wanted to have been cheated out of this." His voice sounded weary as he turned aside to glance out the window at the Grecian-white skyline of Washington. He turned back to Alexis and said with heartbreaking sadness, "I want it back like it was before."

Alexis could not speak, she could only look at him while her heart broke with his.

"If it can't be that way," he added, "I at least want us back the way we were at our best. We can have that back, can't we, Ali?"

She looked at him through a silvery haze of tears and enormous love. "Yes," she said. She had to avert her eyes again for fear that he would see that she had lied.

20

The next morning when the maid came to Alexis's door, she was not carrying the usual breakfast tray. Instead, she informed her that Mrs. Calahan requested that she have breakfast with her in the dining room.

Alexis found her waiting, looking as elegant as ever in her black silk and a single strand of pearls. Breakfast was served almost immediately, and Eleanor wasted no time in getting to the reason Alexis had been summoned.

"You have no doubt noticed Jon's improvement over the past two weeks." She paused only long enough for Alexis to acknowledge with her eyes. "I want to assure you that I am grateful for what you have done." Alexis was struck by how calm she appeared, except for that cold blue darkness in her eyes. "You are a smart young woman, Alexis, so I'm sure I don't have to explain to you the danger in your staying long enough to start tongues to wagging."

Alexis raised an eyebrow. "I would have thought a week would be ample time to loosen those wagging tongues. I've been here over two."

"Let us just say that we are stretching our luck to carry it any further. The complexities of the oil business can only be expected to carry us so far."

"You are telling me that I am to be dismissed." Alexis spoke with a coldness that equaled Eleanor's.

There was a pause, and it was difficult to tell whether the look on Eleanor's face was amusement or chagrin. "The doctor has recommended a recuperation period of several months," she said. "Depending upon Jon's progress, we may find it necessary to return to Coyote Flats."

"So my services may be needed further."

"Miss Runnels, I don't see the need for—"

"Oh, please. I understand completely." She threw her napkin on her plate and pushed back from the table. "You're only thinking of Jon, and we both want the best for him, don't we?" She stood, looking down at Eleanor. "You just take care of his political career and his social life, and I'll take the burden off of you by fucking him for you. You're damned lucky to have me, Eleanor," she said, her voice trembling from the weight of unshed tears, "because good help is hard to find." She hurried out of the room before Eleanor could see the tears fall.

She was at the train station within an hour. She had packed hurriedly, called a taxi, and left without seeing Eleanor again. Eleanor would have some reasonable excuse for Jon as to why she'd left so suddenly. She'd make up some urgent business in the oil field, perhaps. Eleanor could always fix things.

Well, not all things, maybe. The unwanted pregnancy

was something Alexis knew only she could fix, if it wasn't too late. She was slightly more than three months now. That was late, dangerously late, she knew, and she was scared. She was scared not to do it as well. She could not ruin her life and Jon's political career with a bastard child.

Was that the way her own mother had felt? she wondered. And her father as well? Undoubtedly it was, since she had ended up in that orphanage. She had been the bastard who had threatened to ruin everyone's life. Ivy and Langdon had taken her as an act of charity. She had never escaped the feeling that she had been a burden to them as well, especially after their "perfect family" was made.

Or did she have it all wrong? Ivy and Langdon had always been so closemouthed about her real parents. Maybe her real mother had loved her and wanted her. Had her own mother felt as confused about being her father's mistress as she did about her relationship with Jon? Had she been as frightened and uncertain when she found out she was pregnant?

If only her real mother had lived, she would have someone to talk to, someone who understood. Ivy would try, of course. She could never fault Ivy for not being kind. She could only fault her for not having the experience to understand the kind of dilemma she found herself in now. And for not being her real mother. And for what else? Protecting her too much?

What about her real father? The man she knew only by the one worn and tattered letter she had found quite by accident so long ago. He had never come for her. Never even come to see her. Ivy had asked him not to and had explained to her that it was best that he not come, that it would only upset her because he had left her so long ago, abandoned her to an orphanage. He could only hurt her, Ivy had said, if he returned to her life now.

Was that true? That he could only hurt her? She had never believed that was true but had always thought he would come some day and show them all that he loved her. But he had never come. Why? She had asked herself that question over and over again in the past nine years since the letter had arrived. But he had remained in Colorado, in some little town called Eagleton where the family's gold mining interest was. A place she'd never been. A place that seemed somehow farther away than Paris and London and Rome and all the other European cities she'd visited.

"Where to, Miss?"

The question startled her, and she looked up to find that the line at the ticket window had moved along quickly while she was lost in thought, so that she was now face to face with the attendant.

"I said, where to, Miss?"

"Colorado," she said without realizing she was going to say it. "Eagleton, Colorado."

As the train raced through the iron gray industrial East and the patchwork fields and ice-embroidered farmland of the Midwest, Alexis counted the days, knowing that as each one passed, her risk grew in dangerously compounding proportions. It was important, though, that before she severed a link with the future, no matter how impossible and undesirable that future might be, she needed to affirm her link with a cloudy past.

On the morning of the fourth day, Alexis saw pale blue mountains levitating above a sea of winter-ragged clouds in the distance. As the train drew nearer, the hue of the mountains deepened to purple and then to the color of old gold and tarnished silver. Ivy had mentioned her mixed feelings of awe and dismay the first time she had seen Colorado more than thirty years ago. But Ivy had made her legendary fortune there, as the owner of a saloon and the head of the Sweet Ivy Gold Mining Company.

Alexis hadn't known until less than ten years ago that her real father, Alex, would have been on that train with Ivy seeing Colorado for the first time as well. She found she could not in the least imagine anything he might have felt. She had imagined him at one point as a princely figure, who would someday send for her to come reign with him in his kingdom. By the time she was twenty-one she had read the letter enough to catch a glimpse of what was between the lines. He was not a prince or a king, but a man pleading to see a daughter he'd made no attempt to see for sixteen years, and when he was so easily turned away by Langdon and Ivy's refusal, she had resigned herself to the fact that he did not care enough to bother. Now, after hearing Jon speak of his own inability to communicate his feelings to his son, she wasn't sure of anything anymore. Maybe Alex Barton, her real father, had loved her and simply not been able to show it.

In Colorado Springs she changed trains to the narrow-gauge Denver and Rio Grande line, which wound its way around the edges of sheared rock cliffs and climbed steep grades dotted with needlepoint designs of ice encrusted pine trees. The route from

Colorado Springs to Eagleton took her through the mountains past old mines that had long since been abandoned when the gold was all gone. To Alexis they looked like gaping, laughing mouths, as if they were remembering the bawdy dramas that had been played out around them less than a lifetime ago.

Finally, the train approached a wide valley, and Alexis saw the helter-skelter sprawl of a town tarnished and sagging under the weight of past glory. She had been uninterested and only half aware throughout her life of any of the details of the gold mining aspect of the family business, since oil had emerged as the current primary source of their wealth. She had managed to pick up the information, however, that only two mines remained in operation around Eagleton, and that the Sweet Ivy was not one of them, the gold having long since all been extracted.

She stepped off the train carrying only one suitcase, since she had sent the rest of her luggage on to Coyote Flats and wired Nick to pick it up for her. She had not told him where she had gone, only that she was going to take a side trip to visit family before she returned. She had also asked him to meet her at the station in Coyote Flats when she returned in another week. She had added a cryptic message: *Be prepared to take me to see the woman I've been so eager to meet.* She would have it over with soon, but she needed a few more days to prepare herself. Surely a few more days wouldn't make much difference.

The Golden Palace, she remembered, was the name of the business in Eagleton that Alex had mentioned in the letter. He was still there, he said—at least he had been there nine years ago when he wrote the letter. Since there were no taxis in the dilapidated town, she set out on foot, suitcase in hand, to find the legendary Palace.

The streets were lined with fading and vacant buildings that once had obviously housed businesses. There was still a drugstore and a grocery where the few remaining miners and their families could buy necessities. A handful of people milled about the streets and cast curious glances her way. They looked very much like the buildings did, run-down and somehow vacant. She passed a livery stable that boasted one gasoline pump in front, and as she walked past a muddy, snowpacked incline that must have been a street, she could see a large brick building and hear the shouts of a small band of children at play in a school yard. The town was alive, but wounded and limping like a once-beautiful woman in rundown shoes.

She walked two more blocks before she saw the two-story building festooned with baroque designs in plaster and a faded sign of gilded lettering swaying seductively in a breeze. It was the Golden Palace. She stood for a moment looking at the words and felt a moment of paralyzing uncertainty. She should have telegraphed ahead to tell Alex she was coming, she thought. What would she say to him? What would she call him? Alex? Mr. Barton? Certainly not Papa.

It was not too late. She could still change her mind, turn around and get back on the train, and for one moment, for the blink of an eye, she thought she would. Instead she walked on a rising surge of fear and fatalism into the past of Ivy and Alex Barton and, by the connection of some frayed thread, her own past as well.

A BAD GIRL'S MONEY 351

The room was dark and cavernous, strewn with tables and chairs, and the walls were covered with ornate paintings and frescoes. The same baroque designs of the exterior, she saw, were repeated in the gold-inlaid beveled ceiling. A heavily carved bar occupied one end of the room, but its shelves were bare in deference to Prohibition. Another wall of the room was dominated by an ornate staircase leading upward into something dark and secret. Cooking smells and the sound of dishes and utensils being handled wafted from somewhere behind the bar.

Presently a young woman appeared in a doorway to the right of the bar, wiping her hands on a stained apron.

"You looking for a room?" She was very young. Hardly a woman, actually, since she couldn't have been more than twenty. She had strawberry-blond hair falling out of a bun twisted at the back of her head and a fine sprinkling of freckles across her nose.

"No, I—"

"Well, we're not open for lunch yet. Be another hour."

"I'm looking for . . . for Mr. Barton. Alex Barton."

"He's not hiring, if that's what you're after. I advise you to go to Denver if it's a job you're wantin'."

"Can I help you?" Alexis turned around at the sound of the voice and saw an old man at the foot of the ornate staircase. He was impeccably dressed in dark woolen trousers, a crisply starched white shirt, and an old fashioned brocade vest. "I'm Alex Barton," he added in the same accent of the South she associated with Ivy.

She could only stare at him, at the lined face, the

thick mane of white hair, the eyes that came to her, colorless in the semidarkness, but penetrating nonetheless. He was thin, a bit stooped. But the presence of him smote the air like silent electricity.

"I . . ." Her voice failed her. She coughed nervously, awkwardly. "I'm Alexis," she said finally in the weak voice of her fear.

He had not seemed to hear her, or at least not to understand. He turned his head slightly to the right, tilted it as if to catch the sound better, and then, as if the words had come to him slowly, his face changed, and he reached a faltering hand to grasp the bannister. "My God," he whispered. "It's you. Alexis." He said the name as if he were savoring the taste of it.

They stared at each other a moment. He must have said something else, but Alexis could hear nothing except the roar in her ears. Then he smiled and came down off the last step of the stairway. Still looking at her, he reached a hand to his left and flipped a switch. Four crystal chandeliers sprang to a life of incandescent splendor, robbing the room of shadows and showing it for the faded, dingy, and deteriorating relic it was.

"Welcome to the Golden Palace," he said in a voice so decidedly theatrical she wanted to laugh, yet somehow so sadly pitiful she was afraid she'd cry. "She sent you, didn't she?" he said, more a statement than a question. "My dear, sweet Ivy, I knew she would see that you came."

There was a moment of awkwardness in which they both seemed undecided about whether or not they should embrace, but neither of them moved. Alexis looked at him in the dazzling light, and she saw then that his eyes were blue, perhaps once the intense blue of her own, but the blue had begun to retreat behind a smoky haze. There were deep, sallow circles under his eyes and crisscrossing lines at the corners and down his slackening, ashen cheeks. But she could see that he had once been handsome, and did still have an air of handsomeness about him in the flash of his smile and in the boyish vanity he obviously possessed.

"No," Alexis said when she had finally found her voice. "She doesn't know I'm here."

He appeared shocked. "She must have told you about me. She must have—"

"She never told me anything until it was too late," Alexis said, surprised at the bitterness in her voice. "Until nine years ago when your letter came, I never knew you existed."

"You read the letter? I wanted to come then, but I—"

"But you never came." She hadn't meant to say that. She had not expected to confront him so directly, did not, in fact, want to be doing it now, but somehow couldn't stop herself.

He looked away, like a child afraid to face the consequences of some naughty deed, she thought. "Ivy was right. It was best I stay away." He glanced down at his hands. "Best you never knew I existed."

"How can you say that?" She was fighting to hide her anger and hurt and suppress her unwise words, but losing the battle. "How could it be best for me not to know who you were? If I didn't know who you were, how could I know who I am?"

He appeared mildly startled. "Why, I can see that you're a fine young woman. I'm sure you know that."

"I kept thinking you would write to me, but you

never did," she said. "I was afraid to write to you, afraid you wouldn't answer."

"Oh, no," he said, "I would have answered. You must never think that. I have thought of you so often. I have wanted to see you. I have—"

"You gave me away." She said the words simply as her rage began a slow retreat.

"She told you that?"

"Yes. She told me that I am your bastard and that you gave me away. To an orphanage."

"She told you everything, then."

"I don't know. That's why I came here."

"I only did what I had to do. If I don't quite measure up to your expectations—"

"I told you. That's why I'm here. I want to find out some things."

He smiled. "Well, of course you do," he said, putting his arm around her and leading her toward one of the tables. "And it's high time. Let's have some lunch and get to know each other, I'm sure we can—"

"Just tell me," she said, stopping. "Is it true that you gave me away? To that orphanage."

He looked stunned, paralyzed for a moment. "Yes," he said finally. "I gave you away." He spoke evenly and matter-of-factly, but she saw his hand tremble as he tugged at his vest and saw the pulse beat throbbing under the thin blue skin at his temple.

"I have to know why."

He moved his eyes away from hers and then back. He was wearing a little smile now, as if the movement of the eyes had been necessary to get away just long enough to put on the facade. "Of course. But I insist. Let me treat you to lunch. The old Golden Palace isn't what it used to be, but we still serve a good meal."

"I'm not very hungry, and I—"

"Hush, now. You have to eat." He turned toward the kitchen, and Alexis noticed for the first time that the young woman was still there, watching them with an oddly pained expression on her face. Alex placed an arm around the girl's shoulder and led her with him into what was obviously the kitchen. He reappeared a few minutes later, alone, and with two plates of food. "Hope you like fried chicken," he said, setting the plate in front of her. "It's not as good as Ivy cooks it, but it's not bad. Does she still cook southern fried chicken like she used to?"

"Sometimes, I think, for Langdon. But they have Marie, who does most of the cooking."

"For Langdon?" He smiled a little sadly, then laughed, a bitter sound. "I didn't see it happening. I didn't see that I was losing her."

"You're still in love with her," Alexis said, surprised.

Alex put down his fork and pushed his plate back. His mask had slipped, and anguish grayed his face. "Yes," he said finally, unsteadily. "I'll always love her. I never wanted to hurt her. That's why I couldn't tell her about you."

"I don't understand."

"I . . . I couldn't tell her that . . . that I'd fathered a child, I . . . I was wrong, of course. Out of wedlock. I don't suppose you'll understand. It just happened. I never meant for it to—"

"I understand." He looked at her, obviously surprised at her words. "I mean, I know these things happen. It doesn't mean any harm was meant."

"That's right. Of course, no harm was meant," he said, smiling warmly, relieved perhaps that she understood. Alexis felt a surge of kinship and compassion seeing his relief. "I was young, foolish," he continued. "I had to keep it from Ivy so I wouldn't hurt her."

"But she knew. She told me."

"You were two years old before she knew you existed. I'm surprised she didn't tell you that." He laughed, sadly. "No, I guess I'm not surprised. She wouldn't have wanted you to think I was such a son of a bitch. She was always trying to protect me. I guess, in a way, she never got out of the habit." Alexis saw his hand shake as he reached into a vest pocket for a cigarette. "And whether she believes it or not, I was trying to protect her, too. I was afraid she'd be hurt if she knew. I never meant to hurt either of you. I thought you'd be better off with the Sisters of Mercy. I didn't know any other way."

"My mother would not have wanted me in an orphanage, would she?"

"Of course not. Ivy loves children, always wanted—"

"No," she said, surprised that he had thought she'd meant Ivy. "I mean my real mother."

He looked disoriented for a moment. "Lida? No, I suppose not."

Lida. That was the first time she'd heard her name, and the sound of it made her feel shy, as if she dare not try to utter the word herself, lest she trip her tongue. Ivy had never mentioned the name. She'd said only that she was a "poor unfortunate dance-hall girl," and Alexis had been afraid to ask more. She'd been given the feeling that her past was something dark and shameful and not to be explored. But now she couldn't stop herself.

"Tell me about her," she blurted.

Again Alex seemed to have been caught off guard. He drew hard on his cigarette and coughed, a loose, rattling, old man's cough. "I hardly know what to say." He paused a moment as if his mind were drifting back a quarter of a century. "She was right pretty. All plump and dimpled. You might look like her if you had a little more meat on your bones. She had blond hair and blue eyes, I think. Yes, I remember. They were blue. Like yours. But I like to think you get yours from me."

"But what was she like? I mean, was she smart? Was she a good cook? Did she like to read? I just want to know. Everything."

Alex stared through a haze of smoke. "She was . . . I don't know. Smart? She was uneducated. Had a tough life, probably. Most of them did. Not much chance for education. But I think she was . . . I don't know. She was nothing like Ivy, of course."

"You met her in a dance hall?"

"Yes. The Nolton. Or was it the Central? Yes, the Central. I used to like to go over there."

He hardly remembered her, Alexis realized. Had he put her out of his mind because of the painful memories? Or because she was just one of many women he'd had? Perhaps she shouldn't keep pushing him. Yet there was a hunger gnawing at her that wouldn't let her stop.

"The fire. Tell me about that."

Alex shot her a sudden alarmed glance, as if the fire was the most painful memory of all.

"She was burned," Alexis said, prodding him. "Mama told me that much."

"Yes. She . . . she was burned. I saved her, though. Brought her out of the building. Got burned myself.

Still have the scars on my hands." He showed her the scars, shriveled patches on the backs of each hand. He took his hands back, then, and hid them in his lap. "The fire weakened her, of course, so she couldn't survive the birth."

"The whole town burned, Mama said. And no one knows how it started."

Again he looked at her with a pained expression, as if the memory was too much for him. "No. We never found out." He managed a smile. "But we all survived it somehow. Built everything back."

"Was I born in the hospital where they took her?" Alexis asked, relentlessly.

"No. They moved her to Denver. You were born there. And when she died, I . . . I had to find a place for you."

"The orphanage."

His brow furrowed, and she could see that he was sweating. "What could I do? I couldn't hurt Ivy. I couldn't raise you alone. I only wanted to leave you there until I could think of something. I never meant to abandon you." He got up and went to the bar and pulled a bottle from somewhere underneath, then poured himself a drink. "Would you care for some, or has Ivy taught you to be a teetotaler like she was?"

"I'm not a teetotaler, but I'm not up to it right now," she said.

Alex picked up his glass and brought it back to the table. "It's just as well. You never know what kind of poison you're gettin' with this bootleg stuff," he said.

Alexis could see now that the shaking hands and the sallow complexion were most likely due to alcohol. He didn't look well. Perhaps she should show some mercy, but she was in no mood for mercy. "You never loved her, then?" she asked.

He drank deeply of the whiskey in his glass then set it down, staring into its amber light, reflecting fire from the gaudy chandeliers. "I never loved anybody except Ivy," he said. He seemed for a brief moment to be lost in his thoughts, then he glanced at Alexis and said apologetically, "But you mustn't let that bother you. I was fond of your mother, of Lida. And the important thing is I loved you."

"You loved me?"

"From the moment I saw you."

"But how—"

"I was desperate," he said quietly. "I was unwise. I didn't know what to do. I made mistakes. I've spent a lifetime trying to live with that mistake. I've spent a lifetime thinking of you, wanting to get to know you, afraid that if I tried to meet you, you would hate me. You have no idea how much courage it took for me to write that letter."

Alexis looked into his eyes, brimming with tears, and she was angry with Ivy for all of the pain she had caused both of them.

"You mustn't think that I would ever hate you," she said.

He smiled. "I'm glad you're here now. And that's what's important, isn't it? You being here. I want to get to know you. You don't know how many times I've wanted to see you. But I was scared." He stopped, his voice choked. He looked embarrassed for a moment, then he finished off the whiskey and said brightly, "I'd show you around the town, but there's not much to show. I'm afraid this old Palace is about the biggest curiosity around. Unless you count me."

He laughed sardonically. "Did you know this old saloon used to belong to the Sisters of Mercy Orphanage? Ivy gave it to 'em. Now that's a story I'll have to tell you one of these days. I ran the place for 'em for years, and they made a fortune. Bought it from 'em after the gold boom died down and it wasn't worth a damn any more. Heck, I'm barely scrapin' a livin' out of it now, but I couldn't stand to see it go to somebody else. Sometimes I still think I can see Ivy comin' down that staircase in that emerald green dress of hers or sittin' there, where the blackjack table used to be, dealin' cards. Did your mother ever tell you she used to run this place?"

"Yes," Alexis said, "she told me." He had relapsed into referring to Ivy as her mother again. Lida was no more than a shadowy memory to him. Alex studied her face for a moment, as if he was trying to memorize it. "Well," he said, still sounding ill at ease, "Like I said, there's not much to see around here, but I could show you the mine. The old Sweet Ivy claim's not in operation any more, but we can still go see it. Your mother and her old friend Diana Pollard were the ones that opened it up. Now that's a story for you to hear sometime—how those two women found that rich vein of gold. You get Ivy to tell you about that."

"I've heard about Ivy's business partner," Alexis said. "My stepsister is named for her."

"Named for Diana?"

"Yes."

"Well, I'll be damned." He laughed, seemingly at some private joke. His smile faded, and he looked away again. "She had two little girls," he said quietly, but Alexis had the feeling he was not speaking to her. "That's what she always wanted. Two little girls." He was once again lost in thoughts for a moment before he seemed suddenly to remember she was there. "Well, what do you say? Want to go have a look?"

"Yes," she said. "I'd love to. But could we wait until tomorrow? I'm afraid I'm a little tired. The high altitude," she added quickly.

"Of course," he said. "Let me just take your bags up. Make you comfortable. Then when you're up to it I'll show you this old Golden Palace. It was quite a showplace in its day."

She let him show her to her room, and she found that sleep for once came easily. When she had rested, Alex kept his promise and showed her the fading opulence of the Golden Palace, taught her how to spin the roulette wheel, showed her the stage that had once held glittering, bawdy shows, showed her some of the old trunks that were still full of Ivy's opulent, old-fashioned dresses.

"Tell me about yourself," he said, when the tour was done. And she did. She found that she could talk to him easily, and that she was pleased when he praised her for her bravery for her work during the war and for her intelligence and courage for her work as a suffragette. He was amused at her anecdotes about her wealthy, spoiled friends. He laughed at her story of Langdon's disapproval of her plan to buy a nightclub and was genuinely interested in her oil exploration. She told him about everything except Jon. She went to bed that night knowing that he had charmed her and that she had been quite willing to allow it. He was at last, the father she had always wanted to know.

She slept well and was up early the next morning. They had not made definite plans about going to see the mine, but she planned to talk to him at breakfast. She could smell bacon and coffee as soon as she came down. When she went to the kitchen, she saw the same young woman she'd seen the day before standing in front of the large cast-iron stove.

"Hello," Alexis said.

The young woman turned around suddenly. "Oh, it's you. Papa won't be up for awhile. He always sleeps late."

"Who?"

"Papa. Alex."

Alexis felt a moment of paralysis. "Alex is—your father?"

"Yes," the young woman said, her back still turned to Alexis. "Are you surprised?" When Alexis didn't answer she turned around to face her. "I didn't know about you, either. Not until yesterday. I overheard you and Papa talking. But I guess I wasn't surprised. Papa's had a lot of women." She was silent, studying Alexis's face with her sad eyes. "Why'd you have to come?" the girl said finally.

Alexis found it difficult to speak. "Because . . . he's my father."

The girl weighed Alexis' words a moment before she spoke. "I think I heard Papa say you're Ivy's daughter. Everybody in this town remembers her and Langdon. Everybody knows about their gold mine, and then all that oil money in Texas. You have a rich family! Isn't that enough for you?"

The pain Alexis saw in the girl's eyes made her feel uncertain. "That's not it. I . . . I just wanted to know who he was."

"Why?" the girl demanded, then faltered, looked away. "I guess I know the answer to that. But let me warn you," she said, glancing up again, quickly. "Papa's not always easy to love. Mama left him nine years ago. When I was only ten. Took me with her. But I love Papa, and I missed him. Missed Colorado, too, so last year when I turned eighteen I came back. I'm taking care of him now."

"Nine years ago?" Alexis asked, remembering that it had been nine years ago that Alex had written the letter begging Ivy to allow him to see her, claiming she was his only living relative. He had lied. He had wanted her to fill a gap made by this child's leaving, that was all. He had lied then, and he obviously hadn't bothered with the whole truth since she'd arrived either.

"Yes, when I was ten," the girl said. "I missed him so much. Everybody needs a family. I had Mama, of course, but Papa needed me. He always said that. He always said he would die if anything happened to his little girl. He still calls me that sometimes. His little girl." She smiled sadly. "He was sure squirming when I told him I overheard the two of you talking and you claiming to be his daughter. You shoulda seen him grasping for a reason why he never got around to telling me." She waved a hand and went back to her cooking. "Can't let it bother me, though. Papa's like that. Always squirming around trying to get himself out of some jam. That's why he needs me. Why I take care of him."

"What's . . . what's your name?" Alexis asked when she could find her voice again.

"Susan. Susan Elizabeth Barton. And he married *my* mother." She turned around suddenly. "Hey, that wasn't nice of me, was it?" she said softly. "Guess I'm just a little jealous. You showin' up here like this, reminding him of Ivy. She's the one he talks about the most, except for Mama, of course. They were the only two that ever left him," she said, turning back to her cooking. "The rest of 'em, he left. He found somebody a few months after me and Mama left, but it didn't last. Papa says it's because Mama was the only woman he ever really loved."

She glanced over her shoulder at Alexis. "You needn't feel sorry for me being here like this. I'm here because I want to be. But I'll leave some day. Soon as I can get a little savings together, I'm headin' for Denver." She set a plate of food in front of Alexis. "You might as well eat some of that. Papa won't be out of bed for awhile."

She turned back to the stove. "I heard all that stuff he told you yesterday. Papa's good at that stuff."

"What stuff?"

"He can charm the pants off of a person." She laughed. "He means it, though. At least at the time he says it. Can't stand for anybody not to like him. So I guess I'm kinda glad you at least were nice to him." She brought another plate to the table and sat down across from Alexis. "You in some kind of trouble? That why you're here?"

"No, I—"

"'Cause if you are, he can't help you. Believe me, I know. Can't imagine why you'd be in trouble, though. I heard you tellin' Papa you were in business for yourself. That sounds like Ivy. She's near 'bout a legend around here. Guess you're following in her footsteps."

Following in Ivy's footsteps? Is that what she had been doing? Had she, somehow without realizing it, been trying to show Ivy that she was like her, the way David had done with Jon?

She had come to Eagleton looking for something. Perhaps it was to find where she belonged. She had never found it. Not in Houston. Not in Paris. Not with Zane. Not in Coyote Flats. At least, not in Coyote Flats without Jon. But not with Jon, either. He belonged with Eleanor in Washington. She knew she had yet to find where she belonged. And now she realized she had looked in the wrong place. Alex Barton could not tell her. He had charmed her for a few moments, perhaps, but she could now see that he had been no more than the sower of a seed that had grown up without him—first in an orphanage and then with Ivy. The picture had begun to emerge for her now of Alex, irresponsible, thinking only of himself, and of Ivy, taking Alex's abandoned child away to love and protect her.

She had wanted to believe always that she was loved and protected. She knew now that she had only begun to doubt that was true when she realized the past had been kept secret from her. Perhaps she shouldn't blame Ivy and Langdon for that. Perhaps they had, after all, done it out of love, wanting her to believe she was theirs, wanting to protect her from knowing she had a father who was weak and wounded and who had been willing to give her away.

Alex had never come to see her and had only made an attempt when one of his crutches had been knocked out from under him. It was very likely, she realized, that he had never thought of her again once he found another crutch. But she knew now that it didn't matter what he thought. What mattered was love. And she knew love resided in Houston.

"Do you think I can get a train out of here this morning?" she asked Susan.

"If you hurry, but I thought you and Papa—"

"I want to try to make connections in Colorado Springs for Houston."

"Houston?"

"My family is there."

Susan dropped her eyes, embarrassed. "Look, I guess I shouldn't have—"

"I'm very happy to have met you, Susan, and to know I have another sister. But I want you to please tell Alex I've decided to go home." She felt awkward for a moment, not knowing whether to embrace Susan or simply turn away. Finally she reached a hand to clasp her shoulder affectionately. "If you want to write . . ."

"Yeah, maybe I will."

"Just send it in care of Runnels Oil in Houston. It'll get to me."

"Sisters ought to act like family, I guess. When you come right down to it, family's all there is."

Alexis tried to respond, but her throat was too choked for words. She could only manage a smile and a wave.

21

She would keep the baby. Somehow some secret part of her had always known that would be her decision. How could she do otherwise? How could she give up the only little part of Jon she would ever have? How could she give up this part of her family? She would have to tell Ivy and Langdon, of course. Her family had a right to know her decision.

She had rehearsed the speech she would deliver over and over in her mind as she made the journey from Colorado Springs to Houston. She would have to enlist their help in making sure that Jon never knew about the child. That, of course, meant that she would never see him again.

She had wired ahead to tell Ivy and Langdon that she was coming and that she had something important to tell them. She had also wired Nick to tell him she was going to Houston until after the baby was born. She knew she could trust him not to betray her. Nick was, in many ways, the best friend she'd ever known.

He would go along with her idea to manufacture a story about the father dying in an oil-field accident.

Would she tell the child the truth someday when the time was right? When the truth could no longer hurt Jon and when she saw that the hunger for it was gnawing away at her child as it had at her? The answer didn't come so easily, and she saw now that it must not have been easy for Ivy and Langdon either. She prayed that they would be understanding about her decision to keep the baby, and that it wouldn't somehow end up hurting and embarrassing them.

Now as she stepped out of the taxi and walked up the long shadowy walk to the front door of Green Leaves, she was more than a little nervous. She rang the bell and it was not Walter or Marie but Ivy who opened it. She held her arms out wide as if she'd been expecting her.

"You're home, darling! You're home!" She took her in her arms and held her close. "Langdon," she called over her shoulder. "Our little girl is home!"

"Yes, Mama, I'm home." She knew without a doubt that she was home now, with her family. She'd had to learn what love was, even when it had been under her nose at Green Leaves all along. Now she knew there was no need ever to feel invisible again, because love gave a person substance.

Langdon, standing behind Ivy, moved forward.

"Hello, Papa," she said.

"Hello, Ali."

"Papa, I . . . I want you to know that I—"

"You made it big, little girl. Just like your mama. I knew you could do it!"

"Just like my mama," she said, forming her words around the painful lump in her throat. "Papa, I . . . I want you to know that I love you. I want both of you to know how much I love you."

"Don't you think we know that, girl?"

"Well, I—"

"I love you too, you know," Langdon said with a smile. "You've always made my life interesting. A little too interesting sometimes, but I—"

"I'm afraid I'm about to make it even more interesting."

"I know."

"You know? But how—"

"Come in, darling," Ivy said, pulling her forward. "Let's get your things put away before you see who's here."

"Is it Diana and Miller? I want to see them, of course, but not just yet. I have to tell you something first. I . . . I want to tell you both—"

"It wouldn't have hurt for you to stay in touch," Langdon said. "Where have you been?"

"First Washington, because Jon was very sick."

"We know about that," Langdon interrupted. "We tried to get in touch with you in Midland after you left Washington, but you weren't there, and no one in Midland seemed to want to tell us—"

"I was in Colorado."

There was a sudden pall, and Alexis saw her mother's face grow pale. "You saw him? Alex, I mean."

"Yes, Mama, I did, but that's not what I want to tell you just now—"

"We should have told you long ago, before the letter. I realize that now. I was only afraid it would harm you somehow. I was afraid he could hurt you. You don't know him, he's so—"

"It's all right, Mama. I think I understand better now, how you want to protect people. Maybe it's just that we all have an instinctive feeling to protect children. I think I can understand that now, because, you see—"

"It's hard to see one of your kids do crazy things," Langdon said. "Like going off to the war. Going off to West Texas. It's hard to let them take those risks. You just naturally want to protect them."

"Papa, I said I understand. I had to grow up, that's all. I just had to realize how lucky I am to have a family who loves me. Even when I'm . . . well, when I'm hard to love."

"Why, Ali, you could never do anything to make us stop loving you," Ivy said.

"Mama," she said with a deep sigh, "I think we should talk." Suddenly her breath caught in her throat and she felt as if she couldn't move. He had just emerged from the parlor and was standing in front of her, and she spoke his name. "Jon."

"Hello, Ali. I've had a hell of a time tracking you down."

"What are you doing here? You shouldn't have traveled this far. The doctors said—"

"Never mind what the doctors said. I told you, I've decided to live."

"This is who we were trying to tell you was here," Ivy said. "Perhaps you'd like a few minutes alone." Alexis was only vaguely aware that Ivy had taken Langdon's arm and was leading him toward the stairs. Her eyes had not left Jon.

"I came to find you," Jon said. "Came here because this is where Nick said you'd be. Came here, mind you, to my old enemy's castle. I've even made a kind of peace with the tough old bird. And now that I've found you, I'm never going to let us be apart again."

"I don't understand. What about Washington? What about—"

"The governor will appoint someone to serve until a special election can be held. My illness will be the face-saving excuse for me, of course." He laughed softly. "How would it look to say I'm giving it all up for a woman?"

He seemed to be waiting for her to respond, but she found she was too stunned to speak.

"You gave me the quote once, didn't you? *In delay there lies no plenty*?" he continued. "I don't want to delay any longer. That's why I'm here. I've just done the proper thing and asked your father for your hand."

"But Eleanor—"

"Eleanor didn't want me when I told her I didn't want the congressional seat." He smiled, sadly. "I guess it was the first time in our lives we ever spoke candidly to each other. We both cried a little. After all, it was twenty years together coming to an end."

"Oh, Jon, if there's still something there, if you're not sure—"

"Of course I'm sure. I'm just trying to be fair about Eleanor. She only wanted me to be all that she thought I could be. Just as my father did. The trouble is, I never stopped to ask myself what I really wanted. And after you left I couldn't stop thinking about what I had given up, and all for something I never wanted in the first place. I want you, Ali. David's death made me realize how short life is. How important it is to be with someone you love." His voice faltered. "I can see now how right you were about him. I never let him be what he wanted to be either. The chance to do right by him is gone, and I don't know if I'll ever get the chance again to do something right."

She smiled and reached a hand to touch his.

"I don't seem to be saying this right, my dear. I hope you know that I—"

"Jon, darling," she said softly, interrupting him and enclosing both her hands around his, "there's something I have to tell you. . . ."

AVAILABLE NOW

A SEASON OF ANGELS by Debbie Macomber
From bestselling author Debbie Macomber comes a heartwarming and joyful story of three angels named Mercy, Goodness, and Shirley who must grant three prayers before Christmas. "*A Season of Angels* is charming and touching in turns. It would take a real Scrooge not to enjoy this story of three ditsy angels and answered prayers."—Elizabeth Lowell, bestselling author of *Untamed*.

MY FIRST DUCHESS by Susan Sizemore
Jamie Scott was an impoverished nobleman by day and a masked highwayman by night. With four sisters, a grandmother, and one dowager mother to support, Jamie seized the chance to marry a headstrong duchess with a full purse. Their marriage was one of convenience, until Jamie realized that he had fallen hopelessly in love with his wife. A delightful romp from the author of the award-winning *Wings of the Storm*.

PROMISE ME TOMORROW by Catriona Flynt
Norah Kelly was determined to make a new life for herself as a seamstress in Arizona Territory. When persistent cowboys came courting, Norah's five feet of copper-haired spunk and charm needed some protection. Sheriff Morgan Treyhan offered to marry her, if only to give them both some peace . . . until love stole upon them.

A BAD GIRL'S MONEY by Paula Paul
Alexis Runnels, the black sheep of a wealthy Texas family, joins forces with her father's business rival and finds a passion she doesn't bargain for. A heartrending tale from award-winning author Paula Paul that continues the saga begun in *Sweet Ivy's Gold*.

THE HEART REMEMBERS by Lenore Carroll
The first time Jess and Kip meet is in the 1960s at an Indian reservation in New Mexico. The chemistry is right, but the timing is wrong. Not until twenty-five years later do they realize what their hearts have known all along. A moving story of friendships, memories, and love.

TO LOVE AND TO CHERISH by Anne Hodgson
Dr. John Fauxley, the Earl of Manseth, vowed to protect Brianda Breedon at all costs. She didn't want a protector, but a man who would love and cherish her forever. From the rolling hills of the English countryside, to the glamorous drawing rooms of London, to the tranquil Scottish lochs, a sweeping historical romance that will send hearts soaring.

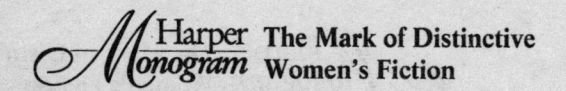

Harper Monogram **The Mark of Distinctive Women's Fiction**

COMING NEXT MONTH

DREAM KEEPER by Parris Afton Bonds
The spellbinding Australian saga begun with *Dream Time* continues with the lives and loves of estranged twins and their children, who were destined to one day fulfill the Dream Time legacy. An unforgettable love story.

DIAMOND IN THE ROUGH by Millie Criswell
Brock Peters was a drifter—a man with no ties and no possessions other than his horse and gun. He didn't like entanglements, didn't like getting involved, until he met the meanest spinster in Colorado, Prudence Daniels. "Poignant, humorous, and heartwarming."—*Romantic Times*

LADY ADVENTURESS by Helen Archery
A delightful Regency by the author of *The Season of Loving*. In need of money, Stara Carltons resorted to pretending to be the notorious highwayman, One-Jewel Jack, and held up the coach containing Lady Gwendolen and Marcus Justus. Her ruse was successful for a time until Marcus learned who Stara really was and decided to turn the tables on her.

PRELUDE TO HEAVEN by Laura Lee Guhrke
A passionate and tender historical romance of true love between a fragile English beauty and a handsome, reclusive French painter. "Brilliant debut novel! Laura Lee Guhrke has written a classic love story that will touch your heart."—Robin Lee Hatcher

PRAIRIE LIGHT by Margaret Carroll
Growing up as the adopted daughter of a prominent Boston family, Kat Norton always knew she must eventually come face-to-face with her destiny. When she travels to the wilds of Montana, she discovers her Native American roots and the love of one man who has always denied his own roots.

A TIME TO LOVE by Kathleen Bryant
A heartwarming story of a man and woman driven apart by grief who reunite years later to learn that love can survive anything. Eighteen years before, a family tragedy ended a budding romance between Christian Foster and his best friend's younger sister, Willa. Now a grown woman, Willa returns to the family island resort in Minnesota to say good-bye to the past once and for all, only to discover that Christian doesn't intend to let her go.

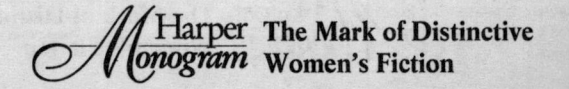

Harper Monogram The Mark of Distinctive Women's Fiction

HarperPaperbacks *By Mail*
BLAZING PASSIONS IN FIVE HISTORICAL ROMANCES

QUIET FIRES by Ginna Gray ISBN: 0-06-104037-1 $4.50
In the black dirt and red rage of war-torn Texas, Elizabeth Stanton and Conn Cavanaugh discover the passion so long denied them. But would the turmoil of Texas' fight for independence sweep them apart?

EAGLE KNIGHT by Suzanne Ellison ISBN: 0-06-104035-5 $4.50
Forced to flee her dangerous Spanish homeland, Elena de la Rosa prepares for her new life in primitive Mexico. But she is not prepared to meet Tizoc Santiago, the Aztec prince whose smoldering gaze ignites a hunger in her impossible to deny.

FOOL'S GOLD by Janet Quin-Harkin ISBN: 0-06-104040-1 $4.50
From Boston's decorous drawing rooms, well-bred Libby Grenville travels west to California. En route, she meets riverboat gambler Gabe Foster who laughs off her frosty rebukes until their duel of wits ripens into a heart-hammering passion.

COMANCHE MOON by Catherine Anderson ISBN: 0-06-104010-X $3.95
Hunter, the fierce Comanche warrior, is chosen by his people to cross the western wilderness in search of the elusive maiden who would fulfill their sacred prophecy. He finds and captures Loretta, a proud golden-haired beauty, who swears to defy her captor. What she doesn't realize is that she and Hunter are bound by destiny.

YESTERDAY'S SHADOWS by Marianne Willman ISBN: 0-06-104044-4 $4.50
Destiny decrees that blond, silver-eyed Bettany Howard will meet the Cheyenne brave called Wolf Star. An abandoned white child, Wolf Star was raised as a Cheyenne Indian, but dreams of a pale and lovely Silver Woman. Yet, before the passion promised Bettany and Wolf Star can be seized, many lives much touch and tangle, bleed and blaze in triumph.

MAIL TO: **Harper Collins Publishers**
P. O. Box 588 Dunmore, PA 18512-0588
OR CALL: **(800) 331-3761** (Visa/MasterCard)

Yes, please send me the books I have checked:

☐ QUIET FIRES (0-06-104037-1) $4.50
☐ EAGLE KNIGHT (0-06-104035-5) $4.50
☐ FOOL'S GOLD (0-06-104040-1) $4.50
☐ COMANCHE MOON (0-06-104010-X) $3.95
☐ YESTERDAY'S SHADOWS (0-06-104044-4) $4.50

SUBTOTAL	$ ____
POSTAGE AND HANDLING	$ 2.00*
SALES TAX (Add applicable sales tax)	$ ____
TOTAL:	$ ____

*ORDER 4 OR MORE TITLES AND POSTAGE & HANDLING IS FREE!
Remit in US funds, do not send cash.

Name _____
Address _____
City _____
State _____ Zip _____

Allow up to 6 weeks delivery.
Prices subject to change.

(Valid only in US & Canada)

H0031

ATTENTION: ORGANIZATIONS AND CORPORATIONS

Most HarperPaperbacks are available at special quantity discounts for bulk purchases for sales promotions, premiums, or fund-raising. For information, please call or write:
**Special Markets Department, HarperCollins Publishers,
10 East 53rd Street, New York, N.Y. 10022.**
Telephone: (212) 207-7528. Fax: (212) 207-7222.